Temperance hardly heard
the duchess as she gazed unseeingly
at the carved legs of the desk,
finally allowing herself to believe
Jack was alive.

Joyful excitement suddenly bloomed in her heart. She
would see Jack again. She would!

New energy surged through her. She leaped to her feet—

And stumbled with shock as she registered what else the
duchess had said.

"Your *son*?"

"Yes, he's my son."

"B-but…"

"Sometimes he calls himself Jack Bow," said the duchess.
"But his full name is John Beaufleur, second Duke of
Kilverdale."

* * *

The Vagabond Duchess
Harlequin® Historical #846—April 2007

CLAIRE THORNTON

The Vagabond Duchess

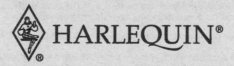

HARLEQUIN®

TORONTO • NEW YORK • LONDON
AMSTERDAM • PARIS • SYDNEY • HAMBURG
STOCKHOLM • ATHENS • TOKYO • MILAN • MADRID
PRAGUE • WARSAW • BUDAPEST • AUCKLAND

ISBN-13: 978-0-373-29446-6
ISBN-10:   0-373-29446-8

THE VAGABOND DUCHESS

www.eHarlequin.com

Author Note

The stories in the CITY OF FLAMES trilogy take place during the reign of Charles II. This was an era of great color, drama and variety. The king scandalized some of his subjects with his many mistresses, but his reign also saw the emergence of modern banking among the London goldsmiths. Actresses appeared for the first time in London theaters, while members of the Royal Society met every week to witness scientific experiments.

Athena Fairchild, Colonel Jakob Balston and the Duke of Kilverdale are cousins, but they've led very different lives. Athena grew up in England, Jakob in Sweden, and Kilverdale spent his childhood exiled in France as a result of the war between Charles I and Parliament.

The cousins' romances take place in various locations, but London is at the heart of the CITY OF FLAMES trilogy. The cousins all meet the one they love in the city— although Athena's happiness is destroyed almost before it begins.

Athena's story, *The Defiant Mistress* begins in May 1666 in Venice and the events span the rest of the summer. Jakob's story, *The Abducted Heiress,* and Kilverdale's story, *The Vagabond Duchess,* both begin in London at the start of September 1666. In the early hours of the morning of 2 September, a fire in Pudding Lane will burn out of control....

While I was writing these books I fell in love with the characters and their world. I hope you enjoy reading their stories as much as I enjoyed writing them.

FAMILY TREE

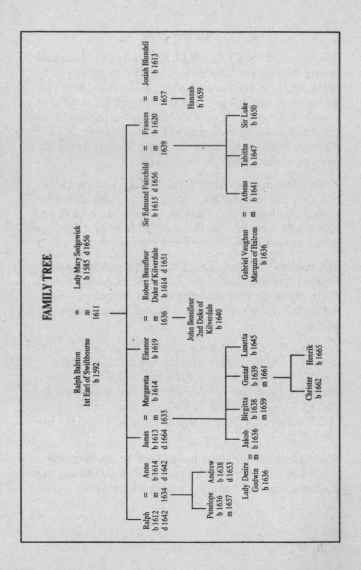

Ralph Balston
1st Earl of Swiftbourne
b 1592

= m 1611

Lady Mary Sedgewick
b 1585 d 1656

Ralph
b 1612
d 1642

= m 1634

Anne
b 1614
d 1642

James
b 1613
d 1664

= m 1635

Margareta
b 1614

Eleanor
b 1619

= m 1636

Robert Beaufleur
Duke of Kilverdale
b 1614 d 1651

Sir Edmund Fairchild
b 1615 d 1656

= m 1639

Frances
b 1620

= m 1657

Josiah Blundell
b 1613

Hannah
b 1659

Penelope
b 1636
m 1657

Andrew
b 1638
d 1653

Lady Desire
Godwin
b 1636

= m 1636

Jakob
b 1636

Birgitta
b 1638
m 1659

Gustaf
b 1639
m 1661

Lunetta
b 1645

John Beaufleur
2nd Duke of
Kilverdale
b 1640

Gabriel Vaughan
Marquis of Halross
b 1636

= m

Athena
b 1641

Tabitha
b 1647

Sir Luke
b 1650

Christer
b 1662

Henrik
b 1665

Prologue

A French youth sang a love song. A group of courtiers played basset around a large table, gambling huge sums with fashionable disregard for the consequences. The King lounged at his ease, amused by the clever, cynical conversation of his noble companions.

The Earl of Swiftbourne stood aloof from the clamour around him. He was nearly half a century too old to be part of the circle of witty young men who entertained the king, and too hard-headed to risk his fortune at the gambling table. He owed his status at court to the fact he'd been one of the men, along with the Duke of Albemarle, who'd helped Charles regain his throne. Swiftbourne was well aware royal gratitude could be fickle, but he was adept at navigating the hazards associated with power. For the time being, he was confident his position was secure.

A few feet away from Swiftbourne, an aristocratic rogue was trying to seduce one of the ladies of the court. From the tone of her responses, Swiftbourne judged the rogue was close to success. He ignored the couple as he focussed on the group around the King. His grandson, John Beaufleur, the Duke of Kilverdale, was among them.

Kilverdale was just short of twenty-six and in the prime of his youth and power. He looked every inch the courtier in his periwig, silk brocade coat and Venetian lace, but he also had the manners and intelligence necessary to hold his own in the Court of Charles II. It was an environment where little was sacred and noble poets could shred the reputation of a rival with a few anonymously circulated verses.

Kilverdale had been the target of such satires in the past, but now he was doing nothing more scandalous than asking the King's permission to leave the country.

'A retreat! Kilverdale seeks a retreat because he has been overmatched by Rochester's wit!' Fotherington exclaimed.

Swiftbourne controlled a scornful curl of his lip. The youthful Rochester was a fine poet and a brilliant conversationalist, but he did not intimidate Kilverdale. Swiftbourne was confident his grandson could match wits or swords with any man present should the need arise.

'I must fetch my cousin from the English convent at Bruges, your Majesty,' Kilverdale said.

'A *nun,* by God!' said Fotherington.

'She is a guest of the nuns,' Kilverdale said, continuing to address the King.

'I visited the convent at Bruges myself, when I was on my travels,' said Charles. 'Remember me to the Abbess.'

Kilverdale bowed gracefully in acknowledgement of the request. His expression, as so often, was courteously unreadable. Swiftbourne knew the English nuns on the continent had done a great deal to help the King's cause when he was in exile. The Abbess might justifiably have expected a little more from Charles than his remembrances now.

'Is she beautiful?' asked Fotherington. 'I have heard rumours her name is Athena and your mother sent her to the nuns because she is so beautiful.'

'You must present her to us,' said the King, his interest caught.

'I thank your Majesty for your kindness. She will be honoured to attend Court—but I must present her to my mother first,' Kilverdale replied. 'Athena has lived retired from the world for several years. She must become accustomed to society by degrees.'

'Is she an heiress?' asked one of the fops crowding around.

'That depends on the quality of the man who courts her,' Kilverdale said, a cold glint in his eye.

The fop opened his mouth and then shut it again. It was well known that, unlike many of the debt-ridden noblemen adorning Charles's court, Kilverdale's title was backed by a large fortune. The implication in his words was clear—if he approved a suitor for his cousin's hand, he would bestow a dowry on her. If he didn't approve of the man, he would be ruthless in preventing access to his cousin.

Of course, Kilverdale's cousin was also Swiftbourne's granddaughter, but Swiftbourne had no intention of interfering with Kilverdale's plans for her. Athena had been living in the convent to hide from her abusive husband, but she'd recently been widowed. It seemed Kilverdale had decided it was time for her to return to England and make a more satisfactory second marriage. Despite his sometimes eccentric reputation, the Duke had always had a well-developed sense of responsibility for those who depended upon him. Swiftbourne was curious to discover what kind of matchmaker his grandson would prove. So far he'd been notably reluctant to enter marriage negotiations on his own behalf.

Kilverdale took formal leave of the King and turned to make his way out of the chamber. As he did so he looked straight at his grandfather for the first time.

Even after fifteen years it still shocked Swiftbourne to be confronted by that flat, hard gaze. There were times when he was convinced Kilverdale hated him, other times when he was sure ruthlessly controlled rage seethed behind the polite stare. And sometimes he caught glimpses of the devastated eleven-year-old boy whose world had been overturned by a few short words. It was those occasions Swiftbourne found most disturbing, though he always concealed his feelings behind the impenetrable mask of the professional diplomat.

'My lord.' Kilverdale paused to acknowledge his grandfather. 'I am glad to see you in good health.'

'Thank you,' said Swiftbourne, allowing just a touch of irony to shade his cool response. 'It's an inconvenient time to cross the channel, now we're at war with the French as well as the Dutch.'

Kilverdale raised one eyebrow. 'I dare say the enemy will come to more harm than I if we encounter each other,' he replied. 'Good evening, my lord.'

'Good evening.' Swiftbourne watched Kilverdale walk away. Two sons and a grandson had already predeceased him—he did not wish to receive the news of this grandson's death. Of all his children and grandchildren, Kilverdale was the one who most resembled him. Swiftbourne had survived seventy-four years with his health and wits intact and his fortune significantly enlarged. He comforted himself with the thought Kilverdale was more than capable of equalling that achievement.

Kilverdale was approached several times as he made his way out by his friends—or those who sought his friendship. Swiftbourne watched with cynical amusement as one enterprising girl nearly tripped up at Kilverdale's feet in her efforts to catch his eye. It was far from the first time such a thing had happened. The young, unmarried and wealthy duke had been a target for matchmaking parents and ambitious daughters ever since he'd returned to England six years earlier.

Kilverdale restored the girl's balance with a deft gesture, spoke a few coolly courteous words and moved on. The next attempt to waylay him was far more determined. The Earl of Windle stepped away from the basset table and moved directly in front of Kilverdale. Even at this distance Swiftbourne could see the bullish expression on Windle's face. It was well known the Earl's fortune was in a desperate state. His plans for recovery centred on finding a rich husband for his daughter. At first he'd tried to lure Kilverdale into marriage negotiations. Recently his attempts at persuasion had become less subtle. Swiftbourne began to stroll towards the two men.

'I regret I do not have time to linger tonight, my lord,' Kilverdale said.

'You can spare the time to take some wine with me, I'm sure, your Grace,' Windle replied unctuously.

'Unfortunately not. I'm bound for Flanders at first light,' said Kilverdale. 'I—' His eyes narrowed as Windle caught his coat sleeve.

The Earl flushed angrily, but released his grip. He was naturally inclined to be a bully, but Kilverdale's prowess with a sword was too well known for Windle to risk forcing a quarrel on the Duke. 'I will be pleased to travel with you to the coast so we can conclude our discussions before you leave,' he said.

'I do not recall starting a discussion with you that cannot be concluded with a simple "good evening",' Kilverdale said, turning away.

'By God, Kilverdale, you must take a wife soon!' exclaimed Fotherington. 'Why not Windle's daughter?' He glanced between the two men, clearly hoping his meddling would incite some entertaining fireworks.

'With all due courtesy to the Lady Anne, I am already committed to another,' Kilverdale snapped. 'Good night, my lords.' He turned on his heel and strode out before any of them could respond.

After a second's shock Swiftbourne found himself the focus of all eyes. He'd been as startled as the rest of them by his grandson's announcement, but his expression remained impassive as he said, 'Do not expect me to reveal Kilverdale's secrets, gentleman. No doubt he will provide further enlightenment when it suits him.'

'Are you in his confidence, my lord?' Fotherington asked. 'I had not realised you were on such warm terms with him these days.'

Swiftbourne raised an eyebrow. 'I am pleased to assure you that Kilverdale and I enjoy terms of more than adequate warmth, sir,' he said, and took even more pleasure in the way Fotherington wilted under his icy gaze.

There was a sudden commotion at the basset table as one of the players won a considerable sum. It was a signal for a general regrouping and a few moments later Swiftbourne discovered the King at his elbow.

'Committed to a bride, or a paramour?' Charles asked, a gleam of amusement in his eyes. 'Either will be something of a novelty for Kilverdale—if there was any truth in what he said to Windle. Let us hope he returns swiftly to Court so we can enjoy the next act in this drama.'

Chapter One

∽∽∽∽∽

London, Friday 31, August 1666

Temperance kept a wary eye on her surroundings as she followed the link boy through the dark streets. It was nearly midnight, and the bustling daytime crowds had long since gone home. Normally she would never venture out so late, but business had been slow all summer. She could not afford to lose the potential sale at the end of this journey. She listened for threatening sounds in the shadows and kept a firm grip on the stout stick she held by her side. She maintained an equally firm hold on the carefully packed goods she carried in her other arm.

The link boy stopped abruptly, lifting his torch to illuminate the sign of the Dog and Bone tavern. Temperance was so startled by the snarling beast revealed in the flickering light she took an involuntary step backwards.

'Here you are,' said the boy.

Temperance released a careful breath. After a second glance, she decided the sign was badly painted, not deliberately vicious. All the same, she wished her apprentice hadn't been taken sick that afternoon. If Isaac hadn't been near blind from the pain in his head, he could have come with her. His presence would have increased her status in the eyes of her potential customer.

She slipped the stick through a side opening in her skirts and hung it from a concealed belt. She took a coin from the pocket, which was also hidden beneath her skirts, and gave it to the link boy. Then she braced herself and pushed open the tavern door.

A thick fog of wine and tobacco fumes and too many closely packed bodies rushed out to greet her. Temperance stepped inside, realising at once that something unusual was happening. She'd anticipated the unpleasant smells. She hadn't expected to be presented with an impenetrable wall of male shoulders the moment she stepped over the threshold. The men were all looking at something she couldn't see, and blocking her from moving any further into the room. For an alarming moment she thought they might be watching a fight.

Her first instinct was to leave. She'd rather lose the sale than risk being caught up in a brawl. Then she realised the mood of the crowd was good humoured. She edged further into the room, trying to see what the men were looking at. She was tall enough to peer over the shoulders of most of those blocking her view, but the crowd was a couple of rows deep. Heads kept getting in her way. It was infuriating.

At last she tapped on the shoulder of one of the men. When he looked around, his eyes widened in surprise. She was about to ask him where the tavern keeper was, but he grinned and said, 'Can't see, lass? I'll wager you'll take more pleasure in looking than most of us will. Come through.' He stepped back so she could move in front of him.

Temperance hesitated for half a second. It wasn't sensible to let herself be hemmed in by a crowd of strangers—but curiosity got the better of her. With a murmur of thanks she accepted his offer. From her new position she could see all attention was focussed on a figure sitting near the unlit hearth. She'd just noticed he was holding a lute when he began to play. The crowd immediately fell silent.

At first Temperance couldn't believe it. What kind of musician could hold a tavern of drinking men in thrall at nearly midnight? But after a few moments the music reached out to her, drawing her in as surely as it held the rest of the audience. She craned to one side, trying to get a better look at him. She saw a head of black hair and the flash of a white shirt before someone got in her way.

Then he began to sing. To her astonishment, she felt goose bumps rise all over her body. His voice curled deep down inside her, stirring nameless urges so intimate and disturbing part of her wanted to run away and hide. The rest of her wanted to get a lot closer. Such a thing had never happened to her before. Half-angry at her inexplicable reaction, but unable to deny her compulsion to look at the singer, she pushed forward until she was at the front of the standing crowd.

She clutched her bundle against her chest and stared at the musician. His black hair nearly reached his shoulders. It glowed like a raven's wing in the candlelight, but it didn't look as if it had ever been tamed by a barber. He'd taken off his coat, and his white shirt was open at the neck. She was fascinated by the movement of his strong throat as he sang. Her fingertips tingled with the urge to touch him there. To explore beneath the plain white linen.

When she became aware of the improper nature of her thoughts she flushed and directed her attention elsewhere. It didn't help much. The soft linen revealed the breadth of his shoulders, and he'd pushed his sleeves back to his elbows. She watched the play of sinews in his forearm as his long fingers plucked the strings. He had clever hands, she thought dazedly, watching the swift surety with which his left hand moved over the neck of the lute. It was both exciting and unsettling to watch him play with such skill. The room seemed even hotter than it had a few moments ago.

He lifted his head and glanced around his audience. His dark brown eyes were set deep under black brows. He had a nose like a hawk, cheekbones to match and more than one day's growth of stubble on his strong jaw. His voice might hold the allure of a fallen angel, enticing her to commit all kinds of sinful folly, but he looked like a vagabond.

His gaze passed over her in the crowd then returned to focus upon her face. His eyes locked with hers. Temperance stood rooted to the spot. He had *seen* her. His dark eyes seemed to pierce straight to her heart. A hot wave of self-conscious awareness rolled over her.

Just for a second she thought she heard a slight hesitation in his supple voice. Then she was sure she'd imagined it, because he continued to sing with utter confidence—and his lips curved in a small, but unmistakeably arrogant smile.

That smile jarred her out of her stupefaction. No doubt he took it for granted he could turn a woman's knees weak with a simple song. He was surely a seducer and a vagabond who left broken hearts and lives behind him without a qualm. Temperance wrenched her gaze away from him, furious and embarrassed she'd fallen under his spell for even a few seconds. She gripped her bundle of goods so tightly her knuckles turned white.

She refused to look at the musician again, but she couldn't stop listening. It was an irritating, tormenting pleasure. She wanted to listen to him, she just didn't want to feed his arrogance by seeming to enjoy his song. She stared at the fireplace to one side of the musician and pretended she was indifferent to him. To her indignation a note of humour crept into his voice. Even though the taproom was full of people, she was certain he was singing to her—and laughing at her. It was insufferable. She glared at the mantelpiece. In an effort to distract herself she focussed on a crack in the plaster of the chimney breast, allowing her eyes to follow it all the way up to the ceiling. The amusement in his voice grew more pronounced; even the lute seemed to be laughing at her as he plucked a lively, teasing melody from its strings.

She realised too late it must have looked as if she'd stuck her chin in the air in response to his initial amusement. Very slowly, by casual degrees, she allowed her gaze to drop until she was once more looking at the mantelpiece. She kept her eyes fixed straight ahead and hoped the song would soon come to an end. How many verses did it have? Was he even singing the same song he'd started with? Or had he slid seamlessly into another one so he could deliberately prolong her discomfort? She stopped looking at the mantelpiece and stared at him suspiciously.

The fellow had the gall to grin at her! His fingers didn't fluff a single note and his voice remained perfectly in tune—but he grinned at her!

How dare he! The urge to box his over-confident ears was almost too strong to resist. She imagined a discordant jangle and the pleasing sight of the dark-eyed vagabond wearing a necklace of lute strings and small fragments of wood around his cocksure neck.

A man beside her chuckled.

'Jack Bow is singing for more than his supper now,' he murmured. 'Does he take your fancy, lass? You've surely taken his.'

'No!' Temperance's denial emerged more forcefully than she'd intended. She saw several heads turn to look at her, and some men began to smile in an obnoxiously knowing way.

Her skin burned. She forgot her reason for coming to the tavern. All she wanted to do was remove herself from the mortifying situation at once. She was about to push through the crowd to the door when the musician ended the song with a flourish.

He was rewarded with applause and whistles. Several men called out to him, offering to buy him a drink. For a moment Temperance lost sight of him as the tavern patrons moved into new positions. She belatedly realised she wasn't the only woman in the room—though at this hour of the night she was most likely the only respectable woman present. And she was only here because the plague that had devastated London the previous year had been so bad for business. The City was almost back to normal now, but if Temperance was to restore her shop to a sound footing she needed every sale she could make.

Where was the gentleman whose servant had roused her to wait on his master? She resisted the urge to glance in the direction of the singer and instead tried to locate the tavern keeper.

A door on the far side of the taproom crashed open. Temperance couldn't see who came out, but then an irritable voice shouted, 'Where the hell's the draper I sent for?'

Temperance pushed her way towards her still-unseen customer. When she got closer she saw he'd just emerged from a private room that led off from the main taproom. He was a fashionably dressed young man, but his clothes were the worse for wear. He was also at least two inches shorter than Temperance.

He scowled at her when she stopped in front of him.

'I want a draper, not an overgrown doxy,' he said.

Temperance swallowed an angry response. His appearance was at least as unappealing as hers. Worse, in fact. She might be unusually tall and no great beauty, but at least she was sober and well groomed and didn't wantonly insult strangers.

'I am the draper,' she said coldly. 'Your man said you want a length of linen and a length of muslin.'

'You have them?' His red-rimmed eyes focussed on the bundle in her arms. 'Show me.' He stepped back into his private room and she had no choice but to follow.

She didn't particularly want to do business in public, nor did she relish the thought of being alone with this well-born lout—but when she entered the smaller chamber she saw he had a friend with him.

'Has that damned caterwauling finally stopped, Tredgold?' the other man demanded.

Temperance bristled with indignation at the insult to the musician. Caterwauling? The dark-eyed vagabond might be as arrogant as the devil, but he had the finest voice she'd ever heard, and his musicianship was remarkable.

'Give me the linen.' Tredgold grabbed the bundle of goods from her arms and tore it open.

'Be careful!' Temperance protested, as the piece of muslin fell into a puddle of liquid on the floor.

Her customer ignored both her and the muslin. He shook out the length of linen and tossed it over his head. Temperance watched in disbelief as he stuck his arms out and swayed from side to side. Then he started to moan and groan.

'*OoooOOOOooooOOOOoooo…Arghhhh….OOOoooooo-OOO!*'

His friend stared at him with an open mouth for several seconds, then clutched his head and cowered in his seat.

'Oh! Oh, I'm so scared. Oh, my poor heart! Oh, I'm *dead*!' At his last dramatic exclamation, he collapsed sideways, disappearing from view beneath the edge of the table.

Temperance's own heart thudded with alarm and confusion. For an instant she almost thought he really was dead, then she realised he had been sitting on a high-backed bench. He'd just fallen sideways on it. Now he was lying there, laughing like a lunatic.

'Do you think it will work?' Tredgold demanded.

'The old goat might die of laughter—but not fear,' his friend replied, sitting up again. 'Whoever heard of a ghost with brown velvet arms? If you take off all your clothes and wrap the linen around you, you could pretend you've risen from the grave. That might work.'

'Hmm.' Tredgold threw the length of linen across the table—where it soaked up some spilled wine—and took off his coat. For a horrified moment Temperance thought he was going to disrobe further but, to her relief, he seemed content to experiment in his shirt sleeves and breeches. He wrapped the linen around himself in untidy folds.

'Give me the muslin, wench,' he ordered, pointing at where it still lay on the floor.

Temperance handed it to him and hastily stepped back. He twisted it round his upper body and head and turned back to his companion.

'Now what do you think?'

'I've never seen a corpse wrapped in pink,' said his friend, looking at the spreading wine stains on both the muslin and the linen.

'It's blood, of course!' Tredgold said impatiently.

'Not that colour. You'll never frighten the old man to death in pink muslin.'

'What are you trying to do?' Temperance asked.

'Scare his grandfather into his grave,' the friend said.

'*What?*'

'He's nearly ninety. Until he dies I can't claim my inheritance,' Tredgold said as if he had a genuine grievance.

'You should be ashamed of yourself!' Temperance exploded. 'I won't be party to such an evil scheme. Take off the linen at once!'

'I am taking it off,' Tredgold snarled. 'It's not going to work. I'll have to think of something else.' He tossed the fabric on the floor, flung himself into a chair, and poured some more wine.

Temperance stared at the stained, crumpled cloth. She couldn't sell it to another customer now.

'You must pay for the goods you have spoiled,' she said, trying to control her anger.

Tredgold laughed. 'I'm not paying for those useless rags.'

'I did not bring you rags. I brought you lengths of fine linen and muslin—as you requested,' Temperance said. 'It is you who have ruined them. You must pay for what you have played with and spoiled.'

Tredgold raised his eyebrows superciliously, allowing his gaze to move up and down Temperance's body in an insulting assessment. Then he shrugged one shoulder. 'Send your master to claim his dues,' he said. He turned away from her, tilting his chair on to its back legs as he reached for the wine jug.

Temperance kicked the nearest chair leg as hard as she could. Tredgold crashed backwards with a shout of alarm. The wine jug flew into the air, its contents drenching Tredgold and splashing Temperance's skirt. It hit the edge of the table, then smashed to the floor.

Temperance stood over Tredgold as he blinked up at her. Her heart was pounding, but she was far too angry to be afraid.

'You will pay me,' she said. 'Get up and give me the money.'

Tredgold stared at her for a few seconds, then his dazed expression turned spiteful.

'You bitch!' he raged. 'I'll teach you—'

She took a step back, reaching through the slit in her skirt for her stick. She was taller than Tredgold, but under no illusion she could match his strength.

Tredgold disentangled himself from the chair and staggered to his feet. He was too dazed to move quickly. There was time for Temperance to flee, but it wasn't in her nature to run away. She cursed her decision to come to the tavern, but she held her stick by her side and kept her watchful attention on Tredgold and his friend.

Tredgold shook his head and winced. Then, without warning, he lunged towards her.

She only just had time to lift her stick and jab him in the stomach. He swore and reeled away. He hadn't realised she was armed.

Temperance released a jerky breath. The first victory was hers. But though the stick extended her reach, she hadn't managed to get as much power behind her blow as she'd hoped. Tredgold wasn't incapacitated, and now he was forewarned.

Since there was no further need to conceal the stick she held it in both hands in front of her, ready to defend herself from Tredgold's next attack.

He came at her in a rush, faster than she'd expected, his mouth drawn back in a snarl of rage. Both fists were raised—

The next instant he was spun around and slammed back into the edge of the heavy table. The table screeched across the floorboards until it hit the end wall. The vagabond musician had come to Temperance's aid. Now he waited, a mocking smile on his lips, for Tredgold to recover.

Tredgold leant on the table, his head bowed over his braced arms as he took several heaving breaths. Suddenly he reared up and around with a feral growl. He threw a wild punch, which the musician easily avoided. He blocked another flailing punch, then replied with a blow of his own that laid Tredgold cold on the wine-soaked floorboards.

Temperance started breathing again, her wits slowly catching up with events. She didn't know when the musician had entered the side room. She'd only become aware of him after his lightning intervention saved her from Tredgold's charging attack. She stared at him. He looked back at her, absently flexing his left hand, the one he'd used to hit Tredgold. Apart from that small gesture he seemed unperturbed by the brief, violent incident.

Temperance's thoughts and emotions were in total disorder. She should be making a dignified exit from the tavern, but she kept staring at the musician. It was the first time she'd seen him standing up. He was a couple of inches taller than her own five feet ten inches. It was so rare for her to have to look up to meet a man's eyes, she couldn't stop looking. He was lean-limbed and graceful, but there was unmistakeable power in his broad shoulders. Even dressed only in shirt and breeches with his hair ungroomed and his chin unshaven, he was the finest figure of a man she'd ever laid eyes on.

His mouth quirked up at the corners as if he was well aware of her admiration.

She jerked her gaze away from him.

'Cocksure,' she muttered, annoyed with him for being so arrogant and with herself for being so easily bedazzled.

He grinned. 'What does he owe you?' he asked, indicating Tredgold with a nod of his head.

'For the linen and muslin,' Temperance replied, trying to collect her wits. Even when she was still half-dazed with shock she was determined the musician understood she was a respectable trades-woman. 'He ruined them.'

'How much?' The musician searched for and found Tredgold's purse.

'Hey!' Tredgold's friend exclaimed.

'How much?' The musician looked at Temperance, ignoring the half-hearted protest.

She told him, and watched as he counted out the coins in full view of Tredgold's friend.

'There,' he said to the gape-mouthed youth. 'You can tell him you witnessed a fair accounting of his debts when he recovers.' Tredgold was already stirring and groaning. The musician dropped the purse on to his stomach and gave Temperance the price of her linen and muslin.

'Thank you.' She blinked at the coins, hardly able to believe she'd been paid after all.

'And now I'll escort you home,' said the musician.

'Escort me?' Temperance looked up. 'Oh, no, sir, there is no need—'

'Are you not here alone? If you have an escort, he did a poor job of protecting you,' the musician said.

'My apprentice is sick,' said Temperance, standing straighter as she consciously gathered her dignity and authority. 'I will hire a link boy—'

'Certainly,' said the musician. 'And I will escort you.' He headed for the taproom as he spoke. The watching men fell back to allow him easy passage.

Temperance followed him. She had no choice. He'd created the only clear path through the room. But she couldn't help being ex-asperated at the way the men parted for him just like the red sea had parted before Moses. After all, he was...

'Just a man who doesn't own a comb,' she muttered. And nearly bumped into him when he stopped suddenly.

He grinned at her over his shoulder. 'But I do have a useful left,' he said. 'And I'm even better with my sword. I doubt a comb would be much protection against footpads.'

Temperance opened her mouth, then closed it again. However much she wanted to put him in his place, she couldn't forget he'd saved her from Tredgold's attack, and made sure she was paid for the spoiled goods. She was in the musician's debt.

She watched as he buckled on a sword belt with a brisk familiarity that suggested he was indeed competent with the weapon.

'Are you a soldier?' she asked.

'A soldier?' He quirked an eyebrow at her. 'No. The only cause I've ever fought for is my own.'

One of the men in the crowd laughed. 'Jack Bow's a soldier of fortune, lass. He goes a-venturing with his sword and his lute. He's got a host of tales to tell about the far-off lands he's visited.'

'Oh.' Temperance's gaze focussed on the musician's hands as she considered that unsettling information. It sounded as if he was a mercenary. He'd saved her from Tredgold when there were witnesses to applaud his actions, but was it wise to be alone with such a man in the dark city streets?

'I'm afraid there are no interesting adventures to be had in Cheapside,' she said, making a final, half-hearted attempt to dissuade him from escorting her. 'You will be very bored, sir.'

'The man hasn't been born who could be bored in your company, sweetheart,' he replied, shrugging into a plain olive-green coat. He slung his lute case over his back and grinned at her dumbfounded expression. 'Let's go.'

Temperance followed him out of the tavern. 'I am not your sweetheart!' she said as soon as the door closed behind them.

'So where is your man?' asked Jack Bow. 'The one with the right to call you sweetheart?'

'There isn't one,' said Temperance. Her public status as a virtuous spinster was essential to her continuing right to trade in the City as a member of the Drapers' Company. It didn't occur to her until too late that she should have been more circumspect with this stranger.

'Why not?' he asked.

'Why…? That's none of your business.' She strode off down the road.

'Such a pretty, hot-blooded wench must have suitors queuing

at your door,' he said, falling into step beside her. 'Do you beat them off with that stick?'

'Just because you helped me doesn't give you the right to make fun of me!' Temperance exclaimed. 'Go away and vex someone else.'

'Oh, sweetheart, the night's young—and I haven't finished vexing you yet,' he replied. 'You do respond so charmingly.'

'What?' She blinked at him in the darkness. 'You are a cocksure knave. I don't believe anyone who speaks so brazenly can possess a scrap of delicacy or proper modesty.'

He laughed.

Temperance walked faster.

'What of father or brothers?' he asked, easily keeping pace with her. 'Why did they send you to answer Tredgold's summons?'

To her surprise she detected an undercurrent of disapproval in his voice.

'Surely a man of your ilk would have no qualms about sending a woman to the Dog and Bone?' Temperance said, dodging his question. 'It ill behoves you to criticise others.'

'A man of my ilk…?' he mused. 'What a pretty picture you have of me. Are your menfolk sick or just lazy?'

'Isaac is sick,' said Temperance, uncertain what to make of his persistence. 'Otherwise he would have come with me.'

'And Isaac is?'

'My apprentice.'

'Your apprentice?' he repeated. 'You are the mistress?' He laughed softly. 'No wonder you did not take kindly to Tredgold's insolence.'

'It is *my* draper's shop,' Temperance said proudly. 'I am my father's only surviving child. I inherited it from him and I manage it in every particular. I do it very well.' She refused to let her voice falter as she made the last statement. There were many things in her life she couldn't claim, including a queue of suitors calling her sweet names, but she had worked hard to learn her father's business. 'I have no wish to marry and be ruled by a man.'

'But you could continue to do business as a feme sole, could you not? As long as your husband had his own trade and took no part in yours?'

'In certain circumstances. But if my husband wasn't a freeman of the City I might lose the right to trade completely.' Temperance paused, surprised by Jack Bow's knowledge of City practices.

'How do you know that?' she demanded.

She sensed, rather than saw, his shrug. 'My great-grandfather was a grocer,' he replied. 'I know a little about the customs of the City.'

'A *grocer*! Why didn't you follow in his footsteps? If you didn't care to be a grocer, there are many trades in which a strong, quick-witted man can prosper.'

'He died before I was born,' Jack explained. 'I followed in my father's footsteps.'

'And he was a rootless vagabond.'

Silence followed her hasty retort. As it lengthened she wished her words back. She hadn't meant to insult a man she knew nothing about. There was something about Jack Bow that prompted her to speak far too recklessly.

'I'm sorry—' she began, wanting to apologise for her slight to his father, though she had no intention of softening her manner to Jack himself.

'Uprooted,' he said at the same instant. 'Uprooted, not rootless. He knew where he came from. He was thwarted in his efforts to return there.'

'I do not know him. I should not have said such a terrible thing,' Temperance said.

'Why not?' said Jack. 'It was me you were describing, not my father, after all.'

'Well…' Temperance swallowed. She could sense the change in Jack's mood. For the first time humour was absent from his voice. He spoke quietly, with perhaps a hint of fatalism in his manner.

'Where do *you* come from?' she asked. The simple question took more courage than she'd anticipated.

'Most recently from Venice—by way of Ostend and Dover,' he replied. 'I must have lost my comb along the way.'

'*Venice*! Truly?'

'Very truly,' he said. 'The biggest wild goose chase I've ever taken part in. I might as well have stayed in London and lined my barber's pockets for all the good I achieved. What's your name?'

'Temperance,' she began, disconcerted by the sudden question. 'Temperance—'

'Temperance?' He started to laugh. 'You were misnamed, sweetheart. Restraint of any kind seems to be completely alien to your character. *Tempest* would be far more apt.'

Chapter Two

Saturday 1 September 1666

It was a warm, sunny afternoon as Jack strolled through the City. The wooden shutters of all the shops were opened for business. It was fortunate Cheapside was such a broad thoroughfare because in some cases the lower boards projected as much as two and half feet beyond the shop front. The upper shutters were raised to provide a modicum of protection for the goods displayed on the lower board. Shopkeepers stood or sat in their doorways to guard their goods and attract the attention of potential customers. Often it was women who occupied the carved seats in front of the shops. Cheapside was one of the fashionable meeting places in the City. It had become famous for the pretty tradesmen's wives who bantered with the men-about-town sauntering past. More trestles and stalls were set up in the street itself, though hundreds of other sellers sold their wares from nothing more than a sack or a basket on the ground.

Jack was in no hurry. He paused to exchange compliments with the blue-eyed wife of a goldsmith, then strolled on a few more yards. He was taller than most of those around him, and an instant later he was grateful for the advantage it gave him. Coming towards him was the last man he wanted to meet in London or anywhere else. He ducked into the nearest shop, which happened to be a mercer's, and watched the Earl of Windle walk past the door and on towards St Paul's. He hadn't seen or spoken to Windle since their encounter at Court six months ago. As far as Jack was concerned, the longer their next meeting was delayed the better.

He left the mercers and continued along Cheapside, his blood quickening in anticipation as he approached Temperance's shop. He'd enjoyed his encounter with the hot-tempered draper the previous night. They were well matched in several pleasurable ways. For once he was in no danger of getting a crick in his neck when he talked to a woman. She wasn't a classic beauty, but he'd felt the pull of attraction to her from the moment he saw her in the taproom. It had been impossible to miss her in the crowd. Her personality was so vivid that, even when she was standing quite still, her thoughts and emotions had been easy to read.

Most of all, he enjoyed the way she challenged him at every turn. She was very different from the women who tried to win his favour at Court. He could not imagine Temperance heaping him with false flattery or pretending to trip up at his feet to catch his attention. She'd thanked him for his help with Tredgold, but she clearly wasn't the woman to gush her undying gratitude. In fact, it wouldn't surprise him to discover she believed she'd been capable of dealing with the contretemps in the tavern on her own.

As he drew closer he saw the shutters of the draper's shop were open and goods were laid out on the board, but Temperance wasn't sitting in the doorway. Mildly surprised by her absence, Jack lengthened his stride.

'Go back to bed, Isaac,' said Temperance.

'But, mistress, I must not shirk my work,' he protested.

'You are not shirking,' she replied. 'You spent all yesterday afternoon and most of the night groaning about the pain in your head or throwing up. You know when these headaches come upon you, you are fit for nothing the next day. Go upstairs and rest. I will expect you to work doubly hard on Monday.'

'Yes. Thank you.' Even though he tried to hide it, she saw the relief in his face.

He was turning to the stairs when the light from the open

doorway at the front was suddenly blocked. They both looked towards the customer.

The newcomer had his back to the light, and his appearance had changed in one, very startling way since she'd last seen him, but Temperance recognised Jack Bow immediately.

'What have you done to your hair?' The disconcerted question escaped before she had time to think better of it.

He grinned. 'I traded it for someone else's,' he replied, stepping into the shop. 'No doubt a buxom country lass was glad to sell these locks for a profit.'

He was wearing a black periwig. The hair was as black as his own but, instead of the wild, shaggy mane of the previous night, it fell in thick, graceful curls around his shoulders. It was longer than his own hair, and changed his appearance considerably. He was smooth shaven as well, and Temperance caught the faint scent of orange flower water when he moved. Today he looked far less like a rogue and a lot more like a gentleman. But he still wore the same travel-creased coat, and his lute case was slung across his back just as it had been when she'd last seen him. His hawklike nose and piercing eyes were those of a vagabond.

Her heart began to beat triple time. She was nervous and excited all at once. She wanted to invite him in. She wanted to send him on his way before he turned her life upside down. She was conscious of Isaac staring at her. For pride's sake she wanted to treat Jack Bow like any other customer, but for several long seconds she couldn't think of anything to say. All she could do was look at him.

He returned her gaze just as intently. She wasn't used to such concentrated scrutiny from a man—not unless he was bargaining with her. But Jack Bow wasn't looking at her like a tradesman. He was just…looking at her. Heat rolled over her body.

'Mistress?' Isaac said uncertainly.

With an effort Temperance wrenched her gaze from Jack's face. She could see from Isaac's expression that he was worried, unsure what he should do.

'Go to bed,' she said. Her voice didn't sound as if it belonged to her.

'Bed?' said Jack. 'It's the middle of the afternoon.'

'He is not well,' Temperance defended her apprentice.

'Ah.' Jack's shrewd gaze rested on Isaac for a few moments. He nodded as if accepting the accuracy of her claim. 'You may safely obey your mistress, lad. I'll not do her any harm.'

'No, you won't!' Temperance retorted. 'And I'll thank you not to make so free with your orders in my shop, sir!'

Jack grinned. 'Why don't we step outside so you can keep an eye on your goods?' he suggested.

Temperance followed him to the door as Isaac went upstairs. She looked across the width of board, automatically checking nothing had gone missing while her attention was elsewhere. She smoothed a piece of linsey-wolsey beneath her hands, then glanced up to see he was watching her with a half-smile on his lips.

'Why were you so extravagant?' she burst out. 'There was nothing wrong with your hair. If you'd only combed and dressed it properly—'

'Don't you admire my new locks?' His long fingers briefly caressed one of the black curls that lay against his shoulder. The gesture reminded her of the preening fops she sometimes saw strolling past her shop, but there was nothing remotely foppish about the wicked gleam in his dark eyes.

'I suppose you're bald underneath,' she said, feeling disgruntled and not sure why.

'Not quite. Are you regretting the lost opportunity to run your fingers through my hair? You should have mentioned your preference last night.'

'Keep your voice down!' Temperance ordered, alarmed at his indiscretion. She glanced around to see if anyone had heard him. Fortunately, Agnes Cruikshank, her neighbour to the left, was engaged with a customer.

'Yes, Madam Tempest.' Jack grinned.

'All my cloth is of the finest quality,' she declared. 'Are you thinking of a new coat, sir? Something to do honour to your fine new hair. This pink would go nicely with the sweet little curls.'

'Black or blue might be more appropriate,' he mused, testing the quality of the fabric between his fingers and thumb. 'To match my bruises when you pull out the stick banging against your thigh.'

'I *never* beat my customers—'

'Unless they refuse to pay,' he reminded her.

'I didn't! I just kicked his chair. It was *you* who—' She broke off. How on earth had he lured her into this ridiculous argument? But all he had to do was look at her with that exasperating, disturbing gleam in his eyes and she forgot all proper reticence.

'What are you doing here?' she demanded.

'I came to make sure you're none the worse for your adventure last night.'

'Thank you. As you can see, I am very well,' Temperance replied, trying for a note of sedate formality.

'Very well indeed,' he said. 'Your eyes are as clear as the summer sky…'

'Blue,' she said weakly.

'Obviously, otherwise I'd have compared them to something else. And your hair…'

'Brown,' she said.

'Are you determined to destroy the poetry of the moment?' He frowned at her. 'I am famous for my sonnets, you know.'

'You are?'

'Humorous, witty or romantic, as the occasion requires.'

'I'll bear you in mind, should I ever find myself in need of a rhyming couplet,' Temperance said.

'Excellent. Would you, perchance, accept a sonnet in praise of your beautiful eyes in exchange for a length of this *nearly* as fine blue broadcloth?'

'No.'

Jack put one hand over his heart and assumed a pained expression. 'You're a hard woman to do business with, Mistress Tempest.'

'I can't buy coal with pretty compliments,' she said, feeling flustered.

'Have you ever tried? The coal merchant might be susceptible to cornflower blue.'

'I don't think so. He… You do talk nonsense!' She pulled herself together.

He smiled, and butterflies swooped in Temperance's stomach. His smile was quite different from his teasing grin. It revealed a kinder, quieter side of his personality and called forth a much more profound emotional response from her than his cocky grin.

'How long have you been mistress here?' he asked.

'My father died nearly two years ago,' she said.

'A difficult time to take on such a responsibility.'

'Yes.' She pushed a strand of hair back from her face, her eyes unfocussed as she remembered that time.

'Did you stay in London?'

'During the plague?' She glanced at him. 'I had nowhere else to go. We all survived.' She shuddered as she recalled some of the terrible things she'd seen. 'But it does seem the worst is past now,' she added optimistically. 'And I pray it will not return.'

'So do I,' Jack said quietly.

'Were you here then?' She looked at him curiously.

He shook his head.

'Venice?' she asked, remembering his comment the previous night and wanting to lighten the mood. 'Or some other exotic location?'

'Last year I was very dull. I went to Bruges…Oxford…but mostly I stayed in Sussex.'

'Oxford? The King and Court went to Oxford to escape the plague.'

'So they did,' Jack acknowledged with a half-smile.

'Did you…? Have you ever played for the King?' Temperance asked, and held her breath waiting for the answer. He would surely laugh at her for asking such a silly question. But he was such a fine musician she could easily imagine him entertaining kings and queens.

Jack grinned.

'What does that smirk mean?' she demanded.

'The King has more appreciation for my sonnets than you do,' he replied. 'The witty ones at any rate. He particularly admired one I composed about a lady's—'

'Never mind,' Temperance interrupted, sure it would be scandalous. 'Have you really spoken to the King? Or are you just teasing me?'

Jack smiled his quiet smile. 'I have spoken to the King,' he said. 'And played my lute for him. I've played for Louis too, though that was several years ago.'

'Louis? The King of France?' Temperance stared at him. 'We're at war with France.'

'We weren't when I attended the French Court,' Jack replied. 'But the war was a cursed inconvenience when I was making my way back from Venice this summer. I got stuck at Ostend, waiting for the packet boat to form part of a convoy. By the time I'd languished in an inn for several days I could hardly afford to pay my fare home.'

'What did you do?' Temperance was half-fascinated, half-horrified by his revelations. She couldn't imagine anything more terrifying than being stranded so far from home.

'Played my lute, of course.' This time his grin was shot through with pure wickedness.

Temperance knew—she just knew—his next revelation would be outrageous, but she had to hear what he did next.

'Did you convince the captain of the packet boat to exchange a sonnet for your passage?' she asked.

'No. It was the good housewives of Ostend who showed the greatest appreciation for my talents,' he replied.

'What?' She looked at him warily. 'They gave you money when you sang?'

'Yes, they did,' he recollected. 'I was sitting on the beach and they came to watch and throw me coins. Then a couple of them invited me to go home with them—to sing for them privately. Because they so greatly admired my talents.'

'You are a rogue and a scoundrel!' Temperance wanted to cry.

'Only if I accepted their invitations,' he said.

'I'm sure I don't care to know how you paid your way home,' she said coldly.

'I was rescued by my cousin,' he said. 'Why don't you sell me some of this blue cloth?'

'Not for a sonnet. And after buying that ridiculous wig I doubt you've enough coins left.' She crossed her arms and glared at him.

'How much?'

When she grudgingly named a price he delved in his pocket and produced the necessary coins.

'Cut me a length,' he ordered.

'Yes, sir.' She mutinously complied.

He leant his hip against the edge of the board and watched her.

'There I was, playing my lute to pay for my supper, wondering how I could afford the packet fare without sacrificing my virtue—'

'Your *virtue*,' Temperance exclaimed, then snapped her mouth shut.

'Indeed. When who should I see approaching but my cousin. A splendid, prosperous fellow. It turned out he was waiting for the packet too. So I prevailed upon him to sponsor me.'

'Really?' Temperance didn't even try to keep the scepticism out of her voice. 'What a coincidence. What was your cousin doing in Ostend?'

'He'd gone to visit another cousin of ours in Bruges. But she wasn't there.'

'*She*? You may cease with this nonsense.' Temperance folded the broadcloth with quick, angry hands. 'And pay for your purchase.'

'I really do have several cousins.' Jack's eyes twinkled at her as he handed over the coins. 'One of them was a guest at the English convent in Bruges for several years. It was her fault I went to Venice this summer. I went to Bruges in April to fetch her home and found she'd already left for Italy, so I had to follow her.'

Temperance held the folded cloth in front of her and looked at Jack. Was it possible he was telling her the truth? He'd already mentioned visiting Bruges, and he'd told her about his trip to Venice more than once.

'Is your cousin a Catholic?' she asked, noting his reference to the convent.

'No. At least, she wasn't when she first became a guest of the nuns. She may have become more sympathetic to their mode of worship over the past few years,' Jack replied. 'But I can assure you she doesn't have horns and a tail.' There was an unusually acerbic tone in his voice. 'My other cousin, the one I travelled with to Dover, is a good Swedish Lutheran. No doubt far more acceptable to your English sensibilities.'

Temperance stared at him, trying to unravel everything he'd just said.

'Aren't you English?' she said. 'I thought you were. You sound like an Englishman. You said your great-grandfather was a grocer here in London.'

'Yes, I'm English. By birth at least,' he replied.

'But you have a Swedish cousin?'

'Half-Swedish. One of my uncles decided to make his fortune in Sweden and married a Swedish lady,' Jack explained. It was only when she noticed a slight relaxation in his posture she realised he'd tensed in response to her earlier question.

'Don't you feel English?' she asked.

'No. Yes.' He lifted one hand towards his head, then abruptly lowered it.

'You nearly forgot it's not your hair,' she taunted gently. 'If you hadn't wasted your money, every time you feel frustrated you'd be able to tug at your hair to your heart's content. As it is…' She let the words fade aggravatingly away.

'Why are you prejudiced against my handsome periwig?' he demanded. 'It is no different from that of any courtier—even the King himself. Would you make fun of his Majesty if he came to buy linen from you?'

'Of course not. But you must cut your coat to fit your cloth.'

'Very apt. Are you ever going to give it to me? Or just clutch it against your breast until Judgement Day?'

'Are you thinking a gentlemanly appearance will help you win another audience with the King?' Temperance asked, experiencing sudden enlightenment. 'I can see, if you believe it will help you win greater advancement, it might be worth the investment.'

'I'm glad I've finally won your approval.'

'I didn't say that. If it was from pure vanity—'

'*Diable!*' Jack snatched the periwig from his head and stuffed it in his pocket. 'There, are you satisfied?'

Her breath caught. His black hair had been cropped close to his head. Now there was nothing to soften his angular features and the predatory jut of his aquiline nose. His dark eyes simmered with impatience. He looked lean and dangerous. A hard, dark man capable of unimaginable deeds. Her first instinct was to take a step back, but she refused to give ground before him. Why had she allowed herself to forget her first impression of him? He was a vagabond.

Then he started to laugh. 'You would try the patience of a saint, Madam Tempest. And Heaven knows, I am no saint. Let us call a truce on the subject.'

'As…as you wish.' Temperance's hands felt unaccountably shaky as she turned away to finish preparing the cloth for him. 'So where is your cousin now?' she asked over her shoulder.

He shrugged. 'Somewhere between London and Dover, I imagine.'

'You left him behind?' Temperance exclaimed.

Jack grinned. 'I was in a hurry. There was only one good riding horse at the inn, so I took it. It was his own fault for going for a walk around the town.'

'You abandoned him after he paid for your passage across the Channel?' Temperance forgot her resolve not to get embroiled in any further arguments with Jack. 'How could you have repaid his kindness so ill?'

Jack raised one eyebrow at her. 'I took his clothes as well,' he said, casting a disparaging glance down at the olive coat he wore. 'Surely you didn't imagine I normally wear such drab attire? But my own clothes had been worn to a thread by the time I reached Dover.'

'You *stole* —' Temperance clapped her hand over her mouth. Accusing a man of being a thief in the middle of one of the busiest shopping thoroughfares of London was a sure way to call unwanted attention upon them.

'How could you be so ungrateful?' she demanded in a furious under-voice, smacking the bundled cloth against his chest. 'Heedless! Have you no conscience? What will you do when he catches up with you?' she asked. 'He'll disown you—or worse.'

'No, he won't,' Jack said. 'And if he did, it would just mean one less relative to worry about.'

'To be worried by you, you mean.' Temperance pushed her hair away from her overheated face. 'You're a heedless knave. If you're not careful, you'll end at Tyburn.'

'Would you come to wish me farewell?'

Temperance glanced sideways at him, furious with herself because she *did* care what happened to him. Just the thought of him meeting the hangman's noose filled her with sick anxiety.

'Folly,' she muttered under her breath. She'd known him for less than one full day, and he done nothing but irritate her the whole time. Except for when he'd saved her from Tredgold and made sure she received fair payment for her linen and muslin. But apart from that….

'I beg your pardon?' he said.

'Stupid.' She turned on him. 'Stupid. Stupid. *Stupid.* Go and play your knavish tricks on someone else.'

He grinned. 'I've played no tricks on you at all, sweetheart,' he said. 'But if you prefer me gone, that is easily arranged. Allow me a moment to restore myself.'

Before Temperance's disconcerted gaze he replaced the periwig on his head and arranged it about his shoulders to his satisfaction. The contrast between his hawkish features and the long black curls now framing his face was compelling.

'Farewell, Madam Tempest.' He bowed and strolled away.

Temperance watched him go, then dropped into her chair. He was gone. She should feel relieved. Instead she felt flat. Disappointed. He'd gone. And even though he was a scoundrel of the first water, he'd taken all the sparkle of the day with him.

Covent Garden, Sunday 2 September 1666

Jack woke to the smell of coffee and muffled sounds from the coffee room downstairs. He climbed out of bed and stretched, bending his arms to accommodate the low ceiling. He'd enjoyed a convivial evening of music and conversation last night, but it was his afternoon encounter with Temperance that lingered in his thoughts. He smiled as he remembered her reaction when he'd told her he'd taken his cousin's clothes and left him behind at Dover. She'd been just as entertainingly scandalised as he'd expected—and perhaps she was worried about his fate if his vengeful cousin caught up with him. Jack had no such fears, but he was flattered by her concern.

During his years of exile before the Restoration of Charles II, he had often travelled under the name of Jack Bow. It had given him a freedom of action he'd lacked when he'd been trying to maintain the dignity of his title without the support of either estates or fortune. But he hadn't meant to assume the guise on his trip to fetch Athena. He'd only done so after he chased her all the way from Bruges to Venice and back again. By the time he'd reached Milan all his entourage had left him for one good reason or another. Once he was travelling alone it had been quicker and more convenient for him to do so as Jack Bow, rather than the Duke of Kilverdale.

He still hadn't spoken to Athena, but he had caught up with the man who'd brought her back to England—and held a sword to his throat. The Marquis of Halross hadn't turned a hair at having his intentions towards Athena questioned under such hazardous circumstances. Jack was reasonably satisfied Halross would make his cousin a good husband, but he couldn't ask Athena if she wanted the marriage because Lord Swiftbourne had taken her to visit her family in Kent. Jack had decided to wait in London for her. He hadn't yet resumed all the usual trappings of his rank, because he'd never before had a chance to wander unnoticed through the crowds of London. From the day he'd been part of Charles II's triumphal return procession to the City, he'd always been surrounded by the pomp and formality associated with his title. It was a novelty to entertain a London tavern audience as Jack Bow, and know their praise for his music and story-telling was genuine—not prompted by the hope the Duke of Kilverdale would reward them for their flattery.

Half an hour later he wandered down to the coffee room. The serving boy had finished sweeping the floor and was scattering fresh sawdust over the boards.

'Morning, Tom,' said Jack.

'Sir!' The boy set aside his pail of sawdust at once. 'There's rumours of a fire in the City!'

'A fire? Where's your master?'

'He went out to hear more. Three hundred houses burned already, so one fellow told me,' Tom said, following close behind as Jack went to the door.

The coffee house was located in Covent Garden, well away

from the heart of the City, but when Jack went outside he saw the street was unusually busy for an early Sunday morning.

'It's down by London Bridge,' said Tom at his elbow. 'They're saying the Dutch started it. Do you think they did? I know you'll want to see for yourself. I'll come with you—to…to summon the lighter if you want to go by water.'

'What about your duties here?' Jack asked, looking at the half-finished floor.

'Oh, Mr Bundle just wanted me to be here to wait on you,' Tom replied. 'Now you're up I can wait on you wherever you like. And I'm sure you'd like to see the fire.'

Jack laughed at the boy's opportunism. 'Fetch me some bread and cheese, then. I can eat while we walk, but I'm not going fire-chasing on an empty stomach.'

'Yes, sir.' Tom tore off to the kitchen.

Jack frowned thoughtfully, then went to get his sword. He didn't put much credence in rumours—at the end of a hot summer fires were a predictable hazard in the crowded timber buildings of the City—but he made it a habit to be prepared for the worst. If the Dutch were about to launch an attack on London, he'd not go to meet them unarmed.

'Even the pigeons are burning.' Tom sounded close to tears.

'Yes.' As Jack watched he saw a pigeon hover too close to its familiar perch. A sudden gout of fire singed its wings and it tumbled down through the smoke-filled air.

'Why didn't it just fly away?' Tom said.

'I don't know. Most of them are.' Jack offered the small comfort without taking his eyes off the horrific scenes all around them.

They were in a lighter on the Thames. All around them the river was full of lighters and wherries loaded with household goods, but some people were as reluctant to leave their homes as the pigeons. Jack saw a man shouting from a window only yards from where a house was already being consumed by the leaping flames. Other people clambered about on the waterside stairs. Even from a distance Jack had the impression they were scrambling from place to place without clear purpose, too confused and shocked to know what they should do.

Some people trembled in silent fear and others shouted and cursed. The roar of the fire made it impossible to distinguish one cry from another. In this area of London the wooden houses were packed tightly together and the narrow alleys made it impossible to get close enough to the fire to fight it. There were timber warehouses near the river, some of which were thatched, and many of which were filled with dangerously combustible goods: pitch, oil, wine, coal and timber. The fire had taken a strong hold, and it burned hot and savage. To make matters worse, a strong easterly wind was driving the flames relentlessly into the City.

The houses on the northern end of London Bridge were also ablaze. Only a break in the buildings caused by a fire over thirty years earlier saved the whole bridge from destruction. The gale blew hard across the flames, sweeping a searing rain of fire droplets over the boats below. The waterman Jack had hired cursed and manoeuvred the boat closer to the south bank. Smoke swirled around them in choking clouds.

Jack covered his mouth and nose with his handkerchief. He heard Tom coughing beside him. The surface of the river was full of objects that had fallen from the overladen boats. A chair smashed against the side of the lighter. Jack pushed it away, then looked up. Above him smoke coiled around the rotting heads of traitors displayed over Bridge Gate. The dead features were hideously illuminated by sulphur bright flames.

''Tis hell on earth!' Tom gasped. 'It was prophesied. 'Tis the year of the number of the beast.'

'Sixteen sixty-six,' Jack murmured. 'Six, six, six.' He was aware that many almanac writers had predicted the year would be significant. But until he had evidence to prove otherwise, he would continue to assume the fire had been caused by human actions—either accidental or deliberate.

'I've seen enough here,' he said to the waterman. 'Take us back upriver.'

* * *

The streets were in chaos. Temperance found her way blocked over and over again by people, carts and horses. A man in front of her, carrying a huge load on his back, tripped and sprawled headlong. One of his packs broke open as it hit the ground. Bits of broken pottery, spoons and a couple of iron pans rattled on to the cobbles. Before Temperance could offer to help, he pushed himself upright and collected the unbroken utensils, cursing continuously. All around people shouted and pushed and got in each other's way—but there were others who wandered or stood aimlessly, clutching their hands and doing nothing of use at all.

The wind plastered Temperance's skirts against her legs and whipped her hair across her eyes. The smell of smoke pervaded everything. The fire was still far away from Cheapside, but it was devouring everything in its path. Temperance pushed her way through the crowds until she was close enough to see the fire leaping and roaring towards her. Even at this distance the heat was intense and the noise deafening. She was so shocked she stared into the horrible, mesmerising flames for several seconds, her thoughts emptied of everything except blank horror.

She gasped and shook herself back into a more practical state of mind, but she understood better now why some people did nothing but huddle close to their threatened homes and wring their hands. The fire was a hideous monster, beyond the scale of everyday human imagining. How could anyone hope to defeat it or even comprehend it?

She headed back to Cheapside. She was nearly home when she heard a shrill shout cut across the confused babble around her.

'It was him! He's one of the devils who started it!' The accusatory voice was so filled with panic and rage Temperance didn't immediately recognise it.

'I saw him here yesterday. With my own ears I heard him call on the devil! He's not English. He hates England!'

Temperance suddenly realised it was her neighbour, Agnes Cruikshank. For an instant she didn't understand, then she remembered Jack Bow's exasperation at her comments on his hair.

'He's a papist French devil!' Agnes shrieked. 'He wants us all to burn in our beds. I saw him throwing fireballs…'

Horror gave Temperance added strength as she forced her way through the increasingly hostile crowd. She broke through a gap to see Jack surrounded by angry, suspicious men and women. The threat of violence crackled in the air. Her neighbours—quiet, reasonable people she'd known all her life—were on the brink of turning into a lynch mob.

Chapter Three

Temperance flung herself forward, almost throwing herself into Jack's arms in her urgency to reach him before anyone else. He reacted to her presence faster than any of his accusers. She saw the flash of recognition in his eyes, then he caught her shoulders and steadied her. She pulled out of his grasp and spun to face her neighbours, holding out her arms to either side to create a barrier between them and Jack.

'He's not French! He's English!' she shouted. 'His great-grandfather was a grocer! Here, in the City. You're an idle gossip, Agnes Cruikshank. But it's *evil* to accuse an innocent man of such a sinful crime... *What*?' she demanded over her shoulder at Jack. 'Why do you keep pushing me?'

'Because I don't normally hide behind a woman's skirts,' he replied mildly, managing to reverse their positions so he was closest to the crowd. 'Even when she defends me as well as you just did, Madam Tempest.'

'*Tempest?*' A man in the crowd repeated, in a snort of half-amused disbelief. 'He's got the measure of Mistress Temperance, right enough.'

'He's got the look of a foreigner,' said another man.

'I'm as English as anyone here,' said Jack. 'My great-grandfather *was* a grocer, but I was born in Sussex.'

Temperance tried to get in front of him again, but he caught her arm and wouldn't let her.

'I heard the rumours the fire was started by our enemies too,' Jack said. 'I came out this morning ready to defend us from the Dutch—but from what I've heard the fire started by accident, in the house of the King's baker in Pudding Lane.'

'Why did you speak in the heathen's tongue yesterday?' Agnes came close and peered up at him through slitted eyes. 'I *did* hear you. You pulled off your wig and called on the devil.'

Jack grinned. 'How long have you lived next door to Mistress Temperance?' he asked.

'Twenty-three years, near enough,' Agnes replied, glowering at him. 'I was there at her birthing.'

'And in all those twenty-three years, haven't you ever felt the urge to clutch at your hair and swear?' he asked.

Several people laughed. Only the improvement in the crowd's mood stopped Temperance from giving Jack a swift kick on his ankle. She'd thrown herself into the breach, determined to save him, despite his annoying behaviour and questionable morals—and now he repaid her by making fun of her!

'In English.' Agnes prodded him in the chest. 'I chastise her in English. Not French.'

Jack caught Agnes's hand and held it. 'But when I was three years old the Roundheads drove my mother out of our home,' he said, his attention apparently focussed entirely on Agnes. 'She fled in fear of our lives. I had to wait seventeen years to return home to England. I am not at fault for what happened when I was still a child in arms.'

'You visited the French Court. After so long there you must have French sympathies,' Agnes said, but she no longer sounded so hostile.

'I went to the French Court when I was fourteen,' Jack said, releasing Agnes's hand. 'That's a long time ago. I am not a French spy.'

'What was your great-grandfather's name?' asked an elderly man Temperance recognised as Nicholas Farley. 'I'm a grocer, perhaps I knew him.'

'Edmund Beaufleur.'

'*Edmund Beaufleur!*' Farley exclaimed. 'He was Lord Mayor in Queen Bess's reign.'

'That's right,' Jack said.

'Well, well, well.' Farley nodded with interest. 'Edmund Beaufleur's great-grandson. Who'd have thought it?'

Temperance couldn't believe it. London was on fire yet, by the looks of things, any minute now Farley would drag Jack off to examine the Company records in the Grocers' Hall. At least most of the potential lynch mob had dispersed.

'It has been an honour to meet you, sir,' said Jack to Farley. 'I look forward to seeing you again in happier times. I'd enjoy learning more about my great-grandfather when we can talk at leisure.'

'Yes.' Farley looked up and Temperance saw the animation in his face replaced by grim anxiety. 'There is much to do.'

'Let's go inside, sweetheart.' Jack took her elbow and guided her towards her door.

'Yes. Yes.' She gathered herself and fumbled with her key. A few moments later they were standing in the shop. With the shutters closed the only light came from the open door. Temperance stared at Jack in the gloom.

'They might really have hurt you,' she whispered, remembering the volatile, angry mood of the crowd when she'd arrived. She started to tremble and wrapped her arms around herself. 'They were going to attack you—just because Agnes Cruikshank always has to push her nose into other people's business and n-never gets her f-facts right.'

Jack closed the distance between them and put his hands on her shoulders. She stood still as he rubbed his hands up and down her back. She was too shaken to protest at his action, and too tall to rest her head on his shoulder and pretend she hadn't noticed what he was doing. She felt the warmth of his breath against her cheek, the solid strength of his body close to hers.

'They didn't hurt me—thanks to you,' he said, his voice soft and soothing. 'And I do thank you. You are a true virago of a draper, Mistress Tempest.'

She felt his lips brush her skin, then he kissed her. A real kiss, even though it was on her cheek, not her mouth. Her heart rate accelerated. For a moment she forgot about the disaster overshadowing London. She felt hot, excited, unsure. In the dark of the night she'd imagined him kissing her—even though she hadn't known if she'd ever see him again. She'd hugged herself, pretending it was his arms around her, wondering what it would feel like if he was really holding her.

She'd been kissed a few times before, but it had always been an awkward, embarrassing experience. She'd been several inches taller than the hopeful suitor who'd pursued her when she was eighteen. The discrepancy in their heights might not have been a problem if he'd been genuinely attracted to her. Unfortunately, it was her inheritance that had appealed to him, and he'd lacked the necessary address to hide his real motivation. Temperance had sent him away without regret.

But Jack was different. In his arms she didn't feel oversized and unfeminine. He was so graceful and sure of himself that somehow he made her feel more confident in her own appeal. She clutched his coat and lifted her head, instinctively turning her face towards his. His lips slid over her cheek in a hot trail, then his mouth found hers.

Temperance felt the jolt of intimate contact all the way to her toes. Yet it was only his mouth on hers. She held his coat in her clenched fist and his open hands lay on her back, but there was still an inch or two of space between their bodies. The only place where their naked skin touched was mouth to mouth. She was astounded that every novel, delightful sensation rippling through her body was generated by nothing more than the movement of his lips and tongue against hers.

It was too dark in the shop to see clearly, but she closed her eyes the better to lose herself in the experience. It was a wonderment she'd never known before. How could a man's lips be so firm and soft at the same time? His caresses so delicate yet compelling? His tongue stroked her upper lip, teasing and exploring until her knees felt weak. Hardly aware of what she was doing, her arm slid around his neck as she leant against him for support.

His hold on her tightened. One hand in the small of her back pressed her against him. His other hand lifted to cup her head, holding her firmly in place as his tongue slipped inside her mouth and the gentle kiss became far more potent. Lights exploded behind Temperance's eyelids. The pleasant feelings rippling through her inexperienced body suddenly became a torrent of hot, elemental sensation. She gasped and pulled back, half-thrilled, half-frightened by the unfamiliar feelings he aroused.

After a second his hold on her relaxed. She felt his chest expand as he drew in a deep, not quite steady breath.

'I'm sorry,' he murmured against her hair. 'I didn't intend that.'

'Oh, no?' Temperance pushed against him, upset by his comment. 'In the dark did you forget what I look—?'

He silenced her with a brisk, almost impatient kiss.

'Of course I remember what you look like,' he said, releasing her. 'Don't insult me. Or yourself. Even I, irresponsible reprobate though you think me, occasionally put practical matters ahead of pleasure.'

Temperance caught her breath as a vivid image of the fire filled her mind. How could she have forgotten it, even for a few moments? Before she could speak, she heard feet clattering down the stairs.

'Mistress, is it you?' Her housemaid, Sarah, burst into the shop, with Isaac close behind. 'What are we going to do?'

'I don't—' Temperance began, for once in her life uncertain what to do next.

'Pack up and be ready to leave,' Jack said.

'What?' She turned to stare at him.

'The waterwheels beneath the bridge have already been destroyed,' he said. 'Burning timbers fell on them from above. I saw the damage myself. No water can be drawn up from the river, even if it were possible to get close enough to the flames to douse them. And people have been smashing open water pipes in an effort to save their own homes. If the wind doesn't abate, nothing will stop the spread of the fire.'

Temperance pressed her fingers to her mouth. A few moments ago she'd been kissing Jack. Her body was still flushed with the sensations he'd aroused. Now her thoughts turned sickeningly to the disaster that had overtaken the east of the City.

'It's still a quarter of a mile away at least,' she whispered. 'Surely…'

'Pray for the wind to drop and a rainstorm to equal the deluge,' said Jack almost brutally. 'Perhaps the fire won't spread this far—but it is better to be safe than burnt.'

In the silence following his words, Sarah began to cry. Temperance swallowed and tried to gather her wits. She looked around the shop. She'd lived here all her life. Through every crisis that had visited London during her lifetime she'd known at least her home was secure.

'Go where?' she asked. 'How far? Everyone I know lives within a few streets of here.'

'In the first instance, to Bundle's Coffeehouse in Covent Garden,' said Jack. 'Bundle's an old friend of mine. It's nearly one and a half miles from the heart of the fire. God willing, it won't spread—'

He broke off at the sound of running footsteps. A second later Temperance saw a woman in the doorway.

'Is my Katie here?' Nellie Carpenter half-sobbed her desperate question.

'Katie? No. Nellie, what—?'

'*Oh, dear God!*' Nellie spun around. She was almost out of the door before Temperance managed to catch her arm.

'Is Katie lost?'

'I went out to hear the latest news.' Nellie heaved in a shuddering breath. 'She was by my side, I swear. I *told* her not to leave my side. But the next time I looked she was gone.' Tears streamed unheeded down Nellie's cheeks. 'I've got to find her.' She tried to pull out of Temperance's grip.

'Who is Katie?' Jack was right beside Temperance.

'Her daughter. She's five,' Temperance said. 'I'll help, Nellie—'

'We'll all help,' said Jack. 'Nellie, show us where you were standing the last time you saw her. And you two...' he glanced over at Isaac and Sarah '...do you know what Katie looks like? Good, come with us.'

They spent the rest of the day searching the streets for the lost child, while ash fell on them continuously and the fire crept closer to Cheapside. By nightfall Nellie was almost collapsing from despair and terror.

'We have to keep looking!' she insisted, her voice harsh with desperation. 'We have to—'

'We will,' said Jack, his voice as firm and confident as it had been that morning. 'We won't give up until she is found. *I* won't give up until she is found.'

Tears filled Temperance's eyes when she heard his avowal. Yesterday she'd almost decided he was a scoundrel without a conscience—today he was steadfastly looking for a child he didn't know. It was true that, unlike many of the other searchers, he didn't have a business to save, but it was still the act of a generous, compassionate man.

After dark, Jack insisted Temperance and Isaac stay together, but otherwise the search continued as before. Finally, well past midnight, Isaac spotted Katie huddled in a doorway. She was almost hidden behind a pile of rubbish. Temperance hadn't seen her. She thanked God for Isaac's quick eyes as she lifted the frightened child into her arms.

A few minutes later Nellie snatched Katie into her own embrace, scolding and crying over her restored daughter.

Jack took the key from her and opened the shop door, lifting the lanthorn he held high to provide light for the others as they stumbled inside.

'Now we eat,' he said. 'What have you got in your larder?'

'Eat?' Temperance rubbed her face, smearing tears and ash across her cheek. 'I don't know. There's some bread. Bacon. Cheese, I think…'

'Now there's a feast for a hungry man. Will you give me a share, even though I can't play for it?' he asked, a hint of his former teasing manner in his voice.

'Of course.' Temperance was too worried to reply in kind. How was she going to save her goods now? All the previous day she'd seen tradesmen packing their wares and household belongings into carts and barrows. They'd found Katie, and she'd never regret the hours they'd spent looking for her, but would there still be time to salvage her belongings?

Fear compelled her up the stairs, past the kitchen and on to the attic. Horror stopped her breath as she stared towards the fire. In the daylight it had been bad enough, in the dark it was a terrifying sight. The flames lit up the sky almost as bright as day. They were closer now, leaping over rooftops, dancing like obscene devils over church spires.

She gazed, transfixed, by the nightmarish spectacle. Jack came to stand by her side.

'You're right,' she said, her voice harsh with anxiety. 'We have to pack up and leave.'

'After we've eaten,' he replied.

'There's no time—'

'There's time to eat,' he said firmly. 'The fire looks more fearsome in the dark, but it is still no closer than Cannon Street.'

By the time dawn was casting a shrouded light over the city, Jack had found a cart for Temperance. She didn't ask how he'd persuaded the carter to go with him, or what he'd paid to hire the cart. She'd seen for herself how the price of carriage had multiplied since the start of the fire. Porters, carters and watermen were all charging whatever their customers were capable of paying—and if one person didn't have the money, another one, richer or more desperate, was sure to accept the exorbitant price.

Temperance didn't let herself think about how deeply she might now be in debt to Jack. She'd ask him later. For now she concentrated on wrapping and loading the bales of cloth from her shop. Sarah had returned to her own family that morning, too frightened to remain close to the advancing flames, so it was only Jack and Isaac who helped load the cart.

She paused to catch her breath and noticed Agnes come out of her shop door. After today Temperance didn't know when she'd see her neighbour again. She'd had many arguments with Agnes, but she didn't want to part on bad terms, so she went to speak to her.

'Where are you going?' Agnes asked.

'Covent Garden. What about you?'

'My niece, Fanny, in Southwark. You remember her?'

'Of course. What about your belongings?' Temperance could see Agnes's shop was already stripped bare.

'St Paul's,' said Agnes. 'No fire will burn the cathedral. I was lucky I managed to get my goods inside in time. Everyone was rushing there yesterday. I didn't know you knew anyone in Covent Garden,' she added suspiciously.

'I don't. Jack does. Where are Ned and Eliza?' Temperance asked, referring to Agnes's apprentice and servant.

'They've gone ahead,' Agnes said. 'I'll be on my way soon. I just came back…' Her throat worked as she patted the doorjamb of the shop, her home for forty years. 'I can't stand here gossiping, girl,' she said. 'I've got things to do.' She went inside without a backward glance.

Temperance walked over to Jack. He paused, one hand resting on the side of the cart.

'We're nearly done in the shop—why don't you start upstairs?' he suggested.

She nodded and went inside. It was agonising deciding between what she could take and what she would be forced to leave behind.

'What's going?' Jack asked from behind her.

She pointed mutely, making ruthless decisions with tears in her eyes. Jack picked up the largest item and started downstairs. They finished loading the cart in silence.

'Is that everything?' Jack asked at last.

'I think so.'

'Good.' He glanced over her shoulder, and she saw his expression change. She spun around, then clapped her hands to her mouth in shock.

The fire had reached Cornhill. For the first time she could see the flames when she was standing at her own front door.

'Oh my God!' she whispered. 'It's nearly here.'

For a moment her feet seemed frozen to the ash-covered cobbles. Then life surged back into her limbs. She dashed inside the building and rushed up the stairs. When Jack caught up with her she was flinging open cupboard doors and dragging drawers from the old dresser.

'What are you looking for?'

'Everything. Nothing. What if I've missed something important?' She stared around in panic, then headed up another flight to her bedchamber. 'What if I've missed something?' she kept repeating, as she tossed discarded items left and right in her distress.

Jack's arms closed around her from behind. 'You can replace anything except life,' he said gently. 'It's better to live to fight another day than to take on a foe you can't beat. Now be still and think quietly. You've already taken a little carved box. I know it's important to you because you put it straight into your pocket. Is there anything else here that means so much to you?'

'My brother made the box,' she said, her thoughts going off at a tangent.

'Where is he now?' She felt Jack's breath against her cheek as he held her from behind.

'He died when I was thirteen.'

'I'm sorry. Then of course you must keep it safe. Is there anything else here so important to you? Just close your eyes and rest a moment.'

His voice was so soothing and unhurried she did as he bid. Just for a few seconds she relaxed enough to let her mind range over her belongings and all the years to see if there was anything she'd forgotten.

'My mother's sewing box.' She made an instant move to fetch it, dismayed she'd forgotten it until that moment. What else had she forgotten?

Jack held her still.

'Anything else?'

'I don't know.' Panic began to rise in her once more, and tears leaked from her eyes. 'I don't know.'

'Fetch the sewing box,' he said gently. 'It's time to go.' He released her and stepped back.

She careered down the stairs and found the sewing box in its familiar place in the alcove by the fire. It had been in full view all the time. She was so used to seeing it there her eyes had passed over it every time she'd scanned the room for important things to save.

She clattered down the rest of the stairs to the shop floor, terrified they'd lingered too long and the fire would be upon them. To her relief, the flames didn't seem much closer. The fire was making inexorable progress through the old timber buildings, but not so quickly a healthy man couldn't stay ahead of it.

That didn't stop the carter cursing them for the delay.

'Be quiet and drive!' Temperance snapped. He hadn't lifted a finger to help them load the cart, but she knew he was being paid a fortune for his services.

She and Jack and Isaac walked beside it as it rattled over the cobblestones. When she looked around she realised they were the last people to leave this part of Cheapside. The fire roared behind them, so loud it drowned out the sound of the cartwheels. Sparks as well as ash showered down on them. High above them the thick black smoked blocked out the sun.

They were halfway to St Paul's when Temperance remembered Agnes.

'Isaac! Did you see Agnes leave?'

'I…' He drew in a breath and coughed on a gust of smoke. 'I didn't see her.' He stared at Temperance. 'But I wasn't looking. Surely she must have—'

'Did you?' she demanded of Jack.

'No.'

'Carter!' She lifted her voice in a cracked shout. 'Did you see an old woman leave the shop next to mine?'

'Wasn't looking.'

Temperance spun around and headed back the way they'd come. She didn't much like Agnes, but she couldn't leave her to burn. Jack seized her shoulder, pulling her to a stop.

She tried to shake him off. 'I have to go back. Make sure she left.'

'You stay with the cart,' he ordered. 'I'll go.'

Before she had time to protest at his high-handedness he was running back towards the flames.

Temperance paused on the verge of following him. 'Carry on to Covent Garden!' she shouted at Isaac. 'Bundle's Coffeehouse. Don't forget.'

'But, mistress—'

'I have to see Agnes is safe. *Go!*' she insisted, when he seemed reluctant to obey. 'It's your duty to make sure everything gets safely to the coffeehouse. I'm counting on you, Isaac.'

She pulled her skirt almost to her knees and started to run. Modesty no longer mattered. She had to catch up with Jack and find Agnes. She was still clutching the workbox to her chest. She wished she'd had the presence of mind to put it in the cart, but it was too late now. As she got closer to Agnes's shop, her pace slowed. The far end of Cheapside was already a roaring wall of flames. As she watched, the fire leapt the width of the wide street. If Temperance hadn't known better, she would have sworn the flames were alive. She wanted to turn and run, but she forced herself to go forward. Jack was ahead of her for sure and so, perhaps, was Agnes.

The shop door stood wide. She rushed inside, shouting their names.

'Here,' Jack called from upstairs. 'Stay there.'

'What? Why?' Horrors flashed through her mind. She started up the stairs.

'We're coming down. *Move, Tempest!*'

She jumped back and Jack emerged into the shop with Agnes in his arms.

'What's wrong with her?' Temperance hurried ahead of him into the street.

'Fell on the stairs and twisted her knee,' Jack said. 'Stay close to me.'

Temperance almost had to run to keep up with his ground-eating strides. She didn't ask any more questions. She had no breath to spare and Jack had Agnes safe. An occasional shudder racked the old woman, and there was a pinched look on her face, but the fire would not get her now.

Jack paused once they were level with St Paul's. There was a stitch in Temperance's side. She wanted to double over to ease her aching muscles, but resisted the urge.

'Where are we going?' she asked.

'Covent Garden.' Jack sounded mildly surprised by her question. His voice was hoarse, and even his breathing was more laboured than usual.

'Her niece lives in Southwark,' Temperance said.

'I can talk for myself, girl!' Agnes snapped.

'Does your niece have room for you?' Jack asked.

'Of course she does. She's family.'

'We'd best take you there, then.' Jack set off again, striding through St Paul's churchyard as he headed obliquely for the river. Temperance kept close to him as they pushed through the crowds around the cathedral. When she looked to her left she was shocked to see they were moving parallel with the fire. It had travelled further west along the edge of the Thames than she'd realised. They'd have to go further than she'd expected to find a boat to take them across to Southwark.

'Perhaps we ought to go to Covent Garden,' she said.

'I'm sure Mistress Cruikshank would prefer to be safe in the bosom of her family,' said Jack.

It occurred to Temperance that, if they took Agnes to Covent Garden, she would still be their responsibility. Whereas, if they took her to her niece in Southwark, they could leave her with a clear conscience. She started to nod in silent agreement and saw from the ghost of Jack's familiar grin he was thinking the same thing.

It was very late by the time they reached their destination. Temperance had been outraged by the greed of the watermen. If she'd been alone she wouldn't have been able to afford the crossing. It was a relief to hand Agnes over to her niece, Fanny Berridge.

'You're welcome to stay here,' said Fanny, looking harried.

'Thank you, but I'm eager to return to Covent Garden,' Jack said, and a moment later Temperance found herself back in the crowded Southwark streets.

Even though it was nearly midnight, people were out of doors, watching the catastrophe unfold on the other side of the river. Temperance's shoulders slumped at the prospect ahead of them. The journey to Covent Garden would be as exhausting and expensive as the journey they'd made from Cheapside to Southwark. She looked at Jack and saw he was carrying the sewing box. She couldn't remember putting it down. She reached to take it from him, even though she was so tired she was almost past caring whether she lost it.

'I'll carry it,' he said. 'Come on.' He guided her with his free arm around her shoulders.

'At least we can sit down on the boat,' she roused herself to say. 'How can they be so greedy?' She was thinking of the iniquitous amount Jack had paid for their last river crossing, but she was too tired to be angry. She was glad she was with Jack. If she'd been alone, there was a good chance she would have found the nearest quiet spot and fallen sleep in the street. She made an effort to be more alert.

'Why aren't you asleep on your feet?' she mumbled, mildly resentful of his stamina.

'It wasn't my house,' he replied.

'What?'

'Everything we've had to do over the past two days would be enough to tire anyone. I feel it myself.' Jack flexed his arms and grimaced. 'I wasn't sorry to deliver Agnes. But I think it is grief which is making you so very tired. There's no shame in that, sweetheart. Grief is a wearisome emotion. But it will pass.'

'Where are we going?' Temperance suddenly noticed they weren't heading for the river.

'To find a room—or at least a bed—for the rest of the night,' he replied.

'But all the inns will be full,' Temperance protested, even though she yearned to lie down and close her eyes.

'We'll find somewhere,' said Jack. 'Even if we have to share an attic with the scullery maid.'

Temperance was so tired she could hardly find the energy to climb the stairs. She lifted one foot on to the next wooden tread and wearily levered her body up another six inches. Only a few more steps and she could go to bed. The familiar staircase was deep in midnight shadow. She pushed open her bedchamber door. The room was ablaze in bright orange fire. She stared in horror. The flames licked towards her. She turned and fled down the stairs. The fire pursued her. She ran through the streets, the flames hard on her heels. Her heart thundered with panic, but her exhaustion was forgotten. She tried to reach the Thames, but over and over new flames leapt up to block her route. At last she teetered on the very edge of the river steps. Black and red water swirled below. A boat bobbed just out of reach. The fire rose in a huge column behind her. She glanced over her shoulder and saw the flames were poised to swallow her whole. She stretched desperately towards the boat, but it floated further away. She overbalanced. Falling towards the terrible river of burning blood—

Chapter Four

Temperance's eyes flew open. Her heart was pounding, her limbs tingling with fear. Now she was awake the terror was even greater than in her nightmare. The dream had been so real she almost expected to be engulfed in flames at any second.

'Gently, sweetheart,' a soft voice murmured from behind her.

She felt a reassuring touch on her arm. Still more asleep than awake, it took several long, panicky moments for her to shake off the remnants of her nightmare. Slowly she remembered who she was with, where they were and what had happened to bring them to this place.

They were in a tiny room, little more than a cupboard, in a Southwark inn. The bed was small and the mattress lumpy. All Temperance could see when she looked straight ahead was the dirty plaster four inches from her nose. It dawned on her that Jack was lying beside her, but she couldn't see him because she was facing the wrong way.

He kept running his hand lightly up and down her upper arm and talking softly to her. He must have realised she was having a nightmare.

She took a deep breath and began to cough. Jack helped her to sit up. She leant against him as she tried to control the paroxysms. At last she was able to sit quietly. She rested her head on Jack's shoulder, too heartsore to care about propriety.

'Did you dream about the fire?' he asked.

She nodded jerkily and started to cry. From the moment she'd realised Agnes had been left in her shop there had been no time to dwell on the fate of her home. Now she knew her dream had shown her the exact truth. She hadn't been standing on her stairs when her bedchamber caught fire, but by now it had burned just as surely as in her nightmare.

'I'm sorry, sweetheart. I'm sorry,' Jack murmured.

She nodded, but she couldn't speak. For a little while her grief was too overwhelming to control. It was the first time since the death of her father that there had been anyone to comfort her. She clung to Jack, uncharacteristically surrendering to the full force of her emotions. She'd been raised to show more self-discipline than this, but Jack didn't seem shocked. He held her close in a strong, steady embrace. He even rummaged up a grimy handkerchief to offer her.

There was a window facing towards the Thames. The inferno burning on the other side of the river cast a flickering, shadowy light over the bed. Temperance kept her head turned away from the window, but the sight of the handkerchief provoked her into an unexpected hiccough of laughter.

'I've got my own,' she said. 'I *am* a linen draper.'

She pulled away from Jack, immediately missing the sense of security she'd felt in his arms. It was tempting to lean against him again, but she sat up straight and concentrated on finding her handkerchief. Finally, she produced the square of linen and dried her eyes and blew her nose. She still had to stifle an unexpected sob now and then, but she felt calmer.

'Thank you,' she said.

'What for?' Jack sounded mildly amused. 'You spurned my chivalrous gesture.'

'For…' She hesitated. 'Never mind,' she said, not wanting to dwell on her loss of self-control. 'I suppose a man with your varied past is always finding himself in unusual situations. I expect weeping women are commonplace in your life.'

To her surprise, Jack started to laugh. 'When all else fails I stick pins in them,' he said. 'Although fresh chopped onion is also—'

'That's not what I meant,' Temperance interrupted crossly.

'It has happened,' he replied, more seriously than she'd anticipated. 'But I hope I am wiser—and kinder—now.'

'Is she…?' Temperance's breath caught at the implication of his words. 'Is she waiting for you now?' She knew so little about Jack Bow, but he had come to mean a lot to her in the past few days. Was she just another interlude in his wayward life?

'No…' Jack paused. 'There's no woman waiting for me,' he clarified.

'Oh.' Temperance twisted the handkerchief between her hands, not sure what to say. She'd been so exhausted when they'd arrived at the inn she'd fallen on the bed without even noticing Jack was beside her. She'd slept heavily for a few hours, but now she was awake and her mind began to run in all kinds of anxious directions. Jack on the bed was only one of her worries.

She glanced up and inadvertently looked in the direction of the unshuttered window. Her stomach clenched at the ominous play of shadows and lurid light flickering across the room.

'It's still burning.' She scrambled forward to see better. 'What am I going to do?' she whispered, clutching the windowsill. 'It's all gone. What are we all going to do? London's gone!'

'Rebuild,' said Jack, sliding to the bottom of the bed to sit beside her.

'That's easy for you to say!' Temperance turned on him. 'You never stay anywhere. You just wander where you please—' Her voice caught on a sob.

Jack's arms closed around her. She struggled for a few seconds, resenting his efforts to comfort her when he was so unmoved by the fate of the City.

'I've wept for other losses,' he said. 'People—not places.'

She heard the truth in his voice and stopped trying to pull herself out of his embrace.

'I don't know what I'm going to do,' she whispered.

'You'll manage.' He rested his forehead against hers for a moment. 'But not tonight. You don't have to manage anything tonight. Come on,' he urged her to move back up the bed. 'Lie down again. Rest. We'll face our next set of problems in the morning.'

It was an awkward realignment. Jack knelt on Temperance's skirt in the darkness and she scrabbled ineffectually against the mattress before she realised what was wrong, but at last they were lying next to each other again.

Temperance turned on to her back and gazed upwards. She gave a gasping groan and rolled on to her side.

'It's on the ceiling!' She couldn't believe the shadows of the fire even danced there. The monster was everywhere. In her home, in her nightmare, and even in the temporary safety of this rathole Jack had found for them.

'I know,' said Jack.

'I can't sleep now.' She bit her lip because she was determined not to cry any more. 'Every time I close my eyes I can see it!'

'Think of something else.' He stroked her arm.

'I don't know anything else.'

'What?'

'I've never been anywhere but London. In all my memories London is there. Now it isn't… You tell me something else.' She laid her hand on his shoulder. He'd removed his coat and she could feel the firm muscles beneath his linen shirt. 'You've been so many places. Tell me about one of them.'

'My home's in Sussex,' he said, after a moment. 'Shall I tell you about that?'

'Yes.' She wondered if his home was in his mind because of her loss. 'Please tell me.'

'It's green,' he said. 'I last saw it in April and everything was green. New buds and leaves. The daffodils made a brave show beneath the trees. Bright sunshine yellow.'

'Good colours,' Temperance murmured, clinging to the image of sunshine-yellow daffodils instead of the hideous red and black of fiery destruction.

'Very good.' He brushed his lips against her forehead. 'The village green was in full bloom.'

'What village?' Temperance moved a little closer to him.

'Arunhurst,' he replied. 'The church is very pretty. Norman…' He kissed her cheek.

'What church?' Her hand slid around his waist of its own volition.

'St Mary's.' His breath caressed her skin.

She turned her head and his lips found hers. The kiss began gentle and comforting, but almost immediately desperate passion exploded between them. Her hand locked in his shirt and she pulled him closer, responding without thought of consequences. Her whole world had collapsed around her ears, but Jack was strong and reassuringly vital. Alive.

He rolled her on to her back and deepened the kiss. His tongue was so bold. She'd never imagined anything like it. Excitement leapt within her. She lifted her hand to touch him and felt the crisp brush of his short hair against her fingers. She tugged desperately at his shirt so she could feel his bare skin. She needed to wrap her arms around him. To get as close as she could to his virile, living energy. When he kissed her like this she couldn't think of anything else. She didn't want to think of anything else. When he kissed her, all her problems vanished into oblivion. Her hands pressed against his naked back, feeling the flex of his taut muscles. Her heart thudded in her ears. Jack filled her senses and her mind until there was only room for the compelling needs he aroused in her.

He kissed her cheek, then bent his head to caress her neck with his lips. She stared up at the ceiling, but she didn't see the flickering shadow patterns of the fire. All her attention was focussed on Jack. His breathing was as fast and ragged as her own. She could feel the hot urgency pulsing through his body.

He pulled up her skirts with an uncharacteristically clumsy gesture and then she felt his hand on her bare thigh. She gasped as almost unbearable tension filled her. He stroked the outer side of her leg, touching her more intimately than she'd ever been touched before. She held her breath, her grip on his back tightening until her nails pressed into his muscles.

His fingers brushed along her legs as he found his way by touch alone. She moved restlessly beneath him, her breath emerging in quick, almost whimpering gasps.

His hand came briefly to rest on her inner thigh—then stroked boldly upwards. Potent sensation flooded her body. She trembled with an unfamiliar mixture of excitement and almost painfully urgent anticipation. She was swollen and aching, and when he touched her intimately air exploded from her lungs in a wordless gasp of pleasure.

Her legs fell bonelessly apart as he continued to stroke her hot, moist flesh. His own breathing was harsh with excitement. Her body responded to his teasing, tormenting fingers with small spasms of pleasure and intensifying need. When he took his hand away she gave a whimper of protest, but a few seconds later he lifted himself over her.

Her breath caught in her throat. The unfamiliar sensation of his erection pressing against her provoked a brief moment of clarity. She'd never thought this would happen to her. She was too tall, her personality too forthright. Men had looked with covetous eyes at her shop, but not at her. Now Jack was poised above her, his lean, muscular body taut with unfulfilled passion.

She closed her eyes and gave herself up to the intensity of the moment. It was so strange to feel Jack inside her, stretching her. She held tight to him, her anchor in the storm of new sensations.

He paused. She could feel the straining of his muscles as he held still. The expansion and contraction of his ribs as he braced himself over and in her.

'Tempest?' His voice emerged as a ragged moan.

She was so overwhelmed by the physical and emotional strangeness of what was happening she didn't speak. Her fingers dug convulsively into his back. Pure instinct prompted her to raise her knees and he sank a little deeper inside her.

His shuddering groan reverberated through her. He began to move, his strokes steady and careful. At first it wasn't quite comfortable, but gradually the discomfort was transformed into deliciously escalating tension. She arched her back, lifting her hips towards him. She was on the verge of something—

Jack's thrusts became faster and less controlled. Suddenly he groaned and shuddered in her arms. She felt his hot release deep within her. His movements slowed until he was still except for his quickened breathing.

Temperance lay beneath him, her body tingling and somehow unsatisfied. She opened her eyes. She couldn't see Jack's expression. His head was a dark shadow between her and the lurid ceiling. She was breathing heavily. So was he. He was still inside her, yet she felt strangely disconnected from what had just happened. She'd dreamed of Jack the first night she'd met him. Now she was half-convinced she was still dreaming. Nothing that had happened in the past twenty-four hours had any place in her everyday life.

She became aware of her hands on Jack's back, the grittiness of the soot and ash still clinging to both of them. In many ways he was little more than a stranger, and now her arousal was waning the unfamiliar intimacy of their position began to feel increasingly awkward. Part of her wanted to cling to him for reassurance, but another part of her wanted to push him as far away as possible.

Before she could do or say anything he withdrew from her, his movements carefully controlled as he lay down beside her as far away as the narrow mattress would allow.

For the first time since she'd met him their silence was oppressive with tension. It stretched taut between them, but it wasn't the breathless, excited tension that had compelled her into his arms. It was darker, awkward and much harder to deal with.

She sensed him move and realised he was rearranging his clothes. Embarrassment burned through her. She hastily straightened her skirts, though she could still feel the imprint of his body on her and in her. She wondered how long it would be before she stopped feeling the after-effects of their lovemaking.

Dawn was casting a pale grey light over the bed. She stared out of the window and wished she was somewhere else. Morning was nearly here, but for the first time since she could remember she had no regular chores to perform. Why on earth had she allowed—encouraged Jack to make love to her? Grief must have addled her brain.

'I'm sorry,' he said quietly. 'I didn't mean that to happen.'

'Are you blaming me?' She was already feeling defensive—afraid she'd let him make a fool of her. She didn't like the implication it was her fault.

'No.' He sat up and put his hand on her arm. 'It was the two of us together. But I find you quite irresistible,' he added.

Temperance folded her arms and looked away. 'If you were a gentleman—'

'You don't mean that.' He urged her to lie down again and propped himself on one elbow beside her. 'To take advantage of you and walk away without a backward glance.'

'Is that your idea of a gentleman?' She looked at him. Now the room was lighter she could see his expression more clearly. What she saw in his eyes reassured her. To her relief it didn't seem as if he regarded the loss of her maidenhead as a frivolous matter.

'Isn't it yours?' he countered.

Temperance thought of some of her well-dressed, well-born customers. Tredgold, the man who'd planned to frighten his grandfather to death in the guise of a ghost, popped into her mind. If he'd been on this bed with her he wouldn't waste any time worrying about her feelings. Mind you, she couldn't imagine any circumstances in which she'd willingly come within ten feet of Tredgold, especially if there was a bed in the vicinity.

'I don't suppose it matters,' she said, trying to make the best of things. 'With London in such turmoil, no one ever will ever know or care what happened to me tonight.'

'I know,' said Jack. 'And I care.' He put his hand on her waist.

Temperance's heart began to beat faster. 'What does that mean?'

'It means I wish we had more time.' He leant closer and kissed her forehead. 'I need to check for the latest news—and see if I can find Jakob. He was supposed to follow me to London. He's Swedish. I hope no one mistakes him for a Dutchman.' A shadow crossed Jack's face.

Temperance remembered how the mob had nearly attacked Jack when they'd thought he was French. She understood his anxieties about his cousin, but she was dismayed he was leaving. After what had just taken place between them she felt awkward in his company, but she was even more upset at the idea of never seeing him again.

'I'll come back as soon as I can,' he said. 'Stay here. As long as you stay in this room and keep the door barred against strangers, you should be safe enough.' He reached for his coat and the periwig he'd laid aside the previous night. 'Here.' He dropped a surprisingly large amount of money on to her lap. 'I hope you won't need it, but if the innkeeper tries to turn you out because he's had a better offer, this should hold his hand.'

'Is this my…fee?' she said, staring at the coins without touching them. 'For lifting my petticoats—'

'No.' His firm denial cut off her words. 'I was going to give it to you anyway. If you don't feel comfortable here, go back to Agnes's niece.'

Temperance flinched at the notion of presenting herself to Agnes this morning. The old woman's sharp eyes were sure to notice something different about her. If she was to protect her reputation, she had to ensure no one knew of her brief liaison with Jack.

'I'll stay here,' she muttered. 'Can't I—' She stopped, biting her lip. She'd been about to ask if she could go with Jack, but if he didn't suggest it she wasn't going to embarrass herself by asking.

'We don't know how much further the fire has spread,' he replied, answering her unspoken question. 'I don't want to take you from safety into danger. Besides, you need to rest. When I've gone, bar the door and try to sleep.'

Temperance sat on the bed and watched as he put on his coat, sword and finally, his periwig. He looked at her and grinned. 'Is it straight?' he asked.

'You are too vain for words,' she grumbled. Despite everything, her mood lightened at his familiar smile. It did far more to reassure her than the money he'd dropped in her lap. Perhaps she was fooling herself, but she thought it was the kind of look a man gave to a woman he cared about—not one he'd used to ease a fleeting physical need. She knelt up, ignoring the strange, unfamiliar twinges between her legs, and rearranged his somewhat woebegone curls.

'Thank you.'

She shifted her gaze from his hair to his dark eyes. He smiled crookedly at her. 'I'm coming back,' he said. 'I promise.'

Southwark, late evening, Tuesday 4 September 1666

Temperance sat on the bed listening to the unfamiliar sounds of the inn around her, and the noisy disturbances in the streets outside. Earlier she'd left the small room long enough to buy food

and drink from one of the inn servants, but she hadn't dared go
further afield. She'd had to give the innkeeper more money before
he'd let her remain in the cramped chamber, and she knew if she
went out she'd lose the room. She was worried about Isaac, but
comforted by the knowledge he was safe at the coffeehouse in
Covent Garden.

The strong gale had continued to blow most of the day, driving
the flames across London. Temperance had fallen into an uneasy
sleep in the early evening, only to be frightened awake by distant
explosions. She'd scrambled to the window, horrified to discover
the fire was burning even brighter than before.

A sudden pounding at the door made her jump.

'Tempest? Temperance, let me in.' Jack's voice sounded harsh
and strained.

She hurried to open it. He put his hands on her shoulders and
moved her back so he could come into the small room too.

'Did I wake you?'

'No.' He'd come back. He had. Her heart sang with happiness—then she sensed his tension and her stomach clenched with
anxiety. 'Did you find your cousin?'

'No. I've just searched the Clink for him.'

'The Clink?' Temperance was sure she'd misheard. 'The *prison*?'

'Yes. Here.' Jack caught her wrist and lifted her hand. 'This is
for you.' She felt him put a heavy weight into her palm. She closed
her fingers around it and realised it was a purse. 'Put it away
safely,' he ordered. 'Where's your mother's workbox?' Without
waiting for a reply he began to feel around for it.

'Why do you want it?'

'I'm taking you to stay with Fanny Berridge.'

'It's the middle of the night!'

'I don't have time to wait until morning,' Jack said. She could
hear the impatience in his voice, feel it in his movements as he
dropped the workbox on to the bed.

'I'm sorry.' He took a deep breath, and she sensed his effort to
speak more gently. 'Take this as well.'

'What?' She held out her hand and felt even more confused
when he didn't give her anything.

'Stand still.' He lifted his hands over and behind her head. A moment later she felt a slight weight pull at her hair. 'Keep this until I come back. You'd best put it inside your bodice for safety.'

She touched her breast and discovered he'd put a chain around her neck. She slid her fingers along the links and found a ring.

'What is it?'

'My ring. I can't stay now, but I *will* come back.'

Temperance reached out to him and her fingers brushed his cheek in the darkness. She couldn't see him clearly, but he radiated impatient, hard-edged anxiety.

'Why were you searching the Clink for your cousin?' she asked.

'That's where they took the prisoners when Newgate burned. Come.' He took her wrist and pulled her towards the door.

'Wait.'

'I don't have time—'

'Jack.' She paused, remembering how he'd helped her overcome her panic in the last moments before she left her shop. Now she must find the words to calm him. 'There is a little time,' she said gently. 'I will go by myself to Fanny's tomorrow morning. I will be quite safe.' She cupped his cheek with her palm. 'So you have that extra time to tell me why you think your cousin was a prisoner in Newgate.'

She felt him take a carefully controlled breath. She sensed it was hard for him to stand still and talk when he was eager to act.

'When I reached Putney, I found Jakob had sent me a message on Sunday,' he said. 'In it he told me he was a prisoner in Newgate and asked me to go and get him out. But when I got back to London I discovered Newgate had already burned. The warders took the prisoners to the Clink, here in Southwark. I followed. I've been searching…searching… I even went to Swiftbourne's house, but he has no news either!' The torment in Jack's voice was unmistakable. 'I keep thinking…perhaps this happened because I stole Jakob's coat at Dover—but why would they arrest the victim, not the thief?'

Temperance couldn't bear to hear the anguish in his voice. She wondered who Swiftbourne was, but she was far more concerned about Jack. She wrapped her arms around him, hugging him fiercely.

'That's foolish,' she said. 'A man arrested at Dover would not be put in Newgate. It's just a mistake and nothing to do with you. And you couldn't find him in the Clink because, if he's anything like you, he's already escaped.'

For a moment Jack held himself rigid, then his arms closed around her, holding her as tightly as she held him. 'That's what I keep telling myself,' he said. 'Jakob's a soldier. It must have been chaos when they tried to move the prisoners. He could easily have escaped then.'

'He may even have been released before the fire ever reached Newgate,' said Temperance, pleased to feel the tension in Jack ease a few degrees. 'He's probably rushing around London looking for you at this very moment.'

Jack sighed. 'Most likely. But it was a hell of a shock when I read his letter. I won't be easy till I've found him.'

'I know.' There were so many things Temperance wanted to say, but she bit her tongue. Jack had come back to her once. She must trust he would return a second time.

'I'll take you to Fanny's,' he said. 'The streets aren't safe for a woman alone.'

Temperance gave a small laugh. 'I've been a woman alone for years,' she pointed out. 'I'm a unremarkable tradeswoman. No one will bother me during the day.'

'Very well, but be careful,' Jack ordered. 'Go to Bundle's as soon as you can and don't let anyone know you have that purse.'

'I'm not a half-wit!' Temperance said in exasperation. 'Besides, although I thank you kindly, I can't take any more of your money—'

'Of course you can. The world is turned upside down. You don't know when you'll be able to reclaim your goods and set up shop again. For God's sake, be practical!'

Temperance considered herself a very practical tradeswoman. Jack, for all his undoubted loyalty and generosity, was hardly a paragon of that particular virtue. Only a few days ago she'd been upbraiding him for the unnecessary extravagance of buying a periwig. But when he ordered her to be practical in that terse, worried voice, she felt a surge of tenderness towards him.

She leant forward and, more by luck than judgement, kissed

his cheek. 'Then I thank you very kindly and accept,' she murmured. 'I'd hate you to think I'm impractical,' she added with a glimmer of amusement.

'Good.' He pulled her back into his arms and kissed her, his mouth fierce and demanding on hers. It was another small reassurance their earlier intimacy was not unimportant to him. Before she had a chance to respond, he lifted his head and stepped back. 'I'll return as soon as I can,' he said. 'In the meantime, be careful. And no matter how bad business is—don't try selling muslin in taverns after dark again!'

Covent Garden, later that night

Even though it was the early hours of the morning, the coffee-house buzzed with activity. Bundle was keeping a careful watch on the progress of the fire, but so far he hadn't opted for flight.

'Coffee or ale?' he asked Jack laconically.

'Coffee,' Jack said, looking around the coffee room. 'Is my cousin here?'

'No one claiming to be your cousin is here.' Bundle gestured to a serving boy. 'We haven't seen you since Sunday.'

Jack spared him a quick glance. 'Were you worried?'

A grin flickered on Bundle's face. 'After only three days? Which cousin? What does he look like?'

'Jakob Balston. Big. A couple of inches taller than me. Blond. Swedish.'

'Ah, yes, I remember. No, he hasn't come here.'

'Diable!' Jack had known it was a long chance. There was no reason for Jakob to suspect Jack had been staying in the coffee-house. For the thousandth time he damned himself for not having received Jakob's message in time. If Jakob died because he had delayed resuming his ducal responsibilities, Jack knew he'd never forgive himself.

'If he comes here…' He stared at the surface of his coffee as he tried to hold his grinding anxiety at bay. 'Send him to St Martin's Lane,' he said.

'St Martin's Lane?'

Jack looked up. 'Send him to Lord Swiftbourne,' he said harshly.

Bundle's eyes widened briefly. 'As you wish.'

'I don't like it, but it's close,' said Jack. 'If he goes there, Swift-bourne can send a message to me at Putney. I'm going back there now. He wasn't there this morning, but they hadn't moved the prisoners then—'

'Prisoners?'

Jack quickly explained.

'I'm proud to serve such a lively, gallant family,' Bundle remarked.

'You have an insolent gift for sarcasm,' Jack said to the man who'd carried him as a three-year-old all the way from Sussex to France.

'Since when has Jack Bow acquired a taste for tedious deference?'

'After tonight, Jack Bow's dead.'

'What?' Bundle sat up straighter.

'That's what you wanted, isn't it?' Jack tossed off the last of his coffee. 'Or did I misunderstand all your hints that I should adopt a more regular style of living? I'll become a paragon of respectability—but first, please God, I must find Jakob.' He stood up. 'I need a horse.'

Chapter Five

'St Paul's burned last night!' said George Pring.

Temperance huddled in the corner of Fanny Berridge's kitchen, listening as Pring told his story of destruction. She'd waited until morning to make her way through Southwark. When she'd arrived she'd discovered that she and Agnes weren't the only victims of the fire who'd sought temporary refuge with Fanny. Pring was a bookseller who, like Agnes, had believed his goods would be safe in the cathedral.

'It started to burn yesterday evening,' he said. 'All my books— my whole stock—were in the crypt of St Faith. But the cathedral roof collapsed and broke through the floor and smashed the roof of the crypt and…the books are still burning.'

'I heard explosions,' said Temperance. 'Was that St Paul's?'

'The stones exploded! Great lumps of rock hurtling through the churchyard like cannonballs. The lead from the roof melted. It ran in a great red, boiling tide down towards the Thames. It smelt like the fumes of hell. I've lost everything,' Pring finished in a whisper.

Temperance looked at Agnes in concern. The old woman had lost just as much as the bookseller. Overnight she had been reduced from a tradeswoman in comfortable circumstances to a pauper. Worse than that. She'd rented her shop and, under the terms of her lease, she would still be expected to pay her rent, even though she'd lost her business.

Agnes locked her hands together in front of her chest. Her papery skin was pulled tight over the bones of her face. Temperance saw Fanny exchange a glance with her husband. He looked resigned rather than truly accepting, but he nodded. Fanny sat down beside her aunt and began to speak softly to her.

Putney, 5 September 1666

Jack left Bundle's horse on the north side of the Thames and crossed the river in a lighter. As he drew closer to the house his swift stride slowed as his anxiety intensified.

'Your Grace! You're back!' Henderson, his steward, greeted him. 'Colonel Balston—'

'Is he here?'

'Yes, your Grace, the green bedchamber—'

'In *bed*, by God!'

'Your Grace, wait!' Henderson followed breathlessly behind. 'Colonel Balston is not *in* the green bedchamber. He was to sleep outside the door—'

'Nonsense!' Jack wasn't interested in anything the steward had to say, especially when he could see for himself there was no sign of his cousin in the gallery.

He reached the chamber and flung open the door. It slammed against the wall, shattering the early morning quiet. He cast one raking glance around the room before his attention focussed on the bed.

'*Diable*! Are you hurt?'

'No,' Jakob replied calmly.

Jack stared at his cousin as the tension drained from his body. Jakob hadn't been burned alive. The crisis was over. At last he took the time to glance at the woman sitting beside Jakob. To his utter shock he recognised her.

Lady Desire Godwin.

Six years ago he'd come close to marrying the lady, but he'd grievously insulted her and provoked her outraged father into trying to force a duel upon him. The duel had never taken place but, from the expression in Lady Desire's eyes, her hostility towards him hadn't abated. What the devil was she doing under his roof, sharing a bed with his cousin?

Temperance slipped unnoticed out of the kitchen. The street wasn't a pleasant place for quiet reflection, but at least she could avoid banging elbows at every turn with distraught friends and neighbours. As she glanced around, her eye was caught by a dishevelled figure stumbling towards her. It took her a moment to recognise her apprentice.

'Isaac!' She seized his shoulders, shocked by his appearance. One side of his face was bruised and crusted with dried blood. His nose and lips were swollen and he breathed heavily through his mouth.

'Mistress?'

'Isaac.' She ran her hands gently up and down his arms. She didn't know what other injuries he'd suffered and she was afraid she'd hurt him if she touched him too firmly. 'What happened?'

He stared at her, his eyes filling with tears.

'Come inside.' She put her arm around his shoulders. 'You're safe now. I'll tend your wounds and—'

'*I failed you!*' he cried out, his words slurred but his anguish agonisingly clear.

'Failed me?' Temperance's immediate instinct was to take care of Isaac's injuries, but she felt a chill of foreboding. 'Failed me how?'

'I lost…I lost the cart!' His confession emerged in gulping gasps. 'Someone offered the carter more. I couldn't stop him. They threw out all your goods. I tried…I tried to collect it all up. P-protect as much as I could. But I c-couldn't…everything was trampled or st-stolen. I'm s-sorry…' Wrenching distress overcame him. He couldn't talk any more, only stand sobbing beside Temperance.

'Everything's gone?' She breathed. A few minutes ago she'd been contemplating a destitute future for Agnes. Now the same thing had happened to her.

'I'm s-sorry…I'm sorry.'

Temperance put her arms around her distraught apprentice. She was several inches taller than the lad and she ended up with his head on her shoulder as he wept out his accumulated shame and fear.

'I know. It's not your fault. Don't cry. You'll make yourself feel worse.'

Isaac was fourteen, but he was neither naturally robust nor confident. She knew he'd done his best, but he wasn't equipped to deal with the disaster that had befallen him. If she'd been there…

She cut off that train of thought before she gave way to anger and grief as uncontrollable as Isaac's bitter sense of failure.

'Stop this now!' she ordered. 'You'll make yourself sick if you cry any more. Did you go to Bundle's?' she asked when he was calmer.

'Where?' He looked at her blearily.

'Bundle's Coffeehouse. That's where you were supposed to take the cart.'

'Oh. I—I forgot,' he confessed. 'When I woke up…I just wanted to find you. I didn't know where to go at first. Then I remembered Mistress Agnes's niece lives in Southwark…'

'What do you mean, when you woke up?'

'I don't…I don't know. I woke up. I was lying on the street, next to the wall of a house. I didn't know where I was!' His voice was sharp with remembered panic.

'You're safe with me now,' said Temperance, resorting to the brisk tones she'd often used in the shop, though she'd seldom felt less safe in her life.

'Yes.' His shoulders slumped with relief. He even managed a slight smile. 'That's it. I found you. What will we do now?'

Kingston upon Thames, Wednesday 5 September 1666

Jack stepped over the threshold of Lady Desire's Kingston house and into pandemonium. When the fire had threatened her home in the Strand she'd sent her most valuable belongings here, and boxes, furniture and paintings were piled everywhere he looked.

He paused, assessing the situation. He'd brought eight of his own men from Putney. He'd sent two to guard the river entrance, two to guard the street entrance and four were at his back.

'You!' He pointed to the nearest startled servant. 'Where is Ar-scott?'

'Ar-Arscott?'

'Her ladyship's steward,' Jack said impatiently.

'Not… He's not here, my lord.'

'Who's in charge?'

'You devil! What have you done with her?' A man barrelled out of an open door towards Jack.

Jack spun to face his assailant, reaching for his sword hilt. Then he saw the man was unarmed, his face filled with raw fear.

'What have you done with her?' The man seized Jack's coat front and tried to shake him.

'If you are referring to Lady Desire, I haven't done anything with her,' Jack said coldly. 'She is under the protection of Colonel Balston, who will guard her with his life. When I last saw them they were on their way back to London.'

'What are you *talking* about?' The man gave Jack another frustrated shake.

Under any other circumstances Jack wouldn't have tolerated the impertinence, but he could see the panic in the other man's eyes. It reminded him of Nellie Carpenter's fear for her lost daughter.

'Lady Desire is perfectly safe,' Jack repeated, taking the man's wrists and compelling him to release his grip, but making no other retaliation. 'Who are you?'

'Benjamin Finch, her ladyship's Gentleman of the Horse.' Finch remembered his dignity and took a step back from Jack. 'And I know you, your Grace. You have no business uninvited here, in her ladyship's house.'

'I am invited,' Jack replied, concealing his discomfort beneath an aloof tone. 'I am here at Lady Desire's request.' It was stretching the truth somewhat. He'd actually come at Jakob's request and the pressing of his own conscience to make amends for his former lack of gallantry to Lady Desire, but saw no need to share that with Finch.

'Why?'

'Where is Arscott?'

'He went back to London in search of Lady Desire. When we left the Strand yesterday he came by river, I came by road. We both thought she was with the other, but then it turned out she wasn't *anywhere.*'

'She didn't want to leave her home,' said Jack, gentling his tone in response to the other man's distress. 'But she came to no harm. Colonel Balston took her to…a place of safety,' he said, judging it would make Finch more suspicious if he realised Lady Desire had spent the night under Jack's roof.

'Who the devil is Colonel Balston? We don't know any Colonel Balston. It's your doing, isn't it, you—'

'Where is Lady Desire's treasure chest?'

'What?' Finch stared in horror. 'You thief! I'll not let you have it!'

'Pour l'amour de Dieu! I've come to protect it—not steal it! An attempt was made to abduct your mistress on Saturday. The man who ordered the abduction wants her fortune. I'm here to make sure he doesn't take the fortune, even though he missed the lady. And before you make the accusation, I am not the guilty party.' Jack took a deep breath and continued more calmly. 'Since you recognise me, you will also allow I owe your mistress some recompense. So…I will guard her treasure until this matter is resolved. Which I trust will not take long. Now, show me where it is.'

Within a few minutes Jack had assured himself the treasure chest had not been tampered with and Benjamin Finch was rushing to London to find Lady Desire.

Jack sighed and sat down, propping his feet on the troublesome treasure chest. He had a similar chest of his own at Kilverdale Hall, which at times could contain as much as six or seven thousand pounds. Lady Desire's income was almost as large as Jack's and, since she lived retired, her expenses were smaller. Jack suspected there could be as much as nine or ten thousand pounds beneath his feet.

Over breakfast in Putney, Jakob had told Jack how he'd been mistaken for a mercenary and recruited to assist in an attempt to abduct Lady Desire on the Saturday before the fire. Jakob had gone along with the scheme so he could help the lady, but the two men with him had been killed by Lady Desire's steward, Arscott, and Jakob had ended up in gaol. Jakob was sure Arscott had set up the attempted abduction so he could rescue Lady Desire and use her fear to persuade her to marry him.

But the fire meant Lady Desire and a sizeable part of her fortune had become separated. There was now a strong likelihood Arscott would abandon his attempt to steal the lady in favour of stealing her money. Jack hoped he would. He hadn't planned on spending the rest of the day guarding a chest of money, but he'd felt guilty about his treatment of Lady Desire for years. Capturing the traitorous steward would be an excellent way to make restitution for his unkindness to her. He also felt a duty to help his cousin.

He rubbed a hand over his chin, wished he'd taken the time to shave before he left Putney, and yawned. He hoped the steward would come quickly. It wouldn't take long to deal with the villain, and his conscience regarding Lady Desire would finally be clear. After that he'd be able to return to Temperance. Just thinking about her made his blood quicken and filled him with impatience for a speedy conclusion to his current errand.

Covent Garden, Sunday morning, 16 September 1666

Temperance squared her shoulders and pushed open the door of Bundle's coffeehouse. After notching up her courage to enter the unfamiliar surroundings, it was almost a let down to discover the coffee room was empty apart from an old man smoking a pipe and a boy scattering sawdust on the floor.

'Good morning, mistress,' he said. 'Can I help you?'

'I…thank you. I hope so,' she said. It was two weeks to the day since the fire had started to wreak devastation on London, and the first chance she'd had to come to the coffeehouse. She'd found work in the shop of one of her father's friends, Daniel Munckton whose own shop in the Royal Exchange had been destroyed. Along with the other merchants who'd traded in the Exchange, he'd been able to set up his business in Gresham College in Bishopgate Street. With suitable lodgings in such short supply, Temperance had to sleep on a pallet in the shop each night, but her situation was much more comfortable than hundreds of other refugees from the fire. She hadn't been able to come to the coffeehouse before because Sunday was the only day she had free from her duties in the shop.

'Would you like coffee?' asked the boy.

'Oh. No, thank you. I'm looking for Jack Bow,' she said, feeling her face heat with embarrassment. It was the first time she'd ever sought out a man for any reason other than business.

'Jack Bow?' The boy stared at her, shock in his eyes.

'Is he here?'

'No…no.' The boy looked shaken by her question, and there was something in his eyes that made Temperance's skin prickle with apprehension.

'Is he… Is he a friend of yours, mistress?' he asked.

'Yes. What's wrong?' Temperance's embarrassment was forgotten as dreadful possibilities darted through her mind. Jack's cousin had been a prisoner in Newgate. Had Jack been imprisoned himself? Or…?

'He… Mr Bundle told me…'

'What?' Temperance half-reached towards the boy, then clamped her arms across her chest to stop herself shaking the information out of him. 'Where is Jack? What did Mr Bundle tell you?'

'Jack Bow's dead,' the boy whispered, tears in his eyes.

'What?' Temperance swayed with disbelief. 'No, it can't be true…' How could Jack—strong, clever, full-of-life Jack—be dead? 'I don't believe you.'

'It is true.' The boy took her arm and pulled her towards the nearest bench. 'Mr Bundle himself told me. Here.' He jerked his head. 'You can sit.'

Temperance sank on to the bench. She felt numb. Jack couldn't be dead. She looked up at the coffeehouse boy and saw him wipe his cheek with the back of his hand. The lad's grief was unmistakable. Pain slashed through her, ripping apart the brittle protection of disbelief.

'How?' she asked hoarsely.

'It was a sword fight.'

'Swords.' Temperance remembered how competently Jack had buckled on his sword. She'd believed him to be as skilled with the weapon as he was with the lute. 'How could someone have killed him in a sword fight? Was he outnumbered?'

'I don't know, mistress. It can't have been a fair fight. Mr Bow was too good, but Mr Bundle didn't tell me exactly what happened. Just…just that Mr Bow was dead.'

'What did Mr Bundle tell you?'

'It was when I asked him when Mr Bow was coming back. He said…' the boy's eyes lost focus as he concentrated on his master's words '…he said, "Jack Bow's dead, lad." Then he said, "God knows I'll miss him, but I was always afraid the sword would be the death of him."' The boy paused, swallowing convulsively. 'Then…then he sent me to serve another customer.'

Temperance rocked back and forth on the bench as she absorbed the finality of the news. Jack was dead. Dead. A sob caught at her throat. She stood up, turning blindly towards the door.

'Mistress?'

She became aware of the boy's worried face. 'Thank you for telling me so…so kindly,' she said. The words emerged as a raspy imitation of her usual voice. 'Goodbye.'

She rushed out of the coffeehouse before he could call her back, or ask any questions of his own. Once outside, she stumbled along the street with no direction in mind.

When she returned to a sense of her surroundings, she discovered she was standing in the ruins of her shop. Only the chimney and the blackened hearth remained of her home. From where she was standing she could see all the way to the Thames and the buildings of Southwark on the other side. The fire had reduced the City to a waste land of rubble, ash and crooked chimneys.

There were already makeshift shops set up in the ruins. Several tradesmen were living in the cellars of what had once been their homes, and they'd set up their stalls where their shops had once stood. If Temperance had had any goods left to sell, and if she hadn't been a woman alone, she might have done the same. But the City was more dangerous than ever. At night it was the haunt of footpads and thieves. There were stories of linkboys lighting the path of their customers straight into the hands of murderous groups of thieves.

Temperance wrapped her arms around herself, still struggling to come to terms with Jack's death. She had known him for such a short time, but the depth of her grief forced her to acknowledge how important he'd become to her. How much she'd been counting on him returning to her. She'd have given anything for him to be standing next to her, teasing and arguing with her. But she was alone again.

She took a deep breath and straightened her shoulders. She'd been alone before and she'd survived. Somehow she would find a way to clear the site of her shop, rebuild and set up her business again.

Southwark, 17 November 1666

'Stay away from me, you bully!'

Temperance had nearly reached Fanny Berridge's house when she saw Agnes standing outside, completely dwarfed by two large men. Temperance recognised one of the men as the rent collector for the old lady's landlord and broke into a run.

'Leave her alone!' She pushed between the men and Agnes. It was one of those occasions when she was glad of her height. She stared down at the rent collector, trying to intimidate him into retreating.

'You have no business here!' she said. 'When Robert Hubert was found guilty of starting the fire last month it made the fire an act of war. That means Lord Windle is responsible for his property—just like all the other landlords in London. Does he think we don't know the law?'

'That's not my concern,' said the rent collector. 'I'm here at his lordship's orders. The widow Cruikshank will pay her rent if she knows what's good for her,' he added unpleasantly.

'No. She'll take her case to the Fire Court,' Temperance countered. 'The judges will find in her favour without a doubt. Now go away and tell Lord Windle—' She saw the rent collector throw a glance over his shoulder and suddenly realised Lord Windle himself was watching their encounter, a dangerous expression on his face. 'Tell your master to acquire some manners,' she finished in a steady voice, though her heart rate increased uncomfortably when she realised Agnes's landlord was present in person. It wasn't the first time he'd done such a thing. She had no idea why he was willing to demean himself in such a fashion, but her only concern was that his men were unlikely to back down when he was watching them.

She wasn't sure what would have happened next, but to her relief Fanny's husband emerged into the street with his two apprentices and one of his drinking cronies. Temperance thought he could have appeared a little sooner, but for now his arrival had the desired effect.

'Take your case to the Fire Court without delay,' Temperance said to Agnes as soon as Windle was out of sight. She saw the old woman was trembling and gripped her hand. 'Daniel Munckton will assist you, I'm sure.'

'Pinch-mouthed old woman,' Agnes muttered. 'I don't need him. You can help. You can—'

'I'm sorry, I can't,' Temperance cut across the old woman's words. She was sorry for Agnes, but it wouldn't be fair to let her think, even for a minute, that Temperance would be able to help her. 'I'm leaving London,' she said before Agnes could launch into complaints. 'I'm sorry, I have to go immediately. I only came to say goodbye.'

'Leaving?' Agnes stared at her in shock. 'You've never left London in your life.'

'But now I am. I must find Isaac and make ready. I am sure all will go well with you. Don't forget, go to Daniel Munckton and get him to help you present your case to the Fire Court as soon as you can. Please give Fanny my best wishes and say I'm sorry I can't wait to speak to her.'

Temperance hurried off before the old woman started asking questions she wasn't prepared to answer. Two months ago she'd believed the only remembrance she had of Jack was his ring. Now she knew that wasn't true. She also carried his unborn child. And her situation had gone from difficult to desperate.

There had been a proclamation in September ordering all occupiers of fire-damaged properties to produce a survey of the ground on which their building had stood. Temperance had spent most of the money Jack had given her on having the ground cleared so she could ensure her claim to what was left of her inheritance was officially recorded. At the time it had seemed an essential investment. But now she was almost penniless—and the situation of a destitute, unmarried mother was dire. If she wasn't careful, she might find herself in the stocks or subject to a public whipping, and there was no one in London she could turn to for help. Munckton was a man of upright but puritanical morals. He'd been one of the witnesses who'd sworn she was a modest virgin before she'd been allowed to enter the Drapers' Company. He would have no sympathy or understanding of her plight.

She had no choice. She had to leave London.

'Didn't she at least say where she was going?' Fanny asked in exasperation.

'No. Just said she was going and went,' said Agnes. 'Selfish, that's what I call it. Now I'll have to get pinch-faced Munckton to help me with the Fire Court.'

'Oh, be quiet. You'd be dead if not for her,' Fanny said. 'A letter's arrived here for her. I was going to give it to her the next time I saw her. How can I send it to her if I don't know where she is?'

Agnes shrugged. 'Don't suppose it was important,' she said. 'Who would she be getting letters from? All her family are dead.'

Kilverdale Hall, Sussex, 19 November 1666

'Her Grace will see you now,' said the very grand senior servant.

'Thank you. But I don't understand...' Temperance was confused and disconcerted by the way she'd been treated ever since she and Isaac had arrived at the village of Arunhurst. She'd asked for directions at the baker's, but she'd never anticipated being ushered into the presence of someone as exalted as a Duchess.

'Come with me,' said the steward. 'The boy can stay here.'

Temperance had enquired at the servants' entrance. Now she followed the steward into the main part of the house and up a broad flight of stairs. She stared in amazement at the carved newel post and then looked up at the ceiling soaring high above her. The Drapers' Hall had been a very fine building, but in her everyday world stairs were narrow and badly lit. Here there was a large window on the first landing overlooking a deer park, and a huge painting of half-dressed people on the wall. Her pace slowed as she peered at the painting. Then she realised the steward had stopped to wait for her.

She flushed and muttered an apology as she hastened after him. The steward continued down a long, broad gallery. The wall on one side was pierced at intervals by huge bay windows that stretched almost from the ceiling to the floor. It was a world away from Cheapside. Temperance was so unnerved by her surroundings that, as she stepped into the Duchess's parlour, she felt as if a whole flock of London sparrows were trapped in her stomach, fluttering against her ribs.

The Duchess was sitting near a window. She was wearing blue silk, which matched her eyes, and she had very pale brown hair. Temperance didn't have time to notice anything else before she sank into a respectful curtsy.

'My steward tells me you're looking for Jack Bow,' said the Duchess.

'Yes…I mean, no, madam.' Temperance bit her lip.

The Duchess arched her elegant brows. 'Did I misunderstand? Hinchcliff said you were asking directions to Jack Bow's house.'

'I was,' Temperance said. 'I am. Is Jack one of your tenants?' She couldn't think of any other reason for the Duchess taking a personal interest in her enquiries. 'Is he… Is he behind with the rent?' she burst out. Jack had been away from Sussex for such a long time she'd been prepared to find his house in poor repair—but it hadn't occurred to her until now he might have left debts behind.

The Duchess stroked the side of her index finger along her lips. Temperance saw the gleam in the other woman's brilliant blue eyes and realised the Duchess was amused by her question. She didn't have time to wonder why before the Duchess asked, 'Why are you looking for Jack's house?'

'Because he's my husband.' Temperance made the declaration boldly, even though she felt sick with anxiety. She'd never expected the first time she publicly claimed they'd married it would be to a Duchess.

During the long, sleepless nights when she'd been trying to decide what to do, she'd remembered how Jack had exhorted her to *be practical*. Claiming to be his widow was the practical thing to do. Jack's child was entitled to the protection of Jack's name—and so was she.

The Duchess's eyes narrowed slightly. Her only other discernible response to Temperance's statement was a slight check in her breathing. Then her breasts continued to rise and fall smoothly beneath the fine blue silk.

'Your husband?' The Duchess raised her eyebrows. 'The marriage must surely be recent?'

'The day before the fire.' Temperance's voice sounded a little over-loud to her own ears. 'We had a licence. He gave me his ring.' She put out her hand to show the Duchess.

The Duchess held out her hand, palm up in silent command.

Temperance stepped closer. She wasn't willing to remove the ring, but she lifted her hand so the Duchess could see it more clearly.

'It does indeed appear to be his ring,' the Duchess observed. She sat back and studied Temperance. 'Why were you married in, as I suppose, secret?'

'That was for my sake,' said Temperance. She'd known this would be one of the first questions asked and her answer was prepared. There was nothing inherently improbable about it. Apprentices who were forbidden to marry before they'd completed their indentures and widows who didn't want to lose their portion often chose to wed in secret.

'Your sake? Why?' The Duchess's gaze sharpened.

'I am a linen draper. That is, I am a member of the Drapers' Company, and I have a shop in Cheapside,' Temperance said proudly. 'Or I did, until the fire destroyed it.' Her shoulders slumped as she recalled her loss. 'Your Grace may not know, but a woman may lose her right to trade in the City if she marries unwisely—'

'You considered marriage to Jack Bow *unwise*? Why did you accept his proposal?'

'Obviously I didn't think marrying him was unwise!' Temperance paused and continued more calmly, 'I am a very practical woman. It was unwise because I could have been thrown out of the Drapers' Company and forbidden to trade if it was known I'd married someone from outside the City. And it would have been dreadful if I'd been unable to trade before he found a suitable position to support us.'

'He was looking for a position?' The Duchess gazed at Temperance in fascination. 'As what, may I ask?'

It was a good question. One which had taken up far too many of Temperance's thoughts until she'd heard Jack was dead and her secret hopes for the future could never come true.

'I think he hoped to be a musician to the King,' she said.

'When did the marriage take place?' the Duchess asked.

'The Friday immediately before the fire. Jack arranged everything.'

Temperance held her breath, ready to explain Jack had kept all the marriage papers if the Duchess asked her to produce them. Many real documents had been lost in the aftermath of the fire.

'I see,' the Duchess said. 'Jack seems to have been even busier than usual these past few months. Who are you, may I ask?' she added without inflection.

'Temperance Challinor…Temperance Bow, I mean.' Temperance flushed.

'You said you have a shop in Cheapside?'

'I did have. I inherited it from my father. It's just rubble now.'

'I'm sorry,' said the Duchess, her voice almost gentle. 'It's hard to lose one's home. But why have you come here now? Why didn't you continue to wait for Jack's return in London?'

Temperance stared at the Duchess, a cold weight settling in her stomach as she realised news of Jack's death hadn't reached Sussex. 'You don't know, do you?' she said.

'Know what? Tell me, girl.' For the first time the Duchess's voice hardened into a command. 'What is it I don't know?'

'Jack's dead,' Temperance whispered.

'What?' Colour bleached from the Duchess's face. 'No!' She gripped the arms of her chair and thrust halfway to her feet before sinking back. 'No. How?'

'In a sword fight.' Tears started in Temperance's eyes as she watched the Duchess struggle with the horrible news.

'When? Where?' The Duchess turned her desolate gaze on to Temperance.

'I don't know exactly. I'm sorry. The boy didn't know the details—'

'Boy?'

'In Bundle's Coffeehouse.' Temperance described her visit there and what the serving boy had told her.

'Bundle told the boy Jack's dead?'

Temperance nodded. Her throat felt tight.

'He told the boy, but he sent no message to *me*?' The Duchess's voice was full of anguish. 'When did you leave London?'

'Two days ago.'

'*Two days?* A fast horse… My God, what does it matter?' The Duchess pressed her lips together and covered her face with her hands.

Temperance took a hesitant step forward, then knelt beside the Duchess's chair.

'I am so sorry,' she murmured awkwardly. 'If I'd known how grieved you'd be by the news, I'd have—' she broke off. There was no easy way to break such tidings.

The Duchess lifted her head. 'Two days he's been dead,' she whispered. 'How could I not have felt it?'

'No, madam.' Temperance was confused. 'That's when I left London. Bundle's boy told me in September.'

The Duchess went quite still, but suddenly radiated strange tension. 'You were told of Jack's death in *September*?'

'Yes, madam.' Startled, Temperance swayed back as the Duchess leapt to her feet and dragged open a drawer in the desk.

'Jack wrote this letter on the fourteenth of November!' The Duchess swung round, triumphant relief blazing in her eyes. 'Now what have you to say?'

'He's alive?' Temperance whispered.

'See for yourself!' The Duchess thrust the letter in front of her face. 'My son was alive and writing to me a week ago.'

Temperance pressed her hands to her cheeks. It was almost as hard to comprehend this good news as it had been to accept the news of Jack's death. 'Really *alive*?'

'*Yes*. See…here…he has written the date. The fourteenth of November. He was at Harwich then, but he's on his way home now.' The Duchess sat down in a billow of silk.

'*Harwich?* Why—?' Temperance started to laugh and cry at the same time, rocking back and forward on her heels, as she absorbed the news Jack wasn't dead.

'What exactly did Bundle's boy tell you?' the Duchess asked.

'What I said. He believed what he told me. I could see how badly he was grieving. That's why I never questioned the news.'

'But does Bundle believe it?' The Duchess frowned. 'If he did, surely he would have come himself to tell me? This doesn't make sense.'

Temperance hardly heard the Duchess as she gazed unseeingly at the carved legs of the desk, finally allowing herself to believe Jack was alive. Joyful excitement suddenly bloomed in her heart. She would see Jack again. She would!

New energy surged through her. She leapt to her feet—

And stumbled with shock as she registered what else the Duchess had said.

'Your *son*?'

'Yes, he's my son.'

'B-but…'

'Sometimes he calls himself Jack Bow,' said the Duchess, 'but his full name is John Beaufleur, second Duke of Kilverdale.'

Chapter Six

'He's a *Duke*?' Temperance had had so many shocks she was past trying to control her reaction to this latest news. 'Of course he is! This is his house, isn't it? I asked at the village for Jack Bow's house and this is where I was sent. No wonder he laughed.'

'Who laughed?' said the Duchess.

'He lied to me!' Temperance began to pace about the room, fury ripping through her at the way Jack had misled her. 'He told me he was a soldier of fortune. He was playing a lute in a tavern the first time I saw him. He stole his cousin's coat. I thought... Oh, I'll box his ears when I see him.' She struck her hands together in frustrated outrage. 'He'll not play his games with *me* again!'

'Did Jack laugh at you?' the Duchess asked.

Temperance shook her head. 'The man in the village baker's. Oh! He is a *villain*! I should have let the mob string him up—'

'*What?* What mob?'

Temperance blinked at the Duchess, suddenly remembering she was talking to Jack's mother.

'They weren't really a mob,' she said. 'Just frightened and confused. There were rumours the French had started the fire and someone accused Jack of being French. But I told them his great-grandfather was a London grocer, and then it turned out Nicholas Farley remembered him. He was the Lord Mayor!' Temperance sat down suddenly on a nearby stool.

'What a fool I've been,' she said. 'I knew his great-grandfather was the Lord Mayor. I should have known he wasn't just a vagabond minstrel—but he had no business telling me he was Jack Bow! How could he?' She dropped her head into her hands in sudden despair.

'I cannot speak for my son on this matter—' the Duchess began.

'No. No, I know you can't,' said Temperance, straightening, certain the Duchess was about to order her to leave. 'I know. I'm sorry. I should not be speaking to you so.' She stood up. It was time to leave. She would worry about what to do next when she and Isaac were safely outside the grand gates.

'But I am sure he would expect me to make your stay here comfortable while you wait for him to return and—shall we say—face the music?' the Duchess continued.

'Stay?' Temperance stared in disbelief. 'You want me to stay *here*?'

'Of course. You came looking for Jack Bow's house, didn't you?' the Duchess said. 'I assume you meant to take up residence when you found it?'

'Yes. But I thought…I thought it would be quite a little house. I thought—since he'd been away for so long—it might be empty. I thought I'd be cleaning and scrubbing and perhaps it would need a few repairs… I was going to set up a small shop in the front room as soon as I'd had time to settle…' Temperance's voice faded away. 'How could he be a Duke?' she whispered. 'How could he?'

Temperance sat on the window seat in one of the many parlours. Her mood swung between fear for her future, giddy relief that Jack was alive and anger he had deceived her. She'd believed he hadn't come back to her because he was dead. Now she knew he hadn't come back because he was a duke and she was just a passing entertainment. If she was lucky, he would think it a good joke she was masquerading as Jack Bow's wife and give her another purse full of gold before turning her out. If she was unlucky—

Fear seized her. She'd always known there was a small risk attached to her plans. Sometimes a woman would pretend to be the widow of a seaman so she could claim the prize money and other wages owing to her late 'husband'. If the woman's deception was discovered, she would be tried at the Old Bailey and, if she was found guilty, could be sentenced to death. Temperance had only been looking for a safe place to live while she raised Jack's child, but in doing so she had falsely claimed to be the wife of a Duke. That must be an even more serious crime than pretending to be a common seaman's widow.

She laid her hand over her stomach and choked back a disbelieving laugh. The jest was on her, not Jack. She'd tried to save herself from public humiliation in the stocks and made herself a candidate for the gallows instead. At least they wouldn't hang her until after the child was born.

'Who are you?'

The unexpected question made her jump. She turned to discover she was being studied by a small boy with shockingly familiar black hair and dark eyes.

'Temperance,' she croaked, shaken to the core. Jack had told her there was no woman waiting for him. It had never occurred to her that he might have children.

The boy's black eyebrows drew together in a frown.

For a few seconds she thought he was angry with her, then realised he hadn't understood her meaning.

'My name is Temperance,' she explained.

As her heart rate slowed to a more comfortable pace she studied the boy as closely as he was scrutinising her. He really did look like a softer, smaller version of Jack.

He nodded, his expression clearing as he understood what she meant.

'My name is Toby,' he said. 'What are you doing here?'

'I'm waiting to see the Duke.'

'He's not here,' Toby said flatly.

'I know.'

'He is doing something very important,' said Toby. 'He has been away for so long because no one else is strong enough and brave enough to do it. He is chasing a bad man.'

'He… Yes, he is brave and strong,' Temperance agreed. 'What bad man?' She still didn't know what Jack had been doing for the past two and a half months.

'He tried to steal a lady. Papa chased him. It was in his letter.' Toby's eyes narrowed. 'Papa won't come back just for *you*,' he said, lifting his chin stubbornly. 'He promised me he'd be home weeks ago. He won't come any quicker just for *you*.'

'No. What…what lady?' she asked. 'Your mother?'

'*No!*' Toby said, his expression a mixture of scorn and irritation. 'A lady in London. Cousin Jakob married her. I don't remember Cousin Jakob, but Gram says he'll visit soon with his new bride.'

'Oh.' Temperance closed her mouth on more questions. It was humiliating to obtain important information from a fierce-eyed child. In her limited experience, most young boys had their fair share of arrogance, and Toby had obviously been issued an appropriately lordly portion of that characteristic.

'Cherry says you're Papa's wife,' Toby said.

'Ah…' The lie stuck in Temperance's throat. 'Um…' She scrabbled for something to say which wouldn't offend her young interrogator.

'Gram said Papa would get married soon and I must be gracious to his wife. He isn't here, so it is my duty to welcome you to your new home.' He knitted his brows together in concentration and bowed to her.

Temperance stared at him in astonishment.

Toby straightened up, looked at her disapprovingly, and bowed again. She hastily slipped off the window seat, shook out her skirts and sank into her best formal curtsy. The last thing she wanted to do was make a bad impression on anyone in Kilverdale Hall—especially Jack's son.

'Thank you, sir,' she said gravely. They stared at each other for a few moments. Temperance knew little about small boys, and Toby had apparently exhausted his repertoire of hostly gestures.

'You are a very fine young man. How old are you?' she said at last.

'Seven. How old are you?'

'Twenty-three.'

'Papa is twenty-six.'

'Is he?' That was a detail she hadn't known before.

'Gram is forty-seven.'

'You mean the Duchess?' Temperance said, thinking Jack's mother looked a lot younger than her chronological age.

'Yes. Cherry is eighteen and Hinchcliff is fifty-two…'

'You've taken an excellent inventory of the household,' said Temperance.

'What's an inventory?'

'In my shop it was a complete list of all the goods I had in stock,' she said. 'In this case I meant you have a good list in your head of all the people who live in this house.'

He frowned as he considered what she'd said, then nodded. 'I do,' he said. 'I know everyone who lives in the house. What do you sell in your shop?'

'Different kinds of cloth,' she said. 'Would you like to know more about them?'

He nodded, so she began to describe her shop and her daily routine before the fire.

'London burned,' Toby said. 'Gram told me.'

'I know. My shop burned.'

'Is it all gone?'

'Only the chimney's left.' Temperance's voice caught as she remembered how forlorn it had looked beneath the open sky.

Toby thought about the problem. 'Papa will know what to do,' he said eventually. 'After I've seen him you can tell him all about it. He'll know what to do.'

'Thank you.' Temperance managed to smile. She shared Toby's conviction that Jack would know what to do—but she was afraid she wouldn't find it very pleasant.

Eleanor, Dowager Duchess of Kilverdale, pretended to read a book while she covertly watched Temperance struggle with some embroidery. The two women had spent several hours together each day since Temperance's arrival. Eleanor had made her expectations on the matter clear partly because she was curious about the woman claiming to be her son's wife—but also as a test. Even a well-born girl, trained from birth for the role Temperance had claimed for herself, might be overawed by spending so much time with her noble mother-in-law. But Temperance wore her woollen dresses in the silk-furnished parlour without embarrassment, and she replied with cheerful honesty to every question Eleanor asked about her life in Cheapside.

Eleanor had spent most of her adult life managing for herself and her family in the absence of her husband. She respected Temperance's pride in her achievements before the fire had stolen her livelihood. She also thought Temperance's lack of pretension would appeal to Jack. Very few people spoke their unvarnished thoughts to the Duke of Kilverdale. Jack valued those who dealt with him honestly.

But how honest *was* Temperance? For all her straightforwardness of manner, Eleanor couldn't believe she was Jack's legal wife. Jack could be impatient to the point of recklessness, but it was years since he'd been heedless of his responsibilities, or the consequences of his actions.

Eleanor had no doubt there was something between Temperance and her son. But he surely hadn't married the girl? Surely that was a story Temperance had invented after the fire left her destitute? She'd come to Kilverdale Hall as Jack Bow's widow. From the way Temperance sometimes laid her hand on her stomach in an unconsciously protective gesture, Eleanor suspected she might be pregnant. Eleanor hadn't asked—that intruded further into her son's life than she was willing to tread—but the possibility made her nervous. A false marriage claim could be dealt with easily. But what if Temperance was telling the truth and Jack had thrown all his hard-earned caution to the wind to wed the fiery-eyed shopkeeper?

Eleanor was resolved not to interfere—Jack was a man who made his own decisions. But she was eager for his return and determined to witness his reunion with Temperance. She was convinced it would be enlightening.

Temperance stirred and cleared her throat.

'Excuse me, your Grace,' she said, breaking the long silence. 'When… Would you mind telling me when Toby's mother died?'

'Vivien?' Startled by the question, Eleanor laid her book on her lap. 'She's not dead—at least not as far as I know. Why do you ask?'

'Not…but, but…' Temperance looked bewildered.

'Her affair with Jack ended soon after Toby was born,' Eleanor said, surprised to realise Temperance must have thought Jack had been married to Toby's mother. There had never been any secret about the circumstances of the boy's birth. It was another reminder Temperance wasn't part of their social world.

'I haven't seen Vivien for six years or more,' Eleanor said. 'Jack gave her some money and forbade her ever to visit Toby,' she added, curious to see how Temperance would react.

'What? Why?' The colour drained from Temperance's face.

'Jack is a devoted father,' Eleanor said. It was true, although it was far from being the full story.

She saw undisguised fear dawn in Temperance's eyes. Temperance jerked to her feet, her embroidery falling forgotten to the floor. It was the first time Eleanor had seen her so close to outright panic.

'I have… I must… I beg your pardon, your Grace,' Temperance said with a very creditable attempt at calm. 'I have forgotten something I must do.'

'I am sure it will wait a few minutes,' Eleanor replied, sliding a note of aristocratic command into her voice. A linen draper had no business leaving the presence of a Duchess without permission and, when she chose, Eleanor could be appropriately haughty.

Temperance hesitated a few seconds. Eleanor was privately pleased the younger woman didn't obey immediately. Despite her reservations about Temperance's relationship with Jack, Eleanor liked her. Whatever the future held for Temperance, she would need all her courage and pride to survive.

Temperance stared at the Duchess, her heart pounding so loudly she was sure Jack's mother could hear it. Her first impulse was to escape before Jack arrived, but it would be foolish to begin her flight while the Duchess was watching.

'Yes, of course, your Grace,' she said. She sat down, her legs shaking as if she faced immediate danger. She was far more frightened than she'd been when Tredgold had attacked her in the tavern. Then she'd been confident she could deal with the physical assault—but how could she overcome the whims of a Duke?

As she considered all the implications of what she'd just

learned, cold dread began to replace her first surge of fear. The longer she remained at Kilverdale Hall, the more her memory of the man she'd known in London receded, to be replaced by the far more daunting figure of the Duke of Kilverdale.

She twisted Jack's ring between numb fingers. It had been her talisman for weeks, but now it weighed heavily on her hand. She'd been confused by the engraving on it for weeks, but at Kilverdale Hall she'd recognised it for what it was—a Duke's seal ring. And a symbol of Jack's true rank and her lies.

She distantly remembered she'd been holding a piece of embroidery. She looked down and saw it lying by her feet so she picked it up, but her hands were trembling too much to stitch.

Jack hadn't been cruel when he'd given her the ring, but then he'd been pretending to be Jack Bow. Would he be different in his true guise as a Duke?

Would he take her baby and discard her?

She swallowed an instinctive cry of protest. Toby was well cared for and secure in his life at Kilverdale Hall. Perhaps her child would be better off with Jack than with her? Her head knew that was very likely true, but her heart rebelled.

Then another realisation turned her blood to ice. Ever since she'd met Toby, she'd assumed he was Jack's heir. That had made her own claim to be Jack's wife seem a little less disastrous because, although it was shocking, it made no difference to the succession. But now she knew that, when her pregnancy was discovered, it would look as if she had been trying to claim Jack's title for her own baby. A destitute linen draper's bastard son usurping a Duke's title.

She gripped the embroidery tightly to prevent herself from laying a hand over her womb. Irrational though it was, she wanted to apologise to the babe for making him a criminal before he'd been born. She was sure Jack wouldn't harm an innocent child, but her own chances of escaping the gallows seemed to diminish with every fearful breath she took.

'Let me take that. Temperance,' the Duchess repeated, 'let me take your stitching.'

Temperance blinked. She saw the Duchess was looking at her

with disconcertingly shrewd eyes, and leaning forward to lift the piece of crumpled linen from Temperance's lap.

'Yes, thank you,' Temperance said. Then she frowned in confusion. 'Why…?'

'You'll need your hands free to greet your husband,' said the Duchess.

'My husband!' Temperance started up, then fell back again, gripping the arms of the chair until her knuckles cracked. 'He's here? Now?'

Her gaze flew to the door. She heard footsteps getting louder as they approached the parlour along the gallery. In her imagination she could see Jack striding towards her. A footman flung open the door. Jack stepped over the threshold.

Chapter Seven

Jack—the Duke of Kilverdale.

Temperance stared at him. At first sight he looked nothing like the man she'd known in London. Nothing like the pictures of the often dishevelled, shirt-sleeved Jack Bow she carried in her mind.

He was wearing a burgundy velvet coat decorated with silver braid and silver buttons. The velvet gleamed in the mid-morning light from the large window. The silver buttons seemed to glint mockingly at her. There was a heavy fall of Venetian lace at his throat. She noticed all this in a confused impression of magnificence.

Then she found the courage to look up into his face.

A black periwig framed his angular features. When she'd first seen him in a wig she'd laughed at him for his extravagance, but she wouldn't dare to laugh at the hard-eyed man standing before her. The contrast between the soft, extravagant curls and his hard, masculine features was even more obvious than it had been in London.

She gazed at him, desperately trying to see her Jack Bow beneath the grand clothes. Was this haughty aristocrat the same man she'd known in London?

He raked a comprehensive glance around the room, and then focussed entirely on her. The moment his eyes locked with hers, she lost all power of coherent thought.

He stared back, his gaze intensifying until she could hardly breathe from the unspoken emotions throbbing between them.

After several seconds he lowered his gaze. It should have been a relief to escape his intense scrutiny, but instead she felt oddly frustrated by the abrupt end to their silent exchange. She drew in a shaky breath, then realised she was still the focus of his attention. He was looking at her hands as she clutched the arms of the chair.

The ring! His ring! He was looking at the evidence of her scandalous claim to be his wife!

She started to push herself to her feet, then froze as he glanced away from her and spoke instead to the Duchess.

'Good morning, Mama,' he said, his voice as cool as a January frost. 'I hope you are in your customary good health.'

'I am, thank you.' Eleanor graciously inclined her head.

Jack looked back at Temperance, his expression revealing only aristocratic aloofness.

'My dear, you've anticipated me,' he said. 'I'm sorry I left you so long unattended in London.'

Temperance dragged in a deep, gasping breath. She didn't understand the nobility, but it seemed there were rules of polite conduct that applied even when a man was about to denounce a woman for being a liar and an adventuress. Well, she wasn't an aristocrat, but she could play by those rules too.

She pushed herself to her feet and took a couple of steps forward. Then she sank into a deep curtsy before him.

'Your Grace,' she said, 'I am…I am glad to see you so well.'

She remained crouched before him while the silence stretched out until her nerves strained like over-tightened lute strings. She imagined him drawing his sword and striking off her head in one clean stroke. Jack wouldn't fumble the blow she was sure, but there would be…

'Blood on the carpet,' she whispered, light-headed with anxiety.

Jack took a step forward and she felt him lay a hand on her shoulder. She started, nearly overbalancing, and his grip tightened. Was he steadying her for the strike?

'Tempest?' he said quietly.

She dragged another breath into her lungs and dared to look up into his face. She couldn't read his expression, but he didn't look like a man about to draw his sword. In fact, he was holding out his free hand to her.

She lifted her own hand and felt his fingers close around hers. His touch was warm and firm, just as she remembered it. His hands were still Jack Bow's, if nothing else. She wanted him to be Jack Bow. She wanted all of him to be Jack Bow. A sob of confused emotion caught in her throat. She swallowed it back. The Duchess was always dignified and controlled, no matter what the circumstances, and Temperance was determined to emulate her.

Jack pulled gently. Obviously she was supposed to stand up. She tried, but her knees felt stiff. Before she could compel her body to obey by sheer force of will, Jack bent forward and shifted his hand from her shoulder to just below her elbow. With his unexpected help she stood, but she couldn't stop trembling.

He drew her closer and put his arms right around her. Every muscle in her body stiffened in surprise. She didn't understand his behaviour. Moments ago he'd spoken so coldly, but now he was holding her. His embrace tightened until she was pressed against the breadth of his chest. He held her to him with one hand as he stroked the other up and down her back.

'Hush, sweetheart,' he murmured against her ear. 'You didn't shake this much in the face of the fire. And I am not a monster.'

Something snapped inside her. When he held her he felt like her Jack, and now he even sounded like him. She sagged against him, unable to stop herself accepting the comfort he offered. For a few moments she was back in her shop the first time he'd kissed her. She'd remembered over and over again how it felt to be in his arms. Dreamed of it and woken in tears because he was dead—or because he was still alive, but he was a Duke and it had all been a lie.

When she remembered his true rank she stirred in his arms, desperately anxious to make amends for what she'd done before he accused her. He didn't release her, so she struggled to remove his ring with her hands pressed tightly between them. He covered her hands with one of his and startled her into stillness by brushing his lips over her cheek in an apparent caress.

'Later,' he breathed in her ear.

Later? What did he mean, *later*?

He lifted his hand to push up her chin. She looked into his eyes, bewildered by his behaviour and overwhelmed by the physical and emotional impact he had on her. Despite everything she wanted to stay in his tender embrace forever.

Disbelief hit her. Nothing was resolved. Her fate still depended on his whim and it was all his fault she was in this predicament in the first place. She felt a surge of indignation and shoved against his chest with both hands, making him stagger back a couple of places.

'You *villain*! You heedless, deceitful *scoundrel*!'

'Ah…' He opened and closed his mouth. The startled look which replaced his self-confident expression was very gratifying, and for some reason fuelled her anger.

'What do you mean by pretending to be dead? Don't you know how much grief you've caused?'

'I didn't pretend to be dead.' He backed up another step and lifted his hands in disavowal of the charge. 'I have no idea—'

'Bundle's boy thinks you're dead. He was breaking his heart over you when I spoke to him.' Temperance marched around the parlour, words she'd suppressed for weeks flying uncontrollably out of her mouth. 'I came here and told your mother… I *never* want to do that again—and you're not even dead! Heedless, thoughtless—'

'I *didn't* pretend to be dead. I told Bundle it was time Jack Bow died, but—'

'And that's another thing!' Temperance strode back and gave him another shove on his velvet-covered chest. 'What did you mean by telling me your name is Jack Bow? Making a fool of me. The man in the baker's laughed… You could at least have had the decency to tell me your real name.'

'I would have when I returned to you,' Jack said. 'It would have been far better if you'd waited for me in London, madam.' His expression became haughty.

'I couldn't wait for you—you were dead, you oaf!' she shouted at him.

She stopped suddenly, staring at him in consternation as she realised how completely she'd lost her self-control. In the midst of her agitation she noted with satisfaction that, despite his arrogant expression, Jack took another precautionary step backwards. And so he should. He was a thorough knave who had seduced her into the kind of behaviour she would never even have considered before she met him.

'Coat thief!' She flung the accusation in passing.

'I'm not—'

'Have you seen Toby yet?' she demanded, rolling over his startled protest.

'Toby?' Jack blinked. 'No. I came straight to find you.'

'He's been waiting for you to come home for months!' Temperance exclaimed. 'You're supposed to see him first. Not me. I promised him. Go and find him at once.' She grabbed Jack's arms and turned him to face the door. 'Go and find him *now*.' To emphasise her words she gave him a hefty shove between his shoulder blades. It was only after the door had closed behind him and Temperance heard the Duchess's soft laugh that she realised how outrageously she'd behaved.

She pressed her hands against her burning cheeks, then forced herself to drop her arms to her sides as she turned to face Jack's mother.

'Your Grace, I'm sorry,' she stammered. 'I don't know what came over me.'

'Relief, I expect,' said the Duchess calmly. 'Once you could see with your own eyes he is alive and well it was safe to berate him for frightening you. I've experienced the same sensation myself a time or two.'

'Yes, but I should not have…' Temperance shook her head in confusion. Had relief precipitated her sudden outburst of temper?

He was so grand—almost unrecognisable—in his fine clothes. All her secret hopes that he might still view her with kindness had withered when she'd met his implacable gaze. And then he'd touched her so gently and told her he wasn't a monster. She'd wanted to burst into tears and fling her arms around him, but instead she'd tried to take off his ring.

What did he mean by *later*? She turned the ring on her finger, worrying over what he'd meant. He was going to take his ring back, of course, but what else was he going to say to her later?

Despite her best efforts, she felt a sob rising in her throat. She pressed her hand against her mouth, in an instinctive, useless gesture to contain her jangled emotions.

'Excuse me, your Grace.' Heedless of propriety, she turned and fled to the privacy of her room.

Alone in her parlour, Eleanor set aside her book and considered all she'd just seen. It was obvious Temperance and Jack were connected by strong, volatile emotions. It was also clear Jack wasn't pleased to find his secret wife at Kilverdale Hall, yet Temperance had turned the tables on him. Eleanor laughed as she pictured her son's face when Temperance scolded him. She looked forward to witnessing their next meeting.

Jack found himself back in the long gallery with no clear idea how he got there, and the imprint of Temperance's hand burning between his shoulders. The sensation where she'd touched him was so powerful he was almost tempted to strip off his coat to see if she'd left a mark.

He wasn't used to being dismissed. He was on the verge of striding back into the room to finish his conversation with his impostor wife when he remembered his mother's shrewdly watchful presence—not to mention the impassive-faced servants currently observing him. So he nodded briskly to Hinchcliff and strode off towards the second floor.

As he'd hoped, the news of his arrival hadn't yet penetrated this part of the house. When he opened the nursery door, Dr Nichols, the Duchess's chaplain and Toby's tutor, looked up, but Jack put his finger to his lips and the chaplain remained silent.

Jack watched his son unnoticed for a few moments. Toby was sitting at the table, his head bent over as he concentrated on the picture he was creating. His hands were covered in charcoal and there was a black streak on his cheek. Despite his preoccupation with Temperance, Jack smiled at the sight. Ever since he'd left England in April there had been a Toby-shaped hole in his heart. Now that nagging ache disappeared.

He closed the door and stepped further into the room just as Toby looked around.

'Papa!' Joy lit up the boy's face, so dazzling in its intensity that for a moment Jack couldn't speak past the lump in his throat.

'I'm home,' he said, holding out his arms as Toby scrambled off his chair.

But the boy's expression suddenly changed. A scowl replaced his joyful smile. Instead of going towards Jack he retreated to a window seat on the far side of the room. The unexpected rejection hurt so badly Jack could hardly draw breath. He'd been tense and angry in anticipation of his first meeting with Temperance, but he'd had no worries about his reunion with his son.

'Toby?' He let his arms fall to his sides. He couldn't order Toby to be happy at his return.

Toby pulled his knees up, wrapped his arms around them and turned his head stubbornly away.

Dr Nichols began to say something, but Jack silenced him with a quick frown. He waited until the chaplain had left the room before he spoke again.

'Toby? What's wrong?' he asked.

Toby shrugged angrily and wouldn't look at him.

'Stand up and remember your manners,' Jack said sharply.

'You *lied* to me!' Toby jerked around to glare at his father. Scornful anger blazed in his dark eyes. 'You promised you wouldn't be gone long, but you left *years* ago. You broke your promise. I hate you.' He turned his head and stared uncompromisingly out of the window.

Jack gazed nonplussed at the back of Toby's head. How could a child who came from him—was part of him—have such a strong, inflexible will of his own?

He sat down on the other side of the window seat, turning sideways so he could look out at the grey November landscape. He'd last seen that view in April. He had not been away years, but in the span of a little boy's life he had been away a long time.

'I didn't lie,' he said quietly. 'I thought I only had to go to Flanders to fetch cousin Athena. As soon as I knew I'd be away longer I sent you a letter to explain. Did Grandmama read it to you?'

Toby continued to scowl at a bare-branched oak tree, but after a moment he gave a brief, reluctant nod.

Jack breathed a little easier. 'I wrote you lots of letters,' he reminded Toby. 'I even sent a letter from Venice, with a drawing of a gondola in it. Did you get that letter?'

Toby hesitated, then nodded grudgingly.

'Good,' said Jack. 'I was particularly proud of my drawing. I am glad it didn't go astray.'

'You've been back in England ages,' Toby said accusingly.

Jack guessed that was at the root of Toby's anger. He was hurt by his father's seeming abandonment while Jack had been in the same country.

'It was a matter of honour and obligation,' Jack said. 'I wanted to come home, but first I had to finish the task I had undertaken.'

'Because no one else was strong and brave enough?' Toby finally twisted around to look at him.

'Something like that.' Jack felt a strange pang as he recognised the same words his mother had used to console him for his father's absences when he was Toby's age. He knew all too well how Toby felt.

'You caught the bad man,' said Toby.

'Yes,' Jack agreed.

'And found Uncle Jakob a wife,' Toby said.

'He found her himself,' Jack corrected, uncomfortable with the turn the conversation had taken. 'Most men prefer to choose their own wives,' he added, then winced internally as he realised what he'd just said.

He'd walked into the house, determined to exert his authority from the beginning. It was outrageous of Temperance to come to Kilverdale Hall and put him in such an impossible situation—but she'd looked so strained and frightened he'd been unable to resist the urge to comfort her. His Tempest wasn't supposed to stare at him with fear in her eyes. She was supposed to square up to him like she had in London. The memory of her high-handedness eased some of his tension and he found himself smiling at the abrupt ending of their reunion. She hadn't let him down after all. And the sensation of holding her in his arms had been so compelling, he'd have kissed her in his mother's parlour if Temperance hadn't berated him over his use of the name Jack Bow.

His smile faded as he wondered what his mother thought about the situation. He'd spared her little attention earlier, but beneath her usual composure he'd sensed worry—and some amusement. On reflection he suspected his mother had been entertained by the dressing down Temperance had given him. A good reason to ensure privacy for his next serious conversation with his impostor bride.

'You've got a wife,' Toby said, breaking across Jack's thoughts. 'She came the other day.'

'I know.' Jack wondered what kind of conversations the two of them had been having, since Temperance had insisted he find Toby straight away.

'I bowed to her, like Gram said I should,' said Toby. 'She used to have a shop, but it burned down. Her name's Temp'rance,' he added as an afterthought.

'Temperance,' Jack corrected.

'That's what I said.' Toby crawled across the window seat to lean against Jack's side. 'I told her you'd know what to do about it. Will you take me riding on Stargazer?' His manner suggested he considered his father's acquisition of a new wife to be slightly less significant than the handsome black thoroughbred Jack had purchased in the Spring.

'Yes,' Jack said. He put his arm around Toby and lifted him into his lap, giving an inward sigh of relief and gratitude that he'd been forgiven for staying away so long. Resolving the situation with Temperance would be far more difficult.

Her false claim to be his wife and, therefore, his Duchess, created a potentially dangerous situation for both of them. What she'd done would be seen by his fellow lords as an offence not only against him, but as an affront to the privileges of the peerage as a whole. If he'd truly been dead and her claim had succeeded, a bastard commoner might have become the next Duke of Kilverdale. The House of Lords were notoriously lax in forgiving their fellow peers for crimes even as serious as murder—but they did not tolerate anything that undermined the integrity of the foundations upon which their privileges rested. An unpunished threat to the Kilverdale title would be, indirectly, a threat to the security of their own titles.

Jack knew that if he denied Temperance's claim he would ruin
her and, if he didn't exact some form of punishment for her crime,
his own reputation would suffer. Such indulgence would be considered weak and he'd lose the respect of the most powerful men
in society. His occasional masquerades as Jack Bow had been
viewed as an eccentricity and done no damage to his reputation or
the dignity of his title, but this was very different. If he mishan-
dled this matter, he could make some dangerous enemies.

The obvious way to defuse the situation would be to focus on
the fact Temperance had claimed to be *Jack Bow's* wife. Society
would have no difficulty believing Jack Bow's wife was a euphe-
mism for the Duke of Kilverdale's mistress. There would be some
delicious scandal to entertain the Court for a week or two, some
bawdy songs would be heard around the corridors of Whitehall
and in the alehouses of the City—and then the matter would be
forgotten in favour of a new piece of gossip.

'Yes, I'll take you on Stargazer this afternoon,' Jack said,
absently responding to Toby's insistent questions as he contemplated a future with Temperance as his mistress.

Dinner was served at two o'clock, nearly two hours later than
usual, because of the disruption to the household caused by Jack's
arrival. Temperance was dumbfounded to discover she was
expected to sit down to a formal meal with Jack, the Duchess and
Dr Nichols. She couldn't imagine why Jack was subjecting her to
such torment. Why didn't he just take back his ring and tell
everyone she wasn't his wife? She'd almost…almost…lost her
fear he meant to deliver her to the nearest gaol—but she didn't understand why he hadn't yet challenged her lies.

She sat uneasily in her appointed place, aware of the surreptitious
glances being sent her way by the servants as well as Dr Nichols. She
found the watchful chaplain an even more disconcerting companion
than the Duchess, but she gritted her teeth, and tried to conduct
herself with the same serene composure that characterised Eleanor.
She was afraid Jack had decided he would reveal her fraudulent
actions during the meal. If that was the case, she would show them
all a Cheapside linen draper could be as dignified as a true Duchess.

She couldn't stop sneaking glances at Jack, trying to see in the velvet-clad aristocrat the man she'd known in London. At first it was difficult because he was so formal and aloof, but then the Duchess asked for a full account of everything he'd done since he'd left in April.

Initially Jack's manner remained reserved but, as he lost himself in his story, Temperance began to catch glimpses of the man she'd first seen entertaining a crowded tavern with his lute. He leant back in his chair, his eyes gleaming with humour as he described the setbacks and adventures he'd had all the way from Bruges to Venice and back again.

He told his story in such a captivating way that, despite her anxieties, Temperance was soon caught up in his tale. But then the story arrived at Dover.

'So I stole Jakob's coat, took the only horse, and rode to London,' Jack said.

Dr Nichols frowned, but didn't say anything.

Temperance saw the quick, grinning glance Jack threw in his direction, and realised he was deliberately provoking the chaplain. Dr Nichols made her nervous, but she still didn't think it was right to tease a man of God.

'You were overcome with remorse when you thought it was your fault Jakob had been sent to Newgate,' she reminded Jack tartly. '*Then* you didn't think it was funny at all.'

'True,' said Jack. 'But as it turns out, I was wrong, and Jakob managed to get himself thrown in gaol entirely on his own account. Such a fate has never befallen *me.*'

'Yet,' Temperance said before she could stop herself.

Jack looked at her.

She stared back at him, a knot of apprehension forming in her stomach. After what she'd done, *she* was the one who would be lucky to escape prison. He held her gaze and she saw it there, in his eyes. The recognition of her crime and the brutal response he was legally entitled to make. She hadn't seen that awareness in his eyes when he'd walked into the Duchess's parlour. At first he'd been aloof, and then he'd comforted her. Now the truth lay openly between them, unspoken but acknowledged by both. Her heart began to race. Was this the moment he would deny her? When Jack opened his mouth to speak she fisted her hands in her lap.

'I seem to recall you scolded me for what I'd done *before* I knew Jakob's fate,' he said coldly. 'You adhere to a rigorous moral standard, madam.'

His gaze remained locked with hers for several heart-stopping seconds—then he looked away. 'Since the meal is over, I will save the story of my adventures in London and beyond for another occasion,' he said, pushing back his chair. 'I promised I would take Toby riding this afternoon.'

'*No!*' The protest burst from Temperance. Had Jack decided to punish her by prolonging her torment? She couldn't bear another second of such suffocating anxiety. 'I will say—'

Jack moved disconcertingly quickly. One minute he was standing beside his chair, the next moment he was around the table and taking her hand. She was so startled she stared at him with her mouth open. He lifted her hand to his lips.

'I am always eager to hear your opinions, my dear,' he said, 'but Toby is waiting for me. Tell me later.' He put his free hand under her chin to close her mouth; then bent to brush a kiss across her lips. 'Tell only me.' His words were little more than a breath against her skin, but they reverberated through every particle of her being.

His message was clear. She was not to speak without his permission. She sucked her lower lip between her teeth, wishing his touch didn't distract her so much—and that his kiss had lasted more than a few brief seconds.

She watched him walk away with her fingers pressed against her mouth. Then remembered where she was and that there were several interested witnesses to their interaction. She was too proud to play the part of a trembling, besotted maid for them, so she lowered her hand and said to his retreating back, 'As it happens, I have a meeting with my apprentice shortly. It may take some time, so it is fortunate you have something else to occupy yourself with.'

Jack stopped just before he reached the door. She held her breath as she stared at his broad shoulders, wishing she'd controlled her unruly tongue. Jack turned slowly and arched one dark, aristocratic eyebrow in her direction.

'Most fortunate,' he said.

The next minute he was gone, and Temperance slumped into her chair.

'Why don't you speak to Isaac in the great parlour?' the Duchess said. 'I will have him sent to you.'

'Oh…!' The last thing Temperance wanted to do at that moment was talk to Isaac, but she could hardly say so. 'Thank you, your Grace,' she said. 'You are very kind.'

Temperance picked up the comb and passed it a few more unnecessary times through her hair. It was past ten o'clock and she hadn't seen Jack since dinner. At supper the Duchess had explained he'd returned from his ride with Toby, only to closet himself with Mr Worsley, his Receiver-General. Apparently the two men were so deep in the estate accounts Jack hadn't been able to join them for supper.

Temperance had been speechless, first with astonishment, and then with growing indignation. She appreciated the need for good bookkeeping, but surely Jack had more important matters to attend to today? Or was he demonstrating how insignificant he considered her?

She wanted to throw the comb across the room in frustration, but she laid it down carefully. She wasn't used to being dependent on the whim of others and she hated it. She wished for the thousandth time that she was back in her shop, in charge of her own life. It hadn't always been easy, especially last year when the plague ravaged London. She'd seen some hideous sights and once watched appalled from an upstairs window as a naked man, maddened by disease, ran screaming along the street below.

But for all the hazards of London life, she'd always been secure in her position as mistress of her small domain. Now she was a reluctant supplicant for mercy in Jack's house. Since she didn't have the resources to leave, she had no choice except to await his judgement.

Her gaze fell on the little box her brother had given her so long ago. It was one of the few objects on the dressing table that belonged to her. All her family were gone. Her parents had married late, and her mother had been forty-four when Temperance was born. Her mother had died three years ago and her father had followed his wife to the grave within the year. Temperance's brother had died of a fever ten years ago, and she still sometimes missed him.

She touched the box, seeking comfort in the familiar feel of it beneath her fingers. As she did so, she noticed Jack's ring. Seeing it sent another surge of anxiety through her. She slipped it from her finger and laid it on the dressing table. Then she stood up and began to pace around the bedchamber, replaying every word he'd said to her since his arrival that morning. One moment she was almost certain he still felt kindly towards her, the next second she interpreted the same comment as a sign he was toying with her before delivering the *coup de grâce*. She was on her twenty-first circuit of the chamber when she heard the door open.

She spun around to see Jack stroll in. Shock cascaded through her, destroying her hard-won composure.

'What took you so long?' she burst out, thinking not only of the agonising hours he'd made her wait since his arrival at Kilverdale Hall, but all the weeks she'd waited for him in London. Beneath her anxiety and indignation was gnawing hurt he had stayed away from her when he had always been in her thoughts.

He closed the door and turned to look at her, raising an unmistakably ducal eyebrow at her intemperate demand. She tensed as she realised in the circumstances it might be wiser to let him set the course of their discussion.

'I'm sorry, sweetheart.' He strolled forward. 'If I'd known you were so impatient for me I'd have carried you off straight after supper but, as it happens, I only finished my business with Worsley a short while ago.' As he spoke he took off his periwig and dropped it on her dressing table.

His own hair was flat and a little damp from being trapped under the wig. He raked his fingers through it, turning it into a spiky black thatch at odds with his elegant clothes. His hair wasn't as long as it had been when she'd first seen him in the tavern but, like his teasing smile, it was a tenuous link to the man she'd thought she'd known in London.

While she watched, he took off his coat and laid it over a carved oak chest.

Temperance stared at him, torn between hope and confusion. She'd expected him to launch into an angry condemnation of her behaviour, not—

'What are you doing?' she demanded, as he tossed aside his lace-edged cravat.

'Catching up.' He strolled towards her.

'Catching up?' She retreated to the other side of the room, looking at him warily. She was acutely aware of the breadth of his shoulders and the triangle of lean-muscled chest revealed by his unfastened shirt.

Before his arrival she'd been trying to imagine the *character* of the man beneath the ducal finery, but she hadn't expected him to give her quite such a good view of his physical body this early in their discussion. She backed away another couple of steps, although she couldn't prevent her eyes from devouring him. He was magnificent in his grand clothes, but she preferred him like this, when she could see the play of his firm muscles beneath the soft linen. She'd wanted to touch him from the first moment she'd seen him in the tavern and, despite her conflicting emotions, she still wanted to touch him.

'You're already prepared for bed,' he pointed out. 'And I know you to be a woman of passionate and impatient temperament—as you demonstrated when you complained how long I've already made you wait. As a gentleman I consider it my duty to ease your frustration without further delay.' His hands dropped to his belt.

'That's not what I meant!' Temperance exclaimed, startled. 'Stop it at once!'

It occurred to her that, if she stayed where she was, she was in danger of allowing herself to be cornered against the wall, so she marched back into the centre of the room, every nerve end tingling as she passed close to Jack.

She turned to face him, her head held high. 'I am not your plaything. I will not allow you to treat me as one. I came here in good faith. Punish me as you see fit, but don't demean me—'

He closed the gap between them so quickly she was shocked into silence.

'How have I demeaned you?' he demanded, fire in his eyes. 'How? Tell me when have I ever demeaned you?' He took her face in his hands so she had no choice but look at him.

She stared at him, her heart thudding so hard she couldn't speak. There was anger in his eyes she hadn't seen before. She didn't understand his mood or what he wanted from her. Tension almost suffocated her as she watched him scan her face with his fierce predator's eyes.

She studied him just as intently as he was studying her—seeing afresh the angular lines of his face. The high cheekbones and determined jaw. The deep-set eyes that could glint with humour, or freeze with aristocratic hauteur. She'd worried for days over what he'd do when he returned home, anticipating all kinds of responses, yet somehow she'd forgotten how unpredictable the flesh-and-blood man could be. He'd startled her several times in London with his unexpected actions. She remembered how he'd argued with her in the street outside her shop and then snatched off his periwig in exasperation when she'd scolded him for extravagance.

The man of her memories and the man standing before her began to merge in her mind. Perhaps Jack Bow and the Duke of Kilverdale were not as different from each other as she'd begun to fear.

'Jack?' she whispered. 'Jack?'

The hard expression in his eyes softened and he stroked a delicate finger over her cheek.

His light touch provoked a maelstrom of emotion within her. His caress was so gentle, so tender she wanted to fling herself into his arms, but she wasn't sure of her welcome—and he had some explaining to do as well.

'Tempest?' he said, rubbing his thumb lightly across her mouth. Her breathing quickened and her tongue instinctively crept past her lips to brush against his thumb.

She saw heat leap into his eyes and felt an answering warmth bloom deep inside her. He stroked the inside of her lower lip with his thumb and she couldn't resist tasting him again. She rested her hand lightly against the folds of his linen shirt. Even though she didn't press hard enough to touch his chest, she could feel the virile heat of his body a fraction of an inch beneath her fingertips.

She felt as much as heard the deep, wordless sound that escaped his throat. The sound disconcerted her, recalling her to herself. She snatched her hand away and took a step backwards.

Jack stopped her retreat by putting his hands on her waist. There was still more than six inches between their bodies, but she was very conscious of the intimacy of their position.

'I thought you were dead!' she burst out.

His grip tightened. 'Did you weep for me?' he asked.

She stared at him, unbidden tears clouding her vision as she remembered how desolate she'd felt.

'I thought you were *dead*!' Her voice held all the vehemence of her grief when she'd first heard the news.

She seized his shoulders and tried to shake him, furious at how he'd frightened her. 'How could you be so heedless, so thoughtless, so—'

He pulled her hard against him and silenced her angry words with a kiss. She gasped and tried to push him away, but he held her close and kissed her with an urgency bordering on desperation. She could sense tension in every taut line of his body.

She kneaded his shoulders, torn between frustration at his refusal to talk to her, and a growing compulsion to surrender to the passion that ignited between them. His clever mouth was irresistible. Within seconds delicious sensation swirled through her, driving out her awareness of anything except Jack.

The events of their night in Southwark had taken on a haze of unreality in her memory. She'd wondered many times if she'd imagined the eagerness with which he'd made love to her. At first their lovemaking had been so compelling. She'd been swept along on a tide of sensation—but the ending had been unsatisfying and Jack had left her so quickly afterwards.

Now she discovered her memory hadn't exaggerated an iota of the passion he could arouse in her. By the time he drew back they were both breathless and Temperance clung to his shoulders for support.

'You wept for me,' he murmured, rubbing his cheek against hers.

Temperance's body was flushed with arousal. It took a few moments for her to register Jack's words. When she did, it wasn't what he'd said, but the smugness she heard in his voice, which caused her to lift her head.

'I shouldn't have had to,' she said. 'I should never have been told you were dead in the first place!'

'That wasn't my fault,' he retorted, releasing her and stepping away. She realised she was still stretching out her hands towards his shoulders and hid her betraying arms behind her back.

'Well, it certainly wasn't mine,' she said. 'And I can assure you I was told you were dead,' she added as it occurred to her he might believe she'd lied about that as well. He hadn't yet challenged her false claim to be his wife, but sooner or later he would inevitably do so.

'I know,' he said, and she felt an immediate surge of relief that at least she was vindicated in this.

'Bundle's boy misunderstood what he'd been told.' Jack thrust a hand through his hair. 'I did tell Bundle Jack Bow was to die that night, but it was a jest—'

'A *jest*!'

'Not exactly.' Jack shot her a brief, sideways glance. It wasn't an apology, but she thought she saw a flicker of regret in his eyes. 'Bundle took my meaning at once. Unfortunately he didn't realise Tom didn't know me by any other name. He thought the boy would understand what he meant—'

'You mean I'm not the only one you deceived with your minstrel games—' Temperance broke off as she saw an unsettling gleam appear in Jack's eyes. Given her own actions, it wasn't sensible to make too much of Jack's failure to disclose all the facts about himself.

'You should have gone to Bundle immediately. At the first opportunity you had to cross the Thames safely,' he said.

'There was no point. All my goods had been lost before Isaac ever reached—'

'Not to fetch your goods! So you could live safely under Bundle's protection until I returned to London! If you'd done that—and spoken to Bundle and not just his boy—the muddle about my supposed death would have been cleared up at once.'

Temperance opened her mouth, then closed it again. It had never occurred to her Jack had meant her to *live* at the coffeehouse.

'Why didn't you come back?' she demanded. 'If you'd come back Fanny would have told you where I was, and—'

'I meant to. *Diable!* You don't think I wanted to spend the past two and a half months chasing all over England, do you?'

'Nobody made you—'

'My sense of honour and duty made me!' He glared at her. 'I thought I'd be gone a day or so at most. But Arscott tried to abduct Lady Desire at pistol point and someone had to hunt him down when he ran—'

'And it had to be you?'

'This time, yes,' he said flatly. 'There was a debt. But it is paid now.'

Temperance remembered Jack's fear for his cousin the last time she'd seen him in Southwark. She knew he'd felt guilty for stealing Jakob's coat and leaving him at Dover. He'd obviously chased after Arscott to make amends for his mischievous behaviour. Some of her underlying hurt eased as she realised he hadn't abandoned her for a frivolity.

'I left a message for you with Fanny Berridge,' she said. 'I had—'

'I sent a letter!' Jack exploded. 'I sent letters to you at Bundle's—where you were supposed to be—and when I discovered you weren't there I sent one to Fanny Berridge. If you'd just stayed where you were supposed to be, there wouldn't have been any problem.'

Temperance swallowed. 'Fanny never gave me a letter.' She'd been so anxious to get away from Agnes when she'd said goodbye she hadn't lingered to speak to Fanny. 'Besides,' she continued with renewed confidence, 'I had nothing but the money you'd given me and your ring—and by the time I'd paid for the survey of my shop most of the money had gone. I had to work, so I served in Daniel Munckton's shop. I would still be there now if it wasn't for—'

Jack crossed to her in two swift strides and swept her back into his arms. 'Later,' he said hoarsely, after a toe-tingling kiss she couldn't resist. 'We'll talk later.'

'No, we won't.' Even though her mouth was wet and swollen

from his kiss, and her body ached with unfulfilled yearning, she found the resolution to slip out of his arms and dodge away from him. 'We will talk *now*. I'm not going through another day on tenterhooks, worrying you might—'

'I'm on tenterhooks now,' Jack said, tugging off his shirt and advancing towards her. 'More than tenterhooks. If you have a grain of compassion in you, you'll assuage the need you've stirred in me.'

'I'll assuage... You're *addled*!' Temperance gasped, backing away, but unable to take her eyes off his naked torso. She remembered the feel of his back beneath her hands as he made love to her, but she'd never seen him without his shirt before. She licked her lips and swallowed. 'I'll do no such thing until—'

'You're underestimating yourself,' Jack said, his expression intensifying as he focussed on her flickering tongue. 'You are more than capable of assuaging my needs. I am the one in the best position to know,' he pointed out, humour glinting in his eyes as he reached for her.

She darted to one side. 'I see what it is,' she said, clutching her dressing gown tightly closed. 'You are trying to take shameless advantage of the situation to...to...take advantage of me.'

He laughed, looking more than ever like the vagabond minstrel she'd first met. Except now he had no shirt on and she just couldn't stop looking at him. His shoulders were every bit as broad as they'd appeared beneath his clothes, his arms and chest were defined by lean muscles and she could see the ridges of his flat stomach. There were short, dark curls on his chest and her fingers flexed involuntarily at the thought of touching him there... anywhere.

'Oh!' While she'd been staring at him he'd caught her arm and swung her round so she was trapped between him and the edge of the bed.

Jack put his arms around her. Her gaze locked on his face and, without being aware of it, she sucked her lower lip between her teeth. Perhaps if she let Jack make love to her this time, she would attain the enticing, mysterious pinnacle that had eluded her in Southwark.

'You claimed the privilege of being my wife,' he said. He

dipped his head and stroked the seam of her mouth with the tip of his tongue until she stopped biting her lip. 'Now I'm claiming the privileges of a husband.'

Chapter Eight

It was the first time Jack had referred directly to her false claim, and Temperance had expected him to do so under very different circumstances.

'We should talk first.' She managed one last, half-hearted protest.

'Later.' As he continued to kiss her, he slipped his hands down to press her hips against him, making her devastatingly aware of just how ready he was to claim his husbandly privileges. Within a few seconds she could barely remember why she needed to talk to Jack—all she was aware of was an aching need to get as close to his virile body as possible.

He bent his head and kissed her just below her ear, then teased her neck with his lips and tongue all the way down to the curve of her shoulder.

'I've spent weeks waiting for the moment I could touch you again,' he said, his breath an erotic caress against her skin. He unfastened her dressing gown and pushed it off her shoulders. She gasped and trembled as his hands stroked eagerly here and there over her muslin-clad body, as if he wanted to touch all of her, all at once.

'You have?' The idea he'd been thinking of her—wanting her—was almost as intoxicating as the feel of his hands on her. She didn't protest when he untied the ribbon and pulled the neckline of her shift down to reveal her breasts to his gaze. 'You've been wanting me—wanting to see me again?' She gripped his naked shoulders, feeling the flex of his muscles beneath her fingers.

'Every night,' he said thickly. 'Dreamed about you, woke up hard thinking about you…'

'Oh…' He'd dreamed of her. Wanted her. Excitement thrilled through her.

He lifted his head and looked into her eyes. 'Did you dream of me? Want me again? Did you?'

She flushed with self-consciousness at his intense demand and snatched her hands away from his shoulders. She saw his lips curve with satisfaction at her unintentional admission. He pulled her closer for another kiss and, for the first time, her naked breasts pressed against his bare chest. She caught her breath at the new rush of sensation. She wanted to rub herself against him. She almost did, but then he said,

'Put your hands back on me. Put your hands on me, sweetheart, before I go mad with frustration.'

She tilted her head away from him and saw the hungry passion in his dark eyes. 'I am a respectable woman,' she said, amazed she could arouse such potent need in him. 'I am not used to men marching into my room and taking all their clothes off and—'

'Good. Now stop talking and touch me.' He kissed her again, his mouth hot on hers.

She laid her hands on his shoulders. His lean, strong muscles flexed beneath her fingers. She'd been desperately afraid of his angry rejection. Now his blatant, virile desire for her was intoxicating. She kissed him back, excited by the way his tongue pressed boldly past her lips. Sensual energy raced through her body, creating an anticipatory ache between her legs. He tore his mouth away from hers long enough to cast her dressing gown aside, and tug up her muslin shift.

'Jack,' she gasped, trying to push his arms down again. 'Stop it.'

'I spent the past three months waiting to see you. I'm not waiting any longer, beautiful Tempest.'

She was so surprised by his words she let him pull the shift over her head.

He stepped back, looking his fill. Her skin heated with embarrassment at his intense scrutiny and she lifted her hands to shield herself. She'd never considered herself beautiful, and the effects of her pregnancy made her even more self-conscious, but the hot appreciation in Jack's eyes as his gaze roamed over her body stunned her into stillness. She'd never thought any man could look at her with such unmistakable desire.

He released her wrists and put his hands on her waist. He touched her stomach and her breath caught. Had he guessed about the babe? Then he stroked lightly upwards until his palms cupped the outer edges of her breasts. Her thoughts fragmented in a wave of pleasure. His thumbs circled her sensitive nipples and she heard herself whimper softly. Her legs trembled. She put her hands on his arms to support herself, and felt the bunching of his lean, powerful biceps.

He uttered a muffled curse and bent to kiss the upper curve of one breast. His breath warmed her naked skin and then his tongue caressed her.

Temperance gave an involuntary whimper of pleasure.

His thumb brushed across the tip of her hardened nipple. She gasped, her fingers digging into his arms as heat leapt deep in her belly.

He lifted his head. In the candlelight his dark eyes were heavy with passion. He stepped back and made short work of removing his shoes, stockings and breeches. Temperance swallowed as she saw for the first time what she'd only felt before. She was fascinated and a little disturbed by the thrusting proof of his arousal. His whole body was full of virile determination, but this part was most intriguing and exciting to Temperance because it had been hidden until now.

She brushed her fingertips hesitantly over his sides, feeling his muscles twitch in response, and then trailed her hand lower. She hesitated.

'Be bold, sweetheart,' Jack said hoarsely.

She closed her hand around him and sensed the convulsive response in every part of his body. Tentatively at first and then more confidently, she explored his hard length. She heard his breathing grow ragged and again experienced a sudden, heady sensation of power. She was holding him so intimately and he wasn't making any attempt to hide how strongly she affected him. She looked up at him, her hand still circling his erection.

He claimed her mouth in a fiercely carnal kiss. Her hand tightened involuntarily as he overwhelmed her with erotic sensation.

A shudder shook his body and he dragged his mouth from hers.

'Sweet, wait,' he murmured. He took her hand in his and lifted it to his mouth. He brushed a kiss across her knuckles. Half-dazed with arousal, she realised his fingers were trembling as much as hers.

He pulled back the bedclothes and together they half-fell, half-crawled on to the mattress. Jack rolled her on to her back and bent over her. His lips closed around a nipple and he began to suckle. She buried her fingers in his hair, arching her body towards him.

His hand swept over her side and along her thigh and stroked unhesitatingly upwards. He found his goal and began to caress and tease her slick, swollen flesh. She cried out at the intensity of the sensation.

'Jack!'

He lifted himself over her. She stared up at him. His features were taut with passion. He met her eyes and held her gaze as he eased slowly into her. They'd made love in the shadows in Southwark. The intimacy of this moment when she could see him was so overwhelming she wanted to look away—but she couldn't. She was snared by the intense expression in his eyes as he began to stroke in and out of her. A new, sublime tension began to build within her. She lifted her hips in rhythm with his thrusts, instinctively seeking to increase the delicious feelings. She was on the way somewhere—and this time she wanted to arrive. She clutched wildly at Jack's arms and shoulders. Her heels dug into the back of his muscular thighs. She rocked her hips, desperately trying to increase the speed of his thrusts. She cried out in a mixture of delight and aching need. His thrusts became quicker, more urgent, pushing her over the brink until her whole body clenched and pulsed with ecstasy.

She gasped and moaned, clinging to him as he continued to drive into her, sending another wave of exquisite sensation rippling outwards from her centre. Then she felt the moment of his release. He shuddered, his hoarse shout of ecstasy mingling with her softer whimpers. His movements slowed until he rested on his elbows above her. Temperance lay panting beneath him, stunned by what she had just experienced. Now she knew what had been missing in Southwark. She felt boneless and drained by physical pleasure.

After a few moments Jack lifted himself away from her. He pulled the bedclothes up over them both and lay next to her, one hand resting lightly on her ribs below her breasts. She closed her eyes. The only noise she could hear in the room was their quickened breathing. Her ears still rang with the sounds of their lovemaking. She was amazed and shaken by what had just happened between them. And hovering on the verge of embarrassment now she was no longer in the grip of irresistible sensation. Why had she allowed herself to be led astray by passion when so much was unresolved between them?

She waited for Jack to say something, but all he did was curl his arm around her and give a deep sigh of satisfaction.

'Are you going to sleep?' she demanded in astonishment.

'No.' He sighed again and pulled her closer. His breathing slowed until he was unmistakably asleep.

Temperance stared at the bed canopy, her body satiated, but her heart and mind unsettled by what had just happened. Nothing had been resolved between them. She still had no idea what future Jack planned for her—but for now he was sleeping in apparent contentment.

To have Jack sleeping peacefully beside her was a secret dream she'd never thought would come true. She laid her hand on the strong arm that circled her waist. She didn't know what would happen tomorrow, but for tonight she would enjoy what she had. She closed her eyes. Jack's unfamiliar presence beside her made it impossible for her to fall asleep completely, but she dozed for the rest of the night.

Just before dawn she roused a little as she sensed him waking. She felt embarrassed by the intimacy they'd shared, so she feigned sleep, expecting any second he would try to wake her. Instead he rose quietly, dressed and left the bedchamber.

As soon as he was gone she slipped out of bed. She'd learned the only way to avoid the pregnancy-induced nausea that afflicted her in the morning was to eat immediately after she woke. She chewed slowly on the dry bread she'd hidden from the maid in her mother's sewing box as she thought about what had happened.

Then she frowned, her gaze sharpening as she realised something was missing from the dressing table. Jack had taken back his ring. She touched the empty space where she'd left it the previous night. It had been her talisman for nearly three months—now it was gone. Her apprehension about the future returned in full force.

Temperance ate breakfast alone in the dining parlour. She still wasn't used to the relentless scrutiny of servants, but she tried to pretend they weren't there. She'd been unquestioned mistress in her shop. At Kilverdale Hall neither she nor the servants were sure of her position in the household. The uncertainty on both sides made every interaction with them an ordeal.

'His Grace requests you join him in the knot garden after your breakfast, madam,' Hinchcliff announced.

'Thank you.' Temperance's appetite deserted her, but she was determined not to scurry to do Jack's bidding. She cut her beef even smaller and worried over what Jack would say.

She'd decided in the night he probably meant to make her his mistress. It was the best explanation for why he'd made love to her rather than immediately announcing his plans. That interlude in her bed had obviously been in the nature of a job interview. Jack had wanted to assure himself she'd be satisfactory in the role before he said anything.

She squeezed the knife until her knuckles whitened. What would she say when he asked her—or told her—to be his mistress? Before the fire and the loss of all her property she would never have contemplated becoming a man's mistress, but brutal necessity had changed everything. Her respectable parents would have been appalled at the direction of her thoughts, but Temperance was grimly certain it would be better to be Jack's mistress than to be destitute.

Rich, generous men were notoriously fickle, and she still didn't know what had happened to Toby's mother. She decided she would have to negotiate carefully with Jack so her future would be assured when he grew tired of her.

A pang of distress at the idea of Jack losing interest in her made her hand tremble. In her dreams he would always be as eager for her as he had been last night. In her dreams he wanted far more from her than just her willing body—but she knew that was a fantasy. She pushed her sadness aside. Above all she was a businesswoman. If the only commodity she had to sell was herself, she would obtain the most favourable terms she could while Jack was still hot for her.

A few minutes later she was nonplussed to find Jack and Toby playing ball.

As she watched, Jack prepared to toss the ball and Toby stretched out his hands to catch it. The ball sailed past Toby's out-stretched hands and struck him lightly on the chest. He jerked and laughed in surprise, then bent to chase it as it rolled across the ground. He threw it at Jack, his aim at least three feet off target, but Jack caught it and tossed it gently back. This time Toby managed to catch it between his bent arms and his body. He laughed up at his father in gleeful triumph.

'Well done,' Jack said, grinning.

Temperance was sure he hadn't noticed her, but then he looked at her, his smile vanishing as he acknowledged her presence.

'Good morning,' he said.

'Good morning.' Her mouth dried up as she looked at him. The last time he'd looked at her or spoken to her they'd both been naked. She had no practice at conversing with a man the morning after such an experience—let alone under the alert gaze of a child.

Toby solved her immediate problem by bowing to her. She curtsied, relieved to be given such an obvious cue.

'Good lad,' said Jack, bringing a flush of pleasure to Toby's cheeks.

'Madam.' He made his own, elegant bow to Temperance. 'We are just enjoying a game of ball. Would you like to sit and watch a while? We'll be finished soon.' He held out his hand, obviously intending to guide her to a nearby stone bench.

Temperance hesitated. She was tired of passively waiting for everything to happen.

'Couldn't I play?' she asked.

Toby's eyes narrowed. 'Girls can't catch,' he said, so confidently Temperance was sure he was repeating something he'd been told.

'Perhaps we ought to put your theory to the test,' Jack said.

Toby frowned. It was the expression Temperance had already learned to interpret as signifying deep thought rather than displeasure.

'Throw the ball to her and see if she can catch it,' Jack said, expanding on his suggestion.

Without any further ado, Toby bent at the waist, holding his arm straight down in front of him. He jerked upright, tossing the ball towards Temperance at the same time. It went high and wide. Her cloak hampered her, but she just managed to touch it with the tips of her fingers before it landed some distance away in a bed of herbs.

'Girls can't catch,' said Toby with some satisfaction. 'That's what Hinchcliff says.'

'You didn't throw straight!' Temperance put her hands on her hips in mock indignation.

'Papa could have caught it,' said Toby. He ran to fetch the ball, crouching as he sought it beneath a bush of sage.

Temperance looked at Jack. He grinned.

'Girls can't catch,' he taunted her. 'Sit down and watch how men do it.'

The undercurrent in his voice made her body tingle and her cheeks flush with awareness of the man in front of her. She should not be thinking of him in this way, remembering how his naked body felt when it was close to hers. They had to talk about her future. At the first opportunity she was going to insist they did so.

He took her hand and bent over it. When she felt the pressure of his lips against her fingers, her legs began to tremble.

'You should be wearing gloves,' he said, and her pleasure at his courtly gesture turned to mortification as she realised he was commenting on the fact she wasn't dressed like a lady.

'Sit on the bench and tuck your hands inside your cloak to keep them warm,' he said. 'I won't be long.'

Temperance did as she was bid, fascinated despite her anxious preoccupation, to see Jack playing with his son.

This morning his appearance was an odd combination of vagabond and aristocrat. He wore neither hat nor periwig, only his own shaggy black hair. His coat was made of black velvet, but it wasn't new and it wasn't adorned with silver buttons.

She enjoyed looking at him far more than she thought she should. He moved so beautifully. Many of Toby's throws went astray but Jack jumped or bent to catch the ball with lithe grace. She knew how strong he was, yet he always tossed the ball to Toby with gentle accuracy. Toby radiated excited happiness. He'd been waiting so long for Jack to return home, and he was revelling in his father's attention.

Temperance felt tears prick her eyes as she watched them enjoying each other's company. Her parents had taken good care of her and her brother, but they'd never played with her like this, so cheerfully heedless of the passage of time and the practical demands of the adult world. She couldn't doubt Jack loved Toby. She thought she understood better now why he'd been prepared to search for hours through the chaotic streets of London to find Nellie Carpenter's lost daughter.

She laid her hand over her womb, wondering how Jack would treat *her* child. After seeing him with Toby, she was even more certain he would never be unkind to the infant—but she wished she knew why he'd sent Toby's mother away. Had the woman failed to satisfy him as a lover? What charms had she lacked that Temperance must strive to display so Jack would be willing to keep her as well as the child she carried?

She was so lost in worry she almost didn't notice when Dr Nichols came to take Toby back to the house. Toby didn't want the game to end and he pouted, sticking out his lower lip in protest. Jack said a few firm, quiet words to his son and Toby went with the chaplain, but his dragging feet indicated his displeasure at being sent indoors.

As Jack approached her, Temperance took a deep breath and stood up.

'Do you feel well enough to go for a walk?' he asked.

She blinked, so startled by the question it took her a moment to respond. 'Of course,' she said. 'But I don't want to walk. I want to talk to you.'

'We'll do both,' he said, taking her hand and leading her towards a gate that opened into rolling parkland beyond the formal gardens.

'Where are we going?' she asked.

'To the top of that hill. I have been away from home so long I feel a compelling need to reacquaint myself with my property.'

Temperance couldn't believe it.

'You are a heedless, wayward rascal!' she burst out, following him willy-nilly because he had such a firm grasp on her hand. 'How can looking at a few deer—' she'd just caught sight of a small herd silhouetted against the low winter sun '—be more important than talking about—'

'Your eyes blaze like the blue heart of a flame when you're angry,' Jack said admiringly. 'I can feel a sonnet begging to be written.'

'*What?*' Temperance was nearly running to keep up with him. 'You want to write a sonnet about my *eyes*? Slow down!'

'Not just your eyes,' he said, reducing his stride to a more comfortable length, but still walking quickly. 'I find many other parts of your beautiful body equally inspiring. Your lips—so enticingly kissable. Your breasts. When I look upon them—and even more gratifyingly when I touch them—they cause such heat to flow through my veins. And your hands...' He paused dramatically, although he didn't stop leading her deeper into the park. 'When I remember the feel of your hands on my body, stroking your way to my—'

'*Be quiet,*' Temperance shrieked. Her face on fire, she jerked out of his grip and put both hands over her ears. It was one thing to consider the possibility of becoming his mistress in the privacy of her own mind, but quite another to hear him speak so boldly of what they'd done together.

He laughed and reached out towards her. She knocked his hand away.

'You are a vulgar, insensitive dolt,' she shouted, furious he was mocking her at such a time.

He was silent for a moment, then said, 'I know. I'm sorry. Tempest?'

She risked a sideways glance in his direction, half-expecting him to be laughing at her. He wasn't, but there was an edginess beneath his teasing that hadn't been there when she'd known him in London.

'Come on,' he said. 'You can say anything you like in a few minutes.'

'I don't understand.' She kept her hands behind her back.

'Tempest, you lived cheek by jowl with your neighbours in Cheapside,' he said impatiently. 'Do you think it is any easier to keep secrets at Kilverdale Hall than it was there?'

She stared at him, remembering all the pieces of her neighbours' lives she'd overheard when she lived in London.

'You think they'd eavesdrop?' she said.

'Possibly. True privacy is hard to guarantee. By now the whole household will know I spent the night in your bed,' he added.

Temperance flushed, recalling the surreptitious glances she'd received from the maid that morning. She turned her back on Jack and marched up the hill to sit on a wooden seat under a bare-branched oak tree. Before her was the house with the formal gardens laid out in front of it and the family chapel nearby. Behind was a broad swathe of grass, and off to the left she could see the spire of the village church. For someone who'd grown up in the narrow streets of London, the amount of open space seemed strange, and even somewhat disturbing.

'There's something I must tell you,' she said, determined to get straight on with business.

'Yes?' Jack sat down beside her.

'I'm pregnant.' She waited, her nerves stretched to screaming point, for his response.

'I know,' he said.

For a few seconds Temperance's mind went blank with shock. She'd steeled herself to deal with Jack's doubts, accusations or anger. She'd not anticipated this calm acceptance.

'You *know*?' She twisted to stare at him. 'How? Was it last night when you…looked…at me?'

'That confirmed my suspicion, but I guessed as soon as I read Mama's letter telling me you were here, claiming to be my widow,' he said. 'She sent it to me at Lady Desire's house in Kingston in case I went there before I came home.'

'You *guessed*?' Temperance struggled to adjust to the unexpected turn in the conversation.

'Despite all the evidence to the contrary, you're not a natural adventuress—though by all accounts you embarked upon your scheme with commendable gusto,' he said, a touch of dryness in his voice. 'Playing a role—any role—with absolute conviction is the most important factor for achieving success.'

'But I haven't,' Temperance said, a shiver of uncertainty tingling her spine at his tone. She'd been right to suspect his teasing hid a darker mood. 'It was never possible. Even more important than conviction is knowing all the relevant information. I didn't know you are a Duke. You lied to me first.'

'You believe the two lies should cancel each other out?' Jack asked.

'No. I want you to understand I did what I did because I had nothing left,' she said. 'I had no money. My reputation would have been destroyed if I'd stayed in London. I might have escaped the stocks and a public whipping, but only if I'd thrown myself on the mercy of my father's friends. I would have lived in shame for the rest of my life. Your child would have been raised in shame.'

'I know that too,' Jack said, more gently.

'I thought...' she drew in a shaking breath '...when I remembered how you'd searched for Nellie Carpenter's daughter, I thought you wouldn't want a shameful future for your son or daughter. I didn't know...' She made a sweeping gesture, which encompassed the whole of their surroundings from the house to the wide expanse of parkland.

'What did you think when you learned the truth?'

Temperance looked at Jack warily, wondering why he was pursing this line of questioning. She saw he was watching her, his gaze keen beneath his half-closed eyelids.

'I thought you were a liar,' she said, seeing no reason not to tell the truth. 'And then I was afraid. Very afraid.'

'Why didn't you leave? Run away while you still had the chance?' he asked.

She looked down at her hands, flexing her fingers as she considered her answer.

'I didn't think I'd get very far,' she said. 'Not if you chased me for retribution. This is the first time I've ever left London. There was nowhere else…besides…'

'Besides…?' His voice sharpened.

'I wanted to explain, so you'd understand why I'd done it. And…'

'And?'

She looked at him, wondering what he wanted her to say. Then she remembered how the previous night he'd demanded to know if she'd wept for him. Was he asking her if she'd stayed because she cared about him and wanted to see him again? It was true, but she didn't want to reveal how vulnerable she was to him.

'You were a saucy knave when you were a minstrel. I wanted to see if you make an equally saucy Duke,' she said tartly.

Surprise widened his eyes and startled a small laugh from him. 'And what is your verdict?' he asked.

'That you are more a knave than a Duke,' she said, ignoring his incredulous exclamation. 'I've been thinking…'

'So have I—'

'I'm sure. But only listen to my suggestion first.' She caught hold of his coat sleeve, desperate to make her own appeal before he decided her final fate. 'If you please.'

He bowed his head in silent invitation for her to continue.

She paused to order her thoughts.

'I lost everything in the fire,' she said at last. 'But I am certain that, although valuable to me, the entire stock of my shop would represent an insignificant sum to you.'

'Yes.' Jack's expression was disconcertingly impassive.

'So perhaps, since this child is yours as well as mine, you would provide me with the means to set up a small shop somewhere else,' she said, hurrying to get all the words out before he lost patience. 'Not in London, of course. Another town where I can pretend to be a respectable widow.'

'You want me to give back what the fire took away from you?' said Jack. 'Except in a different town.'

Temperance nodded jerkily. So far, he didn't seem outraged by her request. Now was the time he would make a counter-offer to set her up as his mistress if that was his wish. She watched him anxiously, not sure whether she hoped or feared he would do so, but with the comfort of knowing she'd already made her bid for a respectable future.

'I still own the plot of land my shop was built on,' she added after a few seconds. 'I can't afford to rebuild, but something must be done or I may lose it now I'm not in London to defend my rights.'

'Do you want to keep it—or sell it?' Jack asked.

'I kept it because at least I'd have had something to go back to if…if…but I can't go back, of course. Not to London. Not for a long time. It will be best to sell it,' she said resolutely, though her heart twisted at cutting the last of her ties to her old life. 'The money can be set against the cost of the new shop.'

'I can see you don't want to part with it,' Jack said. 'We'll keep it and rebuild.'

Her eyes flew to his face. 'What do you mean?'

'Your shop is your inheritance,' he said. 'We'll keep it. But you will have to find a suitable tenant. My Duchess cannot sit in a shop doorway, flirting with every passing gallant.'

Chapter Nine

'**Y**our Duchess?' Temperance's lips moved, but the words emerged as little more than an inaudible croak.

'The wife of a Duke is a Duchess,' Jack said tautly.

'But we're not married!'

'Shush! There's no need to tell the whole of Sussex.'

Temperance clapped both hands over her mouth and stared at him.

'Have you told anyone—anyone at all—your claim to be my bride is false?' he asked.

She shook her head dumbly, her gaze still fixed on his face.

'No one?' he persisted. 'Not even Isaac?'

'I couldn't.' She lowered her hands and swallowed. 'I was afraid of what he'd think of me if he knew the truth,' she confessed. 'I went to the Royal Exchange that Friday morning—the same day we first met at the tavern. I knew you were in London that day, and it was the only time I was out of my neighbours' sight, so I pretended that's when we were married. I wanted to tell your mother the truth. I felt so guilty for telling her you were dead, and I hated lying to her, but it was too late to change my story. I thought she'd throw me out before I ever got to see you if I did.'

'Good,' said Jack. 'It is crucial you never tell anyone we weren't married when you first came here as Jack Bow's widow.'

'What…why?' A whole storm of conflicting emotions and questions began to swirl inside Temperance as her initial shock receded.

'If I marry you, it will create a scandal,' said Jack, 'but that will eventually be forgotten. We will surmount it as long as everyone believes I courted and married you in secret. It will be just another of Kilverdale's eccentricities. But if it was ever discovered you'd made a false claim to be my wife when you believed me to be dead, I don't think society would forgive either of us for our subsequent marriage.'

'Then don't marry me!' Indignation and hurt spiked through her. 'I did *not* ask that of you. Don't—'

'I know you didn't.' Jack didn't stir from the bench, but his shoulders were so rigidly braced it was obvious he was struggling to control his own turbulent emotions. 'I did not mean to offend you,' he said stiffly. 'There will be no problem as long as you continue to keep your own councel. I only mentioned it to make sure you understand the importance of secrecy on the matter.'

'Everyone will laugh at you for being trapped into marriage by a Cheapside shopkeeper!' Temperance exclaimed. 'No one will believe you want me—'

'That's not the difficulty!' Jack took a deep breath, visibly calming his volatile temper. 'One look at you and no one—no man—will have the slightest difficulty believing I want you. That's not the issue.'

Temperance gaped at him. Had he lost his wits? No man before him had ever taken one look at her and wanted her. She didn't know whether to be flattered or insulted.

'Our marriage will cause a scandal, but that can be survived. Society won't care if it thinks I've made the decision to wed you with…ah, not my head,' he said. 'The Court wits will write a whole flurry of vulgar sonnets turning me into the buffoon of the season, but they'll not take the matter personally. But if it was ever known you'd come here as an impostor…'

Temperance saw Jack's eyes narrow as he spoke about the Court wits. She wondered what it signified, but then acute discomfort at hearing her own actions so bluntly described overwhelmed her. She flushed and looked away.

Jack broke off and continued in a gentler voice, 'The lords would be angry I'd made you my Duchess instead of punishing you for pretending to be my wife, because they'd see it as an affront to their own titles and position as well as mine. That's why we must take care they never suspect anything. I only want to make sure you understand that, and then we need never talk of it again.'

Temperance wrapped her arms around herself. Her knowledge of the aristocracy was limited, but she'd seen at first hand how jealously the tradesmen's guilds of London protected their privileges. No one was allowed to conduct business within the City walls unless they were a member of one of the Companies, and the Guilds could be ruthless in dealing with those who transgressed their rules. She'd left London rather than risk their punishment when she'd realised she was pregnant. She didn't know much about the ways of the nobility, but she was convinced they'd be equally ruthless in protecting their privileges. Most likely they'd consider her unpunished actions an insult to all of them. They might even fear it would act as invitation for other women to make false claims upon them and their titles.

But if her deceit was ever revealed, she wouldn't be the one who would suffer the worst consequences. It was Jack who would pay if the truth ever became known. She knew he was wealthy and powerful but, if the rest of the aristocracy decided he had betrayed them and closed ranks against him, his position would become uncomfortable and perhaps even precarious. Civil war was not the only time when a man could be forced into exile. She shivered at the thought of what might happen if the situation turned against them.

'Why?' she said. 'Why do you want to marry me? You must realise why I find it hard to understand?'

Temperance's question took Jack by surprise. He'd been an acknowledged matrimonial prize for so long it had never occurred to him she might hesitate to accept his proposal.

He stared at her, seeing the worried, beautiful woman beside him, but confounded by a flood of past images and unsettlingly unfamiliar emotions. He saw again the moment she'd thrust herself between him and the lynch mob; remembered how she'd searched for the lost child at the risk to her own livelihood; kissed and scolded him. She'd brought Isaac with her to Sussex, even though the apprentice had become little more than a drain upon her resources after the beating he'd received during the fire. As the succession of memories continued, Jack saw Temperance's face, white with dread when he'd first entered Eleanor's parlour, and then recalled the way she'd berated him for calling himself Jack Bow and sent him to see Toby. She'd never once begged for his indulgence, or asked for more than the most basic restitution for what she'd lost.

He told himself he'd made a rational decision in choosing to make her his wife. He already had one bastard son and he didn't want another. He wasn't willing to examine any other, deeper reasons why he'd rejected the idea of making her his mistress. He only knew it wasn't a tolerable solution.

He noticed she'd recovered from her initial shock and now she was looking at him with a disconcertingly clear gaze. He'd spent most of his life concealing his feelings in public, so he instinctively gave a reason he was comfortable admitting.

'I want you in my bed because you greatly please me,' he said. 'You know that.'

Temperance's eyes widened, then she looked away, her cheeks flushing with embarrassment. He felt a pang of guilt at her reaction, even though he'd deliberately replied in a way that would disconcert her and give him a brief advantage. It occurred to him the tactics he'd learned to hold his own in exile and at Court might not always be appropriate when he was talking to his wife.

'I want you as my wife and mother of my children because I believe you will do whatever is necessary to keep yourself and them alive, safe and in comfortable circumstances,' he said gruffly.

Temperance's gaze snapped to his face.

'I don't understand,' she said. 'You want to marry me because I lied and pretended to be your widow, so I could claim your name for the babe?'

'Yes.'

'You want your wife to be a *liar*?'

'No.' Jack hesitated. For years he'd prided himself on never explaining anything, but Temperance deserved better. 'When I was three years old, my mother was forced to go into exile with me and two of my infant cousins,' he said. 'Andrew and Penelope were orphans in her care.'

He stopped for a moment as more memories surfaced, this time from his life in France. He'd been two years younger than Andrew, and they'd been as close as brothers. Andrew had died when he was fifteen and the sense of loss still lingered whenever Jack thought of his cousin.

'Mama had already managed to hide or send to safety the family jewellery and other valuable articles,' he continued. 'When that was done she took us and fled to France.'

'On her own?'

'She had three loyal servants with her. Hinchcliff was one of them, Bundle was another.

'Where was your father?' Temperance asked.

'With the King's army. He earned his dukedom on the battle-field. And because of the money he lent Charles,' Jack added drily.

'I wouldn't have the slightest idea how to get to France,' Temperance said. 'I can't speak French. This is the furthest I've ever been from London.'

'But what you have just done required a courage and determination to match what Mama did,' Jack said. 'And if you'd needed to go to France I'm sure you would have done,' he added as she shook her head. 'But you didn't—you needed to come here and claim to be my widow. I am sure you will be equal to any difficult task that may be required of you in the future.' He paused, and then repeated again what he'd said earlier. 'I decided some time ago I would only marry a woman who would be able to protect herself and my children. If she had to. If I wasn't there to do so. I hope to God it will never be necessary,' he finished with unusual grimness.

He meant what he said. He knew very well what he owed Eleanor. She'd ensured his physical safety and comfort when he was a child, and managed what was left of his inheritance until he'd been of an age to take responsibility for it himself. As soon as he'd given any serious thought to what he was looking for in a wife, he'd known the woman would have to be capable of equalling Eleanor's accomplishments. Temperance didn't yet know how to conduct herself in the elevated company she would soon be keeping, but she already had the spirit and determination to survive whatever fate threw at her.

He'd said all he had to say on the subject, so he waited for Temperance to reply. She was looking at him, weighing his words, an unreadable expression on her face as she rubbed her hands absently against her forearms.

It was years since Jack had put himself in a position where he was in another person's power, subject to their judgement. His heart began to thud. Despite the November chill he began to sweat beneath his clothes. This was how he'd felt when he was growing up in exile, always knowing he was living in sufferance on the generosity of others, keeping his face impassive when his French cousins taunted him for being a Duke with no inheritance; follower of a King with no country. Waiting, too proud to ask for attention, to see whether his French uncle-by-marriage would amuse himself by teaching the English boy to fence—or ignore him for days at a time.

He hated surrendering control to others, but now he had to endure it. He had to wait and see whether Temperance would accept or reject him. Why had he never considered she might not want him?

She opened her mouth and he tensed in readiness for her reply.

'Why do you play at being Jack Bow?' she asked.

Air exploded from his lungs in a startled exclamation. Her question chimed so closely with the direction of his thoughts, running on the years of his exile, he was afraid she could read his mind.

'What has that to do with anything?' he said brusquely. 'You will be my Duchess. There is no more Jack Bow. He's dead.'

'But why did he ever come to life in the first place?' She was watching him so closely he wanted to fidget like a nervous boy, yet he'd learned to control that instinct by the time he was Toby's age.

'For several years while we were still in exile I often used the name Jack Bow. But since regaining my estates I've used it very rarely. There has been no need.'

'But why? Why did you pretend to be Jack Bow?'

'I didn't pretend anything!' His temper slipped its leash. 'I am Jack Bow.'

'John Beaufleur—'

'One extra syllable! Jack Beaufleur—Jack Bow. Hardly a

hanging offence.' He paused to steady himself. 'I was a landless man with limited prospects,' he continued more calmly. 'A title without the means to support it can be a liability.'

'You were only twenty when you came back to England.'

'I matured early. When I was sixteen I travelled alone from France to Sweden to see my Swedish relatives. Jakob's family.'

Jack gazed unseeingly at the horizon as he remembered both the terror and the triumph of that first solo journey. In his own mind that was when he'd taken control of his life and become a man. Until then his fate had been governed by others. He'd lost his inheritance as a result of other men's actions. While Cromwell ruled in England and the King still languished in exile, his future as the Duke of Kilverdale had hung in the balance. So he'd made himself into Jack Bow, deliberately moulding himself into a man who could face any challenge with only his sword, his lute and an outrageous jest.

'It doesn't seem very…disciplined,' Temperance said. 'My father taught me we all have duties and responsibilities we must strive to fulfil. He would never have abandoned the shop simply because the mood took him.'

Jack tilted his head back and gazed up at the sky, thinking of all the stratagems he and his mother had employed to keep his re-maining fortune intact. He suppressed the first, sharp retort that sprang to his lips.

'We spent several years living with my father's sister, who'd had the good sense to marry a French man,' he said. 'Her husband tolerated us, I believe. His temper was improved by the fact we contributed regularly to his coffers. My father was not closely involved in the City like his grandfather, but he'd continued to make investments. We were never paupers, though our income was irregular. At other times, Mama took a house and we lived in Paris. Both alternatives had their disadvantages. When I was sixteen I enjoyed a brief infatuation with the daughter of a French comte—until it was made abundantly plain to me that a man with no estate, an unsteady income and little likelihood of ever return-ing to his own country was not a suitable candidate for a French aristocrat's daughter. What was I to do? Parade around in velvet and lace with an empty belly—and run up debts I might never be able to repay?'

'No!' Temperance exclaimed, shock in her eyes.

He smiled without amusement. 'Many men did,' he said. 'Some of them got away with it—others were ruined. After the comte jeered at my prospects as Duke of Kilverdale, I became Jack Bow more often than not. It was cheaper—and more profitable. At first I paid my way with my lute. After I turned eighteen I was occasionally hired for my skill with a sword as well as my talent for entertaining the party with a song or three. My French uncle is a master swordsman and it amused him to teach me. We had no outstanding debts when we returned to these shores. Is that responsible enough for you, Madam Shopkeeper?'

Temperance locked her fingers together and turned her face away, but not before he'd seen her hands were trembling.

He let out a long, careful breath and covered her hands with one of his. The anger he'd just vented had very little to do with her intransigence over their marriage.

'I'm sorry,' he said. 'I should not have attacked you so. You are not responsible for my exile.'

Her gaze flew to his face. 'I know you ended up travelling as Jack Bow on your way home from Venice because your retinue abandoned you one by one,' she said. 'You told us so at dinner yesterday…'

'They didn't abandon me,' Jack corrected her, not caring for her choice of words. 'They couldn't keep up. And my French valet wanted to see his mother. Enough prevarication. Will you marry me?'

His tone was peremptory, but his heart pounded uncomfortably fast as he waited for her reply. He hoped she wasn't aware of his choppy emotions.

If Temperance agreed to marry him, he would lose that sense of absolute control of himself and his situation he'd spent so much of his life striving to achieve. He'd have legal authority over her, but the unconventional nature of their match meant their marriage could never be the polite formality it might have been if his wife was a well-born lady.

He and Temperance would be bound together by the need to win social acceptance for their marriage and for Temperance herself—and he wouldn't be able to command her heart and mind to obey him. For the first time in his adult life he was voluntarily putting himself in a position where he would have to depend at least partially on someone else.

His mouth felt too dry. His cravat too tight. When he saw Temperance open her mouth, his hand unconsciously tightened over hers. In the next few seconds she would decide their future. In a flash of blinding clarity he realised the only thing more devastating to his peace of mind than her acceptance would be her refusal.

Chapter Ten

Temperance pressed her fingertips against the window, but she didn't see the view. All she could think was that she was now the Duchess of Kilverdale.

Jack hadn't made a big announcement; he'd simply started referring to her as his wife, or by her new title, from the moment they'd returned from the park. At once there had been a subtle but unmistakable change in the way the servants treated her.

They'd dined with the Dowager Duchess and Dr Nichols just as they had yesterday, but despite her new status she hadn't felt any more comfortable in their presence. Yesterday all she'd had to worry about was keeping up a dignified appearance until Jack denounced her, but from now on she had to conduct herself in a manner befitting a Duchess. She'd felt especially awkward when Jack had told Dr Nichols he would be conducting the ceremony renewing their vows in the family chapel.

She leant her forehead against the cool glass and wondered if she'd lost her mind. She was a Cheapside shopkeeper—what did she know about running a house the size of a palace and attending Court balls? The mere thought of mixing in such exalted society filled her with paralysing anxiety. What if she failed in her new role?

She'd taken Jack's warning never to let anyone know she'd made a false claim to be his wife to heart. Now she had to learn in a few weeks everything a nobleman's daughter would be taught from birth. She couldn't bear to let Jack down when he had treated her with such astonishing, flattering…terrifying…generosity.

Despite her initial hesitation when Jack asked her, every instinct had prompted her to accept his proposal. He was handsome, charismatic and honourable and he stirred her blood in a way no other man ever had. All the years she'd tended the shop in Cheapside she'd never aspired to catch the attention of such a man. She was proud of her achievements, but she'd always thought she was too tall and too forthright to win a man's romantic, or even lustful, interest. Jack hadn't made any secret of the fact he desired her—she was still astounded and delighted by his impatient assumption that any man who saw her would want her.

But now doubts gnawed at her as she thought of the challenges ahead. She tapped her fingertips against the window frame, then spun away from the window. She had to talk to Jack again—make certain this was what he wanted before it was too late to change their minds.

She'd heard him tell Hinchcliff he was going to the parlour, so she went there first. The most direct route was through the great hall. Every noon the household and estate workers dined in the large chamber, but it was empty now. She hurried across it towards the connecting door to the parlour, pushed open the door—and came to a dead halt.

Jack was sitting in an elaborately carved chair, talking to a stout man who stood before him.

Shaken, Temperance stammered an apology and started to back out. She'd expected Jack to be alone. He'd looked around at the sound of the door opening and now he smiled at her.

'Come in.'

She froze. She didn't want to talk to him in front of the stranger. But he rose and held out his hand to her, so she had no choice but to go to him. There were bolts of shimmering silk and velvet laid out around the parlour. She remembered, too late, that Jack had mentioned at dinner he was seeing the silk mercer this afternoon.

'I hope you will approve the choices I've made for you,' he said, leading her to the chair he'd just vacated.

'For me?' Her voice emerged as little more than a croak. She looked at the rich abundance of fabric covering every surface. She'd never traded in silk, but she knew the exquisite material lying about her represented many times the value of the linen and wool cloth she'd sold in her shop. The silk mercer obviously had a very prosperous business and, just as obviously, expected to make several sales this afternoon.

Jack picked up a bolt of blue silk taffeta and sent two or three yards of glistening fabric rippling over her lap.

'What do you think?' he said. 'It matches your eyes. It will make a suitable undress gown.'

She touched it lightly, half-entranced by the glorious material, half-overwhelmed at the thought of wearing silk every day. 'It's beautiful,' she whispered. 'Thank you.'

He lifted it aside, replacing the waterfall of blue with the heavy luxury of cream and gold brocade.

'For your wedding dress,' he said. 'For the ceremony in the chapel here. It's a pity there's no time to send for anything finer, but this should do very well.'

'Oh.' She'd come to ask if he truly wanted to marry her, and he'd laid the cloth for her wedding dress in her lap.

'Will it do?'

Temperance looked up, tears misting her eyes. ''It's wonderful,' she whispered. 'Beautiful. I cannot imagine anything finer. Thank you.'

He looked pleased at her response, but shrugged. 'When we go to London I will arrange for Halross to show us his latest stock—but for now this will do.'

'Halross?' she said. The name sounded familiar, though she couldn't quite place it.

'Gabriel Vaughan, now the Marquis of Halross and recently married to my cousin Athena. He was a merchant before he came into his title. His ships still trade in many goods.'

'Oh. Oh, yes, I remember.' Temperance stroked the cloth of gold and cream on her lap, overwhelmed at the thought of wearing something so grand on her wedding day. 'I've met him.'

'You've met him?' Jack's voice sharpened with interest. 'How?'

'What?' Temperance blinked at him. 'Who?'

'Halross!'

'He was Sir Thomas Parfitt's apprentice,' Temperance explained. 'Lady Parfitt has—had, before the fire—a silk mercer's on Cheapside.'

'I was under the impression Vaughan spent most of his apprenticeship in Italy,' said Jack. 'How is it you met him—and remember him so well?'

'He's tall,' said Temperance. 'And it's not often a man leaves Cheapside as a humble apprentice and returns as a Marquis. I imagine half the City is aware of him.'

'Tall men appeal to you?'

'Tall men are easier to spot in a crowd,' she retorted, intrigued by Jack's reaction at discovering she'd met Lord Halross.

'I believe I have a small advantage on Halross in this regard,' Jack claimed.

'I'd have to stand you back to back to be sure.' Temperance couldn't resist teasing him.

'His wife might object.'

'Hmm.' Temperance suppressed a smile, but her heart felt lighter as a result of the brief, bantering interchange. She knew Jack couldn't be jealous of Lord Halross. But her casual observation had caught his attention, and he clearly wanted her to compare him favourably with the other man.

At that moment the silk mercer distracted them both by fussily smoothing out a piece of green velvet. When he saw he had Jack's attention, he cleared his throat and said, 'Your Grace, I have many other fine pieces to show you.'

His voice almost made Temperance jump; it seemed so loud after her quiet interchange with Jack.

'By all means, Tolworth,' Jack replied, raising his own voice. 'My wife will need many new gowns.'

Temperance felt a little thrill at the pleasure and strangeness of hearing Jack call her his wife.

'Of course, your Grace.' Tolworth swelled with satisfaction in a way that made Temperance think he must already be counting his profits.

'I look forward to meeting her Grace,' he said. His eyes fell on

Temperance. 'You must be her maid,' he said. 'Perhaps you may be of assistance to us. Do you know your lady's taste well?'

Temperance's amusement died instantly. She stared at Tolworth, horrified and embarrassed by his mistake. Jack hadn't introduced her to the silk mercer, but surely Tolworth had heard Jack say the cream and gold brocade was for *her* wedding dress?

'This *is* her Grace, my wife,' said Jack in an icy, and surprisingly loud voice as he laid his hand on Temperance's shoulder.

'Eh?' Tolworth stared first at Jack and then at her in obvious confusion. He looked at Jack again. '*She*'s your Duchess?'

'Yes.'

Tolworth's disbelief was palpable as he stared at Temperance. This was the response she'd feared—scandalised disapproval when people discovered her sudden elevation in the world.

'Sell us your silk or depart,' Jack said harshly, 'but do not insult my wife with your impertinence.'

The colour drained from Tolworth's face. He took a step back, dividing his bows clumsily between Jack and Temperance. 'Forgive me. Your pardon. So sorry…'

Temperance turned her face away. Her heart was beating so fast she felt sick. She wanted to run out of the room, but she knew she had to get through the rest of the excruciating meeting with all the dignity as she could muster. This would only be the first of many such encounters. And Jack had defended her.

She looked up at him, but she couldn't see his face clearly. Was he as mortified as she was by the mercer's mistake, or just angry at Tolworth's impertinence? Jack could dismiss the mercer with one curt word, but it would be impossible to silence the gossip that would spread after this incident.

She bit her lip, fervently wishing she hadn't come in search of Jack. She would have done anything to spare them both this embarrassment. At least when she had clothes befitting her new station her humble origins would be less instantly recognisable.

'Enough!' Jack ordered. 'Show us the green velvet, Tolworth!'

The mercer straightened up, almost falling over his own feet to obey Jack's command.

Temperance endured the rest of the meeting with as much

composure as she could muster. Jack kept his hand on her shoulder. She wasn't sure whether he was offering silent support or making sure she didn't leave, but she was grateful he made his claim on her so obvious. It was a relief when the last selection had been made and Jack summoned Hinchcliff to arrange payment for the goods. While the men discussed terms, she slipped out of the chamber. As soon as she was sure she was unobserved, she paused to lean against the wall and let the tension seep out of her body. She closed her eyes for a few moments, feeling more battered by the events of the past twenty-four hours than she had after working a full six days in her shop.

When Temperance opened her eyes, she discovered she didn't recognise her surroundings. She must have taken a wrong turn when she left the parlour. Eleanor was the mistress of Kilverdale Hall, and Temperance would never presume to oust Jack's mother from that role until she was ready to relinquish it, but some time in the future Temperance would be responsible for running the large household.

She pushed away from the wall and began to explore. Within ten minutes she'd forgotten Tolworth. The house was even larger than she'd realised. Some of the rooms were plainly furnished, but others were very grand. Temperance craned her neck to study elaborate plaster friezes on the ceilings and ran her fingers over finely carved wooden panelling. How was such magnificence kept clean? How many servants were needed to keep the household in good order? How were they managed?

Preoccupied with her thoughts, she opened another door. Her gaze immediately fell on Toby. He was holding a horn book and when she glanced past him she saw Dr Nichols. At her entrance the chaplain rose to his feet. Temperance realised she must have interrupted a lesson. Embarrassed, she began to withdraw with a muttered apology, but then her gaze fell on the third occupant of the room.

'Isaac?'

'Mistress!' He leapt to his feet.

Not to be outdone, Toby stood up and bowed to her.

'What are you doing here?' Temperance stared at Isaac in confusion.

'The Duke…his Grace, I mean…summoned me first thing this morning,' said Isaac.

'This morning?' Jack must have spoken to Isaac even before he'd spoken to her in the park.

'His Grace said that, since I am your apprentice and you are now his wife, my training falls under his direction,' Isaac said. To Temperance's surprise, he hardly stumbled over the explanation. Overnight he seemed to have lost most of his anxiety and regained a modicum of self-confidence. 'I am not to train as a linen draper any more,' he continued. 'His Grace says he always has need of men who can keep good and accurate records. I am to study first with Dr Nichols and then his Grace will find a suitable position for me.'

'That…that is excellent,' said Temperance. 'It is an excellent opportunity for you.'

She caught a flicker of dry amusement in the chaplain's eyes. She was instantly sure he'd guessed she'd known nothing about the arrangements for Isaac.

'Ah. Well, I'm sorry to have interrupted your lesson. Please, do excuse me,' she said, backing out of the door.

Once in the passage she smoothed trembling hands over her skirts and hurried away before there was any chance she could be called back.

Jack left Hinchcliff to negotiate with Tolworth and went in search of Temperance. He'd found the session with the silk mercer extremely difficult, and he was afraid she'd found it even more distressing. He'd been so pleasantly distracted by her unexpected appearance he'd neglected to introduce her to Tolworth. He was angry with himself for the omission—but he was also offended by the silk mercer's reaction when he'd discovered Temperance's identity. The man was blind as well as deaf if he couldn't see her true quality.

The only reason Jack hadn't brought the meeting to an immediate end was because he knew it was a small taste of what lay ahead. Much of his early life had been an exercise in learning how to respond to subtle—or even explicit—insults with aristocratic aloofness. Now it was imperative Temperance acquired the same skill.

But it had gone against all Jack's instincts to remain silent while she discussed her preferences with Tolworth. She'd hesitated once or twice, but to his relief she'd quickly taken the mercer's measure. By the time she'd made her final choices Jack was proud of her. He also ached in every muscle from forcibly holding himself in check. He rolled his shoulders, which felt as knotted as old oak, and pushed open the door to Temperance's chamber. To his surprise she wasn't there. After looking around blankly, he went to his mother's parlour. She wasn't there either. He stood in the middle of Eleanor's Turkish carpet, at a loss as to where he should look next.

'Can it be you've mislaid your wife already?' Eleanor asked, raising her eyebrow at him.

Jack frowned, knowing perfectly well his mother was laughing at him. 'I cannot imagine why I ever thought a sense of humour was an asset in a person,' he muttered.

Eleanor smiled. 'Be grateful I have one,' she said.

Her comment broke through Jack's preoccupation and he gave her his full attention. Time had always touched Eleanor lightly. She seemed little older than when her portrait had been painted in the early years of her marriage. It was a source of pride and comfort to Jack that his mother was so impervious to life's uncertainties. As a boy he'd relied upon her calm competence, as a man he entrusted his household and his son into her care whenever he was absent.

'I am,' he said, remembering all the times when Eleanor's capacity to be amused by misadventure had made their lives in exile easier. 'I misspoke a moment ago. If you feel compelled to laugh at me, by all means do so.'

'How can I resist?' Eleanor smiled. 'You are a source of constant delight and entertainment to me. I never know what you're going to do next.'

'I am sorry you ever believed, even for a few minutes, I was dead,' he said. 'Bundle is consumed with guilt. It never occurred to him that Tom knew me only as Jack Bow.'

His mother nodded, but for a few seconds she didn't say anything. He sensed that, for once, it required an effort for her to maintain her customary composure. He felt a stab of remorse for inadvertently causing her such distress. He sat down beside her and took her hand. As soon as he did so she returned his clasp in an almost painfully tight grip.

'Tom is the serving boy Temperance spoke to?' she said at last. 'Temperance said he was grief-stricken.'

'He fell on me as if I was Lazarus risen from the dead when I stopped at the coffeehouse on my way here,' Jack said ruefully.

'I only believed you were dead for a few minutes,' said Eleanor. 'Temperance thought so for two months. She wept with joy when she discovered her error.'

'She did?' Jack was more pleased than he cared to admit to himself at that revelation.

'And then she raged very fiercely when she discovered you weren't a tenant who'd fallen behind with his rent.'

'She…what?' Jack was baffled.

Eleanor laughed and caught his earlobe in her free hand. 'You'd better ask her.' She pulled on his ear until he was close enough for her to kiss his cheek.

'I'm not seven,' Jack muttered with disgruntled affection, but he put his arm around her shoulders and hugged her tightly.

Temperance was lost again. It was going to be difficult to give the impression of duchessly serenity and authority if she kept going astray in her own home, and she was considering asking Jack to draw her a map when she heard voices approaching round a blind corner.

With memories of Tolworth's shocked expression and Dr Nichol's politely concealed disapproval fresh in her mind, she rebelled at the prospect of attracting any more ill-concealed curiosity. As the voices drew closer she opened the nearest door and closed it carefully behind her.

'Your Grace?'

She spun round to discover Mr Worsley, Jack's Receiver-General, staring at her across a large oak desk. She knew who he was, although they had not yet been formally introduced. The Receiver-General oversaw the management of Jack's considerable estates and finances. It was a position of power and responsibility and Worsley was the younger son of a local gentry family. He was far better born than Temperance, and she was already worried he'd be affronted by her sudden elevation over him. She was horrified at bursting in on him in an inelegant fluster.

For a moment Worsley looked as disconcerted as she felt, but then he smiled and stood up.

'Please come in,' he said. 'His Grace told me he wished me to tell you about my duties. I apologise, I hadn't realised it was to be this afternoon, but…'

'Jack told you to tell me?' Temperance forgot to refer to her new husband in an appropriately formal way as she wondered how many more surprises he had in store for her. 'Ah, yes, of course he did,' she said, gathering her wits. 'Thank you. I will appreciate it. But perhaps we should arrange a more convenient time for you?'

Worsley bowed politely. 'Whenever you wish, your Grace. I am entirely at your disposal.'

Temperance saw the slight gleam in his eyes and knew he'd guessed she come into his room by accident. His perceptiveness didn't surprise her—Jack wouldn't employ a fool to manage his fortune—but Worsley's amusement seemed more kindly than Dr Nichols's.

She hesitated. Sometimes admitting ignorance and asking for advice was the simplest and most honest way of gaining a new friend—and she needed allies in her new life.

'I'm sorry. I opened your door by accident,' she confessed. 'If it is ill timed, I will go away, but I'd be very glad if you could tell me about your duties now.'

Worsley came around the table and set a chair for her. 'It is entirely convenient,' he said, and she belatedly realised he couldn't respond in any other way without risking Jack's displeasure.

She sat down, wondering if she would ever again be able to believe anything anyone said to her. At least insults were likely to be honest. Compliments could be dangerously deceptive.

To her relief, she discovered Mr Worsley had no inclination towards extravagant flattery. Their opening exchanges were cautious on both sides as they sought to gain the measure of each other. Temperance was amazed at the breadth of Jack's financial affairs. A large part of his income came from rents, but he also lent money in a similar manner to the London goldsmiths, and he'd supplied the initial capital for several local tradesmen, including Tolworth. He also provided pensions or allowances for a range of elderly servants or the widows of former tenants.

'Edward Summers, Anne Lidstone, Mary Freeman…' Temperance murmured, reading down the list of quarterly payments. 'He *did* go through the books with you yesterday!' she exclaimed, noticing the most recent date beside Jack's signature.

'He always does when he returns from a period of absence,' said Worsley.

'He is a good, careful master.' Temperance had hated the way he'd made her wait, but she was glad there'd been more to his delay than a desire to torment her.

'Yes, he is.'

'When I first met him I did not realise,' she said, speaking more to herself than the Receiver-General as she recalled her first sight of the shirt-sleeved Jack in the tavern.

'His Grace is a modest man,' said Worsley.

'Modest?' Temperance blinked. Modest was one word she'd never associated with Jack.

Worsley smiled faintly. 'His Grace does not boast of his virtues.' He hesitated, then continued. 'Nor does he boast about his vices, but society is often more accepting of vice—and sometimes assumes it where none exists.'

Temperance stared at Worsley, trying to interpret what he'd just said.

'His Grace told me you had an excellent understanding, and I see he was right,' said the Receiver-General. 'It will be my pleasure to talk to you whenever you wish.'

'Thank you. He has achieved so much.' Temperance thought of Jack in exile, living on his wits with his sword and his lute. How had he learned to be such a good landlord? 'Did the Duchess teach him? After his father was killed in battle—' She broke off as Worsley made a slight sound.

'The present Duke's father didn't die fighting,' said the Receiver-General. 'He was hanged by the Parliamentarians after the Battle of Worcester. They claimed he was a traitor because he was loyal to the King. He was not killed in battle. Some would call his death murder.'

Temperance woke by degrees, slowly becoming aware of sounds originating from beyond her dreams. She opened her eyes and stared at unfamiliar red, silk-lined bed curtains. Then she remembered being brought to her new quarters by Jack's mother earlier in the evening. She'd been disconcerted to discover that, as the wife of the current Duke, three magnificently furnished rooms were set aside for her private use: a parlour, bedchamber and dressing room. A door connected her bedchamber to Jack's.

She rolled on to her back and realised she was laying on top of the bed in her clothes. She'd meant to rest, not fall asleep. She sat up, pushing aside the shawl covering her. She glanced around and saw Jack building up the fire. It was odd to see him crouching at the hearth—only on rare occasions had Temperance tended the fire in her shop.

'There's a maid to do that,' she said, her voice still thick with sleep.

'I know.' Jack stood up and wiped his hands clean on a square of plain linen. 'Sometimes I don't have the patience to wait. Don't tell Hinchcliff. It gives him indigestion.'

Temperance rubbed her hand over her forehead. 'You putting coal on the fire gives your steward indigestion?'

'So he tells me.'

'That's impertinent.'

'He's known me since I was a baby. He was one of the men who went to France with us.'

'I don't think he disapproves of me as much as Dr Nichols does,' Temperance said, still too dazed with sleep to mind her words.

'Hinchcliff doesn't disapprove of you,' Jack said. 'His comments have been appropriately discreet—but quite favourable.'

'He approves of me?' The news snapped Temperance fully awake. 'Surely he'd prefer an Earl's daughter for you at the very least?' she said.

Jack came to lean his shoulder against the bedpost. He looked down at her, his face in shadow.

'They tried that. It didn't work,' he said.

'What? You've been married before?' Temperance was startled.

'No. Betrothed—briefly. It came to naught. You'll most likely meet the lady at the wedding party,' he added after a pause.

Temperance pushed her hair out of her face as she grappled with this unexpected—and unwelcome—revelation.

'Who was the lady? Why didn't you marry her? What do you mean—*they* tried that? And why are you telling me this?'

'Lady Desire Godwin—she is now married to my cousin Jakob. I grossly offended her. *They* were my guardian, Lord Heyworth—I was twenty at the time—and Lord Larksmere, Lady Desire's father,' Jack succinctly answered her questions.

Temperance looked up at him, trying to divine his mood. His face was still shadowed by the bed canopy and the coolly spoken words revealed nothing of his feelings. He hadn't answered her last question, she realised. Instead of repeating it, she asked another one.

'How did you offend Lady Desire?'

Jack hesitated, and then said grittily, 'She overheard me say something insulting about her person.'

'Insulting?' Temperance was bewildered. She'd never heard Jack be truly insulting. 'You mean you teased her? You can be infuriatingly impudent—'

'Impudent?' Even though he was still in shadow, she was fairly certain he'd arched an arrogant eyebrow.

'As a vagabond minstrel you were definitely impudent to a respectable tradeswoman.' She stood and moved a few paces from the bed. With luck he would turn towards her—and the candlelight—and she'd be able to see his face.

'And as a Duke?' To her annoyance he didn't alter his position.

'As a Duke you are both impudent and arrogant. Don't prevaricate, sir. How did you offend the lady?'

Jack pushed away from the bedpost. There was a faint, slightly twisted smile on his lips. 'My least honourable hour,' he said. 'I am telling you this only because she is Jakob's wife and I dare say we will see them quite frequently. I'd prefer to avoid further awkwardness—' he broke off.

'What did you say, Jack?' Temperance said quietly. The contrast between his usual, easy fluency and his current hesitation was marked. It was clear he found this a difficult story to tell.

'Her family had supported Parliament...' he paused again, then continued in a clipped voice: 'Lord Larksmere thought marriage to me would give his daughter a secure place in the new reign. And Lady Desire is an heiress, which made the match attractive to my guardian. Unfortunately, I wasn't consulted, and I had no wish to be shackled to a wife at the age of twenty.'

'Because you were...reluctant to marry a lady from a Parliamentarian family?' Temperance said cautiously.

'Partly,' he said, but there was no bitterness in his tone. 'The lady was a child during the Wars. And she'd paid her own price. She has scars on her face—' He stopped and Temperance remembered their night in the Southwark inn, when he'd admitted he'd once been unkind to a lady. Had it been Lady Desire?

'You were used to roaming at will,' she said, trying to make it easier for him. 'Naturally you were reluctant to tie yourself to a wife so young. Were you afraid she wouldn't be able to manage your household and protect your children at need?'

He laughed harshly. 'I'm afraid I can't claim that defence,' he said. 'At that time I hadn't given much thought to what I was looking for in a wife. I had some friends with me. We were playing billiards in the long gallery. I was drunk and I said something cruel about Lady Desire. Unfortunately, the lady and her father overheard. The old man tried to force a duel on me. Then they left.'

'I see.' Temperance watched him stride to the hearth. 'You just spent the past three months hunting the man who tried to kidnap Lady Desire and steal her fortune.' She'd wondered about his motivation for doing so, now she was sure he had acted from a sense of obligation, and perhaps guilt.

'I owed her that much. It was little enough.' Jack nudged the coals with the toe of his boot, throwing up a shower of sparks. 'Jakob and his bride seem pleased with each other. It occurred to me Lady Desire might be a possible friend for you,' he said, returning his gaze to Temperance. 'Despite her rank, she's spent little time in Society. And she lost her home to fire too. If you are to become bosom acquaintances, I would prefer you not to learn about my sins from her.'

'I can't imagine a real lady will want to be friends with me,' Temperance said doubtfully.

'Tempest, unless you are to be very lonely for the rest of your life, you must find a way to be friends with "real" ladies,' Jack said. 'And you'll do better to look outside the Court for such friendships. There is too much intrigue and jealousy in those circles. You need honest, trustworthy friends, who will value you for yourself and not for the unimportant trappings of your life.'

He sounded so serious Temperance felt a rush of tenderness towards him. She remembered what he'd told her about his life in exile. Between his uncertain prospects then and his wealth and influence now, he must have experienced more than his share of jealousy and false judgements.

On an impulse she went to him, put her hand on his shoulder and kissed his cheek.

'What was that for?' He sounded thoroughly startled.

'For wanting me not to be lonely. What time is it?' She stepped away from him, feeling awkward and trying to distract them both from what she'd done.

'About midnight, I think.'

'Oh. I didn't mean to sleep so long,' she said.

'After everything that has happened, it is natural you feel tired,' he said politely. 'And the pregnancy is likely making you more prone to weariness.'

'Yes. Yes, it is.' Temperance clutched her hands in her skirts. She didn't know how to respond to him when he sounded so formal. So…distant.

'Your mother brought me to these rooms,' she said. 'She has been so gracious and kind to me. I will do everything in my power to be a worthy wife to you—and honour the Duchess in every way I can.'

Jack glanced at her and she thought she saw the ghost of a

pleased smile when she spoke of his mother. 'I know you will,'
he said. 'Come.' He held out his hand to her. 'There is something
I need you to do.'

Chapter Eleven

'What is it?' Temperance looked around curiously as Jack led her into his bedroom.

The walls of the chamber were covered with exquisite tapestries, and the bed was hung with midnight-blue figured velvet, edged with deep, silver fringing. Two armchairs and several large stools were upholstered in the same blue and silver. It was a magnificent room, but there was nothing here to remind her of Jack.

He took her over to a walnut side-table with writing implements set out ready upon it. 'Here.' He pulled several documents from his coat pocket and laid them on the table. 'I need some information from you and a signature.'

Temperance bent over the pieces of parchment and discovered they were documents recording her wedding to Jack on the last day of August 1666. She saw Jakob Balston had apparently witnessed the ceremony. Only the spaces concerning her were still blank.

'How did you get these?' she whispered. 'When?'

She knew special licences were easy to come by. That was one of the reasons she'd had the confidence to make her false claim to be Jack's widow. Bishops' registrars sold blank licences to surrogates. Surrogates were beneficed clergy, authorised to issue the marriage licences to the laity. The licences didn't cost much more than a pound and most surrogates were more interested in making a profit from their sale than in checking the truth of the applicant's sworn statement. A man like Jack would have had no difficulty obtaining one—but when had he had time? And why had he done it before he'd even spoken to her?

'After I read the letter Mama sent to me via Jakob and Lady Desire,' said Jack, 'and before I left London for Sussex. It was quite easy.'

'You'd made up your mind even then? Before even *talking* to me?' Temperance stared at him.

'Of course not. I didn't make a final decision until this morning.' He didn't look at her. 'But it pays to be prepared for all eventualities. Write your name and other details here.' He pointed to a plain piece of paper. After a moment of confusion she realised he must be planning to transfer the information to the official document later. 'I didn't realise at first I don't know your surname. I cut you off before you could tell me that night in Cheapside...'

'Challinor.' She reached for the pen, and then hesitated. 'Are you sure?' she asked. 'Are you truly sure this is what you want?'

'The matter has already been decided,' he said, his voice suddenly harsh. 'Write out the details here, then sign this.'

His tone brooked no argument. He was right, they had settled the matter that morning—but she would have preferred a warmer response from him. It wasn't an encouraging beginning to their official married life.

She picked up the pen and wrote down her name, age and the address of her shop in Cheapside. After all, according to these documents, they'd been married before the fire, and her shop was a valuable piece of property which would have been included in any marriage settlements. She also added her father's name. Even though he had been dead two years and his presence in her new life could only amount to a few words on parchment, she still wanted him to be included. Finally, she signed her name where Jack indicated, and then laughed shakily as she looked down at the wet ink shining in the candlelight.

'At least I can read and write and cast accounts,' she said. 'I had no idea a Duchess needs such skills.'

'Yes.'

Jack's response was so brief Temperance looked up at him.

He was staring down at the documents, an unreadable expression on his face.

Temperance's breathing cramped. The only thing that had given her confidence to accept Jack's proposition had been his energetic determination to make her his true wife. His apparent doubts now scared her. She tried to speak, but her throat was so tight she couldn't. They watched the ink dry in tense, suffocating silence.

At last Jack picked up the documents and replaced them in his pocket. Temperance was certain she saw his fingers tremble.

'We can tear them up,' she burst out. 'It's not too late. We can tear them up. Give them to me.' She held out an imperative hand. She could only survive as Jack's Duchess if he gave her his full support. If he was having second thoughts, they had to take action now, before it was too late.

'No.' He tucked the documents safely in his pocket. 'No, it is done. You *are* my wife,' he said. She could hear the implacable will behind his words, yet he didn't meet her eyes as he spoke.

Temperance gripped her hands tightly together, wishing she knew how to break through the wall of icy reserve now enclosing him. She wondered how long it would be before she was familiar with his different moods and knew how to respond to all of them.

He cleared his throat.

'I know you must be weary,' he said stiffly. 'I'm sorry I woke you, but I needed you to sign these documents. I won't keep you from your rest any longer.'

'You won't…?' Temperance realised he was dismissing her back to her own room. She wanted to protest, to shake him until he told her why he'd suddenly become so aloof, but it wouldn't be dignified. 'Goodnight, your Grace,' she said. 'I hope you will sleep well.'

He didn't reply until she was at the door.

'Jack,' he said. 'Call me Jack.'

She turned and saw he was standing in the middle of the carpet, watching her with that same unreadable expression. Despite his unmistakably aristocratic bearing, an air of isolation clung to him, almost as if he was the one who did not feel at home in his surroundings. The idea was so fanciful Temperance dismissed it.

'Goodnight, Jack,' she said, and closed the door.

Her knees were trembling. She walked over to the bed and sat on the edge of the mattress. She bit her lip, struggling not to cry. Last night Jack had been so eager for her he had seduced her outrageously into making love with him. Tonight she was his official wife, but he'd sent her away and she didn't know why. Had he already lost his desire for her?

She remained unmoving as she fretted over the problem. It was only when she caught the faint sound of music from the adjoining room that she roused herself to creep over and listen at the door. Jack was playing his lute. She snuffed out the candles so there would be no betraying light, and eased the door open a tiny crack. Then she slid down to sit with her back against the wall to listen—and wish with all her heart Jack really had been a vagabond minstrel. She'd known how to deal with the lute player, but she had no idea how to deal with the haughty, reserved nobleman.

'The King gives the Duke a piece of gold plate every New Year,' said Mr Worsley. 'If the plate weighs more than the specified amount, then we—that is, his Grace—must pay the difference to the Lord Chamberlain's office.'

Temperance had been carefully ignoring Jack's silent observation of her conversation with the Receiver-General, but now she was startled into looking straight at him.

'The King gives you a New Year's gift?' she exclaimed.

'It is customary,' Jack said, so calmly that she realised he didn't consider it a matter of any particular consequence.

Over the past two days he had held her at a distance with cool, controlled courtesy; but she'd learned to tell the difference between when he truly had no strong feelings about something—and when he did, and chose to hide them from her. She'd discovered that when her husband's emotions were stirred he could, without saying a word, generate the same invisible tension in his surroundings she normally associated with thunderstorms. After two days of dealing with his exquisite manners, trying to decipher his mood, and waiting for the storm to break, she felt strongly inclined to throw something at him.

But she hadn't survived as a tradeswoman by letting herself be intimidated by the incomprehensible or arrogant behaviour of men. Jack had told her she was to be his Duchess. She feared he was having doubts about his decision, but he hadn't shared his concerns with her. Until he did, she was putting all her efforts into becoming mistress of her new role. She was determined to exceed his expectations.

Worsley had surprised her by emerging as her strongest ally in the house. She was sure Dr Nichols secretly disapproved of her. She suspected Hinchcliff and the Duchess treated her kindly for Jack's sake. But, to her delight, Worsley seemed to accept her for her own worth.

'Wait a minute.' Temperance recalled an important detail in the Receiver-General's revelation. 'You have to *pay* for your own present?'

'Only for however much it weighs over the set amount,' Jack replied, leaning back in his chair with such languid grace her fingers itched to snatch up the inkwell and hurl it at him. He wouldn't be so infuriatingly composed with ink dripping down his chin. 'The Lord Chamberlain's Office just gives out what is available in the Jewel House. So it doesn't always equal the exact value laid down for a gift to a nobleman of my rank. In that case I must repay the difference.'

'What do you do with the plate?' Temperance asked.

'Sometimes I keep it, but usually I have it delivered straight to my goldsmith to be exchanged for something of my choice. Last year we settled on candlesticks, didn't we?' Jack glanced at Worsley.

'Yes, your Grace.'

'And what do you give the King?' she asked. 'I can't imagine he hands out plates without expecting something in return.'

Jack smiled, a true smile, glinting with so much amused appreciation it took her breath away.

'You are right, of course,' he said. 'Usually it is a purse of gold, although, on occasions, I've given him a more personal gift. But the purse is customary and easily arranged. Gold is always acceptable to monarchs.'

'Gold is always acceptable to everyone,' said Temperance, her heart suddenly beating so fast she was sure he must sense it. Just one real smile from Jack after two days of formal courtesy and she was in danger of succumbing to trembling incoherence. A Duchess did not become giddy because her husband smiled at her. She laid her hand flat at the base of her throat and tried to compose herself. Jack's gaze followed the direction of her hand and she saw his eyes darken. She was wearing a hastily made new gown, and it exposed more of her shoulders than her old clothes. She hadn't intended her instinctive gesture to draw his attention to her bare skin—had she?

'The purse is made of silk, embroidered with silver,' said Mr Worsley. 'Also his Grace is expected to give gifts of money to the King's servants. It all goes through the Lord Chamberlain's Office. I have the complete list here if you are interested, madam?'

'Oh. Yes.' Temperance wrenched her gaze away from Jack. She took the paper and began to read it by rote but, as she continued, her interest was caught. 'The King's trumpeters, doorkeepers of the House of Lords, porters at Whitehall gate, yeomen of the guards… Good heavens!' She looked up at Jack. 'What would happen if you forgot? Would you be put in the Tower?'

He smiled and her heart gave another little jump. 'Worsley would never let that happen,' he said. 'I don't have to exchange the plate for household items. What jewellery would please you?'

'Jewellery?' Her hand returned to her throat. Had her earlier gesture put the idea into his mind? It had never occurred to her he might interpret it as a silent hint she expected him to give her jewels. Her skin felt hot beneath her fingertips, and then she gripped both hands together in her lap.

'Thank you. But I have no need of jewellery,' she said breathlessly. 'You have given me so much already. I am sure it would be more fitting for you to give the Duchess—'

'You are the Duchess, Tempest,' said Jack quietly. He stood up. Temperance could sense his retreat from her, even though unreadable emotion continued to burn in his eyes when he looked at her. 'A necklace and perhaps a bracelet,' he said. 'Arrange for the plate to be exchanged for jewellery, Worsley.' He turned and strolled towards the door.

Temperance's fingers closed around the inkwell. She heard Worsley's sharp intake of breath and realised she couldn't possibly throw a pot of ink at her husband's head. As the door closed behind him she slumped back in her chair and glanced warily at the Receiver-General. To her relief he didn't appear shocked.

'Since his Grace was not specific in his request, perhaps you would like to tell me your preferences,' he said mildly.

He'd done it all wrong. Jack pulled back the curtains to allow a broad swathe of moonlight to fall across the carpet. He could see it now. Every mis-step he'd taken since his return to Kilverdale Hall. His grip on the velvet tightened as he stared across the park and thought about the woman on the other side of the bedchamber door. So close. So unbelievably, almost disturbingly, close.

In all the years he'd occupied this room, no one had slept in the Duchess's bedchamber. Until now. It was both unsettling and arousing to know the woman he called his wife was so near at hand, so…available.

So inescapable.

He turned to look at the adjoining door and realised he was still clutching the curtain. He released it, but he didn't take a step towards the door. He couldn't go to Temperance until he'd worked out how to overcome the barrier his own clumsiness had created between them.

He knew the exact moment everything had gone wrong. Temperance had seen his hands tremble after she'd signed the marriage documents. He'd watched her write her name on the parchment and the full weight of the irrevocable commitment they'd made to each other had settled on his shoulders. From this point forward his peace of mind, his happiness, the succession of his title, and perhaps even his fortune would be inextricably bound to hers.

Ever since he'd stood in Lady Desire's garden at Kingston and discovered Temperance was pretending to be his wife, he'd been driven by the compulsion to take control of the situation. To find a solution that would withstand future scrutiny and suspicion. So he'd forged ahead, guided by deep-rooted instinct, sweeping aside every practical problem, until he'd stood in the silence of the night and watched Temperance sign the document that meant they would be dependent upon each other for the rest of their lives.

And his hands had trembled. And when he'd realised Temperance had noticed his momentary weakness he'd been mortified. He'd spent a lifetime perfecting an appearance of outward self-assurance, no matter what his inner doubts. For reasons he didn't care to examine too closely, his need to impress Temperance was far greater than his concern for the opinion of society's wits and beauties.

He'd been furious with himself for his lapse, and he'd instinctively taken refuge in the aloof politeness that had served him so well in other circumstances. Now he was stuck behind a barrier of his own making. Feeling like a fool and furious with himself, because he'd been a married man for three days, but he hadn't spent one of those nights in the same bed with his wife.

He rubbed his forehead. He had no experience in courting a woman in earnest. Since he'd regained his inheritance at the age of twenty he'd had no need for the skill. Women at all levels of society had vied to become his mistress, while the parents of respectable young ladies had seen him as a matrimonial prize of the first water. He pulled off his periwig and passed his hand over his head. He was so used to female attention, he hadn't realised until now that the tricks he'd learned to keep women he didn't want at a distance were no help in dealing with a wife he did want.

If his marriage had been the culmination of a loving courtship, he would have wooed Temperance by degrees until they were both at ease with each other and eager for the next stage of their union. At least, he hoped that's what he would have done.

If his marriage had been one of dynastic convenience to a high-born lady, his course would have been equally clear, though considerably less appealing. He'd always recoiled from entering into such a cold-blooded marriage. He'd never been a womaniser. His reputation as a rake rested on the fact he'd acknowledged his first bastard by the age of twenty and he'd never said anything to confirm or deny subsequent rumours.

What it all came down to was that he'd done everything wrong the first night he'd been back at Kilverdale Hall. He'd still been half in the role of Jack Bow and Temperance had still been the shopkeeper he'd teased on a sunny afternoon in Cheapside, and made love to in the lurid shadows of a Southwark inn. He'd been thinking about her all the time he'd been chasing Arscott across England, and when they were together again it had felt natural to take up where they'd left off—in bed.

But the only reason they'd made love that night in Southwark, so soon after first meeting, was because of the extraordinary situation. He was sure Temperance would never have let herself be overcome with passion if she hadn't been devastated by her losses, and under any other circumstances his own self-discipline would not so easily have slipped its leash. He'd wanted Temperance from the first moment he'd seen her, but he'd been controlling his physical desires for years. They'd found themselves in the middle of a cataclysmic situation and they'd both allowed the heat of their feelings to overcome their usual good sense.

But they weren't Jack Bow and the shopkeeper now. And in some ways Jack Bow had never really existed. Jack had created the role to give himself a measure of independence at a time when he'd had very little control over his future as Duke of Kilverdale. He'd enjoyed playing the part of carefree swordsman-musician, but it wasn't a role he could sustain indefinitely through the intimacies of marriage to a sharp-eyed woman like Tempest.

He released an aggravated breath. He couldn't simply walk into her room and make love to her the way he had the first night, because from now on she'd expect more of him than that. He'd seen it in her eyes these past two days. Watching him, considering him, silently questioning him. He'd offered her jewellery that afternoon and she'd protested he'd already given her enough. But that's not what her clear blue eyes said. They told him she wanted more from him. She wanted him to talk to her—and he didn't know what to say.

He threw another frustrated glance at the adjoining door, and then went into his dressing room and lifted a lute down from the wall. He'd spent his life finding solutions for problems. If he just thought about this one a little longer, he was bound to come up with a suitable plan. And he'd better think of it quickly, so he could get on with the far more rewarding task of making love to his wife.

* * *

Temperance paced around her bedchamber. The room was dark apart from a small chink between the curtains to let in some moonlight. She was wearing her night shift and dressing gown, but her feet were bare. Half an hour ago she'd eased open the connecting door an inch, and she didn't want Jack to hear her moving around.

He was in his room, playing his lute, just as he had done for the past two nights. It was insulting he found his lute better company than his wife! Who would have thought the man would be so contrary? Impossible. Frustrating.

She stood still and tried to calm down. Pacing about in the dark would not solve her problems. Then she remembered how he'd left it to Mr Worsley to select the first jewellery she was ever to receive, and her temper boiled up again. She was his wife—and that meant she had rights as well as duties. She turned decisively towards the connecting door.

Jack sat facing the window. His high-backed chair was propped on its rear legs against the bedpost. He kept it balanced with his right foot flat on the floor. His left ankle rested on his right knee. The moonlight cut a broad, silvery swathe across the floor in front of him.

The answer to his problem hit him in an exultant rush. The quickened tempo of the lute music mirrored his emotions as his hands flew over the strings and fingerboard.

It was so simple!

All he had to do was keep Temperance's attention focussed on the two reasons he'd already given for marrying her. He'd remind her he'd married her because she pleased him in bed—which would make her blush in flustered pleasure—and when he wasn't making love to her, he'd distract her with conversations about estate management. He'd keep her so busy she wouldn't have time to look at him in that thoughtfully questioning way. He'd make them both forget his hands had ever been less than rock steady.

Now he'd settled on a course of action, the tension in his muscles eased and the rhythm of the music slowed. He stroked his fingers over the strings and wished he was stroking them over Temperance—or that she was stroking her fingers over him. As his blood heated he realised he didn't need to wait until morning to put his plan into effect. He could stride into her room and make love to her straight away, and then talk to her in the morning, just as he had the first night.

He let the front legs of the chair jolt to the floor, his muscles tensed to stand—

Temperance stepped into the beam of moonlight, directly in front of him.

He dropped back, stunned by her sudden appearance. The lute music must have covered the small sounds of her approach. He gaped at her for a few seconds, then recollected himself and closed his mouth.

'Good evening,' he said, trying to act as coolly as if this happened every night. 'You look beautiful in the moonlight,' he added, thinking that was probably the kind of thing a husband ought to say in such circumstances.

He couldn't see her expression, but she didn't seem as pleased by the compliment as he'd expected. Too late, he realised that, with her back to the window—

'You can't see my face,' she said. 'I must be one big shadow to you.'

'Not at all,' he said, cursing himself for his lack of suavity. Only Temperance could so consistently undermine his powers of address simply by standing near him. 'The light has created the appearance of a halo around your hair. It is quite ethereal.'

'Hmm.' To his chagrin she sounded unimpressed by the revelation.

Without saying anything else she began to pace up and down in front of him. Her behaviour reminded Jack of a predator stalking its prey. Even though he couldn't see her expression he could sense her mood was not at all conciliatory. If she had a tail, he was sure she'd be flicking it in deadly warning to those around her.

He tensed, misliking the image of himself as her prey. Surely her pacing signified anxiety, rather than displeasure with him? No doubt she wanted assurance about the exchange of gifts with the King, or some other such matter.

She stopped and swung to face him. He realised he was still

sitting in the path of the moonlight. He stood up and moved to stand a few feet away from her so the light fell equally on both their faces.

'I want to talk to you,' she announced.

'Yes,' he said. 'What about?' he prompted after a few seconds.

'My wifely rights.'

'Your...*what*?'

Her demand stunned him. He could think of only one wifely right he hadn't bestowed on her since she'd signed the marriage documents. She was stalking up and down in front of him like an angry cat because he hadn't made love to her!

For two days he'd been castigating himself for letting his composure slip in front of her. He'd been afraid she'd noticed his unmanly hesitation and doubt. He didn't like to admit, even to himself, that he was capable of such weakness. But it had never occurred to him that she would believe he'd stayed away from her because she thought his trembling fingers were a sign he was no longer able to satisfy her womanly needs. That he was *impotent*.

After a second's blank disbelief, fury and self-recrimination surged through him as the full extent of the insult struck home. He should never have left it so long before he took her to bed again.

'You came in here to demand I *tup* you?'

'No!' She sounded startled, but he was so angry and mortified that his own behaviour had given her cause to suspect he was incapable of making love to her that he didn't hear her.

'How dare you doubt my ability to perform for you, madam!'

'I didn't—'

'I've treated you like a gentleman and now you're accusing me of being a eunuch!' He seized her shoulders as indignation and frustration surged through him. He should have swept her into bed the moment she'd signed the documents and every night since then. If he'd made love to her as often as he'd wanted these past two days she'd never have doubted his capacity to satisfy her.

'I never did!' She glared up at him. She seemed shorter than usual. 'What on earth is the matter with you?' She jerked angrily, trying to dislodge his hands.

'There's nothing wrong with me.'

'I never said there was! I *said*—'

'I know what you said,' he growled. 'I don't need to hear the words again.'

'Perhaps you heard them wro—' Temperance gasped as he put his hands on her waist and lifted her off her feet. He carried her several paces and then backed her up against the nearest wall. She bumped into the tapestry first. It was hanging six inches away from the plaster, so by the time Jack had her pinned against the wall she was half-buried in the heavy fabric. He flexed his hips, pushing his pelvis even closer to hers.

'Do you doubt my ability to service you?' he said through gritted teeth. 'Is this proof enough for you? Or won't you be happy till I rip the clothes from your back—'

Temperance wriggled furiously beneath him.

Jack was outraged by her dissatisfaction with his lacklustre performance as a husband—not least because it echoed his own dissatisfaction—but he was even more aggravated to realise she'd made him lose command of himself again. How the devil was he to find a dignified way of out this confrontation? He eased his grip on her waist, but didn't step away.

In the meantime, Temperance managed to get her arms free. She stroked one hand across his head. He couldn't hide his start at her unexpected gesture. He tensed, half-expecting her to twist his ear, or take some other equally uncomfortable and humiliating retribution—but her touch was gentle, almost wondering as she explored the planes of his close-cropped skull.

'I didn't know you'd cut your hair again,' she said. 'No wonder you kept your wig on all day. It must get chilly in the winter.'

Jack muttered something uncomplimentary under his breath.

She put her other hand over his mouth. 'Until you've taught me to speak French, it would be polite if you'd talk to me in English,' she said.

He found her prim rebuke amusing in a rather gut-twisting way. Despite his confidence in her courage, he was relieved he hadn't scared her. He'd married her partly because of her fearless personality. On the other hand, he wouldn't have objected if she'd at least *pretended* to be impressed by his entirely justified outrage.

She changed the angle of her hand over his mouth, then let her fingers brush gently over his cheek and behind his head, until both her arms were around his neck.

'These—' she moved her hips against him in such an unexpectedly provocative gesture that he had to suppress another oath '—weren't the wifely rights I was talking about,' she said.

Jack caught the hint of humour in her voice and swallowed a groan. No, she definitely wasn't afraid and, just as certainly, despite the fact he was the one pinning her to the wall, he wasn't in control of the situation. But if these weren't the wifely rights she'd meant, what *had* she been talking about? He looked down at her, then realised what he was doing.

'Why have you shrunk?' he demanded.

'I haven't shrunk. I just haven't got any shoes on and you have.'

'You're walking around with bare feet in winter. Dammit, woman! Haven't you any sense? I could have trodden on your toes!'

'I wasn't expecting you to ram me up against a wall.' There was unmistakable laughter in her voice.

'I haven't rammed—*did* I tread on your toes?'

'No.'

'If I had, it would be entirely your fault,' he said gruffly, relieved he hadn't inadvertently hurt her. He picked her up and carried her to the bed, dropping her right in the middle of it. She bounced gently on the mattress, then tried to sit up.

'Lie down!' he commanded.

'Why?' With typical lack of obedience she sat up to smooth her dressing gown over her legs.

'Because I told you to.' Now he'd managed to get them as far as the bed he was determined not to lose the small advantage he'd gained.

'It is your wifely *duty* to obey me,' he pointed out, kicking off his shoes. Instead of lying down beside her, he climbed on to the end of the bed and knelt at her feet.

'Only if your order is reasonable,' she said. 'You haven't said why—'

He caught both her ankles and jerked her feet up. His action unbalanced her and she fell back on to the mattress. He heard her gasp, then she tried to lever herself up on her elbows. He countered by lifting her feet almost to his shoulders.

'I said lie down,' he reminded her. He sat back on his heels, admiring the way the dressing gown slipped back to reveal her legs. If he'd had the good sense to do this in the daylight, he'd have been able to see a good deal more.

He felt Temperance relax back on the bed, and then she twisted her head to look at him.

'What are you doing?' she asked.

Instead of answering with words, Jack moved a little closer and rested her ankles on his shoulders. He half-expected her to resist. She made an effort to pull free, but he was sure it was only a token attempt to assuage her pride because he was gripping her so loosely she could easily have broken out of his grasp.

Pride was a strange and powerful thing, he thought. His pride had kept him away from her for the past three nights. Her pride had sent her to make as yet undisclosed demands of him. Now here they were, and perhaps both of them were where they'd wanted to be all along, and though they were happy about it, they were still both trying to save face.

The absurdity of it all made him smile in the darkness. He'd been slightly off balance ever since his return to Kilverdale Hall but, as his sense of humour reasserted itself, he felt much more in control of himself and the situation.

'Behave,' he instructed her cheerfully, turning his head to kiss her ankle. 'A good wife doesn't kick her husband in the face like a donkey.'

'Are you comparing yourself to a donkey now?' Temperance said, amazed at how quickly she was becoming aroused by the unconventional position.

She knew it was too dark for Jack to see how much of her body had been exposed when her shift fell back from her raised legs, but she was very conscious of it. She was glad it was dark, but she couldn't deny the thrill of decadent pleasure shimmering through her as Jack kissed her ankle. Her imagination began to supply all sorts of fascinating, exciting possibilities for what he might do next.

'What quick wits you have,' Jack said. 'I warn you, madam. The more you insult me now, the harder it will eventually go for you.'

'Really?' She vividly recalled the pleasure of exploring the contours of his very male body. She wished she could touch him now, but he was out of her reach.

'What are you doing?' she asked, gripping the silk bedcover.

'Interrogating you,' he said, beginning to stroke her outer thighs.

She trembled in response. Heat pooled between her legs. She wanted him to touch her there.

'What about?' she asked breathlessly.

He was no longer holding her ankles in place, but she didn't try to change her position. She closed her eyes, surrendering to the delicious pleasure filling her with every brush of his fingertips against her calves and outer thighs. Until she started to feel frustrated because he was ignoring other parts of her that were just as eager for his stimulating touch.

She opened her eyes and moved one leg until her foot was flat against his shoulder. She began to rub the ball of her foot against his velvet coat in a sensuous caress of her own.

'What are you interrogating me about?' She pushed her foot against his shoulder in a light, but firm, reminder he hadn't answered her question, feeling rather proud she'd managed to cling to the thread of their conversation.

Jack didn't say anything for a few moments. Then she felt him shake his head as if to clear it. The idea he was as distracted as she was by their mutual sensual teasing thrilled her.

'Your wifely duties…ah, rights,' he said thickly.

'According to you, it is my duty to obey you at all times.' She let her foot slide down his body until it was resting on the top of his thigh. She began to knead her toes and heel alternately up and down on his taut muscles.

She heard Jack groan. She was sure it wasn't with pain, and her own excitement grew more intense at this evidence of her effect upon him.

She stroked up and down his leg a couple more times, then the temptation became too strong to resist. She moved her foot higher and inwards until she was able to explore the hard ridge straining the front of his breeches.

Another ragged groan escaped him. Excitement pulsed through her until she was swollen and damp with need. She rubbed her toes against him until he suddenly gripped her ankle and moved her foot aside.

She didn't resist. 'Did I hurt you?' she asked, afraid she'd done something wrong.

'No,' he said hoarsely.

'Oh! You *liked* it!' she exclaimed, reassured and delighted by the discovery.

She tried to move her foot back into position, but he clamped his hand around her ankle and braced her foot on his thigh. 'No more! Or there won't be any wifely rights for you.'

'Hmm.' The threat held no terror for her. She slid her other foot off his shoulder and delicately inserted her toes beneath his coat. The next second he startled her by giving a yelp and jerking backwards.

'Your feet are freezing!'

'You didn't complain just now,' she said, relaxing on to the bed, relieved that was the only reason he'd pulled away from her.

He grabbed her free foot and placed it on his other thigh.

'Don't move,' he ordered.

'Is that a husbandly order I must obey at all costs?' she asked.

'Yes.' He rubbed his hands back and forth over her insteps, and she realised he was trying to warm them. 'When did you become such a brazen hussy?'

'When I met you.'

His hands momentarily stilled. 'What do you mean?'

'What do I *mean*?' she said indignantly. 'You know what I mean.' She curled her toes into his thigh for emphasis. 'You teased me, and provoked me, and walked into my room and took all your clothes off in the most brazen display I've ever seen.'

'I should hope so,' he said, sounding smug. Then he tightened his grip on her ankles. 'How many other men have displayed themselves to you?' he demanded, and for the first time she heard a note of suspicion creep into his voice.

'None, you numbwit! You're the only one.'

'You are twenty-three years old,' he said. 'Hot-blooded. Passionate. Beautiful. How can no other man have tempted you before me?'

She caught her breath, the worst of her indignation fading. No one—no *man*—had ever called her passionate and beautiful before. She knew there were some people of puritanical bent who would consider those to be terms of disapproval—but not Jack.

She still didn't care for the implications of his question, but she cherished the compliment it contained.

'They weren't tall enough,' she said at last.

'Is that all?' He sounded as if he didn't much care for her answer. 'Are you telling me any tall man would do?'

She laughed softly as she remembered the way he'd reacted when she'd commented on Halross's height. 'Of course not,' she said. 'It took a very special and rare combination of qualities to catch my...eye.'

'Such as?' He began to massage her calves.

'Good hands,' she said, her words hitching as he focussed all his attention on her right leg. 'When you were...playing your lute in the tavern. I noticed them particularly. Clever, strong hands.'

'I'm glad you appreciate them.' He enclosed her ankle with both hands and stroked firmly up towards her knee. 'What else?'

'Your broad shoulders.' She lifted her left foot and pushed it lightly against him to illustrate her point.

She could hear how his breathing had grown heavy and ragged. Her dressing gown had long since come undone, and her shift was well above her hips after her earlier efforts to break free of his grip. She knew she was completely exposed to him, but she made no effort to cover herself.

'The way you spent all day and half the night looking for little lost Katie,' she said. 'You are a good, compassionate man—'

'Enough.' Purposefully he moved his hands to her thigh, deliberately stroking as high as he could on both the inside and the outside. As soon as he touched her inner thigh she gasped and quivered in anticipated pleasure. Her blood surged hotly through her veins, and when his fingers danced higher to brush against her damp curls she whimpered softly and turned her head restlessly against the silk bedcover. He parted her gently, and began to stroke her soft, slick inner folds.

Her body clenched and ached for more. This was the culmination of their teasing game. She lifted her hips, pushing insistently against his hand. His movements became urgent. He withdrew briefly, then positioned himself between her legs, and she felt the soft rasp of his brocade breeches against her inner thighs. A second later he was inside her. It increased her excitement to realise he hadn't been able to delay even the few seconds it would have taken to strip off his clothes. She wrapped her legs around him, gasping with pleasure as he began to thrust in and out of her. The hot, intimate slide of his body within hers drove all coherent thought from her head. She seized his shoulders and matched her movements to his until they found an exquisite rhythm.

He filled her world. Together they propelled each other ever upwards to the very edge of the precipice. At last she convulsed in a rush of intense, delicious, sensation. The wonderful feelings rippled outwards through her whole body in wave after wave of ecstasy. Then she felt Jack shudder in her arms as he found his own release.

She lay with her eyes closed, her whole body still humming with pleasure in the aftermath of their lovemaking. All she could hear were the mingled sounds of their quickened breathing and the rapid beating of her own heart. After a little while, Jack lifted himself away carefully from her. Modesty demanded she pull down her shift, but her limbs were filled with such contented lassitude she couldn't find the energy to move. Besides, it was so dark it hardly mattered. She had no words to describe what had just happened, she only knew it had been an exquisitely satisfying experience. She drew in a deep breath and released a long, happy sigh. Then she stirred herself enough to reach for Jack. As she did so, she felt the mattress give as he rolled off the bed and out of her grasp.

Chapter Twelve

Uneasiness pierced Temperance's contented mood. She opened her eyes and tried to see what Jack was doing in the shadows. She didn't want him to turn away from her again. Not now. Not after she'd allowed herself to be so vulnerable and surrendered so completely to him.

As she remembered how wantonly she'd behaved a few minutes ago, her skin began to burn with embarrassment rather than arousal. Thank God it was so dark! At least he hadn't been able to *see* her acting like a brazen hussy, even though he had taken advantage of it. She hadn't behaved like a Duchess. No wonder he'd left the bed. Now he was no longer in the grip of base male lust he was disgusted by her behaviour.

She uttered a soft moan and dived off the edge of the mattress, trying to straighten her clothing at the same time. She didn't realise Jack was standing in the way until the top of her head caught him squarely in his stomach. She flung out her hands to save herself and ended up with one palm resting on his left hip and the other on his right thigh.

He gave a startled grunt, then swore, seized her shoulders and dragged her upright.

'What's the matter with you now?' he demanded.

'Nothing's the matter. I was just...I was just...' Her words trailed off as she realised he was naked beneath her hands. He must have taken his clothes off when he left the bed. She moved her hands, un-thinkingly confirming her first impression, then realised what she was doing and snatched them back as if his body was on fire.

He gave a long-suffering sigh. 'Don't make me *order* you into my bed, wife,' he said.

'You want me to get into your bed?' said Temperance.

'I've just said so, haven't I? Take off your dressing gown first.' He pushed it off her shoulders without waiting for her to respond to his instruction. 'There.' He tossed it aside. 'Now you can get into bed. Hurry up, or your feet will get cold again.'

Still feeling bemused, Temperance did as he ordered, but she couldn't relax. She didn't know what to expect next. Was he going to make love to her again? Or were they going to sleep now?

Jack climbed in next to her. He put one arm around her and drew her close so her back rested snugly against his chest. His body was warm and relaxed, and very comforting after the awk-wardness that had existed between them for the past few days. For a little while Temperance stared into the darkness, trying to antic-ipate Jack's next action, but he didn't do or say anything. At last she closed her eyes and allowed herself to drift into sleep.

Jack rested his hand on Temperance's hip and listened to the gentle sound of her breathing. He liked her very well when she was awake, but just now he was more comfortable with her asleep. He could hold and touch her, safe in the knowledge she wasn't going to throw him off balance with any outrageous demands.

He winced at the memory of how he'd jumped to the wrong conclusion over what she'd meant by her wifely rights. His frus-trated desire had played a part in his misinterpretation of her words, but his overreaction had been foolish. His hand tightened gently on her hip as he recalled how responsive she'd been to his lovemaking.

He smiled crookedly as he acknowledged that perhaps he should be reflecting on how responsive he had been to *her* love-making. Temperance had none of the skills of a practised coquette, but he found her bold sensual curiosity and blunt appreciation of his body extremely stimulating. He was inordinately pleased she liked his hands and his shoulders—and just thinking about how provocatively she had teased him was enough to make his body quicken with renewed arousal. He'd been so overwhelmed by the sensation of losing himself in her at the climax of their lovemaking he'd instinctively pulled away immediately afterwards. He'd needed those few moments apart from her to regain his balance.

He'd never before allowed himself to surrender so completely to a passionate interlude. But this wasn't an interlude from which he could walk away. Temperance was in his bed. Unless he slipped away before dawn as he had done the first night, they would wake to face the day together. The prospect of such mundane intimacy was both unsettling and appealing.

He stroked his hand over Temperance's side and then curved it over her rounding stomach. When she was dressed it still wasn't obvious she was pregnant, but he could feel the slight swell of her belly beneath her shift. He'd decided they wouldn't announce her pregnancy until after the wedding ceremony but, in the quiet darkness, he thought about the babe.

He had no fear of fatherhood. Though he would never have made the unmanly confession aloud, he rather liked babies. He could still remember how surprised and enchanted he'd been by Toby as a newborn. Toby had been so small and fragile; his skin so tenderly soft to the touch. And he had been utterly dependent on the care of others.

Jack hadn't expected to fall completely in love with his son. He'd still been in exile when the child was conceived and, before Toby's birth, he'd supposed he would act as other men did in similar circumstances—providing for his mistress and child with practical generosity without losing his heart to either. Then Toby had arrived and all Jack's assumptions about his lover and his child had proved false.

He'd been dazzled by Vivien when he'd first met her. With hindsight he understood why he'd been susceptible to her charms, though his gullibility still grated on him. Vivien was beautiful and skilled at flattery. At the time he'd thought she'd been attracted to him simply as a man. Now he suspected there was an element of truth in that, but it wasn't a truth he relished.

Vivien's previous protector had been a gout-ridden man in his fifties—and she'd left Jack for another older, wealthier man. Jack had been eighteen when they'd met, with no prospect of regaining his inheritance. When he looked back, he was convinced all Vivien had sought was a brief liaison with a young, virile male before returning to the undemanding security of her older, richer protectors.

She'd resented the unintended pregnancy. She'd endured it with a bad grace and, as soon as she could after Toby was born, she'd sought a more financially rewarding protector. Jack had gone to her lodgings to discover Toby screaming in his crib while the nurse snored in a drunken stupor. Vivien, he later discovered, had been out entertaining her latest lover.

Jack had picked up his son and carried him home and, for the first time in months, he'd felt at peace with himself. In a twisted way he was grateful for Vivien's callousness. If she'd been a better mother, such a simple solution wouldn't have been possible. He'd always known Temperance would be devastated—and furious— if he tried to separate her from her child. He would never have treated her so cruelly.

He cupped her stomach protectively. Toby had come to no harm from the brief time he had spent in Vivien's neglectful care, but this child would never be left to scream unattended.

As for the novelty of waking up in the same bed with Temperance—he would treat it as a matter of simple, married routine. There was no need to discuss it with her. If she mentioned it at all, he'd simply say that, from now on, he expected them to share a bed. It was, after all, one of his original, declared reasons for marrying her.

He frowned into the darkness, wondering if he was being overoptimistic. Unquestioning obedient acceptance was not a quality he associated with his Tempest. He wondered what she'd really meant about her 'wifely rights'. He was glad to know she appreciated his lovemaking, but he wasn't looking forward to finding out how she *did* find him lacking. He kissed the top of her head and closed his eyes. He wanted to be well rested and alert before his next conversation with his wife.

* * *

Temperance woke on a wave of nausea so overwhelming she groaned. She stayed absolutely still, waiting for the first, dreadful rush to recede. She felt Jack move, then he touched her arm.

'Tempest, what's wrong?'

'Sick,' she said through barely moving lips. 'Don't bounce bed. Need to eat bread in sewing box *right now.*'

He slid from between the sheets and she heard him pad barefooted around the bed. She opened her eyes to see him crouching before her, his expression taut with concern.

She'd felt his shorn head the night before, but when they'd made love she'd forgotten his hair had been cut. This was the first time she'd seen him in daylight. His hair was so brutally short it wasn't much longer than the whiskers shadowing his chin. Without his periwig and velvets there was nothing about his appearance to soften the angles of his face. Last night she'd been able to feel the power in his lean, muscular body. Now she could see it. He was so enticing that, if she hadn't felt ill, she'd be tempted to reach out and touch him.

'There's some bread in my mother's sewing box by my bed,' she croaked. 'Please get it for me. I'll be all right when I've eaten.'

He stood and strode into her room. Despite the waves of nausea, she moved her head to admire the lithe power in his naked body. The view was even more compelling when he returned carrying the sewing box.

'Bread in top compartment,' she said.

He opened the box and found the crust wrapped in a piece of linen. He tore off a small piece and passed it to her. She took it, keeping the rest of her body still.

'You don't have to eat dry bread,' he said, his eyebrows drawn together in a frown as he watched her. 'I'm sure there must be something more appetising in the larder.'

She swallowed and reached for another piece. 'This first,' she said, her voice slightly muffled. 'It's the baby. I'll feel better in a little while—when I've eaten. I don't usually feel quite this bad in the morning.'

'It's my fault.' Self-recrimination clouded his eyes. 'I shouldn't have—'

'No,' Temperance interrupted. She was warmed and reassured by his concern, but she didn't want him to blame himself. If he did, he might decide not to make love to her again until after the baby was born. In the midst of her daunting new life, she'd discovered she needed the comfort of his body close to hers in the privacy of the night.

She took a deep, careful breath, looking past him to where daylight streamed in the window.

'It's later than I usually get up, isn't it?' she said.

'About nine.'

'That's why. I usually eat by seven.' She closed her eyes and rested a while. She hoped she felt better soon. She loved the way Jack was taking care of her, but she was afraid he might lose patience if her weakness lasted too long.

'I'll call Mama,' he said. 'She'll know the best thing to do for you.'

'No, don't.' Temperance opened her eyes in alarm. 'You didn't want to tell anyone until after the second marriage ceremony.'

'But I didn't know you felt so sick. There must be something—'

'You already did it.' She managed to sit up, only then remembering she was naked under the bedclothes. She pulled the sheet up to her chin. 'Thank you for fetching the bread.'

'Why are you keeping it in the sewing box?' He sat back on his heels, scrutinising her carefully.

'So the maid won't find it.'

Jack stared at her, then shook his head in disbelief, but he seemed amused rather than disapproving of her subterfuge.

'It's fortunate you remembered the box at the last minute,' he said, 'or it would have been on the cart with everything else.'

'I know. I've thought that many times,' said Temperance. 'If it wasn't for you, I never would have saved it.' To her dismay, tears filled her eyes. She pulled the sheet a little higher in what she hoped seemed a casual gesture, and tried to blot her damp cheeks on the linen. She knew Jack had noticed when he touched her hair in a gentle caress.

'I'm sorry you lost everything else,' he said. 'If I could get it back for you…'

She lifted her head and looked at him, still kneeling naked beside the bed in the chilly December morning. The fires in her rooms were always lit before dawn by the servants, but they didn't light the fire in Jack's bedchamber unless he gave a specific order. When she'd asked him why he didn't have a fire every day, he'd shrugged and said it wasn't worth the extra work when most mornings he didn't spend long enough in his room to notice the benefits.

Over and over again he confused her with the contradictions in his behaviour. He could assume the attitude of an arrogant nobleman as easily as he put on his velvet and lace—and often with less conscious effort—but other times he amazed her with his lack of pretension.

There was nothing grand about him now. He was a magnificent picture of naked masculinity—but she could tell he wasn't impervious to the cold. He wasn't shivering, but she could see goose bumps on his arms. She was about to suggest he get dressed when the revelation hit her.

Jack was kneeling naked beside her in the cold room because he was more concerned about her comfort than his own. This was the man he was beneath his ducal finery. And she loved him.

She loved Jack.

She stared at him, forgetting everything else as the truth of her insight overwhelmed her.

She loved Jack.

Perhaps she always had, though she'd tried to deny or suppress that knowledge for so many good reasons: he'd left her in Southwark, for weeks she'd thought him dead, and then he'd turned out to be a Duke—which was almost worse than being dead in terms of putting him beyond her reach. No wonder she hadn't allowed herself to recognise the truth.

She loved him in all his volatile moods—teasing good humour, high-handed impatience or quick compassion. When she'd believed she couldn't be his wife, she'd settled for being his widow. Now she really *was* his wife. She was married to the man she loved.

It was a stunning discovery. Why hadn't she realised before? When she was pacing her room in frustration at his cool withdrawal, why hadn't she realised what she really wanted was his love, not merely a little more of his attention?

Her mood crashed as she remembered the terms of his proposal. He didn't want her love. He wanted her as his wife because of her practical determination to survive against all odds. And because he lusted after her. Last night was proof enough he enjoyed making love to her.

While she was still grappling with her personal epiphany, Jack stood up. She gazed at him with eyes of love and yearning. She'd found so much pleasure and comfort in his embrace the previous night. As she looked at him, his body began to stir into arousal. She suddenly realised he was not only aware of her intense scrutiny, but responding to it.

Heat flooded her cheeks. She wrenched her eyes away and heard his soft laugh.

'I don't think you are in a fit state to enjoy any more wifely rights at the moment, sweetheart,' he said a little drily.

'Oh, God!' She clamped the sheet against her mouth as she recalled the unwary words she'd spoken, which had precipitated their lovemaking.

'That was *not* what I meant!' she said, her voice muffled by her hands and the sheet, her face so hot she was surprised it didn't set the linen afire. 'I have no idea why you thought I meant what you thought I did—but I *didn't*!'

'Hmm.' Instead of replying, he went into his dressing room. When he emerged he was belting on a robe.

'I don't understand how you could possibly think I would be so brazen, so immodest, so, so—'

'We'll discuss it later,' he interrupted her. 'If I don't bounce, can I sit on the bed?'

Temperance gazed at him. Now she knew she loved him, everything had changed. She didn't know how to behave or what to say to him. Of course, that had been true ever since his arrival at Kilverdale Hall—but for the first time she felt shy.

'Tempest? May I sit?' he repeated.

'Yes, yes, of course,' she said, flustered. 'But please could you give me some more bread first?' she added, more conscious than ever that she was naked beneath the bedclothes.

'When you are feeling better it will be your turn to be naked in

the daylight for my pleasure,' Jack said, the amusement in his
voice suggesting he'd correctly interpreting her reluctance to reach
for the bread herself.

He sounded just the same as ever. Her world had tilted on its
axis and he was still thinking about bread and morning sickness.
The difference between what he was talking about and the new
understanding filling her mind was disorientating.

'You are a rogue and a scoundrel,' she declared, striving to
match his bantering tone. It had been so much easier to spar with
him when he'd only been a charming adventurer—or even an outrageous Duke. It was much more difficult now she knew she loved
him. For all his practical compassion, he was still an experienced
man of the world. If she revealed her feelings, he'd probably be
amused by what he'd see as her unsophisticated sentimentality.

'I know.' He climbed back on to his side of the bed and put his
arm around her shoulders. It was the first time he'd touched her
since she'd realised she loved him. She felt the shock of the
physical connection all the way to her soul.

'I've been a scoundrel all my life,' he said, kissing her temple,
'but I'm sorry you feel so bad. I was going to take you for a walk
this morning, but—'

'I can still go,' she said quickly. 'Soon I will feel completely
better, and it won't take me long to get ready.'

'There's no hurry.' He tightened his grip on her shoulders. 'We
have all day.'

'You want *what*?' Jack stared at Temperance as if she'd lost her
mind.

'Dancing lessons,' Temperance repeated firmly, despite the
fluttering in her stomach. 'I want you to teach me to dance.'

She was sitting on the bench on the little hill overlooking the
house. Jack stood in front of her, looking unnervingly grand in a
brocade coat, periwig and plumed hat. She would never have
guessed from her first sight of him at the Dog and Bone, but she'd
come to suspect he enjoyed the business of dressing in fine clothes.
She'd seen the scented powders and bottles of orange water on his
dressing table and he'd surprised her with his knowledge when

he'd spoken to the silk mercer. His valet even rubbed ointment scented with jasmine into his leather gloves.

So far she'd turned to the Dowager Duchess for guidance on clothes, but now she thought she might do well to ask Jack for his advice on matters of fashion—once he recovered from his present astonishment.

Why was he so put out? Had she offended his ducal dignity by asking him to tutor her?

'You could always—' she began, about to suggest he hire a dancing master.

'You consider dancing lessons a wifely *right*?' Jack demanded in the same instant.

'In our particular circumstances I do,' she said, lifting her chin. 'A true lady would have been taught how to behave in noble company from the moment she was born. I know how to measure and cut cloth, haggle with customers... I don't know *anything* about being a Duchess—and in a few days all the noble guests will arrive for the wedding. You have to help me be a Duchess, Jack,' she said, reaching out to clutch his hand in both of hers as panic at what lay ahead overcame her.

He opened his mouth, then closed it again and sat down beside her, still allowing her to grasp his hand.

'I thought Mama was helping you,' he said. 'And Worsley.'

'They are,' Temperance said. 'Worsley is teaching me about your estates and her Grace is teaching me etiquette. I watch her all the time to see how she conducts herself. She is so serene and elegant. I can never hope to be so elegant. I feel like a carthorse sometimes beside her, but—'

'Ridiculous!' Jack frowned. 'Absolutely ridiculous. Your figure and carriage are admirable. I don't want to hear any more nonsense about carthorses. *Diable!* What a stupid idea!'

He looked so annoyed Temperance's runaway panic eased. She'd spent a lot of time with Eleanor, and she was at least six inches taller than the Dowager Duchess. Whenever she walked anywhere with Eleanor she always felt over-large and clumsy. But she was not taller than Jack. Her unladylike height wouldn't be so noticeable if he stayed close beside her at the wedding ceremony.

'The Duchess does not go to London very often,' she said after taking a few calming breaths. 'She has told me she doesn't know all the latest news and fashions. There is so much I need to know so I won't disgrace myself by saying the wrong thing to the wrong person. You have to tell me about these people, Jack. Your high-born friends.'

His lips curved in a cynical smile. 'Not always friends. No, I do not think I would call them friends.'

She wanted to ask what he meant, but then his gaze returned to her face and his expression softened. She felt a spurt of hopeful excitement that apparently he found it more pleasant to look at her than he did to contemplate the society into which he'd been born.

'You want me to teach you to dance?' he said. He turned his hand within hers and she suddenly realised she was still clinging to him. She tried to draw her hands away, but he claimed her fingers in a strong clasp and she was only able to retrieve one hand. She wondered what it meant. Even the smallest gesture he made seemed so much more significant today—now she knew she loved him.

'Yes, please?' Temperance looked at him hopefully. 'Will you?'

'We'll begin this afternoon,' said Jack. 'May I suggest,' he continued austerely, 'that the next time you have a perfectly reasonable request you make it in a less melodramatic manner.'

'Why?' said Temperance before she could stop herself. 'If I'd been reasonable, you'd have played your lute all night long. Again.'

She felt Jack go rigid as he sat beside her and, when she risked a glance at him, she saw colour staining his cheek. She held her breath, wishing she'd also held her unruly tongue. Why had she said such a provocative thing?

An awful silence stretched between them for several long seconds. Then Jack turned his head very deliberately and looked at her through narrowed eyes.

'So you'd rather make love to me than sleep alone?' he said, his voice so low it was almost a purr.

Temperance's own cheeks burned with embarrassment, but she managed to keep her gaze locked with his. She couldn't speak. She wasn't able to cast aside her modesty sufficiently to agree with him aloud. But nor could she insult him—and lie—by saying she preferred to sleep alone.

He uttered a short, pithy and completely incomprehensible comment. It occurred to Temperance that she really ought to learn French—

Jack plucked her off the bench and on to his lap. She gasped and flung up her arms in surprise, but he barely gave her time to register the heat in his eyes before his mouth found hers in a passionate kiss.

Chapter Thirteen

Even though it was a large chamber and Jack was used to being the focus of attention, the great parlour seemed uncomfortably crowded. He felt as if half the household was watching him, waiting for him to begin the afternoon's entertainment.

Temperance was there because it was her dancing lesson. Hinchcliff was present with his cittern to provide the necessary music. Jack had asked his mother to attend to give Temperance advice on the woman's part in the dance. Dr Nichols was there to partner the Dowager Duchess, so they'd be able to make up a set of four. Toby was sitting next to Isaac on an oak bench, kicking his heels against the carved legs, because it had occurred to Jack his son would also benefit from dancing lessons. If everything proceeded smoothly, Toby and Isaac could make up a third couple, giving Temperance the opportunity to dance in a set of six as well as the basic four.

If everything proceeded smoothly…

Jack took another look around the room, wondering why he hadn't noticed before his fine Venetian cravat was tied too tightly. He'd never taught anyone to dance—and instructing his wife in front of three intrigued adults and two bright-eyed children was a more daunting prospect than he'd anticipated.

When she'd first requested dancing lessons he'd been stunned and then relieved her notion of wifely rights was so innocuous. He'd just been relaxing into the conviction he had everything under control when Temperance had made her casually pointed comment.

He couldn't fool himself now she hadn't noticed his absence from her bed. He was both unsettled and stimulated by the implicit challenge in her words. He awaited the coming night with fierce anticipation. It was going to be a matter of pride, as well as great pleasure, to show her he could satisfy her desires over and over again. But first they had this lesson to get through, and he had no idea how to begin.

He cleared his throat just as Temperance started to speak. He instantly favoured her with what he hoped would appear an indulgently enquiring glance. The kind of glance that indicated to everyone watching he was in command of the situation, but courteously *choosing* to defer to his wife.

'I have been reading this book of dance steps,' she said, holding up a book that he recognised, after a moment's narrow-eyed scrutiny, as Playford's *Dancing Master.* 'I found it in the bookroom.'

He was so pleased with her for making it easy to begin he could have kissed her. Instead he smiled the smile of a tutor rewarding a gifted pupil and said, 'Well done. Let me see.' He flipped through the pages, feeling more confident as he gained a notion of how to proceed. 'This is an old edition. You'll need to learn the latest French dances as well. But we will begin more simply. Mama, will you dance first with me, so Toby and Isaac can see their part?'

He returned the book to Temperance. She was sitting down, so she had to look up to meet his eyes. She had beautiful blue eyes. He'd been fascinated by them from the first. She was looking at him intently, as she so often did, but he couldn't read her expression. He was still trying to interpret what he'd seen in Temperance's eyes as he took Eleanor's hand and led her into the middle of the floor.

'Isaac,' he said. 'I want you to dance the woman's part because I dare say it will be easier for you to switch to dancing the man's part later. Toby has never danced before.' Jack also thought Isaac was more likely to tolerate being cast in the woman's role.

'Your Grace, I will dance any part you wish me to,' said Isaac, so earnestly Jack couldn't help being amused and touched.

'Hinchcliff, music, if you please,' he said.

Dancing with his mother was easy. She was as light-footed as a woman half her age. But by the time they'd danced a few measures, Toby was kicking the bench leg so emphatically it seemed prudent to give the boys the first lesson.

'Your pardon, my dear,' Jack said to Temperance, feeling far hotter than he should have done after the light exercise. It was hard to be debonair when your son was scowling so fiercely he looked as if he might explode with impatience any second.

'I am finding it very helpful to watch and listen to your explanations,' she said.

'Good.' Was she laughing at him behind that serene expression? It was not an entirely unpleasant sensation. Unlike the cutting wit so fashionable at Court, Temperance's humour was never intended to belittle or wound.

'It will be your turn in a just a minute,' he said, thinking he should reward her patience with more than a one-word response.

He glanced at her just in time to see her lips twitch.

'I was always grateful for those occasions when I had the same problem,' she murmured.

'The same problem?' He stopped in the middle of showing Toby a step and stared at her. When had she ever been faced with the task of teaching two boys to dance while maintaining a commanding masculine presence in front of three adult witnesses? Four, if he included her—which he did.

'Several customers wanting my attention at once,' she said. 'As long as they all received satisfactory service, it was good for business. Of course, it's best not to make them wait too long.'

Jack followed the direction of her gaze and resisted the temptation to swear.

'Toby! Don't kick the table! When did you start kicking everything? You are not a mule. Isaac, take your place. Hinchcliff, music!' After instructing them for a few minutes he stepped back to watch. He'd already noticed Isaac learned new skills quickly and he had the knack of holding Toby's interest.

'Excellent,' Jack praised the boys after they'd gone through several measures. At last he was able to dance with his wife.

'Tempest?' He held out his hand to her, and felt a surge of inexplicable excitement as she allowed him to draw her to her feet.

As soon as she was standing in front of him he was assailed by a host of conflicting reactions. When she met his eyes he suddenly understood why she worried about her height. He'd grown accustomed to how well she suited him, but dancing with his mother had reminded him how tall Temperance was. He'd already told her he liked her height, but he'd have to tell her again so she knew he meant it.

When she lowered her gaze and he saw a tinge of pink rise into her cheeks he nearly kissed her. He remembered their audience just in time and pulled her briskly into the middle of the room to start her lesson. It was only when he was directing her in the first steps that it occurred to him there was no reason why a man couldn't show some degree of public affection for his wife. Particularly in the current circumstances, where he wanted everyone to believe the marriage was the result of an extended courtship.

He explained about the rhythm of eight beats and how she should pause a little on every third and seventh beat, while simultaneously considering the novel idea of being romantically attentive to a woman. He hadn't tried to court a woman with sweet words and gestures for years. Not since Vivien had consigned him to the ranks of her discarded lovers. And once he'd returned to England and taken possession of his inheritance, he hadn't needed to flatter women into his embrace. So here he was at twenty-six, well able to entertain the Court with witty sonnets, but completely unpractised in turning the kind of pretty phrase suitable for pleasing his wife in front of his household.

'Like this?' she said, looking to him for guidance.

'Good. Ah…*very* good. You have a naturally graceful carriage,' he said, and was rewarded by her blush of pleasure. Or perhaps she was just warm from the exertion?

'You're doing very well. Perhaps we should try a saraband,' he said.

'Whatever you think best,' said Temperance.

Her composure aggravated him. She'd twisted up his emotions and provoked him at every opportunity, yet she was the one gliding serenely through the dancing lesson. He wasn't surprised she had a natural talent for dancing. He'd seen her move with speed and agility when Tredgold attacked her the night they'd first met, and he'd felt her capacity for sensuous grace on a much more intimate level. With every elegant turn of her hands he was reminded of how entrancingly she'd touched him with those same hands.

Diable! His socially inexperienced wife was seducing him in her dancing lesson. He should be the one seducing her! He was piqued by the silent challenge she offered. The next occasion the dance required her to circle around him he caught her waist and pulled her close for a quick kiss, then released her just in time for the next movement. Her sudden blush and the flustered glance she threw at him sent a surge of triumph through him.

Temperance's first dancing lesson hadn't turned out the way she'd expected. She'd assumed she and Jack would be alone, but she'd felt foolish when she'd seen Hinchcliff with his cittern. Of course there had to be at least one other person present to provide the music. Her initial nervousness at learning in front of an audience had quickly vanished. She was so entertained by the music and watching the others, she didn't at all mind the delay before it was her turn.

Then Jack held out his hand to her and suddenly it wasn't the lively cittern music that quickened her pulse. She tried to concentrate on the steps he taught her. She'd paid close attention to the Duchess and now she tried to replicate Eleanor's movements. She was congratulating herself on how well she'd remembered when, without any warning, Jack kissed her. She was so startled she didn't know what to do. But he kept dancing so, after a couple of faltering steps, she did as well. She glanced at the others. She didn't think it was a regular part of the dance. Dr Nichols wasn't snatching kisses from the Dowager Duchess at every opportunity. It was just Jack, acting more like the impudent rogue she'd first met in the tavern than he had at any time since he'd returned to Kilverdale Hall.

She was delighted and embarrassed in almost equal measure. No one had ever courted her before Jack, or even flirted with her. She held her head up and tried to focus on the dance steps, pretending, despite her fiery face, that she didn't notice each time he brushed his lips over her fingers or her cheek—or even her mouth.

What did it mean? Was it a sign he was developing tender feelings for her? Or was he taking a lover's revenge on her supposed slights to his virility? A man of his experience would be well versed in the art of keeping his lover in a state of excited uncertainty. Temperance loved Jack, but she was determined not to let him reduce her to flustered confusion with a few kisses. Sometimes she couldn't help blushing and self-consciously lowering her gaze, but for the most part she pretended to ignore his seductively distracting behaviour. After a while she realised the more she tried to appear indifferent to Jack, the more he tried to provoke her into responding. It became an intoxicating game between them.

Then the movement of the dance brought Toby directly into Temperance's line of vision. He was scowling at her—and this time his frown didn't indicate deep concentration. The hostility in the dark eyes that were so like Jack's shocked away her giddy pleasure. She moved stiffly through the next few steps, hardly aware of Jack's continued flirting, as she tried to decide what to do. She was sure Jack hadn't meant to make his son jealous. In a distant corner of her mind it occurred to her that perhaps he'd never conducted an affair in circumstances where Toby could be a witness, or he would have learned to be more discreet.

Until now her relationship with Toby had been a mixture of slightly odd formality and the curtsying and bowing ritual they'd developed at their first meeting. She'd been living at Kilverdale Hall for less than two weeks and, for more than half that time, Jack had been absent. Before his arrival, she'd had several conversations with Toby about her shop. As befitted a Duke's son, Toby was accustomed to tradesmen coming to the house, but he'd visited shops in the local village and occasionally gone to Chichester with the Dowager Duchess. He'd never been to London and he responded to Temperance's descriptions of it with a combination of amazed disbelief and an unflagging conviction Kilverdale Hall must inevitably be *better* than anywhere else in the country—or even the world.

But he'd enjoyed hearing about his father's dramatic rescue of Agnes Cruikshank and made Temperance repeat the story several times. He'd been more ambivalent over Jack's search for the lost child. He clearly thought Jack should have been with him, not searching for someone else's little girl, but Temperance had made sure to emphasise Jack's most important contribution had been to take charge of everyone else. It was Isaac who'd actually found Katie Carpenter.

Temperance had liked Toby from the beginning. He was direct in his responses and, unlike the rest of the household, he never tried to conceal his opinion. If he was annoyed with her for forgetting to curtsy, he frowned until she remedied the omission; but when he laughed she knew he was genuinely amused. Before Jack's return she'd been wary of spending too much time with his son, in case it appeared she was trying to ingratiate herself with Toby as a way of mitigating Jack's anger. She realised now that, without intending to, she'd spoken less to Toby since Jack had decided she was to be his Duchess than she had before. She'd felt overwhelmed by all she needed to learn.

Jack's marriage had made less impact on his son's daily life than it would have done in a smaller household. Now Jack was home he spent a couple of hours with Toby every morning, and saw him at other times during the day, but otherwise Toby's routine had continued unaltered. Dr Nichols supervised most of his activities. The Dowager Duchess was the most important woman in his life, and servants performed the basic tasks that would have fallen to a female relative in a humbler family. Until the dancing lesson, as far as Toby was concerned, Isaac had probably been a more significant addition to the household than Temperance.

But Jack's flirting had changed that. For perhaps the first time in Toby's life, he was faced with a rival for his father's affection. The last thing Temperance wanted to do was incite Toby's jealousy. For everyone's sake, she had to bring the flirtatious game to an immediate halt.

'I think it is time we changed partners,' she said, stepping away from Jack. 'May I dance with you?' She smiled at Toby, trying to conceal how anxiously she awaited his response. From the corner of her eye she was aware of Jack's startled expression as he glanced between her and Toby. She hoped he would understand her intention.

'No,' Toby said flatly.

Temperance kept the smile fixed to her face, even though her cheeks began to ache. She was afraid she'd made the situation worse, but not sure what to do next. To her relief, Jack came to her rescue.

'I have some new steps to teach you,' he said to Toby. 'You need to dance with Tempest because this dance only works with a real lady—one wearing skirts. Isaac, you must dance with the Dowager Duchess now.'

Temperance immediately rustled her new silk skirts and sank into her best curtsy. She couldn't imagine anything else she could do with her skirts that Isaac couldn't do with his breeches.

Eleanor smiled and, accepting her cue, curtsied to Isaac. He stammered and blushed and responded with a jerky bow.

The new dance Jack taught them involved so much bowing, curtsying and confusing changes of directions they all ended up breathless with laughter at their mistakes. Now Toby was once again the centre of his father's attention he seemed to forget his earlier jealousy—but the memory of his hostile gaze cast a shadow over Temperance's enjoyment of the afternoon.

The next morning was overcast and damp. After one look out of the window, Temperance chose to walk in the long gallery rather than the garden. She was still worrying about Toby's jealousy. Jack was marrying her for practical reasons, whereas she had no doubt of his deep love for his son. She didn't want her marriage to Jack to hurt Toby; nor did she want to find herself in competition with him for Jack's affection. She wasn't afraid Jack would discard her if Toby started to hate her—marriage could not be so easily set aside, especially when there was the succession to consider—but his attitude to her might change. He could easily decide to leave her at Kilverdale Hall while he took Toby away with him.

She reached the main staircase and started down, so deep in thought she was startled by the sudden clatter of heels on the hall floor. She looked over the banister to see Hinchcliff striding towards the front door, flanked by liveried footmen.

She paused halfway down the stairs, unnoticed by anyone, as

the footmen flung open the door, and a gentleman stepped over the threshold. She couldn't see his face beneath the brim of his hat, but the curls of a light brown periwig fell about his shoulders and his velvet coat and lace were as grand as Jack's.

The well-dressed man must be a guest for the wedding celebrations. The first one to arrive. A nobleman who was well known to Hinchcliff, since the steward was bowing and welcoming, 'Your Lordship'.

Temperance stared at the stranger, transfixed by a moment of pure dread. After a few seconds she remembered to breathe, but her heart was beating so fast and loudly she could hardly hear what Hinchcliff was saying to the visitor.

He would be the first member of grand society Temperance ever spoke to as Jack's Duchess. The first one she had to convince she was Jack's true wife. Would he take one look at her and curl his lip at her lowly origins? Would he, like the silk mercer, Tolworth, know before she said a word that she belonged in Cheapside? She'd always thought Jack would be beside her when this moment arrived. But here she was, exposed on the staircase, with nowhere to hide. She gathered her courage, reminded herself she was now a Duchess, and descended the last few stairs. The visitor turned in her direction.

She faltered, momentarily forgetting everything else in surprise at what she saw. The man standing before her was fair, blue-eyed and old—but in all other respects he was almost the exact image of Jack. He had the same hawkish nose, deep-set eyes and angular cheekbones. He was the same height as Jack, his shoulders were just as broad, and he was still straight-backed, though he must be in his seventies.

Temperance's first, confused, thought was that this was what Jack would look like in fifty years' time. Except he would have fierce brown eyes instead of piercing blue ones. As she stared at Jack's grandfather she saw a flicker of sardonic comprehension appear in his cool blue gaze.

'I see you recognise me,' he said. 'I regret I cannot return the compliment.'

Chapter Fourteen

'Your Grace, may I introduce Lord Swiftbourne,' said Hinch-cliff, earning Temperance's gratitude.

'Your lordship—' the steward turned to Swiftbourne '—may I present her Grace, the Duchess of Kilverdale,' he said with a flourish.

Swiftbourne acknowledged the introduction with a slight inclination of his head. Still stunned by his resemblance to Jack, and overwhelmed by his regal manner, Temperance curtsied, just as she would have done if she'd been back in Cheapside.

No, no! I am a Duchess. I am a Duchess, she repeated silently in her mind as she rose from the curtsy. *I must speak and act like a Duchess.*

'I am pleased to meet you, my lord,' she said, holding out her hand to him. For once she was glad of her height, which meant she could look Jack's daunting grandfather almost straight in the eye. 'I hope your journey was comfortable.'

His eyes narrowed, startling her again. She had seen Jack do the same thing many times, though he had never looked at her in such a coldly assessing way. She lifted her chin, determined not to let Lord Swiftbourne intimidate her. He continued to scrutinise her for several unnerving seconds, and then one side of his mouth twitched in something that could have been the beginnings of a smile, but the expression was so fleeting she thought she must have been mistaken.

'Unexceptional,' he said. 'Fortunately it's not raining. Sussex roads become an impassable quagmire in wet weather.'

Even though she'd come to Sussex for the first time two weeks ago, Temperance bridled at his criticism of her newly adopted county.

'I think it is a particularly beautiful part of England,' she said, withdrawing her hand and grandly ignoring the fact it was the only part of England outside London she'd ever seen. 'The landscape is very graceful and varied. And there are deer in the park.' Since her arrival she'd come to enjoy catching glimpses of the deer from the windows of the house.

Swiftbourne raised an eyebrow, reminding Temperance of Eleanor as well as Jack.

'You like venison?' he said.

She frowned. That was *not* what she'd meant. 'I like to look at the deer—not eat them,' she said. 'They are elegant creatures.'

This time Swiftbourne lifted both eyebrows. She thought perhaps he was genuinely surprised by her comment. As one of the King's ministers, he probably expected people of lesser significance to agree with everything he said.

She was aware of Hinchcliff hovering nearby and hoped he wasn't finding fault with her behaviour. Then she realised that, if she'd still been living in Cheapside, she would immediately have offered an honoured visitor refreshments.

Flustered by her failure as a hostess, she opened her mouth to remedy the situation. Before she could say anything she heard Jack calling her, then his footsteps on the first flight of stairs. A moment later he turned the corner and started down the second flight, taking the steps two at a time.

'Tempest! Oh, you're there. Do you want—'

He saw Swiftbourne and his voice cut off. He didn't stumble, he was too sure-footed, but he visibly checked and the colour drained from his face. After a second, he recovered himself and descended the rest of the stairs one at a time. His expression when he looked at his grandfather was closed, and arrogantly unwelcoming.

'Good morning,' said Swiftbourne. 'I have come to witness the renewal of your marriage vows and the blessing. I believe the event is to take place in two days' time?'

'I did not invite you,' Jack said flatly.

'No,' said Swiftbourne. 'Your mother did. You will not slight her, I trust.'

Jack didn't say another word. He cast Temperance a brief, inscrutable look, then turned on his heel and strode away. She was left standing beside Swiftbourne, unsure whether Jack expected her to follow him, or stay and make his grandfather welcome. She glanced at Hinchcliff, but his impassive expression offered no guidance. Lord Swiftbourne arched his eyebrow sardonically as he looked after Jack. Temperance had the impression he'd received the welcome from his grandson he'd expected.

Jack's mother had invited Lord Swiftbourne. Temperance's chaotic thoughts fastened on that one, simple fact.

'The Duchess is in her parlour,' she said. Presumably Eleanor wanted to see Lord Swiftbourne or she wouldn't have invited him. 'I am sure she is eager to see you. May I escort you to her?'

'Most gracious.' Swiftbourne inclined his head. 'Thank you.'

'And perhaps you would like something to eat or drink after your journey?' Temperance suggested. 'We will be having dinner in an hour or so. But if you are hungry now, Hinchcliff will make sure you are served as soon as may be.'

The steward immediately bowed. 'At once, your Grace.'

'Very hospitable,' said Swiftbourne. 'My needs are simple. Send up a tankard of small ale and, if you have such a thing…' he glanced at Temperance '…a venison pasty.'

She maintained her composed expression in the face of his provocative comment. She was not disposed to like Swiftbourne, but it occurred to her that Jack and his grandfather had more than their appearance in common, though Jack's teasing humour was less caustic.

'What is your name?' Swiftbourne asked.

'Temperance,' she said, noticing he wasn't in the slightest bit winded from walking up the stairs. She sensed he was a man who took care to preserve his dignity, but an aura of energy surrounded him. Despite her other reservations about him, Swiftbourne's vigour pleased her. She liked to think Jack would be as strong in his old age.

'Temperance?' he repeated.

'My name was Temperance Challinor,' she said, assuming he was querying her pedigree. 'Of Cheapside.' She lifted her chin proudly. She wasn't going to pretend to be something she wasn't. 'Now it is Temperance, Duchess of Kilverdale.'

'Indeed,' Swiftbourne murmured. 'I understand your first, private marriage ceremony took place after a lengthy courtship?'

'Yes.' Temperance hesitated. She was reluctant to be drawn into a discussion of the supposed lengthy courtship, but she didn't want to appear ungracious. 'I was—I am—honoured to be Kilverdale's wife,' she said.

Swiftbourne's expression remained inscrutable. 'I thought I heard your husband call you Tempest? Did I mishear? Age takes its toll.'

It would have been rude to challenge his last statement directly, but Temperance let a sceptical glance reveal what she was thinking—that there was nothing wrong with Lord Swiftbourne's hearing.

'He did call me Tempest,' she agreed. 'He often does.'

'I wonder why?' Swiftbourne mused.

'I've never asked him,' she replied.

'No? To me the name suggests a stormy, perhaps even fiery, temperament,' said Swiftbourne. 'What do you think?'

'I think her Grace will be delighted to see you, my lord,' said Temperance, coming to a halt outside the door to Eleanor's parlour.

Temperance didn't know where to look for Jack. He'd gone through the ground-floor hall towards the back of the house, but there were other stairs and he could have gone anywhere. She hesitated, biting her lip. She could go through the whole house, opening doors at random, but Jack was a man, not a lost child. She couldn't search for him like a panic-stricken mother.

She wished she knew why he'd walked away from his grandfather. She wished someone had warned her he *might*.

She went to her own rooms to compose herself before dinner. She was sure Jack would be present for the formal meal. After all, he'd dined with her the very first day and her presence at Kilverdale Hall was far more shocking than his grandfather's. She wondered how he would behave—and how he wanted her to behave.

She walked into her private parlour and pushed open the door to her bedchamber. She took a couple of steps into the room and stopped short in surprise.

Jack was standing by the window with his back towards her. He was wearing a rich blue brocade coat and lace, but he'd discarded his periwig. The contrast between the grandeur of his garments and the curious vulnerability of his closely shorn head struck Temperance forcibly. She'd never before thought of Jack as vulnerable.

She saw from the slight lift of his head and a subtle tension in his posture that he was aware of her presence, but he didn't turn towards her. She hesitated, unsure what to say.

'I took your…I took Lord Swiftbourne to see the Duchess,' she said at last.

'You are the Duchess,' he said, his voice gritty, his eyes still fixed on the view beyond the window.

'What?' His unexpected comment threw her further off balance.

'You are now the Duchess, Tempest. My mother is the Dowager Duchess,' he said.

'Yes. Yes, I know.' Was his observation a criticism of her behaviour? She wished he'd turn and look at her. 'I took Lord Swiftbourne to see her Grace,' she repeated.

'Thank you.'

The silence stretched out again, stretching Temperance's nerves along with it.

'I didn't know what to do,' she said.

'I am sure you did excellently,' he said. He seemed as remote from her as the blue hills on the horizon.

Her anxiety and confusion boiled over into anger.

'Don't look out of the window! Look at me!' She marched over to him. She was about to grab his arm and pull him round to face her, when he turned towards her.

'You are nothing if not direct,' he said. 'And looking at you is always a pleasure.' He took her still-outstretched hand and lifted it to his lips.

She gazed at him, too concerned by the bleakness in his expression to respond to flattery.

'What's wrong?' she asked.

'Nothing. I am famous for my volatile moods. That is a very pretty gown. I'll give you some pearls to wear with it. You will enhance their beauty most delightfully.'

'I don't want pearls. I want you to tell me what's wrong.'

One side of his mouth lifted. 'Not easily deflected, are you? Many women would prefer pearls to a few unimportant words.'

'Don't judge me by others.' She stared at him, trying to see what he was attempting to hide from her.

He touched her eyebrow, tracing lightly outwards to brush his finger tips over her temple.

'Close your eyes,' he said softly.

'What?'

'You have very…piercing…eyes,' he said.

'I…' She wanted to say he'd got it wrong, he was the one with piercing eyes, but when his fingers moved lightly over her eyelids she obeyed his silent command. Her pulse quickened. She was intensely aware of how close they were standing. The lace at his wrist brushed against her cheek and neck. He put his hands on her shoulders and rested his forehead against hers. The gesture seemed to close out the rest of the world and bind them together. Temperance knew it was an illusion, born only of whatever disturbing emotion Jack felt at his grandfather's arrival, but her heart swelled with love and concern. She put her arms around him. He stiffened, and she wondered if she'd been overbold in her need to comfort him. He hadn't admitted there was anything wrong.

He moved his hands to her waist and bent his head to kiss her cheek and then her neck. The caress of his lips against her skin was as delightful as ever, but she sensed his lovemaking was another attempt to divert her attention. When his mouth found hers she pulled her head back and placed her fingers firmly over his lips.

His eyes narrowed with annoyance.

'Don't,' she said. 'I will kiss you all night if you wish, but now you must tell me why you walked away from Lord Swiftbourne.'

'I must?' He arched a eyebrow.

'Yes, you must,' she said. 'For you have promised to help me be your Duchess—and how will I manage if I don't know how you wish me to behave with Lord Swiftbourne?'

'You may behave any way you choose.'

She just looked at him until at last he sighed and moved away from her. 'It is…hmm…untidy. No. Like a drawer that will not close properly and annoys you every time you see it.'

He thumped the window frame with his clenched fist.

Temperance caught her breath at his unexpected action and waited a few seconds for her heart to settle into a calmer rhythm.

'Your grandfather is like a sticky drawer you can't close?' she said.

He shot her a glance full of intense annoyance and a fair degree of hostility. 'Of course not!'

'Umm…' She decided not to point out she'd repeated his own words. 'Why didn't you invite him to the wedding celebrations?'

'I knew Mama would.'

'In a minute I am going to shake you,' Temperance said calmly. 'Then I am going to lock you up in your room and give orders you are not to be released or fed until you give me an answer I can understand.'

Jack looked at her for a few seconds, then she saw the first genuine relaxation of tension in his expression since she'd found him by the window.

'As long as you lock yourself in with me,' he said. 'You may shake me to your heart's content.' He drew in a deep breath and glanced towards the window, but this time Temperance sensed he was gathering his thoughts, rather than avoiding answering.

'My father was for the King,' he said.

'I know,' she said. 'I know he was killed after the Battle of Worcester by the Roundheads.'

Jack looked at her and she bit her lip.

'That's what you're going to tell me, isn't it?' she asked. 'I already knew your family was royalist—'

'Not Swiftbourne. He threw in his lot with the Parliamentarians from the first.'

The revelation stunned Temperance. Jack's father had been executed by Parliamentarians. Jack's grandfather had been a Parliamentarian. Many families had been split by conflicting allegiance to Crown or Parliament, but she'd never expected to find herself in the middle of such a feud six years after the restoration of the King.

'That's why you hate your grandfather—because he fought for Parliament?' For a horrible minute she wondered if Jack's father and his grandfather had met on the battlefield. But if that was the case, surely the Dowager Duchess would have been as reluctant to see Swiftbourne as Jack?

'He didn't fight,' said Jack. 'He was Cromwell's ambassador to Sweden and France. I don't hate him,' he added.

'You don't hate him?' she echoed. 'Then why turn your back on him?'

'I...despise...him,' said Jack, his hesitation making her doubt that was the full answer.

'Why?' Swiftbourne was one of the King's ministers. He was a successful, powerful man. Hating such a man seemed to make more sense than despising him.

'I despise him for being self-serving at the expense of loyalty, principles...everything a decent man should hold dear,' said Jack.

'You despise him for changing sides twice?' said Temperance. 'Because he served the King before the war, then sided with Parliament, before finally supporting the new King's return?'

'Yes,' Jack said more firmly.

Temperance thought about it. She understood his reservations, but she could not help noticing an inconsistency between his attitude to Swiftbourne and his attitude to her.

'Jack.' She put her hand on his arm. 'You married me because you believe I will do whatever it takes to keep myself and our children safe—including lie. You chose me because of my willingness to sacrifice certain principles—'

'To protect those who are weak,' he said, his voice hardly above a whisper. 'Not to advance your own position, regardless of what may happen to others.'

She slipped her arms around his waist and hugged him. After a few seconds she felt his arms close about her and he laid his cheek against hers.

Her heart ached for him, yet his willingness to turn to her for comfort filled her with tenderness towards him. She rubbed her hands up and down his back, wondering if he would tell her the rest of what he was thinking. Nothing he'd said accounted for his reaction when he'd first caught sight of Swiftbourne. She felt his chest expand on a ragged breath, and then he put his hands on her upper arms and set her apart from him.

She felt the chill of separation, but didn't protest. As she watched, he stroked his hand over his head, then let it fall to his side.

'Father was hanged after the Battle of Worcester,' he said. 'In September. But we didn't find out until December. Swiftbourne— he was still Viscount Balston then—came to us in France. He stood in front of me, cold as ice, and announced his allies had murdered my father.'

Temperance could hear in Jack's voice all the raw anger and pain of the eleven-year-old boy he had been.

'He told you?' she said after a moment. 'What about your mother?'

'He'd already told her. I came into the room to find her crying. I had never...' Jack swallowed. 'Never seen her in such great distress. I demanded to know what he'd done to her. Then he told me. I was angry. I told him he was lying.'

Temperance could imagine the scene. Receiving such horrific news must have been devastating for Jack and his mother. But she also wondered about Swiftbourne, who'd taken upon himself the task of telling his daughter and grandson, not only that their husband and father was dead, but that he'd been executed by Swift- bourne's own allies. Despite his caustic manner, she could not believe Jack's grandfather would have taken pleasure in the chore. If he'd been indifferent to Jack and Eleanor's suffering, wouldn't he have left it to others to give them the news?

'Sometimes when I see him unexpectedly,' said Jack, 'it is as if I am back in that room in Paris. I cannot explain it.' He shook his head. 'It doesn't make sense. I am twenty-six, not eleven. Most days I hardly give the matter any thought. Then all at once he is in front of me and I am eleven again. It is intolerable. I despise *myself*!'

'Do you feel like that every time you see him?' she asked.

'No. When I went to his house during the fire, all I could think of was finding Jakob. I didn't think of Father at all. But today on the stairs—' Jack stopped talking, his unhappiness and frustration with himself obvious. After a moment he sighed. 'It will be dinner soon,' he said. 'There is no need for you to fret over me. I will not embarrass you in public.'

'Jack—' she broke off, uncertain what to say. She'd always been afraid she might embarrass him.

'Once I know I am going to see him I am well able to control my reactions,' Jack said. 'We are cold, but perfectly polite to each other. You'll see there will be no problem.'

Dinner was late because Jakob and Lady Desire, and Athena and her husband, Lord Halross, arrived together, just before it could be served.

Jack was furious with himself for the weakness he'd revealed to Temperance. He had never told anyone else about the strange fluctuations that sometimes occurred in his memory when he saw Swiftbourne unexpectedly. He wished he hadn't told Temperance—yet something had drawn him to take refuge in her room. He was honest enough to admit to himself it would have been easy to avoid her if he'd tried.

He didn't want to eat with his grandfather and, even though he was devoted to both his cousins, he would have preferred to dispense with their politely concealed curiosity over his sudden marriage. He was still ill at ease in Lady Desire's company, and she seemed equally uncomfortable at being a guest under his roof again. All in all, it was not his idea of a convivial dinner party.

Under any other circumstances he would have taken refuge behind cold courtesy—but Temperance needed more than that from him. She was scared. He knew by the way her hand had quivered as he escorted her to her chair, though nothing else about her demeanour revealed her anxiety.

Jack's own gaze was drawn time and again to Swiftbourne. He didn't understand his grandfather and what he knew of him, he despised—yet Swiftbourne fascinated him on a level he couldn't comprehend. What had driven Swiftbourne through all the years to bring him to this point in his life—one of the most influential men of the time? Swiftbourne's career had started in 1613 at the time of the marriage of James I's daughter, Princess Elizabeth. Swiftbourne had been part of the Princess's retinue when she'd accompanied her new husband to his home in Heidelberg. A year later, at the age of twenty-two, before he'd inherited his father's viscountcy, Swiftbourne had been elected a Member of Parliament; and in the half century since he had nearly always held some form of public office. He had survived and risen through the reigns of James, Charles I, and the Parliamentarian interlude until now he was a minister for Charles II. He had elevated himself from a Viscount to an Earl and acquired substantial wealth in the process. What depth of ruthlessness did such relentlessly successful survival require? How many people had Swiftbourne abandoned in his wake—and did he even know or care what had become of them?

Jack glanced again at Swiftbourne and found himself under observation by those coldly ironic blue eyes. He held his grandfather's gaze for a few seconds, then deliberately looked away to ask Athena a question.

Since Jakob and Lord Halross claimed their wives were still tired from the journey, the party split up after the meal. Jack suspected the two sets of newly wedded guests were motivated more by a wish to be alone than by weariness, but he accepted their excuses without comment. Unlike Athena and Lady Desire, Temperance really did look tired, and he wanted her to rest as much as possible during the demanding days ahead.

'Good evening,' said Lord Swiftbourne.

'My lord.' Jack inclined his head.

Swiftbourne's smile was as cold as Jack's acknowledgement. 'Shall we continue?' he asked, his gesture indicating the length of the long gallery. 'The season hardly invites a promenade outside.'

'By all means.' Jack fell into step beside his grandfather. It was late evening. The candles had been lit and the large windows had become impenetrable black rectangles.

'You have a rare talent for inciting gossip,' Swiftbourne observed after they'd taken a few silent paces.

Jack tensed, all too well aware of that. 'I have no interest in the world's opinion,' he said. He needed society to accept the truth of his marriage, but he wouldn't achieve that goal by revealing anxiety on the matter.

'Particularly mine,' said Swiftbourne. They reached the end of the gallery and turned.

Jack noticed, almost against his will, that their strides were the same length. He could not remember the last time he'd walked side by side with Swiftbourne—or even if he ever had. 'Anyone's,' he said.

'The whole of London is breathlessly waiting to meet your new bride,' Swiftbourne said.

'They'll have to go on waiting,' said Jack. 'We have no plans to visit London in the near future.' He wasn't surprised news of his marriage had already reached the capital. He'd only invited a few close members of his family to attend the wedding celebrations, but they were all such notable figures their departure for Sussex would have attracted attention. 'I'm not going to organise my life to please the gossips,' he said.

'Indeed not,' Swiftbourne said. 'You may be interested to learn Lady Lacy has recently returned to England.'

'*Vivien?*' Jack's stride checked slightly, before he once more matched his grandfather's pace. 'I thought she was living in Naples under Carthaven's protection.'

'He inconveniently died. I imagine she is now looking for a new patron.'

'Her actions are of no interest to me,' Jack said curtly. 'I have not laid eyes on her for nearly six years. Nor do I wish to.'

'I did not suppose you did,' Swiftbourne said coolly.

Jack relaxed slightly. 'You'd best beware. She favours rich old men.'

'She is not to my taste,' Swiftbourne said, so imperturbably Jack suddenly found himself curious about his grandfather's private life. Did Swiftbourne have a mistress? Even at seventy-four he was far more vigorous than the unfortunately deceased Carthaven had ever been.

'Windle could be more of a nuisance to you than Vivien,' said Swiftbourne. 'Your marriage thwarted his plans for his daughter.'

'Windle?' Jack frowned. 'I would not even enter into negotiations with him. He has no grounds for complaint.'

'I did not say he has,' Swiftbourne replied. 'Only that you have made an enemy. He was already deeply in debt, and his losses in the fire have brought him to the verge of ruin. A few days before I left London he was ranting about a case he'd just lost in the Fire Court. A portion of the Kilverdale fortune would have been a nice bulwark against bankruptcy.'

Jack shrugged. 'By the time I return to London he'll have found another potential bridegroom to bully,' he said. 'I feel sorry for his daughter.'

A smile flickered on Swiftbourne's lips so quickly Jack wondered if he'd imagined it. 'I am relieved you did not take it upon yourself to rescue her,' said Swiftbourne. 'Windle would not be a welcome addition to our family.'

They walked a little further as the wind rattled against the window panes. Jack was determined *not* to ask if his grandfather considered Temperance a welcome addition to the family. In any case, as Duke of Kilverdale, he was the head of his own family.

'With luck the wind will blow the clouds away and you'll have clear weather for the wedding,' said Swiftbourne.

'It will also make your journey back to London more comfortable,' said Jack stiffly. *Diable!* He would *not* ask about Swiftbourne's opinion about his marriage.

'Have you ever considered that you dislike me so much because you are more like me than you wish to admit?' said Swiftbourne.

'What?' Jack slammed to a halt.

'Your father was an idealist,' said Swiftbourne. 'He was also a fool. You…' he arched an ironically amused eyebrow at Jack '…learn from your mistakes.'

He turned on his heel and left Jack staring after him in outrage—and some confusion.

To what mistakes, exactly, was his grandfather alluding? The mess Jack had made over his first unwanted betrothal to Lady Desire? He'd made considerable efforts to avoid similar misunderstandings in his interchanges with Lord Windle. If that was the case, he could live with the implied approval behind Swiftbourne's words—but he was damned if he was like the old man. That was an insult of the first water.

It was mid-morning the day after the guests' arrival when Temperance stepped out of her parlour and nearly walked into Lady Desire.

'Oh, pardon me!' she exclaimed.

'It was my fault,' Lady Desire said quickly. 'I wasn't looking where I was going.'

'Nor was I,' Temperance confessed, wondering what to say next to her noble guest.

She'd been aware of Jakob's many polite attempts to draw her into private conversation the previous day. He had signed the false marriage documents, which meant that, unlike everyone else, he knew she hadn't married Jack in London. She was sure he was suspicious of her. Had he shared his doubts with his wife? She could tell Lady Desire wasn't comfortable at Kilverdale Hall, but she wasn't sure whether that was because her ladyship was still uneasy in Jack's company, or because she disapproved of his low-born bride.

'I'm glad you and Colonel Balston are attending the ceremony tomorrow,' Temperance said. 'Jack—Kilverdale, I mean,' she corrected herself, 'is very attached to Colonel Balston.'

Lady Desire nodded politely.

Temperance decided to tackle head-on one of the possible causes of the other woman's discomfort.

'I hope you are not finding it too awkward to return here,' she said. 'Jack's company manners can be a little stiff at times, but he is truly pleased you've come.'

Lady Desire looked startled, then flushed uncomfortably.

'You know what happened?' she said. 'I didn't expect him to say anything. Never mind—'

'He didn't,' Temperance said quickly. 'That is, I know he said something disrespectful and you left. And I know he is sorry. But that's all. Nothing else. Not...not what he said, or...well, nothing else.'

Lady Desire looked at Temperance, then let her gaze drift around the long gallery.

'It is partly that,' she admitted. 'But his Grace offered me a handsome apology when we saw him in Kingston. And he told me he'd followed me back to London almost immediately after...what happened here all those years ago. He wanted to apologise to me then, but Arscott told him my father had given orders for him to be horse-whipped if he tried to speak to me.'

Temperance gasped and Lady Desire smiled sadly. 'It wasn't true,' she said. 'Arscott was laying the foundations of his future villainy. No...you'll probably think it very odd of me...but if I seem distracted it is because this house reminds me so powerfully of my father. Ever since we arrived, I keep expecting to see him.'

'Your father?' Temperance was bewildered. 'Why?'

'We visited here together,' Lady Desire explained as they began to stroll along the gallery. 'He died several years ago, and I've grown used to his absence at home. I never expect to see him there. But the last time I was here—walking along this gallery—he was walking beside me. So I somehow feel he ought to be here now. But I don't suppose it will take me long to adjust,' she added brightly.

They reached the L-shaped end of the gallery. The billiard table was set back from the main part of the gallery in the short side of the *L*. A huge window rose behind it, revealing a glorious view of the park beyond. Temperance was leading the way to the window when she realised she was alone. She turned to discover Lady Desire had stopped dead and was staring in obvious distress at the billiard table. Too late, Temperance remembered this was where Lady Desire had overheard Jack's unkind comment about her, and her father had tried to force a duel on him. Before Temperance could say anything, Desire gathered herself. She smiled at Temperance and continued walking as if nothing was amiss.

Temperance made an instant decision. Lady Desire did not seem ill disposed towards her, and Jack wanted her to be friends with his cousin's wife. Perhaps it was time to create new memories in the long gallery for both of them.

'Have you ever played billiards?' she asked.

'No.' Desire looked surprised, then intrigued by the question.

'Nor have I. Why don't we try?' Temperance picked up two of the oddly shaped sticks, and handed one to Desire. She examined her own stick curiously. It was long and thin, with a curved block of wood at one end.

'Have you any idea what we're supposed to do with it?' she asked.

'I think you hit the ball with this head bit,' said Desire, demonstrating in mid-air. 'From what I can remember, they were standing at the table with the head on the table surface and the stick rising over their shoulders. But they might have been doing it wrong, of course. They didn't get much else right,' she said tartly.

'Hmm.' Temperance turned her attention to the table. 'Two balls and a hoop. I suppose we're meant to make the balls go through the hoop.' She set one of the balls down on the cloth and gave it a tentative shove with the head of the stick. 'It's a bit awkward,' she said.

Desire had a go too. Her ball went slightly further.

'Men have very peculiar ideas of entertainment,' she observed. 'Perhaps they just like aiming at small holes—wherever they find them.'

Temperance blinked, then gave a choke of startled laughter at Desire's straight-faced comment. 'You could be right,' she said, when she could speak. She squared up to the table, squinted along the stick, and gave her ball a good clout. It cannoned across the table, missing the hoop by a bare inch, and rebounded off the far edge of the table with a loud bang.

Both women jumped in surprise, looked at each other, and laughed.

'I think I hit it too hard,' Temperance said ruefully.

Desire tucked the lace trimming on her sleeves out of her way and lined up behind her ball. 'My turn,' she said.

Chapter Fifteen

'I've got it!' Temperance began to crawl out from under the billiard table. 'Ow!'

'Did you hurt yourself?' Desire crouched down worriedly.

'No. I just bumped my head on the stupid table leg. It doesn't hurt.' Temperance sat on the floor, her ball in hand, and laughed until her ribs ached.

Desire plopped down on the floorboards and laughed too. 'Your face…your face was so funny when the ball jumped off the table,' she gasped.

'It doesn't run true!' Temperance said indignantly. She held up the billiard ball. 'Look—there's a definite lump on this side.'

Desire leant forward and squinted at it. 'You're right,' she said. 'Who'd have thought the Duke of Kilverdale would have unsatisfactory balls…on his billiard table. Oh, I'm sorry.' She slapped her hands over her mouth and gazed at Temperance over the top, an odd mixture of contrition and amusement in her eyes.

'They're perfectly satisfactory elsewhere,' said Temperance, shocking herself. She put her hand over her mouth as well and both women rocked back and forth in slightly drunken hilarity, even though neither of them had taken a sip of intoxicating liquor.

It was the first time in years Temperance had had so much fun. After the tension of the past few weeks, the release of laughter was so overwhelming she felt as light-headed as if she really was drunk. She thought maybe Desire felt the same way.

She heard footsteps and glanced over her shoulder to discover Jack and Jakob approaching them. She looked up at their startled expressions and exchanged a glance with Desire. Then both women went into another gale of laughter.

'*Min älskade,* what are you doing?' Jakob asked.

'We're playing…playing…billiards,' Desire gasped through bursts of laughter.

'You play billiards on top of the table, not under it,' Jakob said, grinning as he dropped on to his heels beside her.

'My ball jumped off.' Temperance held it up to illustrate her point. She leant backwards in an attempt to see Jack's face, and nearly overbalanced. 'Oh.' She put out a hand to catch herself and laughed again as she caught sight of his nonplussed expression. 'It must have happened to you too,' she said. 'When playing b-billiards, I mean.'

'Not often,' he said gravely.

Her amusement dissolved. She wasn't behaving the way a Duchess should. Feeling flustered and overheated, she put a hand down to push herself up, but Jack bent and lifted her to her feet. She couldn't help tensing, afraid of his disapproval. To her surprise he pulled her closer.

'I like to see you laugh,' he murmured against her cheek. 'Even if it is at the expense of my…billiard…balls.'

His unexpected comment—not to mention the feel of his arms around her—sent a surge of pleasure through her. From the corner of her eye she saw Jakob kiss Desire before he helped her up. She could tell their love for each other was mutual, and she wondered wistfully if Jack would ever feel such tender affection for her.

'It's my turn now,' Desire told Jakob. 'Where's my stick? I've got the ball through the little arch lots of times already. I want to do it again before we stop.'

'Stick?' Temperance saw Jakob roll his eyes comically in Jack's direction and looked round to see her husband was responding with a similar expression of male superiority. Temperance didn't mind. She much preferred Jack's cousin to tease her than watch her with politely concealed suspicion. She hoped it was a sign he'd decided to accept her.

'What's wrong with calling it a stick?' she said. 'That's what it is.'

'It's a mace.' Jakob picked it up and eyed the table.

'Hey! Wait a minute!' Desire said indignantly. 'It's my turn to play—not yours!'

'I was just going to show you how it's done.'

'We don't want to know how you do it,' said Desire. 'We were doing very well on our own, weren't we, your Grace?' she appealed to Temperance.

'Yes, we were,' said Temperance, thrilled at this evidence of friendship from the other woman. 'You may watch us, if you like,' she said grandly to Jack. 'And when we've finished you may have a turn.'

As soon as the words were out of her mouth, she felt a *frisson* of anxiety. Wives were not supposed to speak pertly to their husbands in public. To her relief Jack grinned and bowed, his salutation directed equally to her and to Lady Desire.

'Ladies first,' he said graciously. 'And then…' he rubbed his hands together as he looked at Jakob '…we'll show you how it's really done.'

Despite Jack's boast, there was no time before dinner for the men to show off their skills at billiards, and they didn't return to the game that afternoon. A casual comment from Jack led to Temperance discovering the south coast was only five miles from Kilverdale Hall. When she revealed she'd never seen the sea, Jack suggested they ride down to the beach that afternoon.

To Temperance's surprise everyone, including Lord Swiftbourne and the Dowager Duchess, decided to join the party. The winter afternoons were short so they finished their meal quickly and, less than an hour later, rode out of the gates in a sedate cavalcade. Toby and Isaac remained at Kilverdale Hall under the supervision of Dr Nichols. Temperance didn't suggest the boys come too. Even an expedition to the beach was a grand affair when it involved a Duke, a Marquis and an Earl. Jack was always self-assured, but Temperance knew he wasn't entirely at ease in the company of his grandfather or Lady Desire. There was no need to add another layer of complexity to the afternoon when Jack could bring Toby to the sea any time when they were out riding alone together.

The party was accompanied by a number of menservants wearing the liveries of Kilverdale, Halross and Swiftbourne. Since Temperance had never been on a horse before, she rode pillion behind Jack.

'It's so big and open!' Temperance stood on the damp sand, tendrils of hair whipping in her face as she gazed out to sea. The sky was a pearly grey, the sea a mixture of darker greys and greens. The Thames was a tidal river; the water rose and fell twice a day and waves lapped over the mudflats and river steps. But the waves on the sea were different. They rolled up on to the ridged sand from a horizon that stretched as far as she could see in both directions. Gulls walked along the tide line and flew swooping and screeching up into the sky. There was a sharp, fresh tang in the air and she breathed deep to savour it. Further inland the winter afternoon had seemed quite mild, but here on the shore a brisk breeze tugged at her skirts and produced an involuntary shiver.

'Cold?' Jack put his arms around her from behind. 'We won't linger too long.'

'I'm not cold,' she denied, but she leant back against him. It was always an exciting pleasure to be close to him, and it was even more satisfying when there was a chill in the air. His warm embrace made her feel safe and protected.

'Did London seem as…full…to you as the sea seems empty to me? I do not mean empty in an unpleasant way,' she added in case he misunderstood her. 'Only that it is so big and open and…flat.'

'It is not always flat.'

'I know. I can see how restless it is and how frightening it would be in a storm.' She looked at the currently benign surface of the sea and shivered again.

Jack drew her more snugly against him. 'Storms can be exhilarating as well as terrifying—but I confess I prefer fair weather for travelling. And the power of the sea should always be respected. As to your question…' He paused to rub his cheek against hers as they both looked towards the horizon. Temperance's pulse rate increased as his breath warmed her skin.

'Many times London seemed overfull, the houses and people crowded together. But that is more a reflection of my own taste than unfamiliarity with the city,' Jack said.

For a moment Temperance felt disorientated, until she realised he was answering her earlier question.

'I've always travelled between town and countryside,' he said. 'It's a long time since I saw a completely unfamiliar landscape for the first time.'

Temperance sighed.

'Are you tired? We must go back.'

'No, I was wishing I'd seen as many different things as you,' she said.

'You will,' he said.

They lingered longer than they'd intended on the beach and ate supper at a local inn. The landlord was delighted to serve so many noble visitors and prepared an excellent spread. By the time they set off for Kilverdale Hall it had been dark for several hours, but the moon was nearly full and the menservants held up their lanthorns to light the way home.

As they rode up to the house the front door burst open. Hinchcliff ran down the steps, followed by Dr Nichols, and several servants.

Jack's horse side-stepped at the sudden onrush. Temperance gasped and clutched at his coat. A groom went to the horse's head and Jack dismounted by swinging his right leg over the pommel. He was glad he'd remembered she was behind him, but she wasn't comfortable left sitting alone so high above the ground. She didn't protest because of the urgency in Hinchcliff's dash down the steps.

'What is it?' Jack demanded.

'Is Toby with you?' Hinchcliff's shoulders sagged as he saw the answer for himself. 'He's not in his room. We've been searching for him.'

'*Pour l'amour de Dieu!* Who saw him last? Where have you looked?'

Temperance sat forgotten on the horse as Jack rapped out a series of sharp questions. Beneath his anger she could hear fear in his voice. Anxiety knotted her stomach. They'd only been gone a few hours. It was unthinkable anything terrible could have happened to Toby in his own home. But sometimes the unthinkable happened.

'I left him drawing a picture in the nursery,' said Dr Nichols. 'The maid was about to bring his supper. When I returned a short time later he wasn't there. I thought he must have gone to see Hinchcliff…'

'I haven't seen him since this morning,' said the steward. 'We can't find him in the house. I thought he might have gone to see his pony, but he's not in the stables—'

'*Diable!* Is he *outside*?'

'I… We don't know,' said Hinchcliff.

Jack looked around the dark landscape, his expression grimmer than Temperance had ever seen it.

By now everyone else, including the other women, had dismounted, leaving only Temperance sitting aloft. All the men were rapping out questions to Hinchcliff and Dr Nichols—even the servants were distracted by the crisis. In the circumstances it didn't seem right to call attention to herself by asking for help, but it was another small reminder of the difference between her and the true ladies in the party. Eleanor, Lady Desire and Athena were all comfortable in the saddle—no doubt they'd ridden from childhood. It was another skill Temperance needed to acquire.

She was worrying about Toby and wondering how long she would be forgotten when Lord Halross came to assist her down. She was grateful for his consideration, but she was also disconcerted to find herself in such close proximity to the Marquis.

'It is cold out here,' Halross said quietly, 'You must go in—all the ladies must go in—while we search.'

Temperance straightened her spine. Halross's words reminded her of how Jack had organised the search for Nellie Carpenter' child. Now Jack was the anxious parent. She must keep a clea head and help him as he had helped her friend.

'He must be in the house somewhere,' she said, lifting her voice to make sure she was heard. 'He's far too sensible to go outside in the cold and the dark.'

'He's a child,' Jack said, his voice hard-edged with worry.

'But he's not a fool.' Temperance made a deliberate effort to speak calmly. 'He thinks before he does things. What reason could he have for going outside?'

'Have you looked in my rooms, and the Duke and Duchess's chambers?' Eleanor asked.

'Your Grace, we've looked everywhere he might be,' said Hinchcliff. 'At first it didn't seem serious. He often comes to see me or visits Warren in the stables, but…' The steward's face sagged.

Temperance locked her hands together. There were more than three hundred rooms in Kilverdale Hall. She had a dreadful vision of Toby trapped and hurt somewhere they couldn't find him.

'We'll search again,' said Jack. 'Inside the house and out. Warren, rouse everyone under your command and search the gardens and the chapel. Hinchcliff—'

'I know where he is.'

Temperance spun about to see Isaac standing on the edge of the servants crowding around Jack. Hinchcliff and Dr Nichols lashed out with angry questions, but Jack silenced them with a curt order. Temperance's former apprentice looked pale but determined as he met Jack's eyes.

'Is he safe? Is he hurt?' Jack strode towards Isaac.

'Yes, sir. No. He's safe. He's not hurt, sir…your Grace. Not injured, that is.'

Temperance's first, overwhelming emotion was one of relief—followed by confusion. If Isaac knew where Toby was, why hadn't he taken him back to the nursery?

'Where is he?' Jack demanded.

'He's hiding in one of the rooms with covered furniture.'

Hinchcliff began to speak, but Jack silenced him with an upthrown hand.

'Show me,' he ordered.

Isaac hesitated. Temperance saw him swallow. 'Just you, sir…your Grace,' he said. 'Just you come.'

'Very well. Everyone else go to the great parlour.' Jack snatched a lanthorn from one of the footmen and turned back to Isaac. 'Go!'

Isaac obeyed immediately. The rest of the household was left standing in the entrance hall, their voices rising in a clamour of relief and bewilderment. Temperance stood in frozen indecision for a few seconds. Isaac's words had filled her with foreboding. His eyes had slid to her and away again before he'd said only Jack should go to Toby. Was it because of her that Toby had decided to hide from everyone? She had to know. She slipped, unnoticed, after Jack and Isaac.

Isaac led Jack into a seldom-used part of the house.

'How do you know where he is?' Jack said.

'I saw him dragging a candle and a blanket from his room and followed him.'

'A candle and a blanket!' Jack bit off a curse. 'Why didn't you stop him?'

'I...talked to him,' said Isaac. 'I stayed with him until I thought you'd soon be home. Then I had to go into the other wing to look out for you.' He didn't say anything else as he led Jack up a narrow flight of stairs. He stopped abruptly and gestured to a partially ajar door. 'Here,' he murmured, and stepped back into the darkness of the stairwell.

Jack pushed open the door, his heart thudding with hope and anxiety. He lifted the lanthorn aloft, but all he could see were the shadowy shapes of holland-covered furniture, crowded together in the small room.

'Toby?' he said. 'Toby, are you here?'

There was silence, then a gasp and a rustle. A small dark shape flew out of the shadows and cannoned into him.

'Papa! Papa!' Crying hysterically, Toby wrapped his arms around Jack's legs.

'*Toby?*' Shocked and alarmed, Jack managed to disentangle Toby's deathlike grip long enough to crouch down before him. In the lanthorn light he could see tears streaking his son's cheeks, and heart-breaking desperation in his eyes. 'My God, what's wrong?'

Toby flung his arms round Jack's neck, knocking his periwig

askew. Now Jack could only see out of one eye, but he hardly noticed. He was too intent on trying to understand the incoherent plea Toby kept repeating over and over in his ear.

'*Don't throw me away, Papa. Don't throw me away. I'll be good. Don't throw me away.*'

'What?' Stunned, Jack sat back on the floorboards and lifted Toby on to his lap. He held his son tightly, tears coming into his own eyes as he felt the shuddering distress in the small body clinging to him. 'Toby, I will never throw you away. *Never,*' he declared, the force of his emotions almost choking him. 'How could you think such a thing?'

It took a little while for Toby to calm down enough to answer. At last he rested with his head on Jack's shoulder, and one of his hands locked on to the front edge of Jack's coat. He'd managed to get two small fingers through a buttonhole, as if that made his grip even more secure.

'I don't want to go away,' he said, his voice frightened and uneven.

'You're not going away,' said Jack. 'If I have to leave Kilverdale Hall sometimes in the future, you will stay here with Gram and Hinchcliff and everyone else, just like always. Or perhaps you'll come with me. I'll never throw you away, Toby. Never.' Even the mere thought was so devastating Jack instinctively tightened his grip on his son. No wonder Toby was so upset. Anger stirred. Who had put such a cruel notion into Toby's head?

'Why were you sitting in the dark?' Jack asked, deciding to start with a less distressing question. 'Hmm? Isaac said you had a candle?'

'There was a s-spider. After Isaac went away. I moved and the candle fell over. It went dark. I was s-scared it would get on me.' Toby buried his face in Jack's coat.

'I'm here now, and I'm bigger than any spider,' said Jack, giving thanks the candle had blown out, rather than setting the furniture ablaze. 'I won't let anyone or anything hurt you.'

Toby was fearless on his pony, but he had a strong aversion to spiders. It was painful to imagine him crouched in trembling terror in the pitch black after the candle had gone out.

'I'm not your real son,' said Toby.

Jack went absolutely still. 'Of course you are. Who told you differently?'

'I heard the servants talking. The ones who came for the wedding…'

Jack stared straight ahead for several moments, waiting for his fury and self-recrimination to abate. He'd been so focussed on what society scandalmongers would say about him and Temperance he hadn't considered the possibility of Toby being hurt by malicious gossip.

'What did you hear them say?' he asked when he was sure he could speak in a moderate tone.

'I'm not your real son. I'm just a bastard. A bastard is bad. It means now you've got a wife you'll have real sons—'

'Toby!'

'And…and you'll throw me away like a…like an old shoe!' Toby's death-grip on Jack's neck and coat defied any attempt his father might make to discard him so carelessly.

'No.' The single syllable was all Jack could manage until he had his temper under control.

'I'll never be Duke of Kilverdale.'

'No, you won't,' Jack said, a little bleakly.

He and Eleanor had already tried to explain that to Toby. It was a difficult subject for a young child to understand, but they'd thought it was better if he always knew he wouldn't inherit the dukedom. Jack had talked about it matter-of-factly, without dwelling too long on the subject because he didn't want Toby to become bitter about the circumstances of his birth. At the time Toby hadn't seemed to care, but Jack hadn't been married then. Now Jack wondered grimly whether the fact he had himself told Toby he wouldn't inherit the title had made the servants' cruel predictions more believable to his son.

'If I was your real son, I would be Duke. Why won't you let me?'

Jack's heart twisted. He knew Toby didn't understand the ramifications of inheritance. He didn't realise that, before anyone could become the next Duke of Kilverdale, Jack himself would have to die. He only understood he wasn't going to be allowed to grow up to be like his father.

'You are my real son,' Jack said, 'but this decision is not up to me. You remember I told you it's the law of the land? I cannot change it.'

'You can do anything you want.'

Jack heard the echo of his mother's words: *No one else is strong enough and brave enough to do what your father can do.* Jack had discovered his father wasn't invincible in the cruellest of ways. At least Toby was learning the same lesson in a less brutally final manner.

'I can't always do what I want,' Jack said. 'I must obey the laws of England, just as you must obey the rules that I or Hinchcliff or Dr Nichols lay down for you. Everyone in Kilverdale Hall obeys rules. If the cook decided not to make dinner because she didn't feel like it today, we'd all go hungry.'

'I don't see what that's got to do with me being Duke,' said Toby.

'I don't suppose you do,' Jack said, glad his son was regaining a little of his usual spirit. 'But it's the law, and I cannot change it, however much I wish to. But nothing will change the fact you are my son and I love you. I will never throw you away.'

His voice cracked a little as he made his declaration. He had never before told Toby he loved him, though it had always been true.

'I love you too, Papa,' Toby whispered.

Jack closed his eyes and allowed himself to relax a little.

'I love Gram and Hinchcliff too, but I love you most of all.'

'Thank you.' Jack managed to smile. 'Perhaps we should keep that our secret. They love you too, and we wouldn't want them to feel hurt.'

Toby nodded. His head was still resting on Jack's shoulder, and Jack finally noticed the bothersome discomfort of his misaligned periwig. He pulled it off and stuffed it in his pocket.

'Will Temp'rance's babies be Dukes?' Toby asked.

'Only her oldest son,' Jack replied carefully. 'The others won't be.'

'It's not fair. I'm your oldest son.'

'I know. But you'll always be my oldest son—no matter where you are or what you do. It doesn't matter what you're called, that will never change.'

'Do you love Temp'rance more than me?'

'*No.*' Toby's question startled and disconcerted Jack. He hadn't expected anyone, least of all his son, to ask him whether he loved his wife. He admired and respected Temperance, trusted her, *desired* her, but—

'You kissed her,' said Toby. 'When you were dancing. And she went red.'

'That's…different,' Jack said weakly. 'You'll understand when you're older.'

'She's going to have a baby. That's what the servants said.'

Jack was still distracted by the meaning of love and marriage when Toby's announcement jerked him back into the present conversation. His lips twisted in a humourless smile. So much for his attempt to control when that piece of news became public.

'Yes, in a few months' time,' he said. 'It will be your little sister or brother.'

Toby lifted his head and frowned at Jack in the lanthorn light. 'Mine?' he said. It obviously hadn't occurred to him there was any connection between him and Temperance's baby. 'It will belong to you like I do?'

'Yes,' said Jack, squeezing Toby reassuringly. It was clearly taking him a little while to put all the pieces together; for him fully to understand that Temperance's child would also be Jack's. Jack wished he'd told Toby before he found out in such distressing circumstances. All he could do now was encourage Toby to look kindly on the new baby.

'You will always belong to me, Toby,' he said, 'and the baby will belong to all of us—you and me and Temperance and Gram. He or she may have black hair and brown eyes like you and me, or he may have brown hair like Temperance and blue eyes like Gram. Either way, he or she will be lucky to have you as a big brother. You'll be able to teach your little brother and sister how to ride and draw pictures.'

'Babies can't do anything,' Toby said after giving Jack's comment some consideration. 'I've seen them. Brown's baby cries all the time. Except when he's sleeping or eating. And girls can't catch.'

'Babies get older,' said Jack. 'And if it's a girl and you're teaching her, I'm sure she'll learn to catch properly.' He made certain he was holding Toby securely and braced himself to stand up. 'It's cold in here. Let's go back to the nursery.'

Temperance shrank back into the shadows as Jack carried Toby out of the store room. She watched, unseen, as Jack descended the stairs. He was holding the lanthorn in one hand and Toby in his other arm. Toby's head was close to his father's, their black hair so similar it brought a fresh lump to her throat.

Jack turned a corner and she was alone in the chilly darkness. She stood quite still for more than a minute, until at last she noticed how cold her feet were, and sat down on the stairs to put on her shoes. She'd taken them off so Jack and Toby wouldn't hear her footsteps. She buried her face in her hands, still shaken by the intensity of Toby's grief. She'd stood with her back to the wall and cried with him, and she'd heard the unshed tears in Jack's husky voice as he spoke to Toby. Her heart had overflowed with love for her husband as she'd listened to him comfort his son. He had been so tenderly patient with Toby's fears.

She rubbed her hands over her face, trying to tell herself Toby had been found and everything was all right now—but a desolate void was spreading inside her. Jack loved his son. She'd always known that, and she never wanted to come between them. But tonight she'd heard the depth of emotion in Jack's voice as he'd openly declared his love for his first-born child—and the vehemence with which he'd denied he loved her.

Do you love Temp'rance…?

No.

You kissed her.

That's different….

She hugged herself in the dark, assuring herself she was strong and independent and didn't need anyone to love her. Not even her husband. But what about her children? Would Jack ever love them as much as he loved Toby? She'd realised just how much it grieved Jack that Toby wasn't his heir. There had been no mistaking the sadness in his voice as he tried to explain why Toby wouldn't be the next Duke of Kilverdale. In his heart, would he always see

Toby and Eleanor as his real family, and her children as necessary only to ensure the succession?

Another hurt gnawed at her soul. Jack had married her because he'd said she would be capable of protecting his children, yet he hadn't included her in the list of names of people who would care for Toby in his absence. He'd named his steward as guardian for his precious child, but not his wife. It hurt more than she could have guessed. Why hadn't he included her?

She couldn't sit on the narrow stairs for ever. She got to her feet and started downwards, but after she'd descended a few steps she thought she heard movement in the darkness.

'Is someone there?' she said.

There was a moment's nerve-racking silence, then she caught her breath as a dark figure stepped from behind a half-open door. Before she could ask who it was she heard a soft rattle and then a shaft of light spilled from the unshuttered side of a lanthorn. Lord Swiftbourne's angular features were revealed by the pale, flickering light.

'Jack told everyone not to follow him,' she exclaimed, too startled to consider what she said.

'So he did.' Swiftbourne smiled faintly. 'It seems you are no more inclined to obey his orders than I am.'

'Is that why you are so successful—because you spy in corners?' It was a stupid thing to say. She knew it at once, and tensed in anticipation of a cutting reply, but Swiftbourne didn't respond for several moments.

'The child is safe,' he said at last. 'Now you must come back into the warm. If Jack had known you were here, he would not have left you standing in the cold and dark.'

'No.' Her throat clogged with tears. She was half-afraid Swiftbourne was wrong. Jack had not excluded her earlier when he'd ordered everyone not to follow him. Perhaps he would be annoyed by her disobedience. But then she decided she was being unfair to Jack. He didn't love her as he loved Toby, but he'd always been considerate about her physical comfort.

'When is the babe due?' Swiftbourne asked.

His question took Temperance by surprise. Had he overheard

Jack talking to Toby? Or perhaps he'd already guessed on his own account.

'The end of May,' she said. There was no point in prevaricating over the date. She wondered what he made of the information.

'I have eight surviving grandchildren,' he said. 'And so far I have, to my knowledge, four great-grandchildren—but only Toby lives in England. I look forward to meeting the new babe.'

It was the last thing Temperance had expected him to say. Tears pricked at the back of her eyes.

'Thank you, sir,' she whispered.

'Come.' He held out his hand to escort her down the stairs. 'Let us return to the warmth.'

'I was so concerned about what the gossips would say about us I never gave a thought to what Toby might hear.'

'You couldn't have known—' Temperance began.

'Of course I could have known. I kept dragging you up the hill to talk to you, but Toby—' Jack rubbed his hand over his closely shorn head. His forgotten periwig still cascaded untidily from his pocket.

Toby had been reunited with Eleanor and Hinchcliff an hour and a half earlier. The Duchess had been quietly relieved while the far more vocal steward had alternately scolded and comforted Toby. Watching them, there had been no doubting the central place Jack's son enjoyed in the hearts of the most important members of his household. Doctor Nichols had stood silently to one side. He clearly expected Jack to impose a penalty for his negligence, but his employer had ignored him.

Jack had asked Temperance to assure their guests the crisis was over, while he'd stayed to put Toby to bed. He'd ordered Isaac to sleep in Toby's room from now on. In doing so he'd both rewarded Temperance's former apprentice and given him additional responsibility for Toby's care. Isaac had accepted his new role with a quiet confidence that made Temperance proud of him.

As she sat and watched Jack pace up and down in front of her, she wished she felt equally confident about her own position.

'I should have told him there will be a new baby,' he said, bitter self-castigation in his voice. 'He should have heard it from me so it couldn't be used against him.'

Temperance shrank back into her chair. She understood Jack's distress on behalf of his son, but everything he said made her feel worse. Her residual sense of guilt at the way she'd forced herself into Jack's life and household had never completely disappeared and now it returned in full force. Even though she would never have done anything to undermine Toby's confidence in his father's love, she somehow felt what had happened was her fault.

'I tried not to let anyone know,' she said. 'The maid must have found the bread in the sewing box, or...'

'Tempest.' Jack came to crouch in front of her. He laid his hands on her knees and she welcomed the comforting gesture. 'It is not your fault. You have always been discreet. I should not have tried to keep it a secret until after the ceremony. I suppose Isaac told you why Toby hid?' He stood up before she could reply, so she didn't have to admit she'd followed him.

'I have been thinking vengeful thoughts about the servants,' he said with a harsh laugh.

'I'm sure it wasn't your servants,' Temperance said. 'They'd know how much you l-love Toby. They'd never believe you'd hurt him. And they were so worried—'

'Toby said it was the visiting servants. Most of this household have known him since he was a baby. But why should strangers feel kindness towards him? I must teach him to be strong enough to withstand cruel gossip. That is the best thing.'

Temperance looked down at her hands clasped in her lap. She knew she must acquire the same skill.

Jack abruptly returned to her. 'I'm sorry this evening has been so disrupted for you. I wanted to talk to you—but you look tired. Go to bed, you must rest.'

'What do you want to talk about?' Temperance felt a chill of anxiety.

'It will wait. I'm going out.'

'Where?' Alarm sharpened her voice.

'For a walk. I need to clear my head. I'm not restful company at the moment.'

'Outside? It's the middle of the night!'

'I'm not seven,' Jack said impatiently. 'I'm not scared of spiders or the dark. I won't come to any harm.'

Temperance bit her lip. She would not cry just because Jack preferred to clear his head walking alone in the dark rather than stay with her.

'Will you unlace me first?' she asked once she was reasonably sure her voice wouldn't betray her. 'Before you go. I don't want to call the maid tonight.'

'Of course.' His expression softened as he held out his hand to draw her to her feet. 'Come.'

They went into the bedroom and she turned her back to give him access to the points. He unlaced her carefully. She was wearing her bodices very loose because of the babe, but she still couldn't unfasten them herself. She hated that part of the price of her new grandeur was an increased dependence on others for something as simple as putting on or taking off her clothes.

'There.' He touched her arm to indicate he'd finished and she turned to face him. 'Is there anything else you need?'

She shook her head. What she needed was for him to stay. She thought he probably would if she asked, but she wanted him to stay because he wanted to—not out of obligation to her.

'You look tired. Go to sleep—don't wait for me,' Jack said. He cupped her cheek with one hand and lightly kissed her lips. 'And don't worry. I won't be gone long.' He turned and strode out of the room.

Temperance stared after him. Didn't he remember tonight held a special significance for them unrelated to Toby's adventure? She'd tried to comfort herself with the thought he'd been trying to allay Toby's jealousy when he'd told his son he didn't love her. But the fact Jack had forgotten tomorrow was their wedding day clearly told her where she stood in his priorities.

Jack's feet crunched on the gravel. Anger and the aftermath of fear still churned inside him, driving him to lengthen his stride until he was almost running. He forced himself to slow down. Toby was safe and would remain safe. Tomorrow he would talk to Temperance about how best they could make sure Toby didn't feel jealous of the new babe. She was certain to have sensible ideas. He should have told Toby about Temperance's baby before, but he'd thought he had more time—and he could hardly have told his son before he told his mother.

He slammed to a halt. He still hadn't told Eleanor. He'd have to do so first thing in the morning—

Tomorrow.

The day he would make his wedding vows to Temperance before his noble guests and every eminent family in the surrounding area.

He rubbed his hands over his head as he wondered how the hell he'd managed to forget that. Even in the midst of his concern over Toby he'd noticed Temperance was looking unusually anxious and tired. With her pregnancy at the forefront of his mind after his conversation with Toby, he'd assumed that was the cause of her weariness. He'd told her to go to bed because he wanted her to rest. He groaned as he realised she must be fretting about the ceremony tomorrow and he hadn't said a single thing to reassure her. He turned and headed back to the house.

He suffered a brief setback when he reached his chambers and discovered his bed was empty. He'd expected Temperance to be there, as she had been for the past few nights. He was momentarily nonplussed. Had she gone to her own bed because she was angry with him for forgetting their wedding? Or did she have some foolish woman's notion they ought to sleep apart the night before they made their vows?

He frowned at the empty bed, and then decided he was damned if he was going to spend the night alone because of her scruples. He opened the interconnecting door carefully. The room was dark except for the dim starlight coming from the open curtains. Temperance was lying peacefully in bed. He looked down at her shadowy sleeping form, feeling calm for the first time since Hinchcliff had rushed down the steps. He stripped off his clothes, dropped them on the floor, and slid under the covers. Temperance stirred slightly.

'Shush, go back to sleep,' he whispered, slipping his arm around her waist and closing his eyes.

Chapter Sixteen

Dr Nichols conducted the formal wedding service in the family chapel. He announced at the beginning that the Duke and Duchess of Kilverdale had already married in a private ceremony in London some months previously. Today, at the Duke's wishes, the couple were also going to speak their vows in the Duke's ancestral home. The chaplain was uncharacteristically subdued, but he convincingly made the second ceremony sound as if it was the result of an aristocratic whim. His speech made Temperance uncomfortable and she was glad when it was over.

She'd lain awake the previous night, worrying about every aspect of the future. When Jack had returned from his walk she'd pretended to be asleep. After he'd joined her in bed she'd fallen into an uneasy doze, only to wake before dawn, feeling nauseous and anxious.

To her relief, she and Jack had walked to the chapel together. He'd complimented her on her cream and gold brocade wedding dress and told her how beautiful she looked. He couldn't possibly know how much his praise meant to her, even if she wasn't quite sure how much was genuine and how much was intended to boost her confidence. Either motive showed consideration for her, which she hugged to her heart.

As they stood before Dr Nichols she was aware of an undertow of exhaustion, but it was overlaid by nervous agitation that kept her alert. She'd had a brief glimpse of the neighbouring gentry as she'd walked into the chapel. Now they were behind her, but she was acutely conscious they were watching her. Had they already judged her and found her wanting as Jack's Duchess? He was the highest-ranking nobleman in this part of Sussex. Many of the guests had sought, or would seek, his patronage for themselves or their families. None of them were likely to risk openly offending him—but that wouldn't prevent them from gossiping in private.

Jack looked so handsome and relaxed in his fine clothes no one would have guessed there'd been a crisis at Kilverdale Hall the previous evening. She watched him closely as he spoke his vows, remembering how his hand had trembled after she'd signed the marriage documents. She dreaded seeing similar signs of reluctance now—especially after what had happened with Toby. To her overwhelming relief, his voice was firm and he held her gaze steadily as he made the marriage promises.

When it was her turn to make her vows, she discovered her voice was husky with love and earnestness. She was determined to be a good wife to him, to make sure he never regretted his decision to marry her. In her heart she knew she wanted more than that. She wanted him to love her. As the coloured light from the stained-glass window behind the altar fell across their joined hands, she found herself praying that one day he would.

After the ceremony, they emerged from the chapel into a bright December morning. The chapel stood a hundred yards from the house, and there was to be a short wedding procession from the chapel door to the main entrance of Kilverdale Hall. Everyone who worked on the estate, as well as Jack's lesser tenants and most of the local villagers, were waiting to cheer their Duke and his new Duchess. Temperance knew that the villagers would soon be feasting and drinking in the village inn at Jack's expense, but she still took pleasure in their cheers.

She walked beside Jack. Behind them came Eleanor and Lord Swiftbourne, followed by Lord and Lady Halross and Jakob and Lady Desire. All of them were dressed in their grandest clothes. Their smiling presence was an unspoken but powerful signal of approval to the local gentry. She felt a wash of gratitude that

Jack's family—even the initially suspicious Jakob—had accepted her as his wife.

She and Jack stopped just before the entrance to Kilverdale Hall and turned to face everyone. Jack had been laughing and joking with some of the villagers. Temperance admired the way he could set people at their ease, while always acting appropriately to his position. It was another skill she must learn. Then she saw Isaac in the crowd. He was standing next to Toby, keeping a firm hold on the younger boy's shoulder. Isaac was smiling happily but, to her distress, Toby was scowling at her.

Jack took her elbow. She looked at him, and he smiled at her, a hint of apology in his eyes.

'I am sorry for Toby's bad temper,' he murmured, 'but it won't outlive the day. Trust me. He is my son and very like me. Our sulks never last long.'

'Thank you.' Temperance was grateful for his attempt to reassure her. It was true Jack's temper didn't usually endure, but she couldn't forget his hostility to his grandfather had survived for fifteen years. She couldn't bear the possibility Toby might still be hostile to her in fifteen years' time.

'Come.' Jack took her hand and turned to lead her into the house. 'It is time to introduce you to our neighbours.'

It was early evening when Jack took a moment to stand by the doorway between the great hall and the connecting parlour and observe his guests. Musicians played in the minstrel gallery and several couples were dancing in the great hall, while some older guests had gone to sit and talk in the parlour. Both chambers were bright with candlelight, hot and noisy. Bowls of warmed orange water kept the air sweet-smelling.

Before the banquet, Jack had stood beside Temperance, introducing her to members of the local gentry as they approached in order of precedence. After the banquet, he'd danced the first measure with Temperance, guiding her carefully because he knew she was anxious about dancing in public. At first she'd taken several missteps, but he'd smiled at her and gradually she'd become more confident. He didn't care whether she knew the correct angle to hold her head or her hand. It was the trust in her eyes when she let him lead her through the dance that made him feel like a king.

From his position by the door, Jack glanced into the great hall and saw Athena and Halross standing close to each other at the conclusion of a dance. Athena was gazing up at her husband with a world of love in her eyes. The same emotion was reflected in Halross's face. For a moment Jack was transfixed by the intensity of their love, then he turned his head away, feeling like an intruder on their private passion. But the brief interlude had shaken him.

He compared the expression he'd seen in Halross's eyes to the powerful emotion he felt for Temperance—and he remembered Toby's question of last night.

Do you love Temp'rance more than me?

He'd been startled into making an immediate denial because he couldn't imagine loving anyone more than his son. Perhaps even more importantly, for years he'd resisted the possibility he *could* love anyone else as much as he loved his mother and Toby. Love made you vulnerable to pain and loss and disappointment.

But love could not be so easily commanded or denied. He gripped the door frame as realisation rocked through him. He loved Temperance! He looked across the parlour to where she was talking to Jakob and Desire. When he'd asked her to marry him, he'd given only practical reasons for his proposal, and she'd accepted on those terms. He saw now he'd deceived both of them about his true feelings.

But what of Temperance? He knew she was grateful to him, and that she took pleasure in the physical aspect of their marriage, but would she ever love him? He gazed at her, hardly aware of the people thronging around him, as he finally admitted to himself that what he wanted more than anything else from his marriage was Temperance's love.

Temperance's head was ringing with the voices of the strangers to whom she had been introduced. She was cautiously optimistic the day had gone well, but she was dazed from the effort of making formal conversation for so many hours. It was a relief to talk to Jakob and Lady Desire. Compared to most of the other guests they felt like old friends. But after Lady Desire had repeated something to her twice and Temperance still had difficulty forming a coherent reply, she decided she must take a few minutes alone, away from the clamour, to compose herself.

'I'm so sorry. Will you please excuse me? I've just remembered... That is, I need to fetch something from my room,' she said. 'No, no, there's nothing wrong,' she added in response to Desire's concerned enquiry. 'I will be back shortly.'

She stood up and made her way across the room, smiling and nodding to people as she went. She just needed a few minutes away from the voices and laughter and music. With luck she'd be back before anyone noticed she'd gone. Even the pleasant music was beginning to sound harsh and discordant to her amid all the other noise of the party. The air in the hall was cooler and she took a couple of grateful breaths before heading towards the back staircase. She'd only gone a few paces before she heard voices coming from around the corner.

She froze on the spot. She couldn't immediately remember the names of the owners of the voices, but she knew who they were—two or three of the marriageable daughters of the local gentry. One voice in particular she remembered because its owner's cool politeness had not concealed the critical appraisal she'd given Temperance when they'd been introduced.

Dorothea—that was her name.

'It's lust,' Dorothea said, scorn in her voice. 'He'll soon tire of her. He'll be visiting Anne Lidstone again by spring, you mark my words.'

'She has no family here today. I don't believe she's even a gentlewoman. It's an insult to everyone that now she'll be queening it over us,' said another girl.

'But did you see the way he kissed her after the ceremony?' a third girl asked. 'He's so handsome and passionate—'

'And a wealthy Duke,' the second girl interjected.

'Vulgar display!' Dorothea snapped. 'She's a shameless hussy. That's how she caught him in her trap. She probably teased him with her common charms until the only way he could have her was to wed her. Now he can have her any time, he'll get bored with her.'

'But she'll still be his Duchess,' said the girl who'd described Jack as handsome and passionate. 'And you'll have to set your sights on a lower prize, won't you, Dorothea?'

The voices were getting closer. Temperance jerked out of her horrified paralysis. For once her willingness to meet trouble head-on deserted her. She turned and hurried away before the girls realised she'd overheard them.

Who was Anne Lidstone? The name was dimly familiar to Temperance, but she couldn't remember where she'd heard it before. The fact she recognised it disturbed her almost as much as the obvious implication that Anne was Jack's mistress, because somehow she was certain she'd heard it in a context which meant Jack was still in regular contact with the woman.

Jack moved through the great hall, looking for Temperance. He'd been waylaid by the local magistrate, and she'd disappeared before he could extricate himself from the conversation. He was about to ask Lady Desire if she knew where Temperance had gone when he saw her walk back into the parlour.

His heart leapt at the sight of her. She looked beautiful and regal in her cream and gold brocade, but he hardly noticed the details of her appearance. It was her simple presence on the other side of the chamber that filled him with joy. He started towards her, only realising he was smiling as foolishly as any besotted groom on his wedding night when he overheard the low-voiced, ribald jests of a couple of nearby male guests.

Weddings always had a tendency to generate bawdy humour and Jack didn't want the coming bedding to be any more uncomfortable for Temperance than necessary, so he tried to adopt a more inscrutable expression. Soon they could be alone. First he wanted to make sure Toby was safe in Isaac's watchful care, and then the night would belong to him and Temperance.

Temperance had forced herself to return to the party after the briefest absence. She was becoming increasingly frustrated by her failure to remember where she'd heard Anne Lidstone's name. After the silence of her rooms, the clamour of the party grated on her even more than before. She'd spent her whole life living in the heart of London, yet she'd never felt so oppressed by other people as she did tonight. But in London she'd just been part of the crowd. Now she knew all eyes were upon her. Perhaps, like Dorothea, the guests were comparing her attractions unfavourably with those of the unknown Anne Lidstone. She wondered if she would ever again be able to drop her guard in company.

Despite everything, when she saw Jack she felt a surge of love and relief. Even in his grandest clothes he'd become familiar and dear to her. She had to restrain herself from rushing towards him. She knew he couldn't take her away from the party, but if he just stayed by her side for a little while she would feel much more comfortable. Jack knew everyone and he knew exactly what to say.

He smiled at her, looking so pleased to see her that her heart filled with a burst of hope. But then his expression changed, becoming almost blank, though his gaze remained fixed on her face. The change in his countenance from pleasure to something approaching boredom was shockingly unexpected. Temperance caught her breath in confusion and distress. Had he been feeling pleased *until* he caught sight of her? Was he already growing bored with her?

'My dear.' When he reached her side he took her hand in his and lifted it to his lips. 'It is almost time for us to retire,' he murmured.

'Oh. Yes.' Her heart began to pound so loudly she could hardly speak. She'd been sleeping with him for several nights, but the thought of being bedded before all their guests filled her with horror. She wished the next hour was over and she was finally away from all the watching eyes.

'It's time for us to leave the party,' said Jack. 'Lady Desire and Athena will attend to you. I'm just going to see Toby is all right, then I'll join you.'

'Toby?' The day had been so full Temperance had barely had a chance to think of anything except the immediate demands on her attention, but her worries about what had happened last night had never been far beneath the surface. Now it was clear Toby was on Jack's mind as well.

'Shall I…shall I come with you?' she asked. She didn't want to intrude, but she did want to get back on friendly terms with Toby as quickly as possible.

'No.' Jack shook his head. 'He should be asleep by now. I just want to make sure he's where he's supposed to be, and then—' He broke off and smiled over Temperance's shoulder.

She turned to see Lady Halross and Lady Desire approaching.

'Ladies, I give my wife into your care,' he said to them. 'I will join you shortly.'

Temperance found the next half-hour excruciating. She'd considered it bad enough undressing in front of a maidservant. Now she had to strip to her shift before half the female guests. She knew behind their polite expressions they were assessing her body. Her pregnancy was an open secret and she was sure all the women were trying to guess when the child had been conceived. One girl even started to make a joke about the bride needing no advice on how to please her husband—but she was quelled by a cool glance from Eleanor.

Temperance was extremely grateful for the support of her mother-in-law, Lady Desire and Lady Halross. The three women stayed close to her at all times, allowing no one else to attend her.

It was a huge relief when the door opened and Jack strode in surrounded by male guests. He was dressed in a nightshirt and his periwig. Temperance stared at him, momentarily dumbfounded by the sight. She'd seen him covered in soot, she'd seen him dressed in velvet and she'd seen him naked—but she'd never before seen him in a knee-length white linen shift combined with his periwig.

One of the men started to laugh. 'Your bride is overwhelmed by the thought of what awaits!'

Temperance realised her mouth was still half-open and closed it.

'But she already knows!' said a startled voice from among the women. 'They've been married for months—haven't they?'

'Yes,' said Jack. He walked towards Temperance and the women crowding round her fell back to create a path for him.

He put his hand on her waist and pulled her close to him. She could feel the heat of his hard body through nothing more than the thickness of his nightshirt and her shift. She looked at him, startled by his bold action, and he kissed her full on her lips.

'We are both well aware of our marital responsibilities,' he said when he lifted his head. 'And the stockings were thrown months ago in London, so there is no need to do that tonight.' He looked around at the people thronging the bedchamber. 'My wife and I thank you for your good wishes and bid you goodnight.'

It was an unmistakable command, and there was a note in his voice that indicated that, if he wasn't obeyed, it would go ill for whoever crossed him.

Temperance heard a few rebellious murmurs, but then some of the guests began to head reluctantly for the door. The departure of the first few encouraged the rest to leave—especially when Lord Halross and Eleanor exerted their authority. Even Dorothea was intimidated by the Dowager Duchess's cool glance.

When everyone had gone Jack went into Temperance's parlour to make sure there were no loiterers. He locked the outer door to her quarters before going through into his own bedchamber and taking the same precaution.

Temperance wrapped her arms about herself and watched him. After spending so many hours in full public view, every inch of her skin felt over-sensitised—bruised by all the watching eyes. Her nerves were stretched to snapping point. Even the doors Jack had locked seem an inadequate barrier against the strangers filling the house. She was still fretting about the identity of Anne Lidstone, she was so tired she couldn't think straight, and she'd never felt less in the mood to make love.

When Jack tried to take her in his arms, her composure disintegrated.

'Don't.' She pushed at his chest and took a sideways step away from him.

'*Don't?*' He looked startled, then his expression softened. 'Don't worry, sweetheart. The doors are locked. No one will interrupt us.'

He put his arms around her, drawing her close. Temperance could feel he was already aroused.

For the first time ever, she didn't welcome his touch. Usually his virile energy excited her—but tonight she was too tired and anxious to respond the way he expected. She felt so brittle she was sure she would shatter if he tried to rouse her passion.

'I can't.' She braced her palms against his chest, trying to push herself out of his embrace. 'Not tonight. I'm sorry. I can't. *Let me go!*' Her voice rose when he didn't immediately release her.

He dropped his arms so suddenly she staggered as the force she'd exerted against him propelled her backwards.

'What's wrong?' He caught her elbow and guided her to the nearest chair. 'Are you sick? What's wrong?'

'I'm not sick.' She shook her head, but she was trembling so violently her teeth chattered.

'You're freezing.' He gripped her hands in his. 'You must get into bed.'

He reached out to pick her up, but she slapped his hands away.

'I'm not sick. Don't touch me.' She wrapped her arms around herself again. She hated feeling so unlike herself. Tears pricked in her eyes. Her throat felt tight. She could sense herself spinning out of control and she didn't know how to stop it. 'I just want to be left alone,' she whispered, not even sure if it was true. 'To be quiet.' She tried again. Quiet? Yes, that sounded more what she wanted.

'On our *wedding night*?'

'It's not…not really.' She sucked in a breath. 'You can have me tomorrow night,' she said, the words Dorothea had used still echoing in her head. 'And the night after that. But not tonight. I can't…can't…not tonight…'

'I can *have you*?' Jack stared at her. When she looked at him she saw disbelief and growing anger in his eyes. It didn't seem fair he should be displeased with her after she'd spent all day struggling not to let him down in front of his family and neighbours.

'*Tomorrow* night,' she said. 'You can have me tomorrow night. I can't pretend—'

He drew in his breath so sharply it shocked her into silence.

'Pretend?' he repeated. 'Has all your passion until now been *pretended*?'

'What?' She stared at him. Even though her mind was cloudy with exhaustion, she was shaken by the change in his tone.

'You've caught the prize. Now you don't have to waste time pandering to my lust—is that it?'

Temperance gazed at him blankly. She could hardly remember

what she'd said and it took several seconds for her to understand what he meant. When she did she was irritated rather than upset by his accusation.

'*No!*' she exclaimed. 'Of course not! For God's sake, have a little sense!'

'I'm sorry you think so poorly of my comprehension,' Jack said coldly.

Temperance blinked into his hard, questioning eyes, and couldn't recall where the conversation had begun. Disconnected thoughts spiralled through her mind. Dancing with Jack. Dorothea's spite. The faceless Anne Lidstone. Toby's hostility. The images merged until she couldn't distinguish one from another. She swayed slightly.

'You *are* ill.' Jack caught her shoulder to steady her.

'No. I'm just tired.' She shook her head in an unsuccessful effort to clear it. 'Everyone was looking at me. I hated it. I can still feel their eyes crawling over my skin. Like lice.' She shuddered. 'I'm never going to let anyone see me in my shift again. *Never.* I don't think I made any mistakes today, did I? Not big mistakes, anyway.' She caught his wrist.

'You didn't make any mistakes at all.' His voice softened.

'I behaved like a proper Duchess? Even in my shift?'

'Yes, you did.'

'Good.' The tension drained out of her. Her most important goal for the day had been achieved. She sighed and closed her eyes. 'I tried to make you proud…' she mumbled.

Jack caught her as she sagged forward. For a few dreadful seconds he was afraid she'd collapsed, but her pulse and breathing were both strong and steady. It seemed she'd simply reached the point where she was too tired to stay awake any longer.

He picked her up and carried her to the bed. He arranged her carefully under the covers, then sat on the edge of the mattress beside her. This wasn't how he'd planned the night to end.

The stab of horror he'd felt when he'd jumped to the conclusion she'd cold-bloodedly trapped him into marriage was a vivid but fading memory. His doubts on that score had lasted only seconds. Even before she'd looked at him as if he was mad and accused him of having no sense, he'd known she hadn't schemed to become his Duchess. No one could accuse his Tempest of being mealy-mouthed, but her unguarded words had raised other doubts in his mind, which were far less easily banished.

He'd been about to tell her he loved her when she'd pushed him aside and said she couldn't pretend any more. He still didn't know what she'd meant. Surely not that she'd pretended to enjoy his lovemaking? He rubbed a hand over his chest. He was dismayed at how deeply it hurt to think she might not want his love. In its own way the fear she would reject his tender emotions was as incapacitating as a physical injury. He felt exposed and vulnerable.

He gazed down at her. She seemed pale in the candlelight. There were dark shadows under her eyes. He felt another momentary panic that she wasn't breathing, but her chest was rising and falling with reassuring regularity. He released a relieved, shaky breath of his own. This was what love did to you. It filled you with fear and uncertainty. And it inspired hope—hope you learned to keep hidden to protect yourself from mockery when your dreams and plans came to nought.

Temperance clawed her way to consciousness through layers of nausea and an unaccountable sense of foreboding. Her limbs felt as if they were chained to the mattress. She dragged in a deep breath, which made her lungs creak, and finally managed to open her eyes.

She noticed the room was filled with pale daylight before her eyes closed again of their own volition. She took another deep breath. Her brain was still fogged with sleep, but her sense that something important had happened—almost a sense of dread— strengthened. She felt a flare of panic when she couldn't remember why—then memories from the previous few days began to fit together into a coherent story. Yesterday had been her wedding day. She was married to Jack and his hand hadn't trembled when he'd made his vows to her. She sighed with relief and rolled over to look at him.

He wasn't in bed beside her.

Something was wrong. And then she remembered refusing Jack's lovemaking last night. The full picture was hazy, but she knew she'd pushed him away more than once. She closed her eyes, biting back a moan of consternation. How could she have refused Jack on their wedding night? It was a wife's duty to please her husband. She *wanted* to please him. If her nerves hadn't been so jangled over half the neighbourhood seeing her clad in nothing but her shift, she would have been eager to feel his arms around her.

She curled into a ball of misery. Now of all times, when she was worried about Toby and she knew at least some of the local gentry were making spiteful predictions about her marriage, she wanted to be a good wife to Jack. Was his absence this morning a sign of his anger at being denied on his wedding night? She had to find Jack and make him understand she hadn't been rejecting *him*. She'd simply been overwrought at the end of a very demanding day. And perhaps when she'd done that, she would casually introduce Anne Lidstone's name into the conversation. Only a fool would trust anything said by someone as spiteful as Dorothea. Anne was probably an elderly widow he paid an allowance to, or there would be some other innocent explanation for why Temperance recognised her name. But until she knew for sure she'd not be able to stop worrying.

She stumbled out of bed and put on a comfortable undress jacket and skirt that didn't require the assistance of a maid to fasten. Surely a Duchess didn't have to be elegantly trussed up every second of the day? She combed her hair and tried to dress it the way she'd seen the maid do it. As she struggled with a re-calcitrant curl, it occurred to her, in a moment of slightly desperate humour, that Jack's ability to put his hair in his pocket whenever it got in his way gave him a definite advantage.

Then she took a deep breath and went to find him. The first person she encountered was Lord Swiftbourne.

'My lord, are you leaving?' she said in surprise.

Swiftbourne had been walking towards the open front door, but at her question he turned to face her.

She descended the last few stairs as he approached her.

'Good morning, your Grace.' He studied her with keen eyes. 'Your husband said you were resting this morning. I trust you are well now.'

'He…did?' She wanted to ask what else Jack had said—and had he seemed angry when he said it—but she was too proud to appear ignorant about her own husband.

'Yes, I am well, thank you,' she said, steadying herself. 'Yesterday was an unusually busy day. I was a little tired first thing, but now I am very well.'

Swiftbourne continued to look at her searchingly for a moment longer, but to her relief he didn't challenge her assertion.

'Good,' he said. 'Yes, I have tasks awaiting me in London. But, had I known you would soon be rising, I would have waited to take my leave of you.'

'I understand. It's better not to travel too late in the day,' she said. 'Thank you for coming to the wedding celebration. I am pleased to have met you.'

He inclined his head in polite acknowledgement of her comment, but at the same time she saw one of his eyebrows lift. His subtle scepticism annoyed her.

'Perhaps I should say it has been a *comfort* to meet you,' she said, and had the satisfaction of seeing she'd taken him aback.

'A comfort?' he repeated, clearly suspecting her of being sarcastic.

'Indeed. Now I've seen you, I can be confident—even *more* confident than I already was—that my husband will be likewise strong and healthy. And my children.' She laid a hand over her stomach as she spoke.

Complete silence followed her words. Swiftbourne gazed at her, his expression unreadable. He was silent so long, she wondered if she'd offended him, but suddenly he bent into a deep bow.

'Madam, it has been an honour to meet you,' he said, his voice unusually rusty. 'I wish you good health and happiness.' Without waiting for a response he turned back to the door. The footman jumped to open it and the next moment Temperance was alone apart from the servants.

'Hinchcliff! Hinchcliff!'

Temperance spun around to see Toby racing into the hall, Isaac following behind.

'Hinchcliff! Papa's taking me to London! We're going tomorrow.' Toby danced up and down before the steward. 'We're going with Lord and Lady Halross. You have to stay here to look after everything. You don't mind, do you? Lord Halross owns lots of ships. I can't be a Duke, but Papa says perhaps I can be a great merchant and own lots of ships instead.'

'Slow down!' Hinchcliff said indulgently. 'A great merchant must be dignified and speak clearly at all times. I cannot understand half of what you say.'

'Papa's taking me to London,' Toby repeated, emphasising every word with a nod of his head. 'We're going tomorrow.'

'I know,' Hinchcliff said, grinning. 'He told me first thing this morning. You'll have to get up *much* earlier if you want to hear the latest news before *me*, Master Toby.'

Temperance stood by the newel post, ignored by everyone as Hinchcliff teased Toby. Grief washed over her. She hadn't found Jack, but she knew his response to his unsatisfactory wedding night. He was taking his son to London and leaving her behind and she was the last to know. Perhaps he was going to see Anne Lidstone.

She swayed and sat down suddenly on the bottom of the stairs—and discovered she wasn't as invisible as she'd thought. Toby broke off mid-word and stared at her. Isaac rushed over to her. Hinchcliff reached her in two long strides and the footmen tensed, poised to respond to any order they received.

She swallowed a bubble of overwrought laughter, which, if she'd allowed it to escape, would undoubtedly turn to tears. She was a Duchess. Her every action really was being watched at all times by everyone around her.

'Mistress, what's wrong?'

'Your Grace, are you ill? Travis, fetch the Duke.' Hinchcliff threw the order over his shoulder at one of the footmen.

'No, no!' Temperance stretched out her hand in a futile attempt to recall the servant. 'There's no need.' She let her arm fall and smoothed her hands aimlessly over her skirts. As soon as she'd composed herself she was going to return to her rooms. The only reason she didn't do so immediately was because she wasn't absolutely certain her legs wouldn't wobble.

Toby stood in front of her, knee to knee and eye to eye, and frowned. 'Why are you sitting on the stairs? Gram never sits on the stairs.'

'I'm still learning to be a Duchess.' Temperance could feel her lower lip start to tremble, but she was determined not to cry in public.

'Your hair's a mess.'

'I know.' She managed to smile. 'I was thinking how lucky your papa is. He can put his hair on and take it off whenever he likes.'

'Your hair is not a mess!' Isaac exploded. 'Toby, you must not be rude to Mistress Temperance. She is the best, kindest mistress anyone ever had, and you will apologise to her *at once*!'

Temperance burst into tears and buried her face in her hands.

Chapter Seventeen

The Dowager Duchess arrived in the hall in time to hear the last part of Temperance's exchange with Toby, and Isaac's passionate defence of his former mistress. Travis hadn't been able to find Jack—he was in the stables, inspecting the coaches, but the footman didn't know that—so he'd gone to Eleanor instead. She'd hurried to the hall, afraid Temperance was ill. But it didn't seem as if her daughter-in-law was in physical distress, so Eleanor took a moment to watch, unnoticed by the horrified males standing in a semi-circle at the foot of the stairs. Eleanor doubted if Toby had ever encountered adult tears before. He looked momentarily stricken at the possibility he'd made Temperance cry.

Isaac patted Temperance and then awkwardly put his arm around her shoulders. 'He did not mean to be rude about your hair, mistress. He is very young.'

'I'm seven!' Toby said indignantly. 'And *I* don't cry every time someone tells me to comb my hair.'

Eleanor decided it was time to intervene. As she took a step forward, Temperance lifted her head and rubbed her sleeve across her eyes.

'I'm not crying because Toby said my hair is a mess,' she said thickly. 'I know it is. I am crying because…because I am so happy you defended me like a…a knight of old, Isaac. I am proud of you.'

Isaac went bright red and pulled away from Temperance as

if he'd realised it was a breach of etiquette for an apprentice to hug a Duchess.

Toby scuffed his foot on the floor. Temperance looked at him. As she did so, she caught sight of Eleanor. She ducked her ahead, avoiding the Dowager Duchess's gaze, but not before Eleanor had seen her tear-stained cheeks and puffy eyes.

'Isaac, take Toby to the nursery,' Eleanor commanded. 'Hinch-cliff, make sure the Duchess and I are not disturbed.'

She waited until her orders were being obeyed, then sat down next to Temperance. Behind her she heard Toby's shocked exclamation to Isaac. 'Gram is sitting on the *stairs*!'

'Come *on*!' Isaac towed him determinedly upstairs.

'Contrary to my grandson's firm convictions, I have sat on the stairs before,' Eleanor said when they were alone.

'I'm sorry. I didn't mean to cause a scene.' Temperance kept her face averted as she pulled a handkerchief from her pocket.

'Hardly that,' said Eleanor. 'Are you ill? It has been an exhausting few days. I will not think worse of you if you say yes,' she added gently, afraid Temperance might try to conceal any indisposition through pride or anxiety over what was expected of a Duchess.

'No. No. I'm just tired.' Temperance sighed and blew her nose. 'And then Isaac defended me so gallantly and I couldn't help crying. I don't usually.'

'I know.' Eleanor didn't think Isaac's gallantry had caused Temperance's tears. She hesitated, unwilling to pry, but concerned. Before she'd met Temperance she would never have considered a London shopkeeper a suitable wife for her son, but over the past week she'd come to believe they were surprisingly well matched.

'Are you daunted by the thought of the journey?' she asked. 'I did suggest to Jack you might not want to be thrown about in a coach all the way to London so soon after the wedding celebrations, but he was adamant about leaving tomorrow.'

Temperance's head jerked up. As Eleanor met her daughter-in-law's shocked, questioning—and suddenly desperately hopeful—gaze, she was confident she'd discovered the reason for Temperance's distress.

'Shake him,' Eleanor muttered, both amused and exasperated

by her son, who was overseeing every detail of the journey to ensure his new wife's comfort, but hadn't thought to tell her she was going with him.

'I beg your pardon?' Temperance looked confused.

'Never mind. Jack, Isaac and Toby are going with you to London,' Eleanor said. 'You'll be travelling with Athena and Lord Halross. Jakob and Lady Desire are staying here with me over Christmas. I'm going to visit you in Putney once the Christmas festivities are concluded.'

'Putney?'

'Jack has a house in Putney,' Eleanor explained. She stood up and reached her hand down to Temperance. 'Come, we will plan what you need to take.'

For the rest of the day, Temperance had no opportunity to speak privately with Jack. He was always busy making travel arrangements, or occupied with their guests. After a while she came to the conclusion he was avoiding her, but now she knew she was going with him to London she felt calmer. Since she wasn't eager to explain to him why she'd burst into tears, and she still didn't know why he'd decided to leave Sussex, she temporarily abandoned her plan to discuss their wedding night with him. She wanted to have *that* conversation when her head didn't feel as if it was stuffed with straw—and when she wasn't afraid she might start crying again at the slightest thing.

'Go to bed,' said Eleanor. 'I will do everything that's needful.'

'Are you sure she's not ill? Toby said she cried. She never cries!' Jack's hands opened and closed convulsively as he spoke, betraying his worry and uncertainty.

'She's tired,' Eleanor reassured him. 'I sent her to bed to rest. It is not so surprising, Jack. I was very weary in the first months I carried you, and she's had a lot to contend with these past few weeks.'

'I know.' He took a hasty turn around the room. 'I want her to rest. But she…cried? The only time I have known her to cry was when her shop burned. Surely she can't—' he broke off, leaving Eleanor to wonder what he might have said. Jack had kept his own counsel from a very young age, but she could see the turmoil in his eyes.

'Pregnancy often makes a woman more prone to tears,' Eleanor said, 'for good reasons as well as bad.'

'Good reasons?' Jack stared at his mother. 'What good reason did she have for crying this morning?'

'Isaac very stoutly defended her. He said she was the best mistress anyone could have. Such praise would make any tender-hearted woman cry.'

Jack's eyes narrowed. 'Why did Isaac need to defend her? Did Toby say something unpleasant?'

'He was perhaps a little too honest about her appearance,' Eleanor said.

Jack frowned. 'Her appearance is always without fault. She is beautiful and graceful—and I am particularly pleased my wife is tall.'

His final emphatic comment startled Eleanor, until it occurred to her that perhaps Temperance had confided anxieties about her height to him.

'You make a very handsome couple,' Eleanor said, pleased with Jack's consideration for his wife's feelings. 'Now, why have you decided to go to London in such a hurry when you want her to rest?'

Jack stood still for a moment, and then sat down opposite Eleanor.

'For that very reason,' he said.

Eleanor raised her eyebrows.

Jack rested his elbows on his knees and stared at the carpet, obviously picking his words carefully. 'Tempest didn't like everyone looking at her at the wedding. She said their eyes felt like lice crawling over her.'

He looked up. 'I am sure it is only because she is not yet accustomed to her new role,' he said earnestly. 'And she has had to learn so much in such a short time. I am very pleased with her... very pleased...' His voice trailed away.

'She has behaved admirably,' Eleanor said, wishing she knew what had put the shadow in Jack's eyes.

'Yes, she has. I'm proud of her.' He sat up straight, and continued. 'If we stay here, there will be formal visiting after the wedding, not to mention the Christmas festivities. She won't have any respite for weeks. But there won't be any need to draw attention to our presence in Putney. Tempest can enjoy a few quiet weeks without any social demands upon her.'

'I think it is a good idea,' said Eleanor. 'And very considerate. I am proud of you too,' she said, and smiled as he flushed and ducked his head like a bashful schoolboy.

The journey to London astounded Temperance. She'd slept well and risen feeling much more resilient. Jack's sudden decision to leave Sussex still worried her, but at least he was taking her with him. She was daunted by the prospect of arriving in another new household, but Toby had never been to Putney either. She hoped Toby's excitement at his first visit to London would draw attention away from her.

But first they had to get there, and even the expedition to the beach hadn't prepared Temperance for travelling in state with Jack and the Halrosses. Their reception along the way astonished her. Because the party was travelling slowly, it was anticipated for miles in advance along the route. Beggars turned out to cry for alms. Bell-ringers or musicians greeted them at every village they rumbled through. And everyone who opened a gate, held a horse, or simply begged, was rewarded for his or her efforts. Temperance began to understand why Mr Worsley's contribution to the travel arrangements had been several large purses of coins, currently in the charge of Warren, Jack's Gentleman of the Horse.

They separated from the Halrosses before they reached London and, from then on, their progress became a little less flamboyant. Temperance reflected that a Duke and a Marquis travelling together were bound to garner more attention than a Duke alone, but Jack also took steps to ensure their arrival at Putney was relatively unobtrusive.

His first action was to introduce Temperance to the steward and the housekeeper. She sensed curiosity, but no animosity from them. Toby was desperate to see the house so Jack gave them all a quick tour of the most important rooms before announcing it was time for Toby to go to bed.

'It is a smaller house than Kilverdale Hall,' Jack said when he and Temperance were finally alone in one of the parlours.

'Not that small,' she said, thinking of the tall, narrow house in which she'd grown up.

'Well, no.' He glanced at her, and then away. 'We do not have separate quarters here.'

'Oh.' The air between them seemed to thicken until Temperance felt breathless. 'We only saw Toby's room,' she said, realising the omission in Jack's tour.

'I'll show you ours.' He took her hand and led her along a gallery.

It was less imposing than the gallery at Kilverdale Hall, but Temperance was too busy trying to interpret the pressure of Jack's fingers on hers to pay any attention to her surroundings.

'You see.' He dropped her hand to gesture around the chamber. 'It is not on the same scale as the rooms at Kilverdale Hall.'

'No. I suppose…' Inevitably Temperance's eyes were drawn to the bed. Jack hadn't tried to make love to her since their wedding night. She'd slept alone the night before they left Sussex and, although he'd stayed with her last night in the inn, he'd made no amorous overtures. Perhaps she'd killed his desire for her. Anne Lidstone's name slipped insidiously into her mind. She still couldn't remember where she'd heard it before Dorothea had spoken it.

'You may furnish the room as you please,' said Jack.

'I may…what?' Temperance stared at Jack. She was wondering whether he'd come to London to rekindle an old affair, and he was talking about decorating his house. 'You brought me here to *refurnish the bedroom*?'

'Of course not!' His expression was an odd mixture of discomfiture and indignation. 'Obviously not. It's not important. I'm sure you're tired after the journey. Shall I summon your maid or…would you prefer me to undo your points?'

Temperance's pulse jumped, then she became aware of the tension in Jack's body as he waited for her reply. He, too, was unsure of the situation.

'You,' she whispered. 'I'd prefer you.'

He reached towards her. For a moment his hands hovered close to her without touching, as if he wasn't confident of her reaction.

Her breath lodged suffocatingly in her throat. Then he gently laid one hand on her shoulder and turned her around.

She closed her eyes as he eased the edges of her bodice apart. She ought to take this opportunity to talk to him about their wedding night, but the moment seemed so fragile…

She opened her eyes again as she realised there must have been some significance to Jack's comments about furnishings.

'Don't you like the way this room is decorated?' she asked.

'I have no objections to it. It's not much altered from when I bought the house.'

'You *bought* it?' She turned to look at him. She'd assumed this house had been part of his inheritance.

'It was a good bargain,' he said stiffly. 'It was built by a merchant who'd overreached himself. The sale saved him from bankruptcy—he didn't quibble over the price.'

'Sometimes getting information out of you is like pulling teeth!' she exclaimed. 'Jack, what is the significance of telling me I can redecorate this room?'

She was half-afraid he'd withdraw into ducal aloofness. For a moment he did assume an air of cool dignity, then his expression relaxed.

'This is my house,' he said. 'I have always felt Kilverdale Hall is more truly Mama's house. She lost it, grieved for it and returned to it. I will never interfere with how she… But this is my house, and you can furnish it any way you please.'

Temperance drew in a deep breath as she absorbed what he'd just told her, in words and by inference. She didn't think Jack really regarded the Putney house as home. He spent too little time here. And Eleanor had made Kilverdale Hall a home for her family as well as herself. All the same…

'Do you *like* the furnishings in your bedchamber in Sussex?' she asked tentatively, remembering how grand but impersonal it had seemed to her the first time she'd entered it.

He looked at her.

She waited.

Eventually he sighed and gave one small shake of his head. 'I am not partial to French tapestry. Mama bought them for my father, but he never saw them. When we regained the house, she had them hung for me. I have no memory of the house before I returned to it at twenty—' He stopped abruptly.

For the first time Temperance wondered how much Jack remembered of his father—the real man, not the heroic picture created for him by his mother and loyal servants like Hinchcliff. Instinctively she closed the distance between them and wrapped her arms around him.

She felt him stiffen. 'It is of no great importance,' he said, his manner making it clear he rejected even the implicit suggestion he was in need of comfort. 'I am in control of my inheritance, and a few French tapestries are hardly worthy of remark.'

'Of course not,' she said. 'But it would be fun to choose the furnishings for this room. I've never had the opportunity to do such a thing before.'

'Hmm,' he said. 'You can arrange it to your taste so you'll be truly comfortable here. I dare say you'll enjoy bargaining with the silk mercers and carpenters and God knows who else. We will discuss a budget tomorrow.' It was only then, after setting the whole subject on a firmly practical footing, that he put his arms around her and returned her embrace.

Despite Toby's eagerness to go on the river, Jack insisted Temperance do nothing but rest during their first few days in Putney. Toby tried to get Jack to leave Temperance behind, and sulked when his father remained firm, but he cheered up in the course of a thorough investigation of the house and grounds.

'The river comes right up to the garden!' he said, his eyes round with amazement. 'I can see it through the gate. It's full of boats. They shout all the time, Papa! I couldn't understand anything they said. Are they foreign?'

Jack laughed. 'They're Londoners. You're used to hearing Sussex speech.'

'Temp'rance and Isaac are from London, and I understand them,' said Toby.

Jack rubbed the side of his nose. 'Waterman can be somewha'

uncouth in their language,' he said after a moment. 'There's no pressing need for you to understand them.'

At last, to the huge excitement of his whole party, Jack hired a wherry to take them downriver. They left the boat at Queenhithe and walked through the ruined City to Cheapside. Apart from Temperance and the boys, Jack had brought one footman with them, but the manservant wasn't in livery. They were all, including Jack, dressed respectably rather than extravagantly. Jack didn't want to advertise his return to London, nor did he want to attract the attention of any cutpurses hiding in the ruins.

When they reached the site of her shop, Temperance wrapped her arms around herself, remembering how desolate she'd felt the last time she'd stood here.

'I'm so glad you're alive,' she said suddenly.

Jack looked startled, then he put his arm around her shoulders and kissed her cheek.

'So am I,' he said, and for a few moments they stood in silence. 'You had the ground cleared,' Jack said at last.

'Yes, it's been recorded.'

'Agnes hasn't.' He glanced at the untouched rubble on the next plot.

'She can't afford to. Her landlord was trying to force her to go on paying her rent. I told her to take him to the Fire Court—'

'*Beaufleur!*'

The sudden shout made Temperance jump. She turned to see a man hurrying towards them, and was puzzled to recognise Nicholas Farley. She couldn't imagine why he was so pleased to see Jack—or even how he knew him.

'Beaufleur! I *am* pleased to see you again, sir,' Farley said, shaking Jack's hand. 'Edmund Beaufleur's great-grandson. Well, this is a pleasure. After we last met, I took the liberty of looking up your illustrious forebear in our Company records. If I'm not mistaken, you must be quite closely related to the Duke of Kilverdale.'

'Quite closely,' Jack agreed.

Temperance belatedly remembered Farley had been present when Agnes had accused Jack of starting the fire, and he'd obviously assumed, correctly as it turned out, that Jack shared his great-grandfather's surname.

'I'm glad the news of your death was false,' Farley said. 'It is typical of Agnes Cruikshank to misreport such a matter. Though she has had a difficult time of it, poor woman, so perhaps I shouldn't speak ill of her.'

'What's happened to her?' Temperance asked. 'Is she still staying in Southwark?'

'No. Daniel Munckton arranged for her to leave London.'

'Why?'

'She took her landlord to the Fire Court,' said Farley. 'And she won. You'd think that would be the end of it. A great man has no business hounding a poor old woman for a few pounds. But there were some…incidents. Munckton thought it would be safer to send her beyond his lordship's notice.'

'Oh.' Temperance rubbed her hands over her forearms, feeling colder than the day warranted as she remembered Lord Windle's expression the last time she'd seen him. 'I told Agnes to go to the Fire Court.'

'It was good advice,' Farley assured her. 'It means she is no longer accruing debt she cannot pay. Wait! I seem to re-call…Agnes said you're married now?' He glanced from Jack to Temperance for confirmation. 'I congratulate you most heartily on your choice of wife, sir! Mistress Challinor will be an asset to you in any enterprise you undertake. Please forgive me, I am late already for a meeting. Please call upon me at any time if you wish to peruse the Grocers' records pertaining to your great-grandfather. Good day to you both.'

'He thinks I'm an asset,' said Temperance, staring after the voluble grocer in surprise.

'Of course you are,' said Isaac. 'I wonder where Agnes has gone.'

'Munckton will know,' said Jack. 'By the sound of things he was wise to send her out of London. And I'm sure Fanny Berridge's husband is relieved,' he added with a glint of humour. 'Are you ready to leave? We'll take the wherry up to Covent Garden.'

'No, Papa! I want to see St Paul's!' Toby jumped up and down as he clung to Jack's hand. 'And Newgate. Temp'rance says the stones of St Paul's exploded! And Cousin Jakob was in Newgate. I want to see the melted iron bars. If Cousin Jakob hadn't escaped, *he'd* have melted.'

'Hush!' Jack lifted his eyes briefly to the sky. 'You don't want Temperance's old neighbours to think she's married into a family of gaolbirds, do you?'

'We can walk,' Temperance said, unwilling to disappoint Toby.

'No, it will tire you. Toby can see Newgate another day.'

'Papa!'

'It is only a mile or so to Covent Garden,' Temperance said. 'If any of us get tired, we can go the rest of the way by wherry. We'd have to walk down to the river and back up again, anyway.'

'Very well.' Jack took her hand and drew it through his arm. 'Tell me the instant you feel tired. Toby, do not climb about in the rubble! I had in mind that you might want to ask Agnes to take care of your shop when it is rebuilt,' he said as they began to stroll towards St Paul's. 'But that is for you to decide. And after what we've heard, perhaps it would not be such a good idea.'

'I think it was an excellent idea,' Temperance said. 'If it would not put Agnes at risk. I've hardly begun to think about rebuilding,' she confessed.

'There's no great hurry,' Jack said. 'Rebuilding schemes are still being discussed. I understand there are plans to widen Cheapside. We will have to ensure you are compensated for any land you lose.'

They continued towards Covent Garden, but after they left the remains of St Paul's behind them, Isaac withdrew into himself until he was pale and quiet. Temperance realised this was the first time he'd returned to the City. After the fire he'd stayed in Southwark until they'd gone to Sussex. Now they were retracing the route on which he'd lost the cart and all her belongings, and been left bruised and bleeding on the cobbles.

'Your Grace,' he said suddenly, looking up at Jack, his voice so low Temperance could hardly hear him and Jack had to bow his head.

'Yes.'

'Will you teach me to fight instead of play the guitar?'

Jack didn't say anything for a moment, then he put his hand

on Isaac's shoulder and Temperance saw him squeeze it comfortingly. 'I will teach you to do both,' he said.

Temperance experienced her own unpleasant association between place and memory as they approached Bundle's coffee-house. This was where she'd been told Jack was dead. She was eager to meet Bundle, but when she saw the sign she felt a most curious and disturbing sensation, almost as if she'd had an attack of vertigo. It was very disconcerting. But Jack was beside her, real and alive, so she shook off her foolishness.

The door opened, and a man dressed in the height of fashion emerged.

Her only warning Jack didn't welcome the forthcoming encounter was the sudden tension in his arm.

'Kilverdale!' the foppish stranger exclaimed in almost comical surprise. His expression changed immediately to suggest extreme gratification. 'Damnation, man, I *am* pleased to see you. I heard you were buried in the country.'

'Rumours of my demise were exaggerated,' said Jack.

'Eh?' The fop looked blank. 'Oh, not literally. But the country's damned dull for a man of your talents and temperament. Your wit has been much missed at Court.'

'You flatter me,' Jack said, coldly ironic.

The fop turned his attention to Temperance. She forced herself to meet his gaze with calm indifference. He'd said nothing offensive, yet already she'd taken a dislike to him.

'Can it be I have the *honour* of meeting the new Duchess of Kilverdale? What an exquisite pleasure,' the fop gushed. 'I have heard you were recently married, your Grace.'

'My dear, allow me to present Lord Fotherington,' Jack said, his tone suggesting he found the entire conversation unutterably tedious, though the muscles in his arm felt like steel beneath Temperance's hand.

The fop bowed. Temperance calmed her taut nerves by comparing his bow unfavourably with Jack's.

'I am pleased to make your acquaintance, my lord,' she said, trying to inject just the right amount of polite warmth into her voice. She'd already decided it would be a mistake to imitate Jack's cold arrogance—no one would appreciate being treated rudely by a woman who might once have sold them linen—but nor did she intend to demean herself or Jack by desperately seeking the acceptance of fashionable society.

'And I am more than honoured to make yours, your Grace.' Fotherington's gaze darted all over her as he spoke, making her feel he'd noted every windblown curl, all the creases in her coat, and every smear of muddy ash spoiling her skirts. 'The whole Court has been agog to meet you since April.'

'April?' Temperance didn't understand. She hadn't even met Jack in April.

'It was so dramatic.' Fotherington folded his hands together over his heart in a theatrical gesture. 'His Grace informed Lord Windle—and the entire court—that he could not possibly marry Windle's daughter because he was committed to another. And then he left for Flanders. We have all been *panting* to meet Kilverdale's secret bride ever since.'

He lowered his hands, and smiled at her, his eyes glittering with horrible curiosity.

'Why didn't you tell me you were already betrothed?'

'I wasn't—'

'Was it Anne Lidstone?' Temperance swept on, ignoring Jack's denial. 'Is that why you came to London in such a rush, to explain to her—'

'Anne lives in Chichester! I haven't got anything to explain to her. Why the devil are you talking about her now?'

'I—' Temperance stared at Jack as he paced around their bedchamber. While they were in public he'd acted as if he was unperturbed by the meeting with Fotherington, but now they were alone he'd abandoned his pose of cool self-assurance. Temperance couldn't decide whether he was angry, exasperated or worried by what had happened—but he certainly wasn't indifferent to it.

Her own nerves were still jangling. After speaking to Fotherington they had visited Bundle in a private room of the coffeehouse. Despite the anxious questions spinning through her head,

Temperance had smiled and behaved with every ounce of gracious serenity she could summon. Bundle might only be a coffeehouse proprietor but, like Hinchcliff, he was important to Jack. She was determined to make him think well of her. It was only now, safely back in Putney, she could question Jack about Fotherington's devastating revelation.

'Who is she?' she demanded.

'Who? Anne?'

'Yes. No. The woman you denied Lord Windle's daughter for?' Temperance's throat was so tight she could hardly speak. 'The woman you were committed to in April—before you ever met me.'

'No one.' Jack snatched off his periwig and threw it aside. 'There was no woman.'

'There must have been! You told the whole Court…the King… everyone…'

'I spoke in the heat of exasperation!' Jack rubbed both hands over his head. 'Believe me, if you'd had Windle dogging your heels for two months you'd have been driven to extremes.'

'It wasn't *true*?' Despite Jack's denial, Temperance couldn't believe he'd lied to the whole Court.

'No.'

'You lied to everyone.'

'Yes.'

'What were you going to do when you returned to Court without a wife?'

'God knows. Until Fotherington exploded his little firework, I'd completely forgotten I'd said it.'

'You'd forgotten! You made such an important announcement to the entire Court and you *forgot* about it. How could you be so…so—are you sure you're not trying to fob me off with this "I forgot" story?'

Jack opened his mouth, drew in a sharp, angry breath—and then exhaled again.

'Believe me, if I was trying to fob you off, I'd invent a better story than this,' he said more moderately. 'As I recall, I did not actually claim I was *betrothed* to anyone. I simply offered my compliments to Windle's daughter and said I was already committed to another.'

'His daughter was present?'

'No, she wasn't. I've spoken to her exactly once in a room full of people. As soon as I realised which way the wind was blowing I took good care never to be in the same building with her, let alone the same room. It was damned inconvenient.'

'I still don't think it is like you to make a claim you aren't in a position to keep,' Temperance said, although she was finally beginning to believe he was telling her the truth. 'What were you going to do when you went back to Court and discovered everyone taking bets on the identity of your secret bride?'

'Take another trip to Sweden. Tempest—' Jack put his hands on her shoulders '—I *wasn't* betrothed to another woman when I met you. I give you my word of honour. If you'd ever met Windle, you'd know why I lost my temper and said the one thing I could think of to stop him badgering me without resorting to swordplay.'

'I have met him,' she said.

'What?'

'He's Agnes's landlord—or was.'

'Good God.'

'You really aren't betrothed to anyone else?'

'I'm *married* to you!' Jack exploded.

'So who is Anne Lidstone?'

'Why are you asking me about *her*?'

'Don't you want to tell me?'

'I'll tell you anything you want,' Jack said. 'I just don't understand why you leapt to the conclusion I came to London to see Anne. She doesn't even live here.'

'Who is she?'

'She is, or was, the mistress of Edgecroft. He was a friend of mine. Killed in a duel five years ago. Damn stupid affair.' Jack sighed, his tension finally seeming to dissipate. He guided Temperance to a chair and knelt in front of her.

'She was your friend's mistress?' Temperance sat down, watching Jack intently.

'I did share her bed a couple of times soon after Edgecroft died.' He smiled crookedly. 'I took her the news, you see. We were both shocked, and grief can…confuse things.'

'So she became your mistress?' Temperance's nails dug into her palms. She'd been expecting this, but it was still painful to hear.

'No. It takes more than two tear-swamped sessions in bed to make an affair. She didn't want me, she wanted Edgecroft, but when he died he left her with nothing. After I'd regained my commonsense, I arranged for her to receive a regular allowance.' Jack shrugged. 'That's it. That's all there is to tell. As far as I'm aware, she's been raising her daughter in quiet retirement ever since.'

'Whose daughter?' Temperance asked tautly.

'Edgecroft's.' Jack smiled faintly. 'Although we didn't know it at the time, Anne was already pregnant when he died. It pleases the world to claim Emily is mine, because I'm supporting her— and what man in his right mind provides for another's bastard? But anyone who knew Edgecroft would need only one look at Emily to know she's his.'

'Oh.' Temperance took several unsteady breathes as she tried to regain her composure. The tension knotting her muscles began to ease.

'That's all there is to this story,' Jack said. He covered Temperance's hands with both of his. 'Worsley arranges for her allowance to be paid out of the income of the estate—' he broke off. 'What?'

'That's where I saw her name—in Worsley's record books,' Temperance said. 'When Dorothea said it, I knew I'd heard it before, but I couldn't remember—' It was her turn to break off as Jack's eyes blazed with brief but intense irritation.

'Never pay any attention to anything Dorothea Fulbright says,' he commanded. 'Don't you know better than to listen to gossip?'

His words provoked an answering flare of annoyance in Temperance. 'I overheard by accident!' she snapped. 'And if you'd kept me properly informed I wouldn't need to find out about your past from spiteful strangers.'

His eyes narrowed. Her heart thudded against her ribs, but she refused to be intimidated.

'Very well,' he said at last. 'Since you are so determined for me to give you a full accounting… Occasionally, when I go to Chichester, I do visit Anne. We talk about Edgecroft or she tells me about her daughter. We do not, ever, make love.' He paused, with the obvious intention of giving added weight to his next statement. 'She's too short,' he said.

'What?' Temperance looked up, startled.

Jack put his hands on the arms of the chair and leant forward to kiss her cheek. 'I haven't made love to any woman apart from you for nearly two years,' he said against her ear, and stood up.

Temperance's mouth fell open.

For the first time since their meeting with Fotherington, Jack grinned, but there was a hint of wariness in his eyes. 'I never thought I'd be able to shock you into silence,' he said. 'Now you must rest. This has not turned out to be the quiet day I planned.'

It wasn't until he reached the door that Temperance found her voice. 'Jack, why not?'

He stopped. 'The world might consider me a rake—on damn little evidence—but do *you* really think I'd be so heedless of the consequences,' he said, without looking at her. 'I am never again going to tell a child he doesn't have a right to my name and all that is attendant upon it because I put my own fleeting pleasure above all else.'

He left her sitting alone, awash with confused emotions. Anne Lidstone wasn't his mistress. And Temperance herself was the only woman he'd made love to for two years.

Despite her initial shock she believed him. From everything she knew about the fashionable world, he would become an object of ridicule rather than admiration if his self-restraint was discovered. Part of her was thrilled his desire for her had overcome his scruples. But it also created another layer of doubt. His claim he wanted to marry her because he wanted her in his bed took on a new meaning now she knew how long he'd been abstinent. Perhaps he would have been equally eager for any halfway attractive woman once he could make love to her within the protection of marriage?

Jack strode down to the rivergate. He stared into the murky Thames, paying no attention to the shouts of the watermen. He felt edgy and exposed by his revelation to Temperance that she was the first woman he'd made love to for so long. He'd never intended to tell her, but her suspicions about Anne Lidstone, following so closely on their encounter with Fotherington, had shaken him. Even though he wasn't accustomed to sharing his secrets with others, he was becoming more used to sharing them with Temperance. The only secret of any significance he hadn't yet told her was that he loved her. He still shied away from that final revelation, and now something else had happened to disrupt their lives.

He frowned at a piece of driftwood, thoroughly disgruntled with events. He'd brought Temperance to Putney so she could be away from prying eyes and the gossip of strangers. It had been the unkind speculations of visiting servants that had prompted the crisis with Toby. And Temperance had been overwrought after being the centre of attention on their wedding day—although now he wondered if she'd been fretting over Anne Lidstone even then. The only time she could have overheard Dorothea's comment was at the wedding celebrations. Why hadn't Temperance asked him about Anne before? He vented his frustration by hurling a stick into the river. Was it because of Anne she'd cried on the stairs that morning? How could he set her mind at rest when she was worried if she didn't tell him what she was upset about?

He hadn't made love to her since they'd arrived in Putney, although they slept in the same bed. He desperately wanted her to make love to him with the same trusting abandon she'd shown before the wedding night. But she'd been so subdued, cautious even, in the way she responded to him, he'd been afraid to make any demands upon her. He could not bear the thought of hurting or upsetting her.

During their trip to Cheapside he'd started to feel hopeful things were getting back to normal. And then they'd met Fotherington and the day had gone from good to disastrous. Jack was more worried by their meeting with the fop than he was willing to admit to Temperance. He really had forgotten he'd invented a rival for Windle's daughter on the spur of the moment, although now he realised Swiftbourne had probably been alluding to his supposed secret betrothal when he'd said London was eager to meet his new bride. Jack wished his grandfather had been more specific, but took some consolation from the fact Swiftbourne had apparently accepted without question Temperance was the woman he'd been speaking of when he'd made his hasty declaration at Court.

Jack silently cursed Windle for infuriating him out of his usual caution. Under other circumstances it wouldn't have greatly mattered. If Jack hadn't left England immediately, and stayed away so long, he wouldn't have forgotten the throwaway line. And when he'd returned to London unmarried, he would have watched with sardonic amusement as fashionable society scrambled over itself to discover the name of his non-existent bride.

But instead he'd returned to London with a wife. And apparently society had been in a frenzy to find out about her for months. There was no chance now Temperance could make an unobtrusive entrance into society. Fotherington had clearly been trying to steal a march on everyone else when he'd gone to the coffeehouse. Jack had never known the fop to visit Bundle's before, and the most obvious reason he'd done so now was to ferret out information on Jack's new wife. Everyone knew Bundle was closely associated with the Duke of Kilverdale.

Jack clenched his hand into a fist, wishing he could plant it into Fotherington's weasel face—but that wouldn't help matters. The first invitations would start arriving very shortly. Jack knew he'd have to accept several of them, but he could exert his influence to make things easier for Temperance. He went back through the rivergate towards the house. He was sure Temperance would be more comfortable if she made her first public appearance in the home of Lord and Lady Halross. He'd send a message requesting the invitation straight away.

From the window Temperance could see Jack standing at the top of the river steps. She flinched as she saw him throw a stick into the water. The gesture was a vivid indication of his mood. Her own confusion and anxiety had resolved into a knot of cold fear.

She thought Fotherington must have been at the coffeehouse to find out about Jack's marriage. Jack had always said they should allow the world to believe their union was the result of a lengthy, discreet courtship, but she'd never anticipated she'd be the object of intense curiosity before she entered society. If Fotherington was searching for information in Covent Garden—what was to stop him searching in the City? She'd lived in Cheapside all her life. All anyone needed was her unmarried name and they'd be able to learn all about her from her former neighbours or the records of the Drapers' Company.

Temperance Challinor of Cheapside, spinster and linen-draper. She'd lived six days of every week—and every daylight hour of those six working days—on public view. Even on Sundays any visitor to her shop would have been noted by several different pairs of curious eyes. Between them her neighbours could account for almost all her daily activities.

She took a shaky breath as she realised how suspicious it would look if anyone investigated her past. There were no witnesses to the supposed courtship because it hadn't happened, but there would be plenty of people to express astonishment at the notion of her conducting a secret affair. She wondered if Jack had thought of that and whether she should tell him. Perhaps she should come up with a solution first. There must have been some time in the past year he could have courted her without drawing her neighbours' attention.

Chapter Eighteen

Twelfth Night

'I did not expect to meet the King so soon,' said Temperance, smoothing her gloved hands over her gold-and-cream brocade skirt.

They were travelling along the Thames to the Palace of White-hall in the Kilverdale barge.

'Tempest.' Jack put his arm around her shoulders and pulled her close. 'Don't worry, sweetheart.' He kissed her temple. 'The King is very affable. You will do excellently—and after this we will refuse all further invitations.'

'There is no need to do so on my account,' she said. 'We must do whatever is necessary to avoid gossip.'

'You've been wonderful,' Jack said.

'I've been thinking.' She turned into his embrace and laid one gloved hand against his chest as she murmured against his ear. 'You met me during the plague.'

'I did?' He narrowed his eyes in puzzlement. 'Why are you telling me this now?'

'Because I just thought of it.' She took his chin and turned his head away so she could speak into his ear again. 'It's the only time everyone was too worried about contagion to care about their neighbours' morals,' she breathed. There wasn't much chance her words would be heard over the sounds of the river, but she wasn't taking any chances.

Since their meeting with Fotherington they'd accepted several invitations. Even though she knew Jack had selected them carefully, she'd been on tenterhooks that the validity of their marriage would be challenged. There were so many things to worry about. It wasn't just that she hadn't been married to Jack when she'd turned up claiming to be his widow. That was their most dangerous secret and must always be preserved. By contrast, it would be impossible to conceal her humble origins. Temperance was grateful those who knew, including Swiftbourne and the Halrosses, hadn't said anything. But it was only a matter of time before it became common knowledge she'd been a Cheapside shopkeeper. Whenever Temperance went into society, her nerves were stretched tight with the effort of maintaining her poise and guarding her words. And though Jack never lost one iota of his cool self-assurance, she was aware of the tension in the lean muscles concealed beneath his fine clothes.

The only time Temperance had been able to relax in public was when they'd gone to the theatre. Even there she'd been uncomfortably aware she was attracting almost as much attention as the play. Once she'd seen a woman staring at them so intently she'd almost asked Jack if he recognised her, but the woman had disappeared. There were so many who looked at Temperance with open curiosity. She didn't like it, but she was becoming accustomed to it.

'Did you come to London during the plague?' she whispered. 'Or are there gaps when no one knows what you were doing, when you could have come to London?'

Jack turned his head again, which brought their mouths almost into alignment.

'Yes,' he said. He looked at her lips and, even in the dim light of the cabin, she saw his eyes darken.

'Jack, are you thinking about the plague?' she asked uncertainly.

'No.' He kissed her.

Even though she'd seen it in his eyes, he took her by surprise. He hadn't kissed her so fervently since before the wedding celebrations. She responded with instant, grateful passion. She needed him to want her, and apparently he still did. His lips were hot and urgent on hers, his tongue wickedly exciting as he aroused her passion. When he lifted his head, her body was thrumming and her vision hazy with desire.

His kept his arms around her, and for several moments the only sound in the cabin was their ragged breathing. Then he said, 'After tonight we'll take a holiday from our social obligations.'

'Can we?' she asked, although her heart leapt at his words.

'Yes, by God! We're still on our honeymoon. We'll present you to the King, and then we'll consign society to perdition for a while.'

'If you think we can.' Temperance sighed with relief and relaxed against him. As she did so, his comment about perdition reminded her of something else.

'Lord Swiftbourne will be there today, won't he?' she asked.

It was the last thing Jack had expected her to say. He was still almost giddy with relief and pleasure at the way she'd kissed him, but he couldn't help leaning slightly away from her.

'Yes, I dare say he'll be there,' he said, his voice unintentionally growing colder. 'Should we happen to speak to him, we will be courteous.'

'I know,' said Temperance. 'But it occurred to me yesterday… Do you know why Lady Desire seemed so quiet and uneasy her first day at Kilverdale Hall?'

The question threw Jack completely. Of course he knew why Desire was uncomfortable in his house. He'd been unforgivably rude the last time she visited. Before he could reply, Temperance hurried on,

'It was not because of what happened between the two of you. It was because she kept thinking she would see her father.'

'What?' Jack shook his head in bewilderment. 'He's been dead for *years*! Did she think his ghost had taken up residence to haunt me in revenge—?'

'No, no, no.' Temperance put her hand over his mouth. 'You have a very melodramatic imagination,' she said, undoubted amusement in her eyes. Jack decided he must be completely besotted with her, because her teasing created a surge of happiness within him.

'Is it my husbandly duty to let you laugh at me?' he asked, his voice muffled by her hand. He kissed her palm, and was gratified to see her eyes widen in surprised pleasure.

'I'm not laughing at you,' she said. 'In her own home Lady Desire became accustomed to the absence of her father years ago. It was different for her at Kilverdale Hall, because the only time she visited he was with her. She had memories of him there, and no memories of being there without him. That is why I suggested we play billiards.'

'Because her last recollection connected to the billiard table was my cruelty,' Jack said, his mouth twisting as he remembered what he'd said on one of the few occasions in his life he had been the worse for drink. 'And you wanted to give her a happy memory. You are very kind-hearted.'

'Thank you. I am not as kind as you, but I am trying to be worthy of you.'

Jack was so distracted by her comment he didn't say anything. Temperance wanted to be worthy of him, not because he was a Duke, but because she thought he was kind. It was the most moving compliment he'd ever received.

'It was partly because of what happened with you,' Temperance said.

After a moment's confusion, Jack realised she was still talking about Lady Desire.

'But it was also because her father was beside her when they encountered you at the billiard table,' Temperance continued, 'and it seemed to me her memory of him at that moment was even stronger than her memory of you at that time. She's seen you since then in much more favourable circumstances.' Temperance smiled tentatively at him. 'So it occurred to me to wonder whether something similar might be happening with you when you see Swiftbourne unexpectedly. Perhaps you just haven't created enough new memories to drive out the old, painful memory?'

Jack stared at Temperance. He saw her bite on her lower lip and dimly realised she was worried she'd upset him, but most of his thoughts were back in the Parisian room where, fifteen years ago, Swiftbourne had told him about his father's execution.

For weeks after that day, Jack had been overcome with unpleasant sensations every time he'd gone into that room. But the house was small and he'd been unable to avoid the chamber, and eventually it had become just another room. Was Temperance right? It hadn't occurred to him until now that the way he felt when he saw Swiftbourne unexpectedly was a variation on the feelings he'd had about the room where he'd heard the bad news. He hadn't seen Swiftbourne again for nearly nine years. By the memory of hearing his father had been hanged was seared unalterably onto his brain. He could not think about Swiftbourne or look at him without remembering that moment.

'I shouldn't have mentioned it now,' Temperance said. 'Not when we're on our way to Court. I'm sorry. This wasn't the time—'

Jack silenced her with another kiss.

'It was brave and generous of you to tell me this,' he said. 'It is possible…' He hesitated, because it was hard to admit weakness, but she deserved to know what he was thinking. 'It is possible you are right, at least in part.'

'Do you really believe so?' Her gaze intensified for a few seconds, as if she was trying to verify the truth of his words in his face, then a smile lit up her face. 'I'm so glad.'

He caught his breath at her happy, open expression. She was truly pleased she might have said something helpful to him. It made him even more determined to avoid society for a while. If only they could spend some time alone together he was sure he could coax her to love him. But first they had to attend the King's Twelfth Night ball.

Temperance looked around in fascination as they arrived at the Court of Charles II. The hall was lit by myriad candles, and decorated in extravagant swags of leaves, flowers and fruit. The rich clothes and jewels of the courtiers gleamed in the flickering light. Some ladies even wore gowns of cloth of silver, but Temperance was confident the gold-and-cream brocade gown in which she'd been married, and the pearls glowing at her throat, meant she was as well dressed as anyone present. After weeks of practice, she'd learned to wear silk and lace with assured grace, and she believed that, from the top of her carefully dressed hair to her silk brocade shoes, she looked every inch a Duchess.

But it wasn't just her lessons in deportment and her changed appearance that gave her the courage to walk calmly among the courtiers—it was the trust Jack had always placed in her. In the barge she'd suddenly realised the greatest gift he'd ever given her was his unwavering faith in her. Even more wonderfully, he'd kissed her passionately and declared they would take a holiday from the world after this appearance at Court. Now her heart was singing, because even though he hadn't made a declaration of love, surely it was a hopeful sign?

Despite her secret happiness, she still felt sick with nervousness when Jack presented her to the King and Queen. Her knees trembled so much she was afraid she wouldn't be able to rise from her curtsy. But then she wondered what her parents and her brother would say if they could see her now. The thought comforted her, and she was able to reply calmly to the King's genial greeting.

'I'm pleased to meet your bride at last, Kilverdale,' the King said to Jack. 'You've kept her hidden too long. You must permit me to dance with her later.'

'Of course, your Majesty.' Jack smiled and bowed while Temperance's stomach swooped in alarm at the prospect of dancing with the King. She hoped he would forget his whim. She was relieved when they finally escaped the royal presence.

'Well done,' Jack murmured in her ear. 'Now who shall we… ah…'

Temperance looked around and, to her delight, saw the Halrosses approaching them.

They chatted until the King led the Queen on to the floor for the first dance. Temperance danced with Jack first and then Lord Halross, while Jack partnered Athena.

In between dances, she spoke to some of the new acquaintances she'd made in London, but it was a woman with auburn hair who caught her attention. Surely Temperance recognised the lady from engravings in the London print shops?

'Isn't that Lady Castlemaine?' she whispered.

'Yes. Tell me your opinion tonight,' Jack murmured, a hint of amusement in his eyes.

Temperance threw another quick glance at the King's most notorious mistress. She wondered if it was true Charles had once presented Lady Castlemaine to the Queen without revealing the lady was his mistress. It was said the Queen's nose had begun to bleed when she'd realised the truth, and then she'd fainted. Instead of tending to his Queen, Charles had escorted his mistress from the room. Affable Charles might be but, if the story was true, Temperance could not consider him a gentleman.

She was nonplussed a little while later to discover that, gentleman or not, the King did wish to dance with her. Since there was no help for it, she allowed him to lead her on to the floor, and gave every ounce of her concentration to acquitting herself gracefully.

Jack watched Temperance proudly. She showed no signs of nervousness. On the contrary, she appeared to be enjoying herself. Her eyes sparkled as she smiled shyly at the King, and her cheeks were flushed with pretty colour. Jack felt a stir of unease as he noticed the King seemed quite taken with her, but Charles was still entangled with Lady Castlemaine, and he'd been pursuing the virtuous Frances Stuart for the past three years. It was unlikely he'd turn his attentions to Jack's bride—and inconceivable Temperance would welcome the King's advances.

Jack smiled at the vision of an incensed Temperance kicking the King's throne from under him. Then he sobered as he realised that, in the light of what had happened to Charles's father, it wasn't an amusing image. It would be disastrous for England if another king lost his crown.

He caught sight of Swiftbourne standing a few yards away. For the first time, Jack wondered if his grandfather's shifts of allegiance were quite as self-serving as he'd always believed. Swiftbourne had done well out of the restoration of the monarchy, but it had been in England's best interests to invite the King to return. Perhaps Temperance was right and he should make the effort to see his grandfather more frequently?

Jack surveyed the crowd, still pondering the matter. A man emerged from behind a small group of chatting friends. Jack stiffened as he recognised Windle. So far since returning to London he'd managed to avoid the Earl. Although he'd accepted many invitations, he'd selected them carefully, only taking Temperance to houses where he believed she would be treated with consideration. Inevitably that had often meant their hosts were men who hoped in some way to receive his patronage, rather than true friends, but so far the strategy had worked well. Unfortunately, he had less control over who they met at Court.

Jack had no wish to attract Windle's attention, so he took a couple of casual steps sideways, but Windle turned his head and looked straight at him. The undisguised hatred in the Earl's eyes startled Jack. He'd known Windle was angry with him, but he hadn't anticipated such extreme hostility.

Then Windle looked towards Temperance as she danced with the King. His murderous expression made the hairs on the back of Jack's neck stand on end. It took all his self-control to remain still. He was torn between an urge to launch himself at Windle, and an equally powerful impulse to grab Temperance and hurry her to safety. He moved closer to her, ready to claim her as soon as the dance ended.

Windle deliberately turned his back on Jack, addressing a remark to an exquisitely dressed courtier.

Jack divided his attention between Windle and Temperance. Windle's behaviour had roused all his protective instincts, and he was determined to get Temperance safely home as soon as possible. When he saw Swiftbourne on the other side of the hall it took only a heartbeat to decide to request his grandfather's help. He'd not ask for himself, but he would for Temperance.

He collected her from the King almost before the dance was over, forcing himself to smile and respond appropriately to Charles's bantering comments.

'I only made two small mistakes!' Temperance whispered exuberantly when they were out of the King's earshot. 'I don't think he noticed. Jack, *I danced with the King*!' If she hadn't been trying so hard to appear dignified and composed, he was sure she'd be jumping up and down with excitement.

Even though he was distracted by his worry about Windle, her exhilaration in her success delighted him. He wished he could spare the time to enjoy it. He took her arm and started shepherding her towards Swiftbourne.

'Where are we going?' she asked.

'You said I ought to speak to Swiftbourne more often,' he replied. 'Let us start now.'

'Oh, yes, if you wish,' she said, still bubbling with happiness at her success with Charles. 'I wonder if Lord Swiftbourne would like to dance with me? He's tall enough—isn't it fortunate the King is so tall? And I'm sure he—' She broke off, frowning as she glanced past Jack's shoulder. 'Jack, who is that lady? I saw her at the theatre the other day. Her expression is quite…quite unfriendly when she looks at us.'

Jack froze. Then he turned casually, but with a sense of dreadful certainty. The lady met his gaze, and her full lips curved into a gracious, subtly mocking smile. Jack kept his own expression impassive as he looked at Temperance.

'Vivien,' he said, amazed his voice sounded so close to normal when the evening had taken an even more nightmarish turn. 'Lady Lacy.'

'Vivien?' Temperance whispered.

Disaster awaited on every side. Jack shot a quick glance in Windle's direction, afraid the Earl might have disappeared from view while his attention had been focussed on Vivien. He felt only a marginal lessening of tension to discover Windle hadn't moved. Vivien was walking across the chamber with the elegant carriage he'd perfected years ago.

'Toby's mother?' Temperance said.

Jack took her hand and squeezed it tightly. 'I'm sorry. Smile, Tempest. Try to act as if nothing is wrong.'

As Jack watched Temperance struggle to maintain her composure, his mind split between Windle and his former mistress, trying to anticipate and pre-empt whatever mischief they intended. What was Vivien doing here this evening? She was supposed to be searching for another rich, elderly protector. The Court was not her usual hunting ground. She preferred her patrons to be solvent, not waist-deep in gambling debts.

From the corner of his eye Jack saw her approach Windle.

Why was Vivien talking to the Earl? Windle couldn't supply her
with the material luxury she craved. But as he watched them speak
to each other, Jack realised with sickening certainty it was no coincidence Windle and Vivien were both present at the King's
Twelfth Night revels.

He looked back at Temperance and saw she was bravely trying
to smile at him, even though her lips were almost white.

'I didn't know she was a lady,' she said.

'She isn't,' he said, his voice sinking into a growl before he
regained control of it.

Bewilderment mingled with hurt in Temperance's eyes. 'You
called her a lady,' she whispered.

'She married Viscount Lacy in 1657 and she was widowed a
few months later,' Jack said flatly. 'She's the daughter of Sir
Edward Logan—but in every respect that matters, she is not a lady.'

'You…' Temperance stopped, obviously distressed despite her
efforts to seem composed.

Jack abandoned all concerns about Court etiquette. He wanted
to get Temperance far away from Windle and Vivien. Somewhere
she would be safe until he'd dealt with them.

He tightened his grip on her hand and began to draw her
towards the door.

Lord Windle and Vivien suddenly appeared in front of the King

'Your Majesty.' Windle bowed low before Charles. 'I crave
your indulgence for interrupting your pleasure,' said the Earl
speaking loudly enough for everyone to hear, 'but I consider i
my duty to bring to your attention a serious injustice against a
noble, badly used lady.' He gestured towards Vivien. She wa
standing beside him with her head bowed in the attitude of
patient supplicant.

Jack stopped trying to reach the door because it was too late
Many people here knew Vivien had once been his mistress. Severa
heads were already turning in his direction.

He was still holding Temperance's hand and he felt her squeez
his fingers convulsively. He tried to convey reassurance with hi
own, answering pressure, while keeping a coolly disinterested ex
pression on his face for the benefit of everyone watching.

'This is hardly the occasion for such matters, Windle,' said the King.

'I beg but a moment of your time,' the Earl said unctuously. 'Only long enough to present to you the true Duchess of Kilverdale!'

He brought Vivien forward with a flourishing gesture as a gasp echoed around the hall.

'And to declare the Duke of Kilverdale a bigamist and a liar who wilfully tried to deceive your Majesty when he presented his false bride to you earlier this evening.'

For two or three heartbeats Temperance felt numb with disbelief—then waves of horror crashed over her. The courtiers merged into a faceless mass. Her vision narrowed to a single tunnel of overbright light with Vivien at its centre. All along she'd been afraid her marriage to Jack would be challenged, but she'd never expected this.

Jack's wife? How could *this* woman be Jack's wife?

Her first shock passed. Gradually she became aware of herself once more. She began to notice the fast tattoo of her heartbeat, the stiffness in her muscles, and the painful grip of Jack's hand around hers.

She turned her head to look at him. His face was parchment white, his skin stretched too tight across his hawk's face. He was staring at Vivien with something close to hatred. Then he looked at Temperance and his expression changed. Emotions flickered so fast in his eyes she couldn't read them. Apology. Anger. Mortification. Distress.

Their exchange of glances lasted a bare second before he looked back at Vivien and Lord Windle. Temperance looked at them too. At first she'd been so appalled by Jack's former mistress she'd hardly noticed Windle. Now she stared at him, stunned by his vicious determination to hurt Jack. It was only when the Earl looked at her with scalding hatred in his eyes that she realised he recognised her. Even though she'd met him before, she'd assumed he was too insignificant to linger in his memory. She'd been wrong. He obviously recognised her not just as the unknown bride who'd stolen Jack from his daughter—but as the woman who'd helped undermine his attempts to bully Agnes Cruikshank. His rage must be beyond bounds at having been thwarted twice by a common shopkeeper.

She dragged her gaze away from him as she became aware of the reactions of the courtiers. Many people were exclaiming in surprise or condemnation, and turning to stare at her and Jack. For many people present, the Twelfth Night ball had just become considerably more entertaining.

Only the King appeared annoyed rather than scandalised.

'Kilverdale is a man of honour and integrity,' he said coldly. 'Lady Lacy's reputation is quite otherwise. Enough of this nonsense.'

'I have proof,' said Vivien, speaking for the first time. 'Your Majesty.' She curtsied before the King. 'I am sorry to interrupt your evening, but it is often difficult for a wronged woman to put her case.'

'What proof?' The King looked irritable and far from convinced. 'Be quick.'

'Witnesses. The priest who married us in Paris in December 1658 and the guests at the wedding. I also have the marriage licence. The Duke promised me that when he returned to England, I would be at his side. But he broke his promise.' She sent Jack a look of pure venom. 'He stole my child and turned me away. And now he has found another woman to take my rightful—'

'Lies! It is all lies!'

Temperance jumped as Jack's rebuttal cut across Vivien's words. Fierce, but controlled anger, throbbed in his voice. He strode forward to confront Vivien directly.

Taken by surprise, Temperance stumbled, then lifted her head and kept pace with him. He was still holding her hand but, even if he hadn't been, she wouldn't have left his side.

'There was no marriage in Paris or anywhere else.' Jack looked down his patrician nose at Vivien. 'This is a vindictive lie.'

'Hardly that, Kilverdale,' said Windle. 'You've made a habit of clandestine marriages.' He was red-faced and shaking with anger that threatened to erupt at any second, but he controlled himself sufficiently to continue with his accusations.

'The Duchess…' Windle's nod towards Vivien made it wa

clear he was referring to her, not Temperance '…has shown me the documentary proof of the marriage. Your *first* secret marriage, which was conducted by an English priest in France before respectable witnesses. Unlike your latest marital adventure, where your supposed wife didn't even know your real name, it was completely legal, and the priest is ready to bear witness—'

'How much did you pay him?' Contempt saturated Jack's voice.

The sneering reference to her marriage appalled Temperance so badly she lost track of the accusations and Jack's counterattacks for several seconds. She'd always been afraid of this, and now the validity of her marriage was being challenged before the King himself. It was the worst thing she could have imagined.

The very worst.

But then, as Jack continued to hold tight to her hand while he scornfully refuted the charges being laid against him, she realised this wasn't the worst that could happen. Losing Jack would be far more terrible than these threats and public humiliation.

Temperance returned to her immediate surroundings with a snap of clarity, just as Vivien drew herself up, melodramatic indignation blazing in her eyes as she stared at Jack.

'That remark is typical of your cynical, heartless—'

'*Be quiet!*' Temperance was too angry at the insult to Jack to remember the King or the presence of a chamber full of witnesses. She pushed forward.

'He is the kindest, gentlest man in the world, and I will not permit you—or anyone—to abuse him.' She glared down at Vivien, not caring her greater height meant she was looming threateningly over the other woman. She was pleased Vivien took a hasty step backwards, a nervous expression on her face.

'Tempest, hush now,' said Jack in a shaken voice. He drew her back so he could position himself protectively between her and the others. 'I can defend my own honour, beloved,' he said.

'Hiding behind a woman's skirts, Kilverdale?' Windle sneered.

'He doesn't need to hide behind anyone's skirts!' Temperance declared, forgetting herself again. '*He* doesn't bully and threaten defenceless widows. You should be ashamed of yourself! You're nothing but a vile toad—'

'I am the Earl of Windle!' Spittle appeared at the corner of his mouth. 'Whereas *you* are nothing but—'

'My true wife,' said Jack, his voice low and deadly, interposing himself between them again. 'As you value your life, do not insult her, Windle.'

'Enough,' said the King.

Temperance heard annoyance in his lazy voice, and hoped her outburst hadn't made things worse for Jack. But how could she have stayed silent when they abused him so wickedly?

'Since a witness and documents have been mentioned, the matter must be looked into,' said Charles. He glanced around and gestured to Lord Swiftbourne.

'As one of our trusted ministers, my Lord Swiftbourne will investigate your claim,' said the King to Vivien and Windle. 'We suggest you retire with him at once so the matter can be dealt with most expeditiously.'

'He's Kilverdale's grandfather...' Windle burst out furiously.

'Do you question the integrity of our minister?' the King asked coldly.

Windle suddenly seemed to recollect himself and visibly swallowed. 'No, your Majesty.'

'Good. Go.'

Temperance met Swiftbourne's impassive glance as he waited for Vivien and Windle to accompany him from the ball. There was no softening in Swiftbourne's expression when he looked at her, but she comforted herself he could hardly show obvious favouritism before the whole Court.

The King glanced around with displeasure. 'Why has the music stopped?' he demanded. 'Play on!'

Temperance stood close to Jack, wondering if she had disgraced them both by losing her temper in front of the King. But Jack had come perilously close to issuing a challenge in the royal presence, which was probably even more inadvisable.

'Your lady has the protective instincts of a lioness,' the King said to Jack.

'I have been blessed in my marriage,' said Jack. 'My *only* marriage,' he added firmly.

The King smiled slightly, and Temperance thought she saw a look of admiration in his eyes when he glanced at her. She decided the wisest course was to keep silent, so she curtsied as respectfully as she could.

'I had heard tales that yours is a love match, Kilverdale,' said the King. 'Now I see it is true. We will leave the matter of Lady Lacy's extraordinary claims in Swiftbourne's capable hands. No doubt he will deliver his verdict with his characteristic efficiency. In the meantime, let us continue to make merry.'

The next twenty minutes passed in hazy torment for Temperance. She focussed all her energy on maintaining an appropriate dignity while Jack manoeuvred their departure from the ball. Every movement she made, even the smallest turn of the head, must be graceful and composed. There must be no grounds for anyone to claim she wasn't worthy of being Jack's wife.

'You were wonderful,' Athena whispered. 'Windle is a monster. And Vivien is a—' she broke off, but it was obvious she'd been about to say something unladylike.

Jack exchanged a few words with Halross that Temperance didn't catch.

Finally, when her cheeks were stiff from holding a serene expression, and every muscle in her body screamed from the self-control she was imposing on herself, they escaped into the foggy night. The river steps were icy and Jack held her hand firmly as he helped her into the barge. She stood still in the middle of the vessel, listening to him give the order for their departure. In the torch light she could see her own frozen breath on the night air. She shivered and pulled her cloak tighter around her. After the overcrowded, brightly lit ballroom it felt very cold on the river, but she preferred to stand here on the gently rocking barge rather than in the midst of the curious Court.

'Sweetheart, come into the cabin.' Jack put his hand on her back, urging her forward. 'You must not get cold.'

Chapter Nineteen

~~~~~~~~~~~~~~~~~~

Temperance ducked her head to go through the door, and once again she was surrounded by the kind of luxury that had been unimaginable to her when she'd lived in Cheapside. She'd seen such private barges on the Thames often but, until they'd set out for the ball, she hadn't realised how comfortable they could be inside. The floor of the cabin on the Kilverdale barge was carpeted, and the seats upholstered in brocade. There was even a small brazier covered with a perforated lid and filled with hot charcoal to keep the cold at bay.

She sat down and took a deep, careful breath. Suddenly emotion overwhelmed her. She lent forward, giving in to her natural instinct to put her elbows on her knees and hide her face in her hands. Instantly she gasped and straightened up again.

'What is it?' Jack asked, sharp anxiety in his voice. 'Is it the babe?'

'No.' She shook her head and laughed weakly. 'I forgot the bones in my bodice.'

He gave an impatient exclamation, then said gently, 'Take off your cloak a minute, sweetheart, and turn your back to me.' He dropped on to one knee beside her and carefully unlaced her points. She gave a sigh of relief as he pushed the bodice off her shoulders. As long as she kept her back straight, it hadn't been uncomfortable, but that no good posture was the last of her worries, she was glad to be rid of

'Thank you.' She turned to look at him in the lanthorn light, suddenly feeling self-conscious and very unsure of herself. She tried to cover her awkwardness by fumbling to put her cloak back on.

'Wait.' Jack shrugged out of his coat and removed the embroidered waistcoat he wore beneath it. 'Put this on under your cloak. You mustn't catch a chill.'

'Are you comfortable?' he asked when she was wrapped up to his satisfaction. 'Are you hungry? I ordered food to be provided for our return journey. Would you like—'

'Jack.' She put her hand over his as it rested on her knee. 'I'm not hungry.'

'*It's not true!*' The words seemed wrenched out of the deepest part of him. 'Tempest, you must believe me. It's not true, any of it.'

'I know that,' she said, shaken by the anguish in his dark eyes. 'How could you doubt—'

'I don't doubt you!' he said fiercely. 'Never you. My God, you defended me before the whole Court. Before the King himself—'

'Of course I defended you. I'm your wife.' But Temperance bit her lip. She couldn't help worrying their marriage might not stand the kind of close scrutiny with which Swiftbourne was now investigating Vivien's claims.

'You *are* my wife. No one can deny that,' Jack said vehemently, apparently guessing the direction of her thoughts. 'We've got more than written evidence, we've got a chapel full of eminent witnesses, including a King's minister, a Marquis, and two magistrates.'

'Oh, yes. If…' she stopped and swallowed, because this was the hardest thing she'd ever had to say. 'If your marriage to Vivien was proved true—'

'It cannot be!' Jack interrupted impatiently. 'She made the claim from greed and ambition. She left me—'

'But if it was,' Temperance struggled doggedly on, 'Toby would be your rightful heir. He would be the next Duke of Kilverdale.'

Jack went very still. 'What are you saying?' he demanded. He sounded confused, disbelieving.

'I know it is a great grief to you he is not your heir,' Temperance said. Somewhere in the midst of her appalled, incoherent thoughts she had fastened on this single notion. Vivien was Toby's mother. A proven marriage to her offered Jack the one way he could make Toby his heir. Jack might hate his former mistress, but if acknowledging her allowed Toby to—

Jack scattered her thoughts with a furious oath. '*Pour l'amour de Dieu!* You are not thinking straight. I will *never* allow their lies to stand. Vivien was never my wife—'

'Not even for Toby?' Tears crowded Temperance's throat as she remembered the bleakness in Jack's voice when he'd explained to his son that he'd never be Duke.

'No! What is wrong with you? Do you *want* me to set you aside?'

'Of course not—'

'How can you even suggest such a thing? How could you contemplate it even for a second? Do you think I have no honour? No loyalty?' Jack's voice rose to a shout.

'No.' Temperance's lips trembled as suddenly her chaotic emotions slipped beyond her control. She covered her face with her hands again, but she couldn't prevent a sob escaping.

She felt Jack's arm come around her shoulders and he pulled her firmly against him. 'Beloved, don't cry. I will never let anyone hurt you. Shush. It was a horrible scene, but it is over now. You were magnificent. My brave Tempest. I am so proud of you…'

He rubbed his hand comfortingly up and down her arm, kissed her temple and held her hand, all the while keeping up a stream of reassuring comments and compliments.

Temperance leant against him. It was a blissful relief to feel his strong arms around her, to feel the uncompromising certainty in his voice as he claimed her as his wife. To know that he wouldn't put her aside, not even for Toby's sake.

'It grieves you so much that he isn't your heir,' she said, her voice muffled by his coat.

Jack's hand paused in its rhythmic stroking of her arm. 'Why do you say so, sweetheart?'

'Well…because I heard you, that night Toby hid and you comforted him.' She lifted her head to look at him. 'You were so sad. It breaks my heart to hear you so sad. But I wish…' She looked away, tears filling her eyes again. 'Will you love my baby too?' she whispered.

She'd never meant to ask him that, but tonight she couldn't keep the question and the fear inside. Not when her world was tumbling about her ears again.

'Tempest.' He didn't say anything else, only her name in such a shaken voice. What did it mean when he spoke to her like that? Her heart leapt and then settled into a quicker, anxiously hopeful rhythm.

He laid his hand over the gentle swelling of her stomach and rested his forehead against her temple.

'Of course I will love your babe,' he whispered. 'I already do. How…?' He paused and seemed to change what he'd been about to say. 'What about you?' he asked. 'Do you…care… whether I love you?'

For three heartbeats Temperance remained silent, then she said in a hesitant voice, 'Do you…care whether I care whether you… love me?'

Jack's arm tightened around her shoulders, and his lips began to caress her cheek in such a tender, intimate way that she started to tremble from the intensity of her feelings. She turned towards him and he found her mouth. It was the most emotional, heartfelt kiss they'd ever shared. At first they were both tentative, asking questions of each other which neither had fully spoken aloud, and providing answers in the same silent, tender way. The kiss lengthened and became increasingly passionate as their mutual certainty grew, until at last they were both gasping for breath.

'I love you,' Jack said raggedly against her lips. 'I will never let anybody separate us—not even you.'

'Jack.' Temperance flung her arms around his neck, planting kisses all over his face as she cried and laughed with uncontrollable happiness.

'Tempest, beloved. You're overwrought.' He held her close and made an ineffective attempt to soothe her.

She pulled back a little way and discovered he was looking at her with his periwig crooked and a smile as broad and uncontrollable as her own soaring emotions. Then she saw the tenderness shining in his eyes. The love she'd felt for him for so long burst the last of the boundaries she'd imposed on it. It seemed to her that it swelled to fill the cabin and then reached beyond, warming even the foggy night outside the barge.

'Yes, I'm glad,' she said, her smile just as foolishly, uninhibitedly happy as his. 'I love you so much. I think I always have. Why else would I ever have been bold enough to claim to be your wife?'

'I knew too,' he said. 'I gave you my seal ring in Southwark without a second thought—I'd never let it out of my possession before. It took a little longer for my mind to understand, but in my heart I've always loved you. When you pushed me away on our wedding night—'

'I'm sorry. It wasn't you. All those eyes…'

'Like lice.' He smiled at her. 'That's what you said.'

'I don't remember. I know I love you.' She framed his face in her hands and kissed him with all the love in her heart and soul.

'Tempest, how could you ever imagine, even for a second, that I would recognise Vivien as my wife?' Jack asked. He was propped up on one elbow, looking down at her as they lay in bed together. As soon as they'd arrived home he'd made sure she still wasn't hungry, then he'd been adamant she must rest immediately. Temperance had refused to go to bed without him, so now they were both cosy beneath the covers.

'Did you ever, even for a second, think she was telling the truth?' he asked.

'No, it wasn't for her, it was for Toby,' said Temperance, 'but I wasn't thinking clearly. If it was proven true, you'd be put in the Tower or worse—which would upset Toby even more than not being your heir! But I suddenly remembered him crying that he didn't want you to throw him away…'

Jack bent his head and brushed his lips gently over hers. 'I'm not going to throw you away either,' he said. 'Not for anything or anyone.'

Temperance slipped her hand behind his head and held him in place for a more thorough kiss. He indulged them both until his whole body was shimmering with anticipation.

'Enough of that,' he said at last, his breathing distinctly uneven. 'You must rest.' He smiled and stroked her hair back from her face. 'Don't fret about Toby,' he said. 'If you and I have more than one son, only the oldest will be Duke after me. The younger sons will have to make their own way in the world, just like Toby. His situation is not so very different from theirs. And I will always provide for my children. Perhaps they will train to be merchants, like Halross. There is more than enough time for us to worry about that in the future.'

'I wasn't thinking very sensibly,' Temperance said, her voice gruff with embarrassment. Why hadn't she thought of that before? It was obvious only one of Jack's sons could inherit his title.

'You're always sensible,' said Jack, kissing the tip of her nose.

Temperance still felt almost weightless with happiness because he loved her. From the lack of tension in Jack's body and his tendency to kiss and caress her at the slightest provocation, she was gloriously sure he felt the same. Tomorrow they'd have to confront the disaster threatening them, but tonight she wanted to celebrate their newly confessed love for each other.

She slipped her hand beneath his nightshirt and rested it gently on his thigh.

Jack caught his breath. 'What are you doing?'

'Nothing.' She smiled. 'I don't want you to think about Windle or Vivien any more tonight.'

'You're tired,' Jack told her, but she felt his muscles flex responsively under her fingers.

'A little,' she admitted, stroking upwards a little hesitantly. 'Do you mind?' she asked, pausing in her caress, wondering if she was being too bold in demonstrating her love for him.

'No,' he said hoarsely.

'Good. I like to touch you.' She continued her exploration of his upper leg and then his side. His muscles had been hard with tension when she'd begun her caresses and they were still taut beneath her hand, but she sensed the reason had changed.

'I love you touching me, but you need to rest,' he said doggedly, and then groaned as she closed her hand around him. 'Sweetheart, beloved, I really don't think…'

'That's all right.' She explored his aroused body with increasing confidence as she watched the effect her caresses were having upon him. 'I don't need you to think just now.'

'But we are going to take it slow and ea—uh—easy,' he said roughly as he capitulated. 'And then you are going to go straight to sleep.'

'Yes, husband.' Temperance smiled up at him with misty eyes as he joined his body with hers.

Temperance sat in the garden of the Putney house, watching Toby and Isaac nearby playing in the clear January morning. It was two days after Windle and Vivien's accusations at Court. At first Temperance had been so euphoric with joy at discovering Jack loved her, the threat hanging over them had seemed almost insignificant, but now she was becoming increasingly worried. Jack had gone to London to see Lord Swiftbourne and she was waiting on tenterhooks for his return.

She noticed the boys were standing by the rivergate, talking through the bars to someone on the Thames below. Toby suddenly became agitated. His voice rose, although she couldn't hear what he was shouting through the bars, then he turned and hurtled across the frosty grass towards her with Isaac following him.

'Temp'rance! Temp'rance!' He slammed up against her knees and she caught his flailing arms, both to steady him and protect her stomach from an unintentional punch.

Words tumbled out of his mouth so fast she caught only disjointed phrases.

'…singing about Papa…wicked witch Vivien…spelled…steal the boy…Kilverdale's child…*that's me*!' Toby clutched at her sleeve, staring at her with huge eyes. 'He's singing about *Papa and me*—but Papa's not here!'

'I am,' said Temperance firmly. Sharp concern filled her at seeing Toby's alarm, but it was mingled with relief that he'd come to her for help in Jack's absence. She did so want him to trust her and turn to her when he was upset. 'I am here, and I can deal with this. Now, who sang this nonsense to you?'

'The waterman. He's in a boat by the gate.'

Temperance stood up and took Toby's hand in hers.

'What are you going to do?' he asked.

'Talk to the waterman,' she said.

'Are you going to give me to him?' Toby pulled back fearfully.

'Of course not!' Temperance exclaimed. 'I won't give you to anyone and I won't let anyone take you! But I want to hear his song for myself.'

Toby accompanied her rather reluctantly to the gate. 'Stay here with Isaac,' she instructed him. She could see the wherry was still by the wooden jetty at the bottom of the stairs, so she asked the gardener hovering nearby to unlock the gate. She walked through to stand at the top of the river steps, closing the gate behind her as an added reassurance to Toby that she would not suddenly drag him through it and hurl him into the boat.

The waterman looked up at her. He visibly measured her height with his eyes and then began to grin.

'The Doughty Duchess who felled Lord Vile Toad in front of the King, I dare swear!' he exclaimed.

'Lord Vile Toad?' Temperance repeated, briefly confused. Toby had been gabbling about wicked witches and Kilverdale's child being stolen. *'Doughty Duchess?'*

'…but the Doughty Duchess could bear no slight to her lord, so she smote Lord Toad with the hilt of a sword…' the waterman sang.

'I did no such thing!' Temperance took a deep, steadying breath as the wherryman laughed.

Thames watermen were notorious for the outspoken lack of respect with which they treated everyone. It didn't surprise her that he was sufficiently impudent to give a rendition of his song under the gates of its subjects.

'Start from the beginning and sing it all,' she ordered.

'Why should I?' His eyes glinted as he cocked his head at her.

'For this.' She reached into her pocket and pulled out a gold coin. He raised his eyebrows, and then held out his hand.

'The song first.'

He grinned, tipped back his head and lustily sang several verses.

'Is that all of it?' Temperance said when he was finished. 'You cannot hold a tune.'

To her relief, though the song over-dramatised the events at court, it was largely favourable to her and Jack—although she didn't think Jack would like the image it painted of him as a callow, exiled youth briefly snared by the witch Vivien's calculating charms. The verses vividly, if somewhat vulgarly, described a spider-like woman who trapped men in her web and sucked them dry before moving on to her next victim. The song included both the thinly disguised names of some of Vivien's lovers and the various European cities she'd visited, which gave added weight to the scandalous claims. Whatever Vivien's reputation had been in London before this, it would soon be irredeemably shredded.

'I have heard your noble husband has a voice that can charm angels from the sky,' said the waterman cheerfully. 'Therefore I shall not take your criticism to heart. Besides, even if he sang like a crow, you would still find his voice more pleasing than mine.'

'Yes, I would.' Temperance tossed the wherryman the coin. 'You can go now.'

'But I haven't got what I came for.' He caught it neatly.

'What's that?' Temperance looked at him warily.

'My noble patron, and the author of my little song, would like your opinion of his verses.'

Temperance stiffened. 'Who is your noble patron?'

'He wishes to remain anonymous.'

'I'm sure he does,' Temperance muttered. 'Tell him I appreciate the valiant picture he painted of me and my husband,' she said more loudly, 'but his verse is sadly clumsy. I believe he needs to study the art more carefully before presenting his next work to the world.'

'I will convey your message. Good day to you, Duchess. May you fell many more greedy, dishonest men with your doughty blow.' The waterman pushed the wherry away from the steps and began to row downriver.

Temperance watched him thoughtfully before going back into the garden and telling the servant to lock the gate. For the first time she wondered whether common Londoners might be more sympathetic to her than she'd feared. The crisis would not be over until powerful, influential men were assured Jack had told the truth and Vivien had lied—but it would not hurt their cause if the topic of songs and pamphlets circulating among common Londoners generally favoured Jack.

'Did you really hit Lord Windle with a sword?' Isaac asked

'I didn't hit him at all!' Temperance said. 'With a sword or anything else. You know better than to believe everything you hear, Isaac.'

'Isaac said you used to wear a stick inside your skirt to hit people with if they tried to hurt you,' said Toby. 'Are you wearing it now?'

'No,' said Temperance.

Toby scowled. 'Why not? How are you going to stop wicked Vivien stealing me when Papa's not here if you haven't got your stick?'

Temperance led him back to the bench. She sat down and drew him close to her.

'Vivien is *not* going to try to steal you, Toby,' she said in a quiet, firm voice.

She didn't think Toby fully understood the waterman's song, and she wasn't sure if he realised Vivien was his mother, so she kept her reassurances simple and direct. It would be up to Jack to decide how much and when he told Toby about Vivien.

'That was just a made-up part of the waterman's song,' Temperance said. 'Like the claim that I hit Lord Windle with a sword. Where would I have got a sword from at the Twelfth Night Revels? It's just in the song to make the story more exciting, but it's not true.'

'It's a lie,' said Toby.

'Yes. No one is going to take you away. But if anyone tries, I will stop them. I promise.'

Toby stared at her. She looked back very steadily, her heart beating rapidly with hope as she willed him to believe her, but knowing she couldn't force his trust. Eventually, when he seemed to accept what she'd said, she put her arms around him and hugged him. He stood very still for a moment, and then leant against her. That silent moment of acceptance filled her heart with warmth and caused tears to scald her eyes. She hugged him tighter, determined never to let anyone hurt him.

He put his hands on her shoulders and pushed back a little to look down at her. 'You must wear your stick while Papa's not here,' he said. 'We'll go and get it now.'

'Well…' Temperance hesitated despite Toby's tug on her hand. Her stick was ashes in the rubble of London, and she'd never

replaced it. But it shouldn't be difficult for one of the servants
make her a substitute and a belt to hang it from beneath her skirt
Or even on top, since its main purpose was to make Toby feel saf

'She doesn't need a special stick to defend you, Toby. Ar
object that comes to her hand will do.'

Both Temperance and Toby jumped, and Toby clung tight to h
until he recognised Lord Halross standing on the path a few fe
away. Reassured they hadn't been accosted by a child thief, Tob
loosened his grip slightly, but still stayed close to Temperance.

'I beg your pardon, my lord, we didn't see you,' she said.

'I didn't want to interrupt.' He waved away her apology and s
down on a low wall nearby. 'Toby, you may be sure her Grace—
Temperance—will be fearless in defending you,' he said, speakir
directly to Toby. 'Now, look at me. Do I seem to you to be a bi
strong fellow—not to be trifled with?'

Toby gazed at Halross before nodding slowly. 'Papa's not afra
of you,' he said staunchly. 'He'd win if you fought him.'

Halross grinned. 'We won't argue the matter because it's n
going to happen,' he said. 'But you agree that lesser mortals tha
your papa might be scared to make me angry?'

Toby nodded again. Temperance bit her lip, sure she kne
where Halross's story was going. Ever since she'd discovered I
was married to Jack's cousin she'd been afraid the Marquis mig
remember their one previous encounter eight years earlier, whe
he'd been a cocksure twenty-two year old and she'd been mindir
her father's shop alone.

'Good. Well, there was a time when I was younger than I a
now, but just as big and strong, when I visited your—Tempe
ance's—shop and behaved…ah…naughtily,' said Halross.

Temperance glanced from Isaac to Toby and saw that both
them were staring at Halross with open mouths. They obvious
had difficulty imagining such a grand and imposing man ev
being naughty.

'What did you do?' Toby demanded.

'I ate a meat pie in her shop and spilled gravy all over her floo
boards after she'd expressly told me not to,' said Halross.

Isaac gasped. Toby, no doubt because he was a Duke's so

who'd been waited on by servants all his life, was less impressed. 'Is that all?'

'It was a grave discourtesy to her,' Halross corrected. 'And caused her unnecessary work.'

'What did she do?' Isaac breathed. He'd been Temperance's apprentice and knew she didn't lightly tolerate insults.

'Hit me across the shoulders with her yardstick,' said Halross. 'And ordered me out of the shop. So you see, Toby, you need not be afraid when you're with her, for she will always defend you just as stoutly as she defended her floorboards from me, and just as bravely as she defended your papa two nights ago before the whole Court.'

'I thought you'd forgotten,' said Temperance when the boys were playing ball. 'I am so sorry, my lord.'

'You shouldn't be. I deserved it,' Halross replied. 'There was no need to mention it before. But I thought it was a good, simple story to help convince Toby you're able to protect him. I confess I did overhear quite a bit of your conversation with him before I interrupted.'

'Thank you.' Grateful tears clogged Temperance's throat. 'I do thank you.'

'Jack has gone to see Lord Swiftbourne,' she said after a moment. 'I just…I hate…I hope it will all be resolved soon. If I could, I would beat Windle and Vivien black and blue with my yardstick,' she admitted. 'I cannot bear they should hurt Jack like this.'

'Swiftbourne is in command of the investigation, but the King has a vested interest in Lady Lacy's claim being proved false,' said Halross.

'He has? Did the King ever—' Temperance began, wondering Halross meant Vivien had once been Charles's mistress.

'No.' Halross glanced around and then lowered his voice. 'But there have been rumours that while the King was in exile, he secretly married Lucy Walter. If that was proved true, Lucy's son would be heir to the throne, not the King's brother, James. Those rumours may well be what gave Lady Lacy and Windle the idea for their scheme.' Halross smiled sardonically. 'It obviously didn't occur to them that Charles won't want their claims against Kilverdale proven. It would encourage those who either want him to claim Lucy Walter's son as his heir, or deny his marriage to the Queen, to pursue their cause more energetically.'

'Oh.' Temperance absorbed what she'd just heard. 'Isn't there a chance the King might want to put aside the Queen?' she asked hesitantly, remembering not only the Queen's failure to have children, but Charles's many mistresses.

'No,' said Halross. 'Charles will not set the Queen aside. I don't believe it will be long before this crisis is well behind you.'

'Lady Lacy and Lord Windle have been proven liars,' said Swiftbourne. 'The English priest who claimed to conduct the marriage ceremony in Paris was a debtor in the Fleet prison here in London at that time. It would have been quite impossible for him to visit France, let alone conduct a wedding ceremony there.'

'Thank God for that!' Jack said fervently. 'I am grateful to you, sir,' he continued stiffly. 'And to you, my lord,' he said to Halross.

Swiftbourne inclined his head in acknowledgement of Jack's thanks, while Halross smiled and nodded in a less formal manner. It was five days after Twelfth Night and the two men had just arrived in Putney to share their news with Jack and Temperance.

Temperance felt almost dizzy with relief. She'd not allowed herself to believe Vivien's claim would be successful—the possibility that Jack might be put in the Tower for bigamy while Vivien flaunted herself as the rightful Duchess of Kilverdale was a nightmare that hadn't borne thinking about—but she'd not been able to banish all anxiety until this moment.

'What's happened to them?' Jack asked

'Lady Lacy made a public retraction yesterday,' said Swiftbourne. 'She is now on her way to France via Flanders.'

'*France?*'

'I happened to mention to her that one of her old lovers had recently inherited his brother's title,' said Swiftbourne blandly. 'And a considerable fortune. Lady Lacy immediately expressed a wish to congratulate him. I took it upon myself to ensure she will be able to do so at the earliest opportunity.'

'And Windle?'

'Lord Windle claimed he was grievously deceived by Lady Lacy. To be fair to Lady Lacy, she claimed it was Lord Windle who approached her with the scheme,' said Swiftbourne. 'It is their misfortune that their greed and, in Windle's case, his unreasoning animosity towards her Grace, completely outstripped their competence. Both of them appear to have had very limited ambitions.'

'It didn't seem so to me,' said Temperance, shuddering.

'It would if you'd had the tedious task of questioning them,' said Swiftbourne. 'The evidence was relatively well fabricated—though easy enough to disprove to anyone with a modicum of resourcefulness—but Windle was obsessed with the thought of gloating over your ruin. And, I regret to say, maddened beyond reason at discovering Kilverdale had made such an admirably sensible choice of bride…'

Temperance smiled wryly at the favourable slant as she realised Swiftbourne had put on Jack marrying a Cheapside shopkeeper—something that Windle would never have accepted.

'Windle should be drawn and quartered for putting Tempest through so much distress!' Jack exploded. 'He—'

'Is now on the way to Italy for the good of his health,' Swiftbourne said smoothly.

'What?' Jack broke off in mid-tirade.

'His health?' Temperance said, bewildered.

'Certainly,' said Swiftbourne. 'I pointed out that his health would benefit greatly from an extended visit to foreign soil. He's now on one of Halross's ships bound for Livorno. I dare say he'll be grateful for the chance to take up residence in Florence. He'll find it so much cheaper.'

Temperance drew in a breath as she considered how effectively Swiftbourne had dealt with the threat Windle posed. She didn't know exactly what punishment the law would have decreed for the Earl, but she had no doubt Swiftbourne had made it clear to Windle his life would be forfeit if he remained in England. Such ruthlessness was somewhat disconcerting, but she was glad Swiftbourne was on their side.

'What about Windle's daughter?' Jack asked. 'She's barely seventeen. You haven't sent her to Livorno as well?'

'No.' Swiftbourne paused, and then continued in his usual unemotional manner, 'Before he left, Windle was persuaded to make me her legal guardian. She is now in my care.'

'*Your* care?'

'Indeed.' Swiftbourne raised haughty eyebrows before flicking a piece of fluff from his immaculate sleeve.

'What are you going to do with her?' Jack asked.

'Nothing,' said Swiftbourne. 'Except provide her with the necessary appurtenances of a comfortable life. I imagine a husband will be forthcoming for her in due course. Since I am sure Halross will be able to answer any further questions you have, I shall now take my leave—'

'No, don't,' said Temperance, going over and hugging him quickly before she lost her nerve. She knew Swiftbourne wasn't a demonstrative man, but she wanted him to know she was truly grateful for what he'd done.

Swiftbourne's face froze. He stiffened as if she'd just insulted him rather than begged him to stay—but then he patted her awkwardly on the shoulder as she stepped away.

He cleared his throat. 'Well, I dare say I could spare you a few more minutes,' he said with unaccustomed gruffness.

'We would like that,' said Jack, putting his arm around Temperance as she went to stand beside him. 'In fact, why don't you join us in a game of billiards?' he suggested. 'Duchess of Kilverdale's rules.'

'Duchess of Kilverdale's rules?' Swiftbourne was far too experienced a diplomat to reveal his confusion, but he did glance from Jack to Temperance with an uplifted eyebrow.

Jack grinned. 'You have to see them to believe them,' he said. 'But I think you'll find them far more entertaining than the standard game. It will be the first time Tempest has played on the table here in Putney,' he added.

'Very well, you have intrigued me,' said Swiftbourne.

'Good. Henderson will escort you and Lord Halross to the billiards room. We'll join you in a just a moment.' Jack waited unt he was alone with Temperance, then he picked her up and spun her in an exuberant circle. 'He's done it!' he exclaimed. 'The old devil's done it!' He set her on her feet and kissed her soundly.

Temperance kissed him back, then hugged him fiercely, sharing his profound relief that the worry of the past few days was over. At last she drew back and smiled at him. 'And you've invited Lord Swiftbourne to play billiards,' she said. 'That was very well done of you.'

'It was, wasn't it?' said Jack. 'And now I'll have the pleasure of watching him try to keep that impassive expression on his face while you explain the very peculiar rules you invented. It will be better than a play.'

Epilogue

River Thames, early June 1667

Early summer morning sunlight glittered on the Thames as the wherry pulled steadily up river. Swiftbourne folded the letter he'd just re-read and put it carefully into his pocket. The news it contained greatly pleased him and before he'd left home he'd given orders for his departure for Sussex as soon as he returned.

'The Duchess of Kilverdale has given birth to a girl,' he told the lone waterman propelling the craft. 'Both mother and daughter are strong and healthy.'

'Of course they are,' said the waterman. 'And what of the little lad with black hair who stood at the gate?'

'You are a rogue who exceeded his orders,' said Swiftbourne. 'My grandson reports that Toby is enchanted by his new sister.'

'As well he might be, if she takes after her mother,' said the waterman, and began to sing as he rowed towards Whitehall.

The song had begun life as 'The Doughty Duchess', but it had undergone several transformations in the months since then. Words had been changed to improve the rhymes, extra verses had been added to include a legendary exploit or two of Jack Bow— and someone, somewhere, had decided Vagabond Duchess was more fitting appellation for Kilverdale's wife.

Swiftbourne smiled faintly as he listened. He still didn't know the truth of his grandson's shadowy courtship of the Cheapside shopkeeper, and one day he hoped to find out. But the drama surrounding Windle and Vivien's false accusations had given Swiftbourne the opportunity to emphasise in several subtle ways the legitimacy of Jack's marriage to Temperance. Swiftbourne was very fond of his grandson's wife; partly because, to his surprise, she seemed to like him, and partly because he was sure it was thanks to her that he was now on terms of cautious friendship with Jack.

'Her Grace was right, you cannot hold a tune,' he told the waterman as they arrived at the river stairs.

'No, my lord,' said the waterman, grinning. 'But, as I recollect, she wasn't greatly impressed by the quality of the verse either.'

'You're an insolent rogue,' Swiftbourne said mildly.

He left the river behind and strolled towards St Martin's Lane. Considering it was sixty years since he'd last tried to rhyme a couplet and he'd composed the song at seven-thirty in the morning after working all night to establish Jack's innocence, he was rather proud of his poetic accomplishment. Naturally, if anyone tried to ascribe the original verses to his pen, he would respond to the suggestion with cold disdain. He smiled again and went into the house to summon the carriage that would take him to Sussex to see his new great-granddaughter.

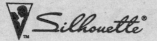

Silhouette®
Romantic
SUSPENSE

**Sparked by Danger,
Fueled by Passion.**

*This month and every month look for
four new heart-racing romances
set against a backdrop of suspense!*

Available in May 2007

Safety in Numbers
(Wild West Bodyguards miniseries)
by **Carla Cassidy**

Jackson's Woman
by **Maggie Price**

Shadow Warrior
(Night Guardians miniseries)
by **Linda Conrad**

One Cool Lawman
by **Diane Pershing**

Available wherever you buy books!

Visit Silhouette Books at www.eHarlequin.com

REQUEST YOUR FREE BOOKS!

 Harlequin® Historical
Historical Romantic Adventure!

2 FREE NOVELS PLUS 2 FREE GIFTS!

YES! Please send me 2 FREE Harlequin® Historical novels and my 2 FREE gifts. After receiving them, if I don't wish to receive any more books, I can return the shipping statement marked "cancel." If I don't cancel, I will receive 6 brand-new novels every month and be billed just $4.69 per book in the U.S., or $5.24 per book in Canada, plus 25¢ shipping and handling per book and applicable taxes, if any*. That's a savings of close to 15% off the cover price! I understand that accepting the 2 free books and gifts places me under no obligation to buy anything. I can always return a shipment and cancel at any time. Even if I never buy another book from Harlequin, the two free books and gifts are mine to keep forever.

246 HDN EEWW   349 HDN EEW9

Name _____ (PLEASE PRINT) _____

Address _____ Apt. # _____

City _____ State/Prov. _____ Zip/Postal Code _____

Signature (if under 18, a parent or guardian must sign) _____

Mail to the **Harlequin Reader Service®**:
IN U.S.A.: P.O. Box 1867, Buffalo, NY 14240-1867
IN CANADA: P.O. Box 609, Fort Erie, Ontario L2A 5X3

Not valid to current Harlequin Historical subscribers.

Want to try two free books from another line?
Call 1-800-873-8635 or visit www.morefreebooks.com.

* Terms and prices subject to change without notice. NY residents add applicable sales tax. Canadian residents will be charged applicable provincial taxes and GST. This offer is limited to one order per household. All orders subject to approval. Credit or debit balances in a customer's account may be offset by any other outstanding balance owed by or to the customer. Please allow 4 to 6 weeks for delivery.

Harlequin is committed to protecting your privacy. Our Privacy Policy is available online at www.eHarlequin.com or upon request from the Reader Service. From time to time we make our lists of customers available to reputable firms who may have a product or service of interest to you. If you would prefer we not share your name and address, please check here. ☐

SIR0407

HH(

HARLEQUIN®

Mediterranean NIGHTS™

Tycoon Elias Stamos is launching his newest luxury cruise ship from his home port in Greece. But someone from his past is eager to expose old secrets and to see the Stamos empire crumble.

Mediterranean Nights
launches in June 2007 with...

FROM RUSSIA, WITH LOVE
by *Ingrid Weaver*

Join the guests and crew of *Alexandra's Dream* as they are drawn into a world of glamour, romance and intrigue in this new 12-book series.

COMING NEXT MONTH FROM

HARLEQUIN®
HISTORICAL

- **HIGH PLAINS BRIDE**
  by **Jenna Kernan**
  (Western)
  A lost love, an unknown daughter… Thomas West must save the
  family he hadn't known he had—and in doing so find his own
  redemption!

- **KLONDIKE DOCTOR**
  by **Kate Bridges**
  (Western)
  Sergeant Colt Hunter finds it hard enough to be ordered to guard a
  spoiled little rich girl on the deadly trail to the Yukon—but his task
  becomes impossible when he realizes that she's a beautiful, feisty
  grown woman!

- **A MOST UNCONVENTIONAL COURTSHIP**
  by **Louise Allen**
  (Regency)
  He hadn't anticipated Alessa's propensity to get herself into a
  scrape, and now, in order to rescue her, this elegantly conventional
  English earl will have to turn pirate!

- **HER IRISH WARRIOR**
  by **Michelle Willingham**
  (Medieval)
  Lady Genevieve de Renault turned to the arms of a fiercely
  powerful Irish warrior *only* for protection…. She didn't expect to
  lose her heart in the bargain!